perspectives

TOOLKIT TEXTS | Short Nonfiction for American History

Industrial Age and Immigration

SELECTED BY

Anne Goudvis and Stephanie Harvey

Heinemann
DEDICATED TO TEACHERS™

DEDICATED TO TEACHERS™

Heinemann
361 Hanover Street
Portsmouth, NH 03801-3912
www.heinemann.com

Offices and agents throughout the world

Library of Congress Cataloging-in-Publication Data
Names: Goudvis, Anne, compiler. | Harvey, Stephanie, compiler.
Title: Industrial age and immigration: short nonfiction for American
   history / [compiled by] Anne Goudvis and Stephanie Harvey.
Other titles: Short nonfiction for American history
Description: Portsmouth, NH: Heinemann Publishing [2020] |
Series: Toolkit text; book 5 | Includes bibliographical references. | Audience: Grades 4–6 |
Identifiers: LCCN 2020029523 | ISBN 9780325105000 (spiral bound)
Subjects: LCSH: United States–History–1865–Juvenile literature. |
   United States–Emigration and immigration–History–Juvenile literature.
   | United States–History–Study and teaching (Elementary)
Classification: LCC E178.3.I63 2020 | DDC 973.8–dc23
LC record available at https://lccn.loc.gov/2020029523

Editor: Heather Anderson
Production: Kimberly Capriola
Cover Design: Suzanne Heiser
Typesetter: Eclipse Publishing
Manufacturing: Steve Bernier, Val Cooper

Printed in the United States of America on acid-free paper
1 2 3 4 5 6 7 8 9 10 MPP 25 24 23 22 21
March 2021 Printing

Acknowledgments

As longtime history buffs, we are deeply fascinated by American history, not to mention what is happening now as "history in the making." Our *Short Nonfiction for American History* texts now include articles about both the past and the present. Part of the Comprehension Toolkit series, this resource would not have happened without the commitment, diligence, and hard work of our Heinemann team. Most of all, we are extremely grateful to our fabulous editor Heather Anderson for her prodigious research skills, sharp eye for engaging material, and boundless enthusiasm. We can't thank Roderick Spelman enough for his enthusiastic support of our vision, his wicked sense of humor, and his willingness to connect us with social studies organizations. Patty Adams, Sarah Fournier, Krysten Lebel, Kimberly Capriola, Lynette Winegarner, Elizabeth Silvas, Suzanne Heiser, Steve Bernier, and Val Cooper put forth the energy and creative thinking that has brought this resource to life. We thank the entire Heinemann team for their ongoing support of our work.

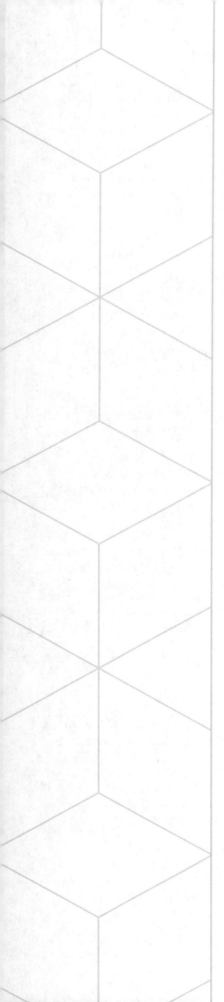

Contents

LESSONS FOR HISTORICAL LITERACY

Articles

Chapter 1: Industry, Inventions, and Innovation

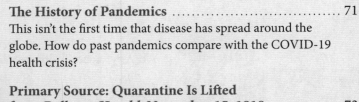

Chapter 2: Child Labor and Social Reform

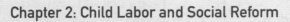

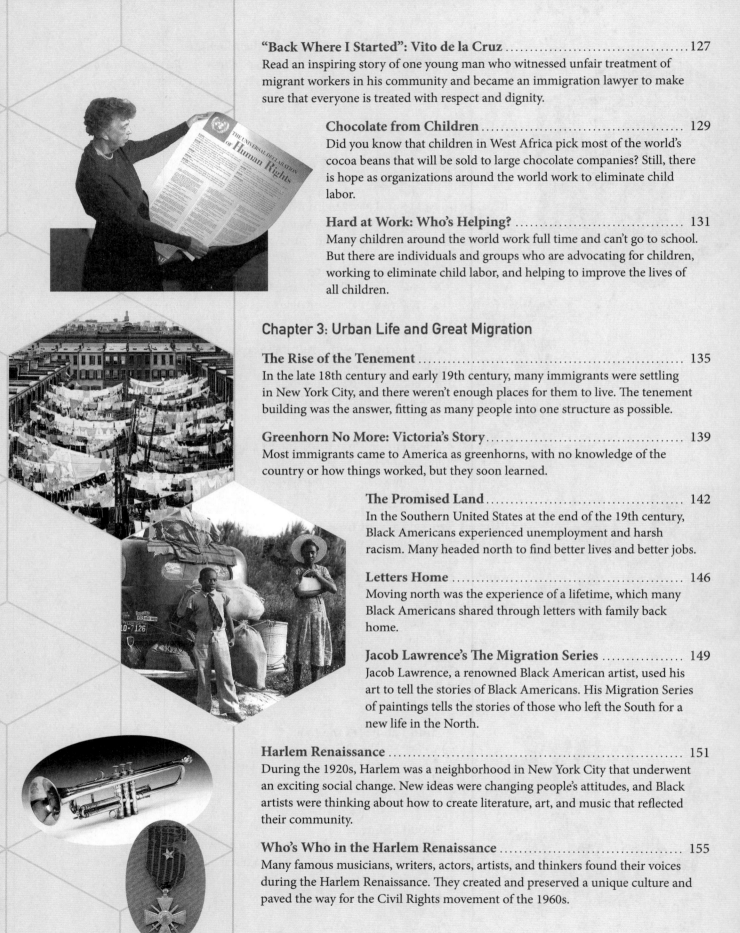

Chapter 3: Urban Life and Great Migration

Chapter 4: A History of American Immigration

Chapter 5: Immigration from 1965 to Present Day

The **DIGITAL COMPANION RESOURCE** includes:

- lessons for historical literacy,
- all of the articles in full color,
- primary source documents,
- a full-color bank of more than 60 historical images,
- "Teaching for Historical Literacy," by Anne Goudvis and Stephanie Harvey (*Educational Leadership*, March 2012),
- "Ten Myths About Immigration" from *Teaching Tolerance*, and
- "What Will the U.S. Supreme Court's Ruling on DACA Mean for Teachers and Students?" by Robert Kim.

For instructions on how to access the Digital Companion Resource, turn to page xxix.

Introduction

Reading, writing, viewing, drawing, listening, talking, doing, and investigating are the hallmarks of active literacy. Throughout the school day and across the curriculum, kids are actively inferring, questioning, discussing, debating, inquiring, and generating new ideas. An active literacy classroom fairly bursts with enthusiastic, engaged learning.

The same goes for our history and social studies classrooms: they, too, must be thinking and learning intensive. To build intrigue, knowledge, and understanding in history, students read and learn about the events, mysteries, questions, controversies, issues, discoveries, and drama that are the real stuff of history.

History is a field that now is striving to reflect the perspectives and voices of many. Yet many history textbooks still do not share the stories of a wide range of diverse populations. Kids need and deserve to see themselves in history texts. In this resource, we highlight those important, lesser known and often under-recognized, perspectives and diverse voices in history and in the current issues and events addressed in this resource.

Content Literacy

When students acquire knowledge in a discipline such as history and think about what they are learning, new insights and understandings emerge and kids generate new knowledge. Fundamental to this understanding is the idea that there's a difference between information and knowledge. Kids have to construct their own knowledge: only they can turn information into knowledge by thinking about it. But we educators must provide the environment, resources, and instruction so kids become curious, active learners.

From Anne Goudvis, Stephanie Harvey, Brad Buhrow, and Anne Upczak-Garcia (2012). *Scaffolding the Comprehension Toolkit for English Language Learners.* Portsmouth, NH: Heinemann.

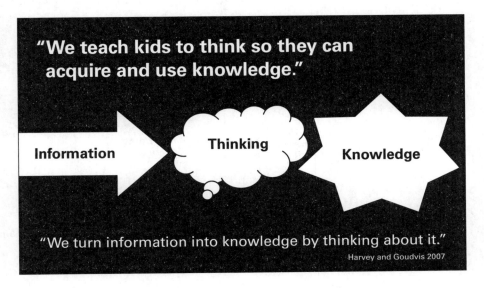

"We teach kids to think so they can acquire and use knowledge."

Information → Thinking → Knowledge

"We turn information into knowledge by thinking about it."

Harvey and Goudvis 2007

Too often students experience history as a passive slog through the textbook, with a "coverage" curriculum that's a mile wide and an inch deep. Instead, students should be reading and actively responding to a wide range of historical sources; viewing and analyzing images; reading historical fiction, first-person accounts, letters, and all manner of sources; and engaging in simulations so they can understand and empathize with the experiences of people who lived long ago and far away, as well as those living today and experiencing history as it happens.

In this approach to content literacy, students use reading and thinking strategies as tools to acquire knowledge in history, science, and other subject areas. P. David Pearson and colleagues (Pearson, Moje, and Greenleaf 2010) suggest that:

> Without systematic attention to reading and writing in subjects like science and history, students will leave schools with an impoverished sense of what it means to use the tools of literacy for learning or even to reason within various disciplines. (460)

Reading and thinking about historical sources and introducing students to ways of thinking in the discipline of history teaches them that there are many ways to understand the people, events, issues, and ideas of the past. But we also want students to understand the power and potential of their own thinking and learning so that they learn to think for themselves and connect history to their own lives.

Content Matters

Cervetti, Jaynes, and Hiebert (2009) suggest that reading for understanding is the foundation for students acquiring and using knowledge. In the figure below, Cervetti, Jaynes, and Hiebert explain the reciprocal relationship between knowledge and comprehension—how background knowledge supports comprehension and in turn, through comprehension/reading for understanding, we "build new knowledge" (83).

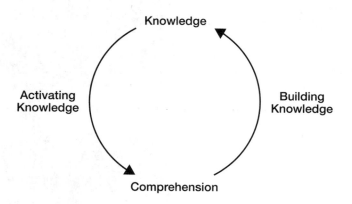

Research (Anderson and Pearson 1984) has long supported the strong relationship between background knowledge and school learning: Students' prior knowledge about content supports their new learning. From our perspective, history, more than many subjects, demands that students have a context for their learning, that they understand the essential ideas that emerge within a larger time span, and that they can discern the big picture.

But activating background knowledge is just the beginning. Researchers emphasize the knowledge-building side of this figure, which underscores the idea that when we comprehend, we add to and enhance our store of knowledge. "Knowledge, from this perspective, does not refer to a litany of facts, but rather to the discipline-based conceptual understanding . . . [which] engage students in becoming experts on the world around them" (Cervetti, Jaynes, and Hiebert 2009).

This is a reciprocal process that occurs as students build their knowledge in many content areas and disciplines. In conversations with P. David Pearson, he sums it up well with his quip: "Today's new knowledge is tomorrow's background knowledge." The more students know, the more they will learn, and even more important, the more they will want to learn!

Historical Literacy

Our approach is to embed reading and thinking strategies in our social studies and history instruction, so that comprehension and thinking strategies become tools for learning and understanding content, as well as engaging with it in ways that go beyond merely answering end-of-the-chapter questions. Teaching historical literacy means we merge thoughtful, foundational literacy practices with challenging, engaging resources to immerse kids in historical ways of thinking.

In the first column we summarize foundational comprehension strategies that foster student engagement and understanding as they read, listen, and view. As students build their own repertoire of reading and thinking strategies, these become tools they use 24/7. The second column describes how students use these strategies to acquire knowledge and deepen their understanding of history.

Comprehension strategies for content literacy	Students use these in history when they:
Attend to one's thinking and follow the inner conversation while reading the text. Monitor understanding.	Stop, think, and react during reading. Learn new information and leave tracks of thinking by annotating the text. Respond to and discuss the text by asking questions, connecting to prior knowledge and experiences, drawing inferences, and considering the big ideas.

Comprehension strategies for content literacy	Students use these in history when they:
Activate and build background knowledge.	Connect the new to the known; use background knowledge to inform reading. Recognize misconceptions and are prepared to revise thinking in light of new evidence. Consider text and visual features. Pay attention to text structures and different genres.

Ask and answer questions.	Ask and answer questions to:
	
	  ▫ Acquire information.
	
	  ▫ Investigate and do research.
	
	  ▫ Interpret and analyze information and ideas.
	
	Read with a critical eye and a skeptical stance.
	
	Explore lingering and essential questions.

Draw inferences and conclusions.	Infer ideas, themes, and issues based on text evidence. Analyze and interpret different perspectives and points of view.
Determine importance.	Sort and sift important information from interesting but less important details. Construct main ideas from supporting details. Evaluate the information and ideas in a text. Distinguish between what the reader thinks versus what the author wants the reader to understand.
Summarize and synthesize.	Analyze, compare, and contrast information across sources to build content knowledge and understanding. Evaluate claims and supporting evidence. Generate new knowledge and insights.

Adapted from Anne Goudvis and Stephanie Harvey (2012). "Teaching for Historical Literacy." *Educational Leadership* March 2012: 52–57.

What might this instruction look like? Students:

- read and reason through many different kinds of sources about the past, connecting to the experiences, dilemmas, discoveries, and reflections of people from other times and places

- ask their own authentic questions, just like historians do

- learn to read critically—to understand different purposes and perspectives, asking, "Who wrote this? Why did they write it? What are the authors' biases, points of view, and purposes?"

- try out ways of thinking about history—inferring, analyzing, and interpreting facts and evidence to surface themes and important ideas.

We believe these practices, above all, promote engagement with the discipline and motivate kids to want to find out more. When kids actively read, think, debate, discuss, and investigate, they have the best shot at becoming enthusiastic students of history. Not incidentally, zeroing in on content literacy in this way will go a long way in helping students meet district and state standards.

To really engage in and learn from history content, kids need a multisource curriculum. We envision the active literacy classroom awash in engaging historical resources of all kinds: maps, timelines, photographs, artifacts, songs, poems, journals, letters, interviews, feature articles, biographies, and so on. Allington and Johnston (2002) found that students evidenced higher achievement when their classroom focused on a multisource, multigenre, multilevel, multiperspective curriculum rather than a one-size-fits-all coverage approach.

Text Matters
SHORT TEXTS FOR LEARNING ABOUT IMMIGRATION AND THE INDUSTRIAL AGE

Kids need engaging texts and resources they can sink their teeth into. These articles offer rich, engaging content that paints a vivid "big picture" of these events and issues in the past and present. In this resource, we have included families of articles on a common topic, theme, or issue, with the understanding that the more widely kids read on a common topic, the more they learn and understand.

Included here are informational articles in a number of genres: first-person accounts, interviews, poetry, historical fiction, and feature articles. Images, portraits, and paintings, and all kinds of features, such as maps, charts, and timelines, provide visual interest and additional information. Primary sources, including historical letters, images, and documents, can be found for each topic. We have also included a short bibliography of books, magazines, documentaries, and websites for investigation. We encourage you to add as many other texts and images on a topic as you can find, to bring history to life and encourage important research skills and practices.

WHY THESE SELECTIONS?

We considered the following criteria in selecting the articles, primary sources, and images:

Engaging content Kids love to learn about the quirky, the unusual, the unexpected, and the surprises that are essential to the study of history. We chose these articles to capture kids' imaginations as they discover the drama, the controversies, and the mystery of history. We anticipate that these articles will ignite kids' interest as they explore historical ideas and issues, as well as current ones.

Identity All kids need to experience history texts as mirrors of their own lives. Chimamanda Ngozi Adichie explains that we must seek diverse perspectives —and writers must tell the stories that only they can tell because of their own personal experience. Until very recently, many kids did not have access to stories that reflected their lives. In order to engage with history, kids must connect to it.

Accuracy and writing quality When we think back to history class, we remember writing that was dull and voiceless—too often full of the generalizations and information overload common to textbook writing. To get kids excited about history and current events so they are motivated to dig deeper and learn more, we searched for articles that had vibrant language and active voice. Variety makes a difference, so we include a rich assortment of nonfiction texts and visual features. Each article has been carefully vetted for accuracy by content experts.

Visual literacy Images provide another powerful entry point for students to access historical texts. Projecting the color versions of the historical images or articles rich with art for students to view closely is one way to generate a conversation about students' background knowledge. We also use images to introduce a particular theme or concept and model interpretation and analysis. Historical and recent images and photographs are located throughout the book. Additional images can be accessed on the Digital Companion Resource or through further research online.

Reading level/complexity Differentiation is key. Included in the collection are articles at a variety of reading levels to provide options for student practice. For example, there are shorter, more accessible articles and longer, more in-depth ones on the same or similar topics. All articles have carefully chosen images designed to enhance the content. This allows for differentiation according to students' reading proficiency levels and background knowledge, as well as their interest.

We have also carefully selected primary source documents that will give students an authentic view of and unique insights into the topics in this resource, both past and present. Arcane or unusual vocabulary and unfamiliar sentence structures can present significant reading challenges. We recommend building background knowledge and historical context (see Lesson 3) before digging into these authentic documents with your students. We offer strategies for approaching the close reading of primary source documents with your students in Lesson 4.

Assigning a grade level to a particular text is arbitrary, especially with content-rich selections, particularly in nonfiction with all of its supportive features. Some of these articles may be challenging for fifth or sixth grade readers, and you might try reading them together in an interactive read-aloud or during small-group work.

We suggest you look carefully at all the articles and choose from them based on your kids' interests and tastes as well as their reading levels.

SOCIAL STUDIES STRANDS

This resource provides a range of reading in the different social studies strands: history, culture, economics, government, and geography. A chart correlating the articles to the social studies strands appears on pages xxii–xxiv.

History Learning about history helps students understand how people and societies behave. It also allows students to make connections between themselves and others who lived long ago. In addition, history helps students to understand the process of change and better prepare themselves for changes they will encounter in their lives.

Culture Learning about culture helps students to better understand and relate to others. By examining their own cultural traditions, students can understand the values of their society. By examining the cultural institutions of other groups, students can gain an appreciation of people who live differently from themselves and also see similarities they might not have otherwise realized.

Economics When students learn about economics, they learn how individuals, groups, and governments all make choices to satisfy their needs and wants. Understanding economics helps students to make better financial decisions in their own lives and also helps them to make sense of the economic world we live in.

Government By learning about government, students are preparing themselves to be good citizens and take part in their political system. Not only does understanding government help students understand the modern-day world and its events, it also gives them the power to change that world through public actions.

Geography Understanding geography helps students understand the physical world in which they live. It helps them see how different parts of their environment are connected and how all of those parts impact their lives and the lives of others.

Read across the chart to determine which social studies strands are covered in each article.

Toolkit Texts: Short Nonfiction for American History, Industrial Age and Immigration

Article	History	Culture	Economics	Geography	Government
Chapter 1: Industry, Inventions, and Innovation					
The Industrial Revolution: A Time of Change	Yes	Yes	Yes	Yes	Yes
Inventing a Revolution		Yes	Yes	Yes	Yes
Hearing Opportunity Knock	Yes		Yes	Yes	Yes
Captains of Industry or Robber Barons?	Yes		Yes		Yes
Ida Takes Aim	Yes	Yes	Yes		Yes
Unions in Tough Times	Yes		Yes		Yes
Strikes in the Mills	Yes		Yes		Yes
Model T: A Car for the Masses	Yes	Yes	Yes	Yes	
Brilliant Breakthroughs	Yes	Yes	Yes		
Awesome Inventions		Yes	Yes	Yes	Yes
Inventions That Bring Music to Our Ears: The Personal Music Player	Yes	Yes			
Edison, Telsa, and the Battle of the Currents	Yes	Yes	Yes		
Inventive Minds: Women Inventors	Yes	Yes	Yes	Yes	
A Woman in the Machine Shop	Yes				
An American Triumph	Yes			Yes	Yes
A New Industrial Revolution		Yes	Yes	Yes	Yes
Shattering the Glass Ceiling		Yes	Yes		
Technology Challenges		Yes	Yes	Yes	
Hooked on Games		Yes			
How the Industrial Revolution Affects You	Yes	Yes	Yes	Yes	Yes
Roy Allela, Inventor of Sign-IO Gloves		Yes			
Kids Can Invent Solutions				Yes	
School Interrupted		Yes			Yes
The History of Pandemics	Yes	Yes		Yes	Yes
Born to Invent: Bishop's Great Idea		Yes	Yes		

Article	History	Culture	Economics	Geography	Government
Chapter 2: Child Labor and Social Reform					
Help Wanted Ads and Spotlight on Child Labor	Yes	Yes	Yes	Yes	Yes
Working Days: Child Labor in American History	Yes	Yes	Yes	Yes	Yes
Mill Girls: Harriet Hanson's Story	Yes	Yes	Yes		
Dear Mama: Letters from a Mill Girl		Yes	Yes		Yes
Triangle Shirtwaist: The Fire Danced on the Machines	Yes		Yes	Yes	
A Day in the Coal Mines	Yes		Yes		
Breaker Boys: "I Could Not Do That Work and Live"	Yes		Yes		Yes
Champions for Reform	Yes	Yes	Yes	Yes	
Lewis Hines: What the Camera Captured	Yes	Yes		Yes	
Kids Fight Back!	Yes		Yes	Yes	
Extra! Extra! Newsboys Strike!	Yes	Yes	Yes	Yes	
Child Labor: It's the Law	Yes		Yes	Yes	
Back Where I Started: Vito de la Cruz		Yes	Yes		Yes
Chocolate from Children			Yes	Yes	Yes
Hard at Work: Who's Helping?		Yes	Yes	Yes	Yes
Chapter 3: Urban Life and Great Migration					
Rise of the Tenement	Yes	Yes	Yes	Yes	Yes
Greenhorn No More: Victoria's Story		Yes	Yes	Yes	
The Promised Land	Yes	Yes	Yes	Yes	Yes
Letters Home	Yes	Yes	Yes		Yes
Jacob Lawrence's The Migration Series	Yes	Yes			
Harlem Renaissance	Yes	Yes	Yes		Yes
Who's Who in the Harlem Renaissance	Yes	Yes			
Migration's Legacy	Yes	Yes	Yes	Yes	Yes
Muddy Waters and the Blues	Yes	Yes	Yes		Yes

Article	History	Culture	Economics	Geography	Government
Chapter 4: A History of American Immigration					
Four Themes of Immigration	Yes	Yes	Yes	Yes	Yes
Waves of Immigration	Yes	Yes	Yes	Yes	Yes
Family Reunion: Ellis Island Experience	Yes	Yes	Yes	Yes	Yes
From Eastern Europe to America	Yes	Yes	Yes	Yes	Yes
An American Welcome: Mexican Immigration in the 1800s and 1900s	Yes	Yes	Yes	Yes	Yes
The Push and Pull of America: Immigration in the 19th Century	Yes	Yes	Yes	Yes	Yes
Voyage of Hope, Voyage of Tears	Yes	Yes	Yes	Yes	Yes
How Curious George Came to America	Yes			Yes	Yes
Interview with Louise Borden		Yes			
Not Those Huddled Masses	Yes	Yes	Yes	Yes	Yes
Louie Share Kim, Paper Son	Yes	Yes	Yes	Yes	Yes
Poetry Carved on the Walls	Yes	Yes			
In Search of Peace and Prosperity: Japanese Immigration	Yes		Yes	Yes	Yes
Angel Island West Coast Stories	Yes		Yes	Yes	Yes
Chapter 5: Immigration from 1965 to Present Day					
Neighbors North and South	Yes	Yes	Yes	Yes	Yes
Celebrating Our Southwest Heritage: A Talk with Khristaan Villela	Yes	Yes			Yes
Recent Arrivals from Asian Countries	Yes	Yes	Yes	Yes	Yes
Building a Library of Books: An Interview with Kha Yang Xiong		Yes		Yes	
Path to Citizenship				Yes	
The Dreamers: Here to Stay?		Yes		Yes	
Marissa Molina: First Dreamer to Sit on the Metropolitan State University Board of Trustees		Yes		Yes	
For Kids, Crossing the U.S. Border Illegally Involves Fear and Hope			Yes	Yes	
Refugees: Who Is Helping?			Yes	Yes	Yes
The Power of Music		Yes		Yes	
Old Towns, New Life		Yes	Yes	Yes	Yes
Fleeing from the Weather			Yes	Yes	Yes
Young Climate Activists				Yes	Yes

TWELVE LESSONS FOR HISTORICAL LITERACY

In this resource, we have designed twelve lessons that merge effective, foundational content-literacy practices with thoughtful approaches to reading historical articles, viewing images, and reasoning through documents. These lessons encourage thoughtful reading and discussion that go far beyond answering the questions at the end of the chapter. By teaching these twelve lessons, teachers will guide students to use reading and thinking strategies as tools to acquire and actively use knowledge in history.

Lesson	Title	Page
1	Read and Annotate: Stop, think, and react using a variety of strategies to understand	L-1
2	Annotate Images: Expand understanding and learning from visuals	L-3
3	Build Background to Understand a Primary Source: Read and paraphrase secondary sources to create a context for a topic	L-6
4	Read and Analyze a Primary Source: Focus on what you know and ask questions to clarify and explain	L-9
5	Compare Perspectives: Explore the different life experiences of historical figures	L-12
6	Read Critically: Consider point of view and bias	L-15
7	Organize Historical Thinking: Create a question web	L-18
8	Read with a Question in Mind: Focus on central ideas	L-21
9	Surface Common Themes: Infer the big ideas across several texts	L-24
10	Synthesize Information to Argue a Point: Use claim, evidence, and reasoning	L-27
11	Read to Get the Gist: Synthesize the most important information	L-31
12	Form an Educated Opinion Distinguish between an opinion and an informed opinion	L-34

TEACHING WITH THIS RESOURCE

We trust that teachers will know their students and how to find the articles that are most appropriate for them. Both the levels and text complexity of these articles are highly variable. Some of these articles may be too difficult for fifth and sixth graders to read on their own. Others may have a more accessible reading level but contain complex and sometimes intense information and issues. For middle and high school readers, many of these articles can be read independently but merit discussion led by the teacher. For younger children, teachers need keep a watchful eye. In fact, all the selections in this resource are best read with some level of discussion. The rich, textured, often sensitive nature of the articles calls for readers to talk about their thinking and reading. So rather than simply handing out articles for students to read on their own, here we share several ways to more effectively teach with this resource.

Interactive Read-Aloud

In an interactive read-aloud, the teacher and students co-construct meaning as the teacher reads and thinks aloud about a piece of text. The teacher models her own questions, connections, thoughts, and reactions initially. Kids turn, talk, and jot about their thinking. The teacher guides kids as they continue to read and think about the article together. Then, kids finish the article independently or in pairs. During interactive read-aloud, all kids can access the ideas and issues that arise, regardless of their reading levels. As kids process the information throughout the instruction, the teacher can support the conversation and guide the discussion toward the big ideas. Interactive read-aloud is a particularly useful instructional technique for this resource, since many of the articles call for deep, extensive discussions to better distill the underlying issues and ideas. Interactive read-aloud also allows for teachers to share some important information that may be out of reach for striving readers. Lastly, some of the issues explored in these selections are delicate, and discussing them with a teacher's guidance will likely help kids wade through some difficult issues.

Partner Reading

There are different forms of partner reading with different purposes. Sometimes kids choose to read in partnerships so they can share their thinking with a friend. Sometimes teachers choose to assign partnerships so a striving reader can get the information when they are not able to read the text on their own. No matter the purpose, our primary goal for reading partnerships is to foster purposeful conversation about the issues and ideas in the text.

Often when kids are partner reading, they take turns reading paragraphs. Sometimes, the student reading is focused on the text while the partner stares off into space; when the reader taps the classmate on the shoulder to say "your turn!" the partner is startled and unprepared. To avoid this kind of behavior, we launch partnerships by modeling and explaining that the listener always has the biggest job. We share what active listening is and give the listener a pad of sticky notes to jot down their thinking as the partner reads. We encourage the listener to jot or draw anything he or she

- wonders
- learns
- is surprised by or
- is confused by.

Then when the reader is done with the section, the listener leads the discussion based on the notes taken during the reading. Active listening keeps the listener participating and engaged. The partners switch roles once they finish discussing that section. Striving readers who can't read the text assume the role of active listener throughout the piece. However, pairing them with more proficient readers frequently cuts into the amount of time they spend reading and they need voluminous reading to grow as readers. So be judicious about this and make sure strivers have text they can read most of the time.

Read, Write, and Talk

Read, Write, and Talk (RWT) is a practice that gives readers an opportunity to read, think, record their thoughts, and then talk about what they have read. RWT encourages kids to merge their thinking with the information and share it with others to better learn, understand, and remember the information. We model the practice by reading, sharing our own thinking, and annotating our thoughts in the margin or on sticky notes. As we read aloud, kids jot their thinking, turn and talk with a partner, and then several share out what they discussed. After modeling this practice, we give kids a chance to try it on their own. They choose among three articles on the topic at hand, such as "immigration today," and read and jot their thinking. When they finish reading, they find a classmate in the room who read the same text and discuss it, using their annotations to fuel the discussion. Teachers move around the room and confer with these small groups. When kids notice and annotate their thinking while they read and engage in purposeful talk after reading, they comprehend more completely and think beyond the text. The articles in this resource are organized by topic, and lend themselves well to the RWT practice. Lesson 1 Read and Annotate is a useful one to model before introducing RWT.

Independent Reading

For kids who can and want to read these articles independently, let them have at it! But be sure to offer them a choice. Choice matters, particularly if our goal is engaged reading. When reading independently, kids can choose virtually anything under the sun that they can and want to read. In this resource, the reading material relates to immigration, industrialization, and innovation. So, we subscribe to Dick Allington's notion of "managed choice", which might look like offering four or five articles on innovation that include similar themes from which kids might choose. We also know that it is essential for readers to have enough background information to comprehend the article they have chosen. So, reading these in the context of a unit of study will give them a leg up.

You might do an interactive read aloud with the introductory overview pages to build enough background for kids who can and want to read other subsequent articles independently. In reviews of the research, Cervetti and colleagues (Cervetti and Hiebert 2009) argue that "knowledge building is the next frontier in reading education" because "evidence is beginning to demonstrate that reading instruction is more potent when it builds and then capitalizes upon the development of content knowledge." As students build their knowledge of the big ideas in this resource, they create a foundation that promotes ongoing learning and understanding.

Collaborative Reading in Small Groups

This version of independent reading convenes small groups where kids read largely independently, but then come together to discuss the information and ideas in a small group. There are several ways this might work:

Small-Group Jigsaw Four kids form a group, with each student getting a different article on a common topic. Kids read and annotate their articles on their own, ferreting out the most important information, summarizing important ideas, asking questions that come up. Then each student contributes to the collaborative conversation. Sometimes kids are asked to respond to questions about the bigger ideas and issues suggested by the topic. This process can work well with articles that illustrate different perspectives, such as primary sources about a variety of immigrant experiences. This kind of group work ensures that each student assumes responsibility for doing lots of reading and thinking and also participates in a conversation to get every student's take on important ideas and issues.

Article Clubs Like book clubs, a small group of students reads a common article and comes together to discuss and respond to it. The goal is to eventually share out their learning and ideas with the whole class in a whole-group jigsaw. After reading, kids create a response of some kind—a small poster, mind map, chart, illustration, or infographic. Responses depend on the goals for the process—but oftentimes, kids surface bigger issues or come up with answers to essential or guiding questions. And groups have been known to get creative with their responses. Drama and artistic creations keep kids engaged and enthusiastic about sharing their ideas with others.

Guided Reading in History Small groups of kids who read at the same reading level choose an engaging text that they will read together with a teacher's guidance. It is an opportunity to address skills development in content literacy and, specifically, historical literacy.

A caveat: please keep in mind that some of the issues in the upcoming selections are sensitive and could be triggers for previous traumatic experience. So, it is important that we know our kids well and that we know the articles, particularly if kids choose them for independent reading. We want to be close by to support kids as they dip into some of these more emotional issues.

HOW TO ACCESS THE DIGITAL COMPANION RESOURCE

The Digital Companion Resource provides all of the reproducible texts, plus primary source documents, and a bank of more than 60 additional historical images in a full-color digital format that is ideal for projecting and group analysis. We've also included the professional journal article, "Teaching for Historical Literacy" (Goudvis and Harvey 2012).

To access the Digital Companion Resource:

1. Go to www.heinemann.com.
2. Click on "login" to open or create your account. Enter your email address and password or click "register" to set up an account.
3. Enter keycode TTSNFII and click register.
4. You will receive a link to download the *Industrial Age and Immigration* Digital Companion Resource.

You can print and project articles and images from the Digital Companion. Please note, however, that they are for personal and classroom use only, and by downloading, you are agreeing not to share the content.

These buttons are available at the top of each article for your convenience:

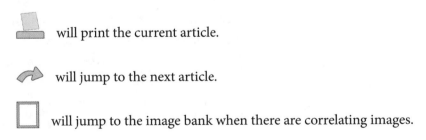

will print the current article.

will jump to the next article.

will jump to the image bank when there are correlating images.

For best results, use Adobe Reader for Windows PC or Mac. Adobe Reader is also available as an app for iPad and Android tablets. However, the Print function will not work on tablets.

Professional Articles

Here are two articles that provide more background information on immigration and offer a few tips for instruction.

Ten Myths About Immigration

Debunk the misinformation students bring to school—and help them think for themselves.

By: Teaching Tolerance Staff

ISSUE 39, SPRING 2011

Editor's note: While originally published in 2011, this story was updated in 2017 to reflect current statistics, policies, and conditions in the United States.

Myths about immigration and immigrants are common. Here are a few of the most frequently heard misconceptions—along with information to help you and your students separate fact from fear.

When students make statements that are unfounded, one response is to simply ask, "How do you know that's true?" Whatever the answer—even if it's "That's what my parents say"—probe a little further. Ask, "Where do you think they got that information?" or "That sounds like it might be an opinion, not a fact." Guide students to find a reliable source for accurate information and help them figure out how to check the facts.

1. MOST IMMIGRANTS ARE HERE ILLEGALLY.

With so much controversy around the issue of immigrants who are undocumented, it's easy to overlook the fact that most of the foreign-born people living in the United States followed the rules and have permission to be here. Of the more than 43 million foreign-born people who were living in the United States in 2014, around 44 percent were naturalized U.S. citizens. Those who were not naturalized were either lawful permanent residents, also known as green-card holders (27 percent of all foreign-born people), or immigrants who were unauthorized (some 11 million people, representing 25.5 percent of all foreign-born people).

2. IT'S EASY TO ENTER THE COUNTRY LEGALLY. MY ANCESTORS DID; WHY CAN'T IMMIGRANTS TODAY?

If you hear students making this statement, ask them when their ancestors immigrated and if they know what the entry requirements were at the time. For about the first 100 years, the United States had an "open immigration system that allowed any able-bodied immigrant in," according to immigration historian David Reimers. Back then, the biggest obstacle that would-be immigrants faced was getting here. Some even sold themselves into indentured servitude to do so. Today, however, many rules specify who may enter and remain in the country legally. There is also a rigorous process for obtaining documentation to enter the United States as a resident, including applying for immigrant visas and permanent resident/green-card status. Many students' immigrant ancestors who arrived between 1790 and 1924 would not have been allowed in under the current policy. Generally, permission to enter and stay in the country as a documented immigrant is limited to people who are highly trained in a skill that is in short supply here and have been offered a job by a U.S. employer, are escaping political persecution, are joining close family already here or are winners of the green-card lottery.

3. TODAY'S IMMIGRANTS DON'T WANT TO LEARN ENGLISH.

While most first-generation immigrants may speak their first language at home, 35 percent of those age 5 or older speak English "very well" and 21 percent speak it "well," according to the U.S. Census Bureau. Nearly 730,000 people became naturalized citizens during the 2015 fiscal year. They had to overcome such obstacles as traveling to the United States, finding a job, tackling language barriers, paying naturalization and lawyers' fees and dealing with an ever-changing immigration bureaucracy. Immigrants must speak, read, write and understand the English language, not only for the naturalization application process, but also so they can pass a lengthy civics test that has both oral and written components.

It's also worth discussing with students that the current demand for English instruction is greater than the services available in many parts of the country. Also explore with them false assumptions about "today's" immigrants versus those who arrived in prior generations. For example, ask students to find out how long it took their ancestors to stop using their first language. "Earlier immigrant groups held on to their cultures fiercely," notes Reimers. "When the United States entered the First World War [in 1917], there were over 700 German-language newspapers. Yet German immigration had peaked in the 1870s."

4. IMMIGRANTS TAKE GOOD JOBS FROM U.S. CITIZENS.

Ask students what kinds of jobs they think immigrants are taking. According to the American Immigration Council, a nonpartisan group, research indicates there is little connection between immigrant labor and unemployment rates of native-born workers. Two trends—better education and an aging population—have resulted in a decrease in the number of workers born in the United States who are willing or available to take low-paying jobs. Across all industries and occupations, though, immigrants who are naturalized citizens and non-citizens are outnumbered by workers born in the United States.

Another version of this myth is that it is undocumented immigrants who are taking jobs. However, the U.S. civilian workforce included 8 million unauthorized immigrants in 2014, which accounts for only 5 percent of the entire workforce. Compared with their small share of the civilian workforce overall, immigrants without authorization are only overrepresented in service, farming and construction occupations (see Table 1). This may be due to the fact that, to fill the void of low-skilled U.S. workers, employers often hire undocumented immigrant workers. One of the consequences of this practice is that it is easier for unscrupulous employers to exploit this labor source, paying immigrants less, refusing to provide benefits and ignoring worker-safety laws. On an economic level, U.S. citizens benefit from relatively low prices on food and other goods produced by undocumented immigrant labor.

5. "THE WORST" PEOPLE FROM OTHER COUNTRIES ARE COMING TO THE UNITED STATES AND BRINGING CRIME AND VIOLENCE.

Immigrants come to this country for a few primary reasons: to work, to be reunited with family members or to escape a dangerous situation. Most are couples, families with children, and workers who are integral to the U.S. economy. Statistics show that immigrants are less likely to commit serious crimes or be behind bars than native-born people are, and high rates of immigration are associated with lower rates of violent crime and property crime. For instance, "sanctuary counties" average 35.5 fewer crimes per 10,000 people compared to non-sanctuary counties. This holds true for immigrants who are documented and undocumented, regardless of their country of origin or level of education. In other words, the overwhelming majority of immigrants are not "criminals."

According to the American Immigration Council: "Between 1990 and 2013 the foreign-born share of the U.S. population grew from 7.9 percent to 13.1 percent and the number of undocumented immigrants more than tripled. . . . During the same period, FBI data indicate that the violent crime rate and property crime rate declined 48 percent . . . [and] 41 percent [respectively]." The truth is, foreign-born people in the United States—whether they are naturalized citizens, permanent residents or immigrants who are undocumented—are incarcerated at a much lower rate than native-born Americans.

6. UNDOCUMENTED IMMIGRANTS DON'T PAY TAXES AND BURDEN THE NATIONAL ECONOMY.

Ask students to name some ways U.S. residents pay taxes. They might come up with income tax or sales tax. Immigrants who are undocumented pay taxes every time they buy taxable goods such as gas, clothes or new appliances (depending on where they reside). They also contribute to property taxes—a main source of school funding—when they buy or rent a house or apartment. A 2017 report from the Institute on Taxation and Economic Policy highlights that undocumented immigrants pay an estimated $11.74 billion in state and local taxes a year. The U.S. Social Security Administration estimated that in 2010 undocumented immigrants—and their employers—paid $13 billion in payroll taxes alone for benefits they will never get. They can receive schooling and emergency medical care but not welfare or food stamps. Under the 1996 welfare law, most government programs require proof of documentation, and even immigrants with documents cannot receive these benefits until they have been in the United States for more than five years.

7. THE UNITED STATES IS BEING OVERRUN BY IMMIGRANTS LIKE NEVER BEFORE.

From 1890 to 1910, the foreign-born population of the United States fluctuated between 13.6 and nearly 15 percent; the peak year for admission of new immigrants was 1907, when approximately 1.3 million people entered the country legally. In 2010, about 13 percent of the population was foreign-born. Since the start of the recession in 2008, the number of immigrants without documentation coming into the country has fallen each year and, in more recent years, the number has stabilized. Many people claim that immigrants have "anchor babies"—an offensive term for giving birth to children in the United States so that the whole family can stay in the country (and a narrative that contributes to the myth that the immigrant population is exploding).

According to the 14th Amendment of the U.S. Constitution, a child born on U.S. soil is automatically a U.S. citizen. However, immigration judges will not keep immigrant parents in the United States just because their children are U.S. citizens. In 2013, the federal government deported 72,410 foreign-born parents whose children had been born in the United States. U.S. citizens must be at least 21 before they can petition for a foreign-born parent to receive legal-resident status. Even then, the process is long and difficult. In reality, there is no such thing as an "anchor baby." The vast majority of the 4 million immigrant adults without documentation who live with their children who were born in the United States have no protection from deportation.

8. WE CAN STOP UNDOCUMENTED IMMIGRANTS COMING TO THE UNITED STATES BY BUILDING A WALL ALONG THE BORDER WITH MEXICO.

Ask students, "How do you think immigrants come to the United States?" Immigrants who enter the United States across the United States-Mexico border without authorization could be from any number of geographical areas. The majority of unauthorized immigrants in the United States are from Mexico, but their estimated number—5.8 million in 2014—has declined by approximately 500,000 people since 2009. In 2014, 5.8 million Mexican immigrants were living in the United States without authorization, down from 6.9 million in 2007. Additionally, the number of immigrants from nations other than Mexico who are living in the United States without authorization grew to an estimated 5.3 million in 2014. Populations of immigrants who are undocumented increased from Asia, Central America and sub-Saharan Africa. So, a wall along the border with Mexico would not "stop" undocumented immigrants from coming to the United States. Building a wall or fence along the entire Mexico border is unlikely to prevent unauthorized entry. Details aside, history has shown that people have always found ways to cross walls and borders by air and sea as well as over land.

9. BANNING IMMIGRANTS AND REFUGEES FROM MAJORITY-MUSLIM COUNTRIES WILL PROTECT THE UNITED STATES FROM TERRORISTS.

A recent executive order, issued by President Donald Trump in March 2017, blocked the entry of citizens from six Muslim-majority countries for 90 days, ostensibly to protect Americans from terrorism. The title of this executive order, "Protecting the Nation From Foreign Terrorist Entry Into the United States," seems to equate the people most affected by the ban—Muslims—with the term *foreign terrorists*, implying that barring Muslims from entry would protect the United States from harm.

10. REFUGEES ARE NOT SCREENED BEFORE ENTERING THE UNITED STATES.

Ask students what the screening process is for refugees. Refugees undergo more rigorous screenings than any other individuals the government allows in the United States. It remains an extremely lengthy and rigorous process, which includes multiple background checks; fingerprint tests; interviews; health screenings; and applications with multiple intelligence, law enforcement and security agencies. The average length of time it takes for the United Nations and the United States government to approve refugee status is 18 to 24 months.

What Will the U.S. Supreme Court's Ruling on DACA Mean for Teachers and Students?

By Robert Kim

On November 12, 2019, the U.S. Supreme Court heard oral arguments in a case, *Department of Homeland Security v. Regents of the University of California*, that has already impacted the fate of thousands of immigrants to the United States—including students and teachers—under the Deferred Action for Childhood Arrivals program, or DACA.

- An **oral argument** is a live hearing in which lawyers for the plaintiffs and defendants of a case explain why the court should agree with them and not the opposing party. In the U.S. Supreme Court, oral arguments are usually delivered in front of all nine justices.

WHAT IS DACA?

DACA was established by the Obama Administration in 2012. It allowed **undocumented immigrants** who came to the United States as children and who meet certain requirements to apply for two-year periods of protection from **deportation**.

- An **undocumented immigrant** is a person who is not a U.S. citizen and who has not been granted legal permission to be or remain in the United States.
- **Deportation** is the process for removing an immigrant from the United States.

DACA did not provide any legal path to citizenship or permanent residency. But DACA did allow recipients to do things like go to college, pursue work, and get a driver's license or health insurance without the constant risk of deportation. In 2019, there were nearly 700,000 active DACA recipients. DACA recipients are often referred to as dreamers.

HOW DID DACA END UP IN THE COURTS?

On September 5, 2017, the Trump Administration moved to end DACA. It believed the policy established by President Obama was unlawful because only Congress, not the executive branch, has the power to provide legal status to undocumented immigrants. The Trump Administration stopped any more people from receiving DACA. But there was still a question of what should happen to existing DACA recipients. Trump's action was challenged by a number of different plaintiffs—including the National Association for the Advancement of Colored People (NAACP), a DACA recipient named Martin J. Batalla Vidal, and the University of California—in what became the *Regents of the University of California ("Regents")* case before the Supreme Court. Basically, their argument was that if the Trump Administration wanted to end DACA, it had to provide a satisfactory explanation; it couldn't just suddenly leave thousands of DACA recipients stranded by the roadside with a bare-bones reason for ending their DACA status.

During the November 2019 oral arguments, the Supreme Court asked both parties to address two key questions: (1) Was the decision by the Trump Administration to end DACA a matter that courts had the authority to weigh in on at all? (2) If so, did the Trump Administration's decision to end DACA violate the law? Solicitor General Noel Francisco answered the first question on behalf of the Trump Administration by arguing that the Department of Homeland Security had the absolute right, without any judicial oversight, to "simply end" its previous (Obama Administration) policy under DACA to suspend the deportation of certain undocumented immigrants. He answered the second question by arguing that the Trump Administration had provided a sufficient explanation for its actions as required by law; it had considered the needs of current DACA recipients but had decided that those needs were outweighed by its belief that DACA was unlawfully established by the Obama Administration.

Theodore Olson argued on behalf of plaintiffs that the government's decision to end DACA caused harmful consequences and disruptions in the lives of 700,000 individuals, their families, employers, communities, and members of the military. He also argued that this decision required the government to provide an accurate and reasonable explanation—and that it had failed to do so, which was a violation of the law.

WHAT DID THE SUPREME COURT DECIDE?

On June 18, 2020, by a vote of five to four, the Supreme Court ruled on behalf of the plaintiffs to preserve DACA. Writing for the majority, Chief Justice Roberts held that, first, whether the Trump Administration's decision on DACA violated the law was something that the courts had the power to decide, and second, Trump Administration's decision violated the law because its decision to end DACA was "**arbitrary** and **capricious**."

- Under federal law, the government agencies must engage in "reasoned decisionmaking"; their actions may be stopped by courts if they are "arbitrary" or "capricious"—which generally means that courts thought the government made a "clear error in judgment."

The Court explained that it was arbitrary and capricious for the government not to consider and explain why it was ending *both* parts of DACA—the eligibility of DACA recipients to receive certain benefits (like work authorization and government-provided health insurance and retirement income) *and* the protection of DACA recipients from deportation—before ending DACA in its totality. The Court also explained that the government failed to consider how rescinding DACA would impact DACA recipients who had gone to school, found jobs, purchased homes, and even started families as a result of becoming a DACA recipient.

The dissenting justices (those that did not agree with the five justices in the majority) made several points, including the opinion of three justices that the Trump Administration was correct in rescinding DACA because DACA itself was unlawfully created by the Obama Administration. Had their view prevailed, it is likely no future U.S. president would have been able to continue or restart the DACA program.

HOW WILL THE SUPREME COURT'S DECISION AFFECT SCHOOLS?

First and foremost, an estimated 700,000 DACA recipients, many of them K–12 and college students, have been at least temporarily spared the risk of immediate deportation, not to mention the loss of their current education, jobs, and benefits. This includes an estimated 20,000 immigrants with DACA-protected status working as educators. Moreover, there is likely to be a sense of relief for those teachers who, according to a UCLA study, have experienced enormous stress and secondary trauma from having to manage and respond to the threat of immigration enforcement targeted at their students.

But the battle is not over. None of the parties in the *Regents* case disputed that the government has the ability, generally speaking, to end DACA—as long as it does so in the right way. As guided by the Supreme Court's opinion, as of June 2020, the Trump Administration plans to provide a more complete justification to rescind DACA. In the meantime, people who wish to renew their DACA status (or apply for DACA for the first time) still face uncertainty. They will likely require the advice of legal and policy experts, who will be closely tracking further developments in the courts and federal government in order to advise both current recipients and new DACA applicants.

Finally, it's worth remembering that DACA itself does not provide a pathway to permanent resident status for undocumented immigrants; it merely "defers" the deportation of DACA recipients from the country. Only Congress can provide that pathway through federal legislation. That effort will continue, regardless of the fate of the DACA program.

Editor's Note: On January 20, 2021, in one of his first acts as president, President Joseph Biden issued an executive order that the Department of Homeland Security take all appropriate actions to "preserve and fortify" DACA. This allows DACA recipients, many of them students, to remain in the United States—living, working, serving in the military, and going to school. In addition, President Biden has urged Congress to pass legislation making

Dreamers eligible to apply for permanent residence in the United States with a path to citizenship in five years, a message of hope for all Dreamers.

To read the full *Regents* opinion, visit https://www.supremecourt.gov/opinions/opinions.aspx.

For more information on services, resources, and advocacy for immigrant students and families, visit: Immigration Legal Resource Center, Immigrants Rising, and United We Dream.

For educator resources—including lessons, toolkits, video, and dialogue guides related to immigrant students—visit the websites of iNation Media or Teaching Tolerance or American Federation of Teachers.

Robert (Bob) Kim is a leading expert in education law and policy in the United States.

A former civil rights attorney, Bob is the author of *Elevating Equity and Justice: Ten U.S. Supreme Court Cases Every Teacher Should Know* (Heinemann, 2020) and co-author of *Education and the Law, 5th ed.* and *Legal Issues in Education: Rights and Responsibilities in U.S. Public Schools Today* (West Academic Publishing, 2019 and 2017).

From 2011 through 2016, Bob served in the Obama Administration as Deputy Assistant Secretary in the U.S. Department of Education Office for Civil Rights, which enforces federal civil rights laws in K–12 and postsecondary institutions nationwide.

Read and Annotate

Stop, think, and react using a variety of strategies to understand

Text Matters

Kids can leave tracks of their thinking on every article, primary source, and historical image in this resource. Teachers model by peeling back the layers of their own thinking; then they guide kids to give it a go and practice annotating on their own.

ANNOTATING TEXT WHILE READING can be a powerful thinking tool. The practice of responding to the text—paraphrasing, summarizing, commenting, questioning, making connections, and the like—actively engages the reader in thinking about the main issues and concepts in that text. The purpose of this lesson is to encourage students to leave tracks of their thinking so they better understand and remember content information and important ideas.

Resources & Materials

- enough copies of an article for all students

Connect & Engage

Ascertain kids' prior knowledge about the text topic.

Today we are going to read about [topic]. What do you think you know about this? Turn to someone near you and talk about [topic]. *[If the topic is unfamiliar, we project or post one or two images on the topic and allow all kids to engage in a discussion through observation and questions.]*

Model

Show readers how to annotate thinking.

When we annotate a text, we leave tracks of our thinking in the margins or on Post-its. I'll read a bit of the text out loud and show you my inner conversation, the thinking I do as I read. I'll annotate by taking notes to leave tracks of that thinking. These tracks allow me to look back so I can remember what I read and fully understand it. *[We read the beginning of the text out loud, stopping occasionally to ask kids to turn and talk about their own thinking and to model some of the following.]*

- Stopping to think about and react to information
- Asking questions to resolve confusion or to consider big ideas or issues
- Paraphrasing the information and jotting our learning in the margin
- Noting the big ideas or issues
- Inferring to fill in gaps in information in the text
- Bringing in prior knowledge that furthers understanding

Guide

▰ **Monitor kids' strategy use.**

[After reading a paragraph or two, we turn this over to the kids by asking them to annotate.] Now I want you to take over jotting your thinking on your copy of the article—or on Post-its if you prefer. I'll continue reading the text and stop to let you turn, talk, and jot down your thoughts. *[As we pause in the reading, we circulate among the kids to check to see if and how they are using the strategies we modeled and if they are coming up with their own thoughts and annotations.]*

Collaborate/Practice Independently

▰ **Invite kids to finish the article.**

Now I'll stop reading. Continue to read and annotate the article, either with a partner or on your own.

Share the Learning

▰ **Invite kids to share, first in small groups and then as a class.**

When you have finished the article, find two or three others who have finished. Form a group to share out your reactions to the article. Think about the important ideas in the article as well as any issues, questions, or thoughts you have. *[After groups have had time to discuss, I ask kids to share out their thinking with the whole class, especially important ideas and questions.]*

Follow Up

▰ Kids might read related articles independently or investigate questions or gaps in information on this topic, continuing to annotate to leave tracks of their thinking.

▰ Inspire kids to assume the role of historians in search of information on a particular topic, locating information online or in print, annotating their thinking as they research, and summarizing what they learned for their cohistorians.

LoC, 3a43333

2 | Annotate Images
Expand understanding and learning from visuals

Text Matters

Images enhance kids' understanding of history. They spark purposeful discussion and authentic questions. Historical images, paintings, and photographs from the image bank, as well as those in articles, all lend themselves to careful viewing and analysis.

VISUAL LITERACY IS CRITICAL TO LEARNING because graphic and pictorial elements often carry or enhance the message in print and digital media. In this lesson, we encourage close viewing and reading using a variety of entry points and aspects of visual images to gain historical information and to further understanding.

Resources & Materials

- a copy of an image for each student (Use the images in the text to be read as well as those from the image bank or other sources.)
- Anchor Chart with three columns headed What We Think We Know, What We Wonder, and What We Infer
- Anchor Chart: Questions to Consider When Viewing an Image

Engage

Invite students to study and respond to a shared image.

[We choose one image and provide students with copies of that image or project the image for class discussion.] Look carefully at the detail in this image and really think about what you notice, infer, and wonder about it. Be sure to think about what you already know about this topic to help you understand.

Chart students' thinking.

Now turn and talk about what you know, wonder, and infer from the image. Also discuss questions and inferences that the image prompts you to think about. Keep in mind that we are always learning new information, and what we already know may be limited or even inaccurate, so be prepared to change your mind in light of new evidence. After talking, we'll come back together and share out our observations, inferences, and questions. *[We jot kids' thinking on a chart as we share out.]*

What We Think We Know	What We Wonder	What We Infer

Model

■ **Show students how to annotate the image with reactions, inferences, questions, and connections to prior knowledge.**

[We use kids' responses to guide our think-aloud and annotate the image with some of the important information we want them to know.] Watch me as I jot down my inner conversation about this image—those are the thoughts that go through my head as I view it. Notice the language I use to jot my thinking—and how I annotate my thoughts right on the copy of the image. I might choose a small part of the image and view it more closely.

As I look at the image, I notice . . . and have a strong reaction to it. I think this is about. . . . When I read the caption here, it tells me more about what this is. Additional text will certainly add more important information. But I respond to the image first, to get a sense of what it's all about. And I ask myself some questions: What's the purpose of this image? Who created it and why? I can infer the answers to these questions, and I may get them answered when I read on, but I may even need to do further research when I am finished to get a more complete understanding.

Guide/Collaborate

■ **Encourage kids to work in pairs to annotate their copies of the image.**

Now it's your turn. Choose from among the remaining images and work with a partner to discuss and record your thoughts. Annotate your copies of the image with your own ideas: what you notice, what you learn, questions you have, connections to your background knowledge. You might want to look back at our original thinking about the image that we recorded on our chart. I'll come around and listen in on your conversations and post some questions you might consider as you annotate your image.

Questions to Consider When Viewing an Image

Who created this and why?

What do you learn from it?

When I looked at this part of the image, I wondered. . . .

What can we infer from this image and other features?

What can we infer from other information we viewed or read?

How do images such as this help us better understand the topic?

Share the Learning

■ **Record kids' thinking as they share ideas and questions about the images.**

Come back together now and let's discuss our background knowledge, questions, and inferences. [*We call kids' attention to the* What We Think We Know, What We Wonder, *and* What We Infer *chart we began earlier.*] Do we understand who created these images? Do we now understand some different perspectives on this topic? Turn and talk about how images such as these enhance our understanding of the topic. Did your thinking change after closely viewing these images and talking about them?

Follow Up

■ Find more images for students to choose from that are related to the topic under study. (See the table of contents for the image bank for some possibilities.) Encourage kids to work in pairs or independently to study the images closely, guided by the Questions to Consider When Viewing an Image chart. As kids share out what they learned from each of the images, the whole class learns from multiple images.

■ What images or artifacts of today will historians of the future study to learn about us? Invite students to create a time capsule of images—personal photographs, print images, artifacts—and imagine what future historians will infer about our times.

Library of Congress, 03565

LESSON 3 | Build Background to Understand a Primary Source

Read and paraphrase secondary sources to create a context for a topic

Text Matters

Background knowledge makes a difference in kids' understanding of historical texts. In order to get the most out of primary sources, kids need to understand the context surrounding them. Secondary sources that accompany primary sources are appropriate for this lesson.

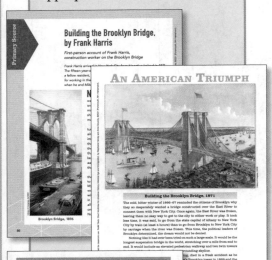

PRIMARY SOURCES can only be read in historical context. Just like working historians, students with background knowledge about the events, people, and ideas behind a primary source are far better able to interpret and understand it. Historians read secondary sources extensively to get a better understanding of historic events and ideas. Then they use the knowledge they have built to interpret and understand the primary source, ultimately using all sources to arrive at a more robust understanding. This lesson is preparation for Lesson 4; here, students build background knowledge by getting the gist of secondary sources to prepare for study of a primary source document in Lesson 4.

Resources & Materials

- a copy of a primary source document or artifact to project or show
- several secondary sources related to the time period in which the primary source was created, enough copies for all students
- chart paper

Engage

▬ **Define primary source and surface background knowledge.**

[We briefly project a copy of a primary source document.] What you see here is a copy of what is called a *primary source*. A primary source is an original document or artifact that is created at a specific point in history by someone who lived at that time. When we read or study a primary source, it's important to have some context for it—who wrote or said or created it, why it was written or created, and what historical events surrounded it.

This primary source was created by [creator] in [time period]. Turn and talk about what you know about this time period, this person, and what was happening at the time. *[Kids share background knowledge with a partner.]* Let's come back together and share out some of your prior knowledge about this. *[We list some of the ideas and information that kids come up with on a chart for all to see.]*

Model

- **Demonstrate how to annotate secondary sources to build knowledge about a topic.**

To prepare for studying this primary source, we'll be reading two articles about this person/this time period/these events. The articles are known as *secondary sources*; they are nonfiction articles written to inform us about a historical time. We'll use what we learn from reading them to inform our reading of this primary source.

As I read, I'm going to read for the essence of what's happening during this time period, with these people. My purpose is to get the gist—to capture the important events and big ideas to add to my store of knowledge. So I'm going to read a small section of the text, stop and think about it, and then write in my own words what is going on or what I learned from this section.

[We read the beginning of the text aloud.] After reading this part, I'm going to paraphrase, or put into my own words, what happened. I'll write a short phrase or two in the margin about this. Notice how I bracket this section of the text and jot down the gist as I read. From this section, I learned . . . and I'm thinking this will help me understand our primary source because I now have some historical context for it.

Guide

- **Continue reading as kids paraphrase information and annotate in the margins of the text.**

Now it's your turn. I'll keep reading aloud, but I'll stop to let you turn and talk, annotate your thinking, and write down the gist of this next section of the text. Remember to focus on the most important information and ideas that you think relate to the primary source we're going to read. *[We listen in to partner talk and glance at marginal annotations to make sure kids are getting the point. We then ask kids to share out what they have learned from the reading so far.]*

Collaborate/Practice Independently

- **Invite kids to continue reading secondary sources to build background about the time period under study.**

[We let students continue independently with the same article or—for more experienced classes—encourage them to choose among additional related secondary sources.] Keep reading about . . . , and continue to paraphrase and annotate in the margins as you read. Note that we don't always have to read sources word by word, but can skim and scan to find the parts that are most helpful to our purpose.

Share the Learning

■ **Chart students' learning.**

Let's come together and discuss the information we found. We'll write down some of what you discovered as you read to get the gist. Remember, share out what you think will help us most with reading our primary source. I'll add to our list so we can keep this information and these ideas in mind as we read.

Follow Up

■ Read a primary source that relates to the information that students learned in this lesson. Use Lesson 4 to further support primary source reading.

■ Challenge kids in pairs or teams to summarize—as historians might—the key information behind the topic under study and present their findings to the rest of the class in a creative, memorable format (e.g., art, diorama, poster).

Japanese American National Museum
(Gift of Madeleine Sugimoto and Naomi Tagawa, 92.97.108)

Read and Analyze a Primary Source

Focus on what you know and ask questions to clarify and explain

Text Matters

Any of the primary source articles or images work well with the thinking routines and strategies in this lesson. Strategies like asking questions and drawing inferences guide discussion as kids reason through these sources.

PRIMARY SOURCE DOCUMENTS can offer unique insights into the time period students are studying, but they often present significant reading challenges. Created in different time periods and for a variety of purposes, these documents are often characterized by unfamiliar formats, arcane language—both archaic or unusual vocabulary and unfamiliar or difficult sentence structures—and content beyond the experience of today's reader. This lesson offers a strategy for approaching the reading of primary source documents. It is important to do Lesson 3 to build a historical context before we ask kids to analyze a primary source, because students need a great deal of background knowledge about the topic at hand. We would not consider having them read a primary source cold without any knowledge of the historical context.

Resources & Materials

- a primary source document, enough copies for every student
- Anchor Chart: Reading Primary Source Documents

Connect & Engage

Review the definition of primary source.

For a while we've been studying about [time period], right? So we already know a bit about it. One way to understand even more about that time is to read *primary source documents*. Who can remind us what a primary source is? Turn and talk about that for a moment. *[We let students share their background knowledge and define primary source as "information—an original document or artifact—created at a specific point in history." They should know this from the previous lesson.]*

It's important to have a good deal of background knowledge about the people and events of the time period before tackling a complex primary source because these documents often have words and expressions that we don't use today. We call this arcane language. It's common for readers to come to an unfamiliar word or an idea and get stuck. Even if we read on to clarify understanding, reading on in a primary source sometimes leads to even more confusion because there are so many unfamiliar words and concepts.

Model

- **Explain a strategy for reading a primary source containing arcane language.**

Let's take a look at this example of a primary source document. I'll read aloud the first couple of sentences. *[We read aloud enough to give kids a taste of the language.]* Wow. Pretty hard to understand, isn't it? That's why when we read primary sources we usually need to read it several times to make sense of it and get the right idea. However, just reading it over and over doesn't help. We need to read it closely and use strategies to understand what we don't know. We particularly need to think about any background knowledge we already have.

Have you ever come to a word or an idea you didn't understand when you were reading? Turn and talk about a time you remember that happening and what you did to understand what you were reading. *[Kids turn and talk and share out a few examples of ways they figured out difficult words and language.]*

One of the best ways to understand a primary source with a lot of unfamiliar words and ideas is to focus on what we do understand the first time we read it, and perhaps think about what we have already learned about the content. Too often we get stuck on an unfamiliar word and that's it. So we focus on what we do understand the first time we read it and get a general idea of what the source is mostly about. Then when we reread it, we think about our questions and address those.

- **Model how to write notes on what you know and questions you wonder about.**

OK, so let's try it. *[We read a paragraph of the document.]* As I read this part of the document the first time, I don't have a clue what this word means, so I am not going to try to read it over and over. But I do understand this one, because I have some background knowledge about it. I can tell that the writer must have meant . . . when writing this. Thinking about what I know helps me get through this difficult text. So although there are quite a few words here that I do not understand, I can at least begin to get an idea of what this is mainly about by focusing on what I know. I'll also jot down any questions I have. We will get more information when we read this again.

So here is an Anchor Chart with some guidelines to help as we read primary sources. *[We review the process for each of the readings outlined on the Anchor Chart and then use the beginning of our document to model the first step. As we model, we make clear that any annotations focus on what we understand and on questioning difficult parts.]*

Reading Primary Source Documents

Reading #1: Focus on what you know. Annotate the text with what you do understand and ask questions about what you don't.

Reading #2: Use what you have come to understand to figure out the answers to your questions and infer the meaning of puzzling parts.

Successive Readings: Fill in the gaps by noting previous annotations, asking and answering questions, and making inferences for a more robust understanding.

Guide/Practice Independently

■ Monitor kids' primary source strategy use as they continue on their own.

Now work in pairs to think through this primary source document. Continue reading it with a partner, thinking about what you already know to understand new information. Annotate any important ideas you understand and write questions about the parts you need to come back to figure out. *[We circulate to make sure students can actually annotate and make progress with the text, pulling them back together to tackle it as a group if not.]*

Share the Learning

■ Call kids together to pool their knowledge and questions.

Let's get together and share our learning and our questions. *[We go back through as much of the document as students have read, noting our understandings, answering each other's questions, and making a chart of the questions we want to figure out in the next reading.]*

Follow Up

■ The first reading of primary sources that contain particularly arcane language might take more than one session to finish. Give kids plenty of time to discuss things they understand. On subsequent readings, go back and model the process of reading for answers to questions and using known information to make inferences about the time period and the document's meaning.

■ Involve kids in a reenactment—either dramatizing or creating a tableau—of the creation of the primary source.

5 | Compare Perspectives
Explore the different life experiences of historical figures

Text Matters
Texts that reflect varying perspectives on the same time period or historical events shed light on unrecognized or overlooked people throughout history. Many articles work for this lesson. Here are several that offer a variety of perspectives on child labor at different times in history.

WHEN WE LEARN ABOUT HISTORICAL EVENTS or a time period, it is important to understand that historical time from a variety of different perspectives. History is very much about the "untold stories" of people whose perspectives and experiences may not get top billing in the history books and that too often go unrecognized. But history is about all of us, so an important goal of this resource is to include voices, people, and perspectives that can provide kids with a fuller understanding of historical times and the people who lived in those times. The purpose of this lesson is to provide students with opportunities to compare and contrast life experiences of people living in this period so as to better understand their perspectives.

Resources & Materials
- images of different people within a particular time period
- chart paper
- a three-column chart and matching Thinksheets for each student: Person/Experiences & Perspective/My Thinking
- articles reflecting different experiences of several people

Connect & Engage
Introduce the idea of different perspectives.

[We post images of different people of the times—children, women, and men, for example.] Let's take a look at these different people. Turn and talk about what you notice about these pictures. Who do you see? Who is not here? What do you think you know about some of these people?

Even though all these people lived at the same time, let's consider how they might have experienced life in these times. Who has some background knowledge or some ideas about this? *[We record kids' background knowledge and thoughts on a chart, guiding them to understand that each person pictured experiences life in a different way.]*

We're going to read a variety of different articles today and compare and contrast the lives of different people who lived in this time period. We'll consider what might be similar about peoples' lives and what might be very different. Let's read part of one account together and then you'll read another account with a different perspective with a small group.

Model

■ **Record text evidence reflecting a person's experiences and perspective in a historical time.**

[To prepare kids to compare and contrast different perspectives later in the lesson, we model how to think about a historical figure's experiences.] I'm going to read this article that is written from the perspective of [person or people]. The authentic information here shows us what these people's lives were like.

I'll begin by identifying who this is about and then read this account aloud. I'll read to find out what important experiences they had and how these shaped the person's perspective, or point of view. Using evidence from the text, I'll also jot down my thinking about their experiences and point of view. I can organize my thinking on this chart:

Person	Experiences & Perspective	My Thinking

Guide

■ **Guide pairs to jot down text evidence for important aspects of a person's experience.**

[We hand out a three-column Thinksheet—Person/Experiences & Perspective/ My Thinking—to each student.] Now I'll keep reading and ask you to work with someone sitting near you to sift out more of these peoples' experiences as well as their perspectives on the times. You and your partner can discuss this and also record your thinking. Remember, the thinking column includes your interpretations and inferences as well as your questions and connections from your reading.

Collaborate/Practice Independently

■ **Ask kids to work in small groups to study other historical people.**

Now choose another article about a different person living in this same time period. Get together with three or four friends who are interested in the same article and record your thinking on your Thinksheets. As you read, think about how your historical characters' experiences affected their points of view, their perspectives on the times. Be sure to tie their experiences and perspectives to the text and also include your thinking.

Share the Learning

■ **Invite students to talk about historical people and compare them to others.**

[Once students have surfaced a variety of perspectives, we reconvene the group to compare and contrast the different lives of the people they read about.] Now let's talk about the historical people in your articles. We consider how their experiences influenced their view of the world, and how people differ based on these life experiences. *[Kids love to work big, and large posters can be very helpful for sharing out the experiences/evidence information that kids have gathered.]*

Questions to guide sharing:

- What experiences did your person have?
- How did this person's experiences shape their perspective?
- How are their experiences alike or different from other people we read about?
- Do you think this person's life experiences and perspective might have been, to some extent, "unrecognized" in general historical accounts of these times?
- Discuss why their perspective and life experiences are important to an understanding of people of this time period.
- Why do you think it might be important to consider a lot of different experiences and perspectives when studying history?

Follow Up

■ Provide additional groups of articles organized to highlight different viewpoints and perspectives on the same time period and engage students in comparing and contrasting different views.

■ Ask students each to assume the role of a historical character they have read about. Put two or three different characters together and prompt them to discuss an event or condition of their time from the perspective of their character: "What do you think about . . . ?"

■ Encourage students to conduct independent research on a lesser-known historical figure and craft a biography and portrait.

National Child Labor Committee collection, Library of Congress, 02314

Read Critically
Consider point of view and bias

Text Matters

This lesson works well with articles or primary sources that have clearly articulated points of view. We want kids to consider the author's perspective as well as possible biases.

As we read historical sources, it is important to read with a critical eye and a skeptical stance. Some articles provide balanced, "objective" information on a topic or issue. Several different perspectives and points of view are represented. Other articles may be written from a specific point of view with a definite perspective or even bias. Many articles fall somewhere in between. One way to support kids to become questioning readers is to show them how to discern the purpose of the sources they read. In this lesson, we help kids surface the author's intent and discuss why the article was written.

Resources & Materials

- Anchor Chart: Considering Point of View and Bias
- copies of two articles and historical images representing different perspectives on the same person, event, or time

Connect & Engage

Introduce questions that explore purpose, point of view, and bias.

[We project or share a copy of an article and discuss the title and its author. We pose questions to prompt kids to think about the point of view.] Before we read an article, it is helpful to discern whether the intent of the article is to be objective and offer information from several points of view or if it is written from a particular perspective. We ask ourselves questions like these.

Considering Point of View and Bias

- What is the author's purpose for writing the article? Is it written to inform us about a topic? To persuade us to have a particular opinion or view? For some other reason?

- Are several points of view or perspectives on the topic expressed? Or is there just one?

- What is the source of the information in the article or image?

- Can we detect any bias given the ideas in the article and the sources the author used to write the article?

Turn and talk about some of these questions. *[Kids do.]* This last question asks about bias. Who can tell me what *bias* is? *[We discuss the term* bias *and define it as "a preference or prejudice," noting that it usually refers to a point of view that doesn't recognize opposing or balanced views.]*

Model

■ **Read and think aloud to uncover the author's point of view.**

[We hand out copies of an article to each student and read the beginning aloud, keeping in mind the questions posed on the chart. We think out loud about both the information and the point of view to begin to uncover the author's purpose for writing the article.] The author of this article is writing about [historical events]. Based on what's happening here, it sounds like the author has some strong feelings and a definite perspective. Now that I read on, I learn that the information we have about these events comes from [source of information]. The actual words make me think. . . .

From the information the author includes and the sources they reference, I'm thinking the author may be biased. That's what I think so far.

Guide

■ **Guide students to read with a critical eye and a skeptical stance.**

Now I'll keep reading. While I do, keep our questions in mind *[We reference the Considering Point of View and Bias Anchor Chart.]* and jot notes in the margins of your copy. What's the point of view? Can you detect any bias?

What does text evidence tell you about the article's purpose?

Practice Independently

■ **Invite students to finish the article independently and/or read a second article with a different point of view.**

Go ahead and read the rest of the article, jotting your notes in the margins. Keep our list of questions from the chart in mind.

Share the Learning

■ **Listen in on small-group sharing.**

Join together with two other people and share out your thinking about the questions on the Considering Point of View and Bias Anchor Chart. Did you all come to the same conclusions? What are some different points of view that you noticed? Why do you think people believed the way they did? How did their personal experiences affect their point of view?

Follow Up

- Provide kids with pairs or groups of articles, images, or combinations of both that depict the same event. Encourage them to compare these, focusing on the perspectives of their creators.
- Create a dramatic interpretation of a scene from the life of a particular person. Keep in mind the point of view of each character as you write the scene.

UN Photo/UNHCR/R Chalasani (384472)

Organize Historical Thinking
Create a question web

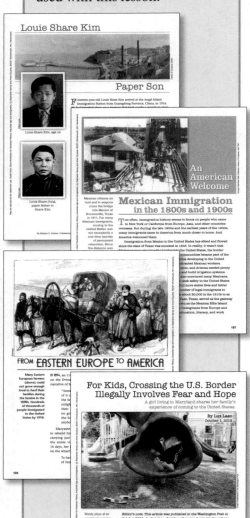

Text Matters

This lesson works well with multiple articles that could be discussed in relation to a central focus question. For example, if kids are to consider why people left their original countries to live in a new country, a variety of articles in this resource about why people emigrate can be used with this lesson.

KIDS' HISTORICAL THINKING often begins with their authentic questions. We encourage kids' curiosity and engagement in history by keeping a list of their questions as we find out more about a topic or time period. We add to our knowledge of the topic as we find answers and create a list of lingering questions for research and investigation. This lesson suggests ways that students can organize questions for further study.

Resources & Materials

- an article containing illustrations, photographs, or other images as well as text that will stimulate students' questions
- a board or chart on which to create and display a question web
- a collection of articles on a variety of related topics

Engage

Let kids know that their own questions are the most important ones.

Sometimes when I read about an unfamiliar topic or learn new information, I find myself asking a lot of questions. Sometimes I ask questions to help me fill in gaps in my knowledge or explain something I don't understand. Other times I wonder what might have happened if circumstances were different, so I might ask, "What if . . . ?" or "What might have happened if . . . ?" Sometimes my questions go unanswered and require further investigation; we call those *lingering questions*. What I do know is that our own questions really help us dig deeper into a topic and further our understanding.

Model

Demonstrate how viewing and reading can prompt questions.

We're going to do some viewing and reading—and pay special attention to our questions while we do. First, let's take a look at the image in this article. What questions does it raise for you? Next, go ahead and look over the article to see what it's about. Turn and talk about your thinking. Maybe you have some background knowledge or some thoughts about this. *[Kids share out briefly.]*

I'm going to begin viewing and reading. I'm going to stop right here because I already have a question. I'm wondering . . . I'll jot that down *[I write the question on one of the stems of the question web.]* and keep going. This section of the article leads me to wonder something else. *[Again the question is written on the web.*] As I think about these questions, a bigger question comes to mind. I'm going to put that in the middle of what we'll call our question web—it's a visual map of our questions. My bigger question goes right in the middle here:

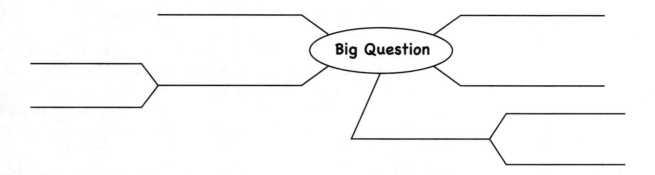

And then as I view and read, I'll add my other questions on stems around it—they are related to the big question—and put related questions near each other.

Guide/Share the Learning

▬ **Read and view together, adding kids' questions to the web.**

[We read on, asking kids to turn and talk to surface their questions.] Let's keep reading and viewing together . . . . Let's stop here. Go ahead and turn and talk about your questions. Jot them on a Post-it so we can share them and add them to our web. *[Kids generate questions and jot these on Post-its. As they share, we have them put the questions on our group question web, guiding them to place related questions near each other.]* These are related to our big question, so we'll place them around our bigger question.

I noticed that as we kept reading, we were able to answer a couple of these questions. I can jot a short answer or response right on the web. It's just a brief thought to capture our thinking.

▬ **Share out questions that were answered as well as lingering questions.**

Now that we've finished the article, let's add any final questions to the web. Now go ahead and turn and talk with your partner and discuss if we've discovered some information that provides some insight into our big question. *[We discuss what we've learned about our big question, wrapping up the conversation by identifying lingering questions that remain.]*

Collaborate/Practice Independently

■ **Give kids a choice of investigations.**

You're going to have a choice for continuing this work. Some of you seem quite intrigued by a couple of these lingering questions—questions that remain after our reading. If you'd like, go online and see if you can find a source or two that might give you some information about your question.

Another option is to read an additional source on a topic you choose. I have a whole bunch of articles right here, so if you'd like to tackle a different article or topic, come on up and peruse these. You can work with a partner, in a small group, or on your own, but be sure to pay special attention to your questions. Try organizing them on your own web.

Follow Up

■ Question webs are great investigation starters. Kids often gravitate to questions and topics that matter to them, and researching answers provides the perfect opportunity for students to use their developing repertoire of reading and thinking strategies.

■ Kids love to make their thinking visible. They can create many kinds of visuals—on posters, on the computer, with a collage of images and illustrations— to share the new information they are learning.

Library of Congress, Lomax Collection, 00277

LESSON 8

Read with a Question in Mind
Focus on central ideas

Text Matters

Kids are always encouraged to stop and ask questions as they read. Questions help kids zero in on what they may not understand initially, and also foster ways for kids to think beyond the text and do further research. Any articles in this resource work well with this lesson.

OFTEN WHEN WE READ to understand big ideas and important information, we read with a question in mind. When we keep one or two focus questions in mind as we read, we can more easily zero in on the information and ideas that are most important to understand and remember.

Resources & Materials

- images related to the topic currently under study, some with labels or captions, others without
- Post-it notes
- copies of an article on the topic for every student
- Anchor Chart, Reading with a Focus Question in Mind, and matching Thinksheets for every student
- a selection of additional articles on the topic

Connect & Engage

Engage students in a gallery walk.

[We post images at different points around the room.] We have placed a variety of images around the room, all of which relate to the article we will be reading. Move around the room, look at the images, and discuss what you notice or wonder with others gathered around each image. This is called a gallery walk where images are arranged like they might be in an art gallery or art museum. After talking, jot down on Post-its any inferences or ideas you have about the image as well as any questions that come to mind. Stick these right on the image.

You might put your initials on the Post-its you write so you can keep track of your own thinking.

Model

Relate the kids' thoughts about the images they just observed to the topic of the article to be read. Show kids how to read with a question in mind and use a Notes/Thinking scaffold to take notes that will address the focus question(s).

Did you guess from the pictures in your gallery walk what topic we're going to begin studying today? *[Students name the topic.]* Right! Now, let's take a quick look at this article, its title and features. What is it mostly about? Are there one or two important ideas that stand out? Turn and talk about what you were thinking and wondering about as you looked at the images in our gallery walk. How do your questions and inferences relate to the topic of the article?

■ **Demonstrate how to turn the big idea of the article into a question—one that gets at the big ideas in the article.**

So, from the images and a quick look at the text, I'd guess that one of the big ideas that is important to understanding this time in history is. . . . I can turn this big idea into a focus question and ask. . . . Keeping a focus question like this one in mind will guide us to find out important information about the topic.

[We hand out the Thinksheets and call attention to the matching Anchor Chart.] To keep my thoughts organized, I'm going to write our question(s) at the top of my Reading with a Focus Question in Mind page. It has two columns, Notes and Thinking, because both the information from the article and our thinking about it are important!

Listen and watch as I read and take notes on the article. I'll make sure the information I record relates to the focus question. So in the Notes column, I'll write facts and information about our question(s); in the Thinking column, I'll jot down what I think about the information—my reactions and responses. Maybe I'll have some additional questions or some background knowledge, all of which I can jot in the Thinking column. *[We read the beginning of the article, picking out information that relates to our question, writing it on the chart, and recording our responses.]*

Reading with a Focus Question in Mind

Focus Question: _____

_____

Title: _____

Notes	Thinking

An example of a big idea is that "All men are created equal." We turn this into a question by asking, "What are the Bill of Rights?" and "Why are these important?"

Guide

■ **Continue to read the article aloud as kids take notes.**

Now I'll keep reading this article while you take notes. Be sure to keep the focus question(s) in mind, jotting down only information that will help you understand the answers. Remember, including our thinking as we take notes means we'll process and understand the information more thoroughly. *[We continue reading, stopping occasionally to give kids time to turn and talk about the focus question before recording their ideas on the Thinksheet.]*

Collaborate/Practice Independently

▦ **Give kids an opportunity to study related sources, taking notes on and responding to the focus question.**

On your own or with a partner, finish reading this article and writing down your notes and thinking about this article. Next, choose one of these other articles or images and continue to think about our focus question. *[We call attention to the images posted for our gallery walk as well as a collection of related articles.]* Does this new source add to your knowledge on this topic? Read it with the focus question in mind and take notes on it.

Share the Learning

▦ **Ask kids to discuss the focus question in small groups, summarizing their learning.**

[We help kids form groups of three or four, making sure that among the members of the group, they have read several of the articles so they can discuss each knowledgeably.] Let's get into groups to discuss what we have learned about our focus question. Get together with two or three other people; make sure that together you have read and taken notes on several articles and images. Share with your group your learning and thinking about the articles you have read.

After you discuss the focus question using each article, take a look at the questions and inferences you jotted on the images at the beginning of the lesson. How has your thinking changed? What do you know now that you didn't when you first viewed the images? What questions that you asked still linger?

Follow Up

■ In small groups, have students do follow-up research to try to resolve any lingering questions. There are many websites rich with historical information; check out the recommended resource list on pages 283–286 to get started. If their queries are still unanswered, students might try contacting historical museums or other institutions. Researchers are often willing to answer questions, especially those of engaged, curious students.

■ Kids love to share their new findings. They can give presentations or create short movies to share the new information they are learning.

Grace Murray Hopper Collection, Archives Center, National Museum of American History, Smithsonian Institution

Text Matters

Kids learn to synthesize big ideas and themes across articles when they read several on a common topic. Using evidence to support these themes encourages discussion of important ideas and issues. There are many themes that surface throughout this resource, but here are four related articles about invention and innovation.

IN REAL-WORLD READING, we rarely read simply one text on a topic. Generally, we read a wide range of texts on a common theme to learn more about it and to understand a variety of perspectives. We infer the big ideas across these various texts to learn more about the overall topic or issue. The purpose of this lesson is to guide students to use evidence from several texts to infer broad historical themes.

Resources & Materials

- two-column Anchor Chart—Evidence from the Text/Big Ideas—and matching Thinksheets for each student
- a set of resources (e.g., an expository article, a piece of historical fiction, and an image) on the same historical topic for each group of three students

Connect & Engage

Engage the kids and review what it means to infer.

Today we're going to interact with several texts on a single topic to get more information. The more texts we read and the more images we view, the more we learn. To better understand the issues and information, we're going to infer the big ideas across several of these texts. Does anyone remember what it means to infer? Turn and talk about that. *[Kids turn and talk and share out some thoughts.]*

Inferring is the strategy we use to figure out information that is not explicitly stated in the text. To infer the big ideas, we need to think about what we already know and then merge our background knowledge with clues in the text to make a reasonable inference, draw a conclusion, and surface some big ideas or themes about the topic or issue. If our inference doesn't seem reasonable, we can gather more clues and information from the text. If we ignore text clues and rely solely on our background knowledge, our inferences could be off the mark. So we're constantly looking for clues, text evidence, and more information to make reasonable inferences and come up with big ideas. Reading a number of articles gives us more background knowledge, which gives us more information upon which to base our inferences.

Model

■ **Model how to use text evidence to infer big ideas.**

[We display a two-column chart on which to record evidence and big ideas.]
While I'm reading this article, I'll closely read the words, and I'll pay attention to the images and features, searching for clues to help me infer the big ideas. When I find some evidence that supports a big idea, I'll write it on the chart. We can find evidence for big ideas in words, pictures, features, actions, and details that are included in the text. Usually, there are several big ideas that bubble to the surface in an article.

Evidence from the Text (words, pictures, features, actions, details)	Big Ideas

[We read the article aloud, stopping when a big idea or theme is apparent.] I think these words are good evidence for the big idea of _____. So I'll write the words from the text in the Evidence column and the big ideas that I infer in the Big Ideas column. Here, these images help me to infer the big idea of _____. So I'll record information about the images in the Evidence column, too. My background knowledge may be helpful here. All of these clues are evidence for the theme of _____.

Guide

■ **Invite kids to come up with text evidence for some big ideas.**

OK, now it's your turn. Let's read a bit together before you go off and try this in a small group. *[We read through a page of text.]* Now that I have read a page, turn and talk about what you think are some of the big ideas here. Look for clues and cite that as evidence for your big ideas. *[Kids share their ideas with a partner.]*

Who has a big idea they would like to share? What is the evidence for that idea?

Let's add to our chart. Sometimes the evidence came from words quoted directly from the text, and other times from pictures and features in the text.

Collaborate

▰ **Support kids as they infer big ideas across several texts.**

Now you can get together in groups of three. I have three pieces of text; they are all different, but they focus on the same topic. Since they are grouped around a common topic, they are likely to have some similar big ideas, and all will likely include evidence for those big ideas. As you read through these articles, they will add to your background knowledge, increasing the likelihood that you will make reasonable inferences when you are inferring the big ideas. Share your thinking with each other; note the text clues and the big ideas that occur to you based on your reading and viewing and jot them on your Thinksheets. *[We distribute three related resources to each group and Evidence from the Text/Big Ideas Thinksheets to each student.]*

Share the Learning

▰ **Record kids' evidence and big ideas.**

[We gather kids in a sharing session to talk about their group's big ideas and evidence.] What are some of the big ideas you inferred as you read and viewed? As you share them, I'll add them to the class' Evidence from the Text/Big Ideas Anchor Chart.

Did you find some similar ideas across all of the articles and images?

Great thinking about using text evidence to infer the big ideas. We can continue to make inferences beyond the book, especially if there is some good evidence to support them.

Follow Up

▰ Add related resources to the original three and have kids continue to look for corroboration of their big ideas—or for new ones.

▰ Students might create dramatic tableaux to support their inferred themes: a series of frozen scenes carefully crafted to represent evidence of the big ideas.

G.H. Grosvenor Collection of Photographs
of the Alexander Graham Bell Family (LC)

Synthesize Information to Argue a Point
Use claim, evidence, and reasoning

Text Matters

Many texts in this resource provide information and evidence for supporting important ideas and taking a stand on an issue. The following texts are a few examples of articles that would work well with this lesson.

A GOOD ARGUMENT expresses a point of view, uses information as evidence to support that view, and applies the information to persuade others. To make a good argument, the arguer must turn information into knowledge, gathering evidence about the ideas in the text and synthesizing that information to make a claim that will convince others of the validity of the argument. To make a valid claim, however, the arguer must have some background about the issue; before making a claim and sharing the evidence, the claimant needs to have viewed or read several sources on the topic so that they know enough to make a reasonable claim about it. As a result, this lesson on synthesizing information to argue a point is best taught near the end of a unit of study.

Resources & Materials

- several articles on the same topics or with similar themes (some read beforehand)
- three-column Anchor Chart with columns headed Claim, Evidence, and Reasoning and matching Thinksheets for each student
- Anchor Chart: Questions to Guide Effective Arguments

Connect & Engage

Invite students to share what they already know about argument.

How many of you have ever heard the word *argument*? Turn to each other and talk about what you know about arguing. *[Kids turn and talk, then share out, mostly about personal disagreements they have had with others.]* Today we're going to talk about a more formal kind of argument.

Define the term *argument*.

Have you ever believed in something so much that you have wanted to convince others to agree with you? It is common to feel that way. Sometimes it happens outside when we want to make rules for a new game. Sometimes it happens at home when we are trying to get one more dessert out of Mom. And sometimes it gets a little unpleasant, with people getting mad at each other. Well, the type of argument we are talking about today is about convincing others to see the issue from your point of view. But rather than getting mad and fighting about it, in this kind of argument we gather evidence to make a point and try to convince the other side based on valid information.

So writers make arguments all the time, and they do it without fighting. They share evidence that helps them make their case. They might argue that we should eat healthier foods and support their argument with statistics showing the health risks of eating junk food. Or they might argue that soccer is a safer game than football, and to make their case share information about the danger of concussions that come from getting tackled in football. This kind of argument is based on a claim—that we should eat healthier food or that soccer is a safer game, for example. Turn to each other and talk about something you believe and would like to make a case for or a claim about. Share evidence that would back up your case. *[Kids turn and talk and then share out.]*

Model

■ **Read through a piece of text and show students how to use text evidence and reasoning to make and support a claim.**

When we make a claim, we need to provide evidence in support of the claim, valid evidence from a text or other source. And to make a decent argument, we need to know quite a bit about our topic. So we read about the issue or topic a bit and form an opinion. Then we merge the evidence in the text with what we already know to convince others of our claim. So let me show you how it works as I read through this article on. . . . I have an Anchor Chart here with columns headed *Claim, Evidence*, and *Reasoning*. As I read through the article, I'll collect evidence for the claim I'm making and add it to the first column.

Claim	Evidence	Reasoning

I have read a bit on this topic over the past week or so, and I already have a belief or opinion about it that I can turn into a claim. I'll state my claim—that is, the argument that I am going to try to make about the issue—in the first column. *[We write a claim in the first column and continue reading.]*

Here is some evidence for my claim. . . . supports my claim because . . . I'll jot this in the second column.

Now in the third column, I'm going to show my reasoning—how I interpret the evidence to support my claim. I believe . . . because the evidence shows me that. . . .

It helps that I have learned about this topic beforehand. I already knew . . . from previous readings, so I can reasonably make this claim based on the evidence from this article as well as from my background knowledge.

Reasoning is an important part of this process because if my goal is to make a case for my point of view and convince others, I need to be able to reason through this issue or topic myself in order to understand it well enough to persuade others. And always remember, an argument is not just our opinion, but our point of view supported by evidence.

Guide/Collaborate

- **Encourage students to work in pairs to read through an article, make a claim, and support it with evidence and reasoning.**

So it's time for you to give it a whirl. With partners, choose one of these articles on *[the same topic or issue]*. Talk about what you already know about the topic based on the article we just read together as well as other things you've learned. Think about an argument, or claim, you would like to make.

Write your claim on your Thinksheet. As you read this additional article, look for evidence that supports your claim and jot that down as well. And talk with your partner about your reasoning.

Questions to Guide Effective Arguments

- What is my point?

- Who is my audience?

- What might the audience already think about this argument?

- Does the evidence back up my claim? If so, how?

- Which evidence will most likely convince my audience of my claim?

- What would be a good counterargument? Is there evidence to support the other side? If so, what is it?

Think about some of these questions as you reason through the text. [*We display guiding questions and read them aloud.*]

Go ahead and get started. I'll come around and check in with your partnerships as you reason through the text, thinking about your claim and the evidence you find to support it. Remember, if you can't find evidence to fit your claim, you might need to revise your claim to fit the evidence!

Share the Learning

■ **Bring kids back together to share their claims, evidence, and reasoning.**

[Kids share their forms and we discuss their claims as well as possible counterarguments.] Whenever we make an argument, we need to be prepared for a counterargument—a claim that contradicts our own. When faced with an opposite opinion, we need to address it with more evidence in support of our own claim or with evidence that disproves the opposite claim.

Follow Up

■ This is an introductory lesson on synthesizing information to present an argument. Since making an effective case is a complex process, it requires repeated discussions and practice. So teaching this lesson a number of times with a wide variety of issues and articles comprises the next steps.

■ Teaching kids to write a paper with a strong argument is an eventual goal. A good resource to support that process is available at the University of North Carolina Writing Center http://writingcenter.unc.edu/handouts/argument. This site will support you as you engage kids in claim-and-evidence writing, although it needs to be adapted for kids younger than college age.

©Kent Knudson/PhotoLink/Photodisc/Getty Images

11 Read to Get the Gist
Synthesize the Most Important Information

Text Matters

When readers annotate and leave tracks of their thinking, they are building a synthesis of a text as they go. Putting important ideas into their own words means kids fully understand and learn from the texts they read. Readers should be doing this 24/7.

In this world of information overload, readers need to synthesize important information as they read or risk getting lost in a sea of details. In this lesson, readers put the most important ideas and information from a text into their own words—getting the gist of it. Then they add their thinking: questions, inferences, and connections. They synthesize the most important information and ideas in their own words and add their thinking to the mix. When readers merge their thinking with the information, they are much more likely to understand and remember it.

Resources & Materials

- copies of the article for each student

Connect & Engage

■ **Ascertain and discuss kids' background knowledge about the topic of the article.**

We'll be reading about _____. Take a look at the article and be sure to notice the images and graphics. *[Kids preview the article.]* Go ahead and turn and talk with someone about what you think you know about this.

Model

■ **Show readers how to annotate the gist and their thinking right on the page.**

Let's talk about the word gist. Who has an idea of what it means to "get the gist"? *[Students offer their idea of the meaning.]* Right! It means to get to what is most important about a text, or maybe even a speech. It's to understand the essence of what someone is saying or what we're reading.

When we read for the gist, we synthesize the most important information and the big ideas in a text. We pare down the information, eliminate some of the less important details, and come up with what's most important.

But we can't forget to include our thinking as well—our questions, inferences, reactions, and connections. When we respond to the information with our thinking, we have a much better shot at understanding it.

Let me show you. *[I read and stop after a paragraph or two to model my thinking.]* Now I'm thinking about what's most important. I'll put that information in my own words and write it in the left margin. But having read this, I've got a question. I'll put that in the right margin. I also have an inference that I'll jot down as well.

Notice that I don't write down every detail. I'm paring my thoughts down to what is most important.

Guide

- **Continue to read aloud as kids give it a go. Guide them and make sure they understand the strategy, especially the difference between getting the gist and recording their thinking.**

Let's try this together. I'll keep reading and we'll stop after this next section. You and your partner can talk about the gist and your thinking, writing these in the margins. Then we'll discuss what you wrote down. *[As kids have a go, I circulate around the group to see if they are understanding how to paraphrase the gist and write down their thinking.]*

Let's talk about some of the ideas and information we should include in the gist, as well as your thinking. *[Kids share out briefly.]*

Collaborate/ Practice Independently

- **Kids finish reading the article in pairs, recording their gist and thinking.**

As you continue reading, you'll probably begin to synthesize some of the big ideas throughout the whole text. Ask yourself: What is the article mostly about? What are the big ideas or the most important information you gleaned from the whole text?

Share the Learning

- **Kids come together in small groups to share the most important ideas and any questions, connections, inferences, and reactions they have. They discuss the entire article and the overall gist.**

Let's hear from each group. It's interesting that we can probably agree on many of these ideas. But your groups also came up with some different insights into this topic, because we have different questions, inferences, and reactions. That's what is so cool about reading—we can agree on the big ideas but we can each have our own take on the information. Nice job today!

Follow Up

- The gist/thinking strategy works well for any informational article, as well as images and nonfiction features such as historical images, diagrams, or maps. Try this strategy with images that students can choose from an assortment of possibilities. Enlarging texts, images, and features so kids can write on them graffiti style—or using Padlet or another digital annotation tool—encourages kids' conversations about their new learning.

Division of Work and Industry, NMAH, Smithsonian Institution

12 | Form an Educated Opinion
Distinguish between an opinion and an informed opinion

Text Matters

Reading changes thinking. And this is especially true when reading articles that prompt strong reactions, responses, and, of course, opinions. Kids need to know the difference between an off-the-top-of-the-head opinion and a more reasoned one that's based on information and evidence. These articles, among many in this resource, may spark kids to investigate further as they form more informed opinions.

WE LIVE IN THE INFORMATION AGE. Information abounds whether we are reading online, viewing TV, or reading newspapers. As they grow, students will be blasted with information. Unfortunately, in our digital world, much online information is unvetted and "fake news" proliferates. This generation of youth must be able to discern facts from opinions, certainly, but also to distinguish opinions from informed opinions. Its easy to have an opinion on just about anything, and everyone seems to. Kids definitely need to know that their thinking and opinions matter, but they also need to understand that the more they learn, the more their thinking evolves. As we gain knowledge, our understanding and opinion about a topic may change.

Resources & Materials

- copies of an article for each student
- a three-column Thinksheet, Opinion/Reasons & Thoughts/Informed Opinion

Connect & Engage

▬ **Flip through the article, pointing out the title, a few subheads, and some images.**

We have a really interesting article here. I'll read aloud the first section of this article. Cool, right? Flip through and preview the rest of the text to get an idea of what it is mostly about. *[Kids preview the article.]* Turn to each other and talk about what you think this article is mostly about and what you think you already know about this topic. *[Kids turn and talk.]*

Model

▬ **Discuss the difference between an opinion and an informed opinion. Demonstrate how one expresses an informed opinion.**

How many of you know what an opinion is? Turn and talk about that. *[Kids turn and talk and several share out.]* Exactly, an opinion is something you believe. Today we are going to talk about the difference between an opinion and an informed opinion. Opinions are not necessarily based on fact. Opinions carry more weight if there is information and evidence to back them up. When an opinion is based on facts and evidence, it is a more informed opinion. When people read, study, and learn about an issue, they develop a more informed opinion.

Let me show you how it works. "I am of the opinion . . ." *[I pick up text and read.]* But when I read this, I find that the facts don't back up my initial opinion. I will need to learn more about this issue to gain a more informed opinion.

Oh, now after reading, I've changed my opinion. Sometimes when we learn more about something, we change our opinion. Turn and talk about the difference between an opinion and an informed opinion.

Guide

▬ **Continue to read aloud and elicit kids' opinions about the topic.**

So, what do you think? What's your opinion? Do you think this is a good idea or not so much?

It's OK not to develop an opinion right away. Sometimes we simply don't have enough information. We call that NEI, for not enough information.

Opinion	Reasons & Thoughts	Informed Opinion

[We hand out the Thinksheets.] Here is a thinksheet titled Opinion/Reasons & Thoughts/Informed Opinion. If you are in favor of the idea here, jot *Pro*. If you are against it, jot *Con*. If you are not sure yet, write *NEI*. In the second column, jot down your reasons for that response. You can leave the final column blank until you have read more about this topic. Notice if your opinion is the same or has changed somewhat.

Collaborate/Practice Independently

▬ **Ask students to continue reading the article in partnerships, explore the pros and cons of the issue in the article, and jot additional thinking on the Thinksheet.**

As you read this article, you will discover new information about this topic. You may change your opinion; you may believe even more strongly in your original opinion or you may need more information. Whatever you decide, you will be more informed after reading this. That's a cool thing about reading!

Share the Learning

▪ **Kids share out their thinking on the Thinksheet.**

So, how many of you found evidence that made you stick to your opinion? How many changed your opinion? How many need more information to gain an informed opinion? One thing for sure, your opinion is more informed now after all of that reading and thinking.

Follow Up

▬ Find more articles in the resource or primary sources online that share further information about the issue explored in this lesson and encourage kids to read further about the issue. Check out the recommended resource list on pages 283–286 to get started.

▬ After further study, have kids choose a side and debate the issue. Share suggestions for debating including:

- Come prepared with information on the topic.
- Share your side of the argument and state your claim clearly.
- Cite evidence for your argument.
- Speak in a convincing, enthusiastic tone.
- Argue your point with confidence and show you care about your claim.
- Show respect and disagree agreeably.
- Listen to the other side closely and take the debate seriously.

National Portrait Gallery, Smithsonian Institution; gift of Margaret Carnegie Miller

Telling Our Stories in Words and Pictures

Honoring Family Stories

There are many good reasons to encourage kids' to share their personal and family stories. Eleven-year-old Dontae suggests one, saying, "It's very hard for us to find books that relate to our own situation" (Ehrenhalt 2019). When children share their stories, our classrooms become communities where many different voices and perspectives are listened to, relished, and understood. Our students—especially kids who are new to the classroom or community—may find they have a lot more in common than they realized. Indeed, there are a burgeoning number of books capturing the experiences of human migration— stories of "hope, courage, and humanity." Often told by refugees and others journeying to new lives and places, these can become mentor texts for kids' writing about their own lives, families, and experiences.

Award-winning Nigerian author Chimamanda Ngozi Adichie suggests other reasons to bring stories to life in her 2009 Ted talk, *The Danger of a Single Story*. Adichie explains that inherent in the power of stories is a danger—the danger of only knowing one story about a people or culture. She says, "*The single story* creates stereotypes, and the problem with stereotypes is not that they are untrue, but that they are incomplete. They make one *story* become *the only story*."

> **Donald Graves famously said, "Every child has a story to tell. The question is whether they will tell me, or whether they will tell you (2003)."**

The examples shared here focus on creating an inclusive, welcoming classroom with many stories and illustrate several ways for kids to tell their own—from the past or present, about themselves, their families, their experiences, their cultures. UCLA's Re-imagining Migration project believes that "sharing stories helps students take ownership of their own narratives, builds community in the classroom, and makes students feel less invisible to their peers and school faculty." And these stories also remind us that "beyond the stories themselves are issues related to identity, safety, trust, confidentiality and, for some, trauma (www.reimaginingmigration.org)." With this in mind, be sensitive to information that families may want to keep private. Encourage kids to share their stories in a safe, welcoming environment where many perspectives and opinions are valued. The project suggests some ways to create these learning environments and begin with stories from literature and oral history collections before asking kids to share their personal and family stories. Check out www.reimaginingmigration.org for great ideas about how to do this.

This story cloth illustrates a child's memory of a special dance performance celebrating Korean heritage and traditions. In her writing, the child describes how happy she felt to share this tradition with her class and how proud her parents were to attend her performance.

Ways to Tell Our Stories

Here are some suggestions of ways to honor, preserve, and share these stories. The examples included here are from educators who have worked with children and young people to tell their stories and build understanding across cultures, traditions, and history.

CREATING STORY CLOTHS: STORIES THROUGH WORDS AND PICTURES

Children and young people can tell their stories through words and pictures. What kids can talk about, they can write and draw. Teacher Lauren Hoyt asked kids learning English to tell a short story or a vignette that they remembered. Next, kids sketched an image that "tells" the story. They created collages of their experiences with fabric and then wrote about these. Another option is to have kids create a "story cloth" with cut-out paper and illustrations. Lauren's students posted their stories in the hallway to be read and enjoyed by others and to create a welcoming community for the many cultures represented in the school.

Based on the Hmong tradition of embroidering tapestries (*pa'ndau* in the Hmong language) that illustrate traditional patterns, images of wildlife and plants, or a story, Hmong story cloths serve as mentor texts for kids as they create their own.

FAMILY STORIES AND INTERVIEWS

One way to share family stories is to have students interview family members about their family history and experiences. We work with kids to think of something they want to ask their parents, grandparents, or family friends about. Then we help them craft questions to ask. Kids can record answers to the questions on a phone or tablet. Or they can have a written list of questions and jot down answers as notes to eventually write up the story. Kids who plan to record interviews with their families might find the StoryCorps app helpful (https://storycorps.org/).

Here we share a family story that is a collaboration between seventh-grade student Kent P., and his sister, May, who illustrated the story. Kent wrote this personal narrative about his father for his seventh-grade language arts class. He spoke with his father, Kit, about the family's journey as they fled Laos at the end of Vietnamese War. Kit was just seven years old the time.

A Story in the Jungle

By: Kent

It was a peaceful morning, the village sleeping contently when they heard a scream… "Fighter jets!" An old lady shrieked in terror at the top of her lungs. Jolting out of their sleepy state, they scrambled to some boars sitting in the riverbank. They had feared this day for days on end. People crammed in on the rowboats, going in the Vietnam War. Sure, their boat was a little over the weight limit, causing it to sink dangerously close to the river, just barely afloat. Waves crashes against the side of the little rowboat, water seeping in from every little crack. The boatmen rowed like their lives depended on it, maybe because it did.

Overwhelmed with adrenaline, Kit and my three uncles, Pete, Jack, and Shawn*, were scooping river water out with their bare hands as fast as the water flooded in. Nobody spoke, for when fleeing to another country as illegal immigrants, no one would dare say a word, unless they wanted to die with a bullet through your skull. Down the Mekong river they went, strong currents pushing them faster than they'd like. The river was merciless, sending them flying over every cascade, smashing them against the river floor. Blasts echoed throughout the landscape as bombs fell from the sky, tearing at the canopy, sending shockwaves that seemed to vibrate the rowboat. Gunfire was heard in the distance. It was then that my father said farewell to the only home he knew.

* * *

They were found by some Thai soldiers, who stuffed them in an unsanitary refu It was a giant white tent, about the size of a football field with people crowded inside outside. The soldiers assigned spots for the family, splitting them apart. There, my se old dad would scream and bawl and would only stop when his mom, my grandmothe

Find Kent's entire essay of his father's journey on the Digital Online Resources.

TELLING TALES: ACCOUNTS OF MIGRATION AND REFUGEE EXPERIENCES

There are many collections of migration stories, both published in books and online. Self-publishing a school or classroom collection honors the diverse voices that are an important part of our communities. We know many districts that have options for kids and teachers to publish their work; websites are another way to take kids' work public and share it with others.

Telling Tales: Immigrants' Refugees' Multilingual Stories of Transition, Resilience, and Hope, edited by Deborah Romero, is a collaboration of University of Northern Colorado professor Deborah Romero and Weld County School District educators Jessica Cooney, Laura De Groote, and Sally Reid. Their goal

was for students to "share with passion and enthusiasm their tales of adventure and strife as they found themselves forced to relocate, to abandon their hometowns, their countries and families, for an array of reasons. . . ." The book captures—in each student's words and illustrations or photographs— the resilience and optimism of people who find themselves facing huge challenges as they enter into a new culture and way of life.

The project grew out of Family Literacy events for English language learners, newcomers, immigrant students, and their families. The authors capture stories in the students' own words, as they are learning English, and emphasizes how the project forged ties and increased "diversity outreach" between the university, the school district, and the community.

Resources

"Authors of Their Own Stories" by Jey Ehrenhalt in *Teaching Tolerance*, Issue 63, Fall 2019.

The Danger of a Single Story by Chimamanda Ngozi Adichie in her 2009 Ted talk: https://www.ted.com/talks/chimamanda_ngozi_adichie_the_danger_of_a_single_story?

The Whispering Cloth: A Refugee's Story by Pegi Deitz Shea, Boyds Mills Press, 1995.

Telling Tales: Immigrants' Refugees' Multilingual Stories of Transition, Resilience, and Hope, edited by Deborah Romero.

Yanet and Natali Gutiérrez

We are Yanet and Natali Gutiérrez and we are twin sisters. We were born in February the 23th of 1995 in Houston, Texas.

Our parents are: Pedro Rodríguez and María Concepción García, who when we were one year and nine months took us to their hometown: Arandas, Jalisco, México. It is a village full of traditions and above all characterized by the Tequila. We lived there for a long time and studied Primary and Secondary School. But studying Secondary School was not that easy because we lived in the edge of the village in a ranch and they had to take us to school every day so we kept studying.

Our father works in agriculture and we didn't have enough economic resources to buy all we needed for school or gas, and since we are five brothers it is more difficult to have money for all given that it is only Dad who works.

But my sister and I were always encouraged and always got good grades. After finishing our Secondary School we decided to come to our country, the U.S.A., thanks to the support of our aunt to keep studying since it would be impossible in Mexico because our father didn't have money and wouldn't keep helping us with our studies.

It hurt when we came because we had always been with our mum and we didn't have friends here. But we have always thought that if you want to be somebody in your life you have to suffer. We hope we learn English quickly. We are putting a lot of effort to study and (salir adelante) [get ahead] and not have to struggle in a hard job like our dad's. We miss so much our brothers Alberto and Alfredo, also twins, our sister Joyana and of course our parents, who unfortunately are in Mexico and don't

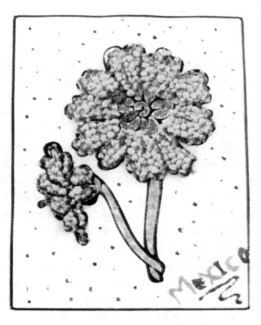

41

Continued on next page.

have the papers nor the resources needed to come. But fortunately, like we said before, my aunt and uncle offered us their house here in the States and are giving us the opportunity to keep studying. We are very thankful for that. We are currently in High School and are doing well in school. The teachers are good people, but some classmates keep bothering us, but anyway we are (echándole para adelante)[trying hard]. We hope see our dreams come true and our family in better life conditions someday. Hoping that, the twins say goodbye to you. Natali and Yanet.

Nuestros nombres son Yanet y Natali Gutiérrez y somos gemelas. Nacimos el dia 23 de febrero de 1995 en la ciudad de Houston, Texas.

Nuestros padres son: Pedro Gutiérrez Rodrieguez y Maria Concepción García. García quienes a la edad de 1 año con 9 meses en el año 1996 nos llevaron a su ciudad natal Arandas, Jalisco, México, un pueblito llena de tradiciones y lo caracteriza sobretodo el tequila. Ahí vivimos por mucho tiempo y estudiamos la escuela Primaria y secundaria. Pero estudiar la escuela Secundaria no fue tan facil porque nostrosviviamos a las orillas del pueblo en un rancha y todos los días nos tenian que llevar hasta el pueblo con tal de seguir nuestros estudios y además mi papi es apicultar y no teníamos los recursos económicos suficientes para comprar todo lo necesaria para la escuela o para la terminar nuestra

escuela Secundaria, decidimos venir a nuestra país E.U., aunque gracias al apoyo de nuestra tia para continuar con nuestros estudios yo que en México. Sería imposible hacerlo porque nuestro papá no tenía dinero y no nos sequiría apoyando más en eso.

A nosotros nos dolia mucho venirnos porque siempore estábamos al lado de mi mami y aunque no teníamos amigos de todos modos es difícil venirte y dejar sola a tu familia sola pero yo siempre he dicho que si quienes ser alguien en la vida le tienes que sufrir mucho. Esperamos y ojalá aprendamos a hablar inglés rápido. Le estamos echando muchas ganas para estudiar y salir adelante y en un futuro no batallar en un trabajo difícil como el de nuestro papá.

Extrañamos mucho a nuestros hermanitos Alberto y Alfredo tambien gemelos, a nuestra hermana Jovana y por supuesto a nuestros papas que desafortunadamente se encuentran en México lejos de nosotros y no tienen papeles ni los recursos suficientes para venir. Pero afortunadamente como ya antes dijimos, mi tia y mi tio nos abrieronlas puertas de su casa aquí en Estados Unidos y nos están dando la oportunidad de seguir estudiando. Les agradecemos mucho por esto. Ahorita estudiamas la High School y nos va muy bien en la escuela. Las y los maestros son muy buenas personas, solo que algunas que otras compañeras no dejan de molestar, pero de todos modos estamos echándole para adelante. Esperamos algún dia ver nuestros sueños realidad y nuestra familiaen mejores condiciones de vida. Esperando que esto suceda se despiden de ti las gemelas.

42

Duba Ebessa

My name is Duba Ebessa, I am 18 years old. I was born in 1993 in Somalia in a refugee camp. I have four brothers and three sisters. I don't remember a lot from the camp because I was very young, but sometimes there was fighting.

My sister and I left Somalia when I was 14, but my brothers and sisters stayed in Somalia. We went to Kenya and lived in a refugee camp called Isle. We lived with people we did not know. Life in the camp was hard because there was no food and no school. My parents left Somalia before us and lived in Ethiopia. I have not seen my parents since 2006.

I came to the United States in 2008. First, I lived with my bother in Minnesota. I went to school for first time in my life when I was 15 years old. The first semester was hard because the classes were in English and I did not know English. In January of 2010, I moved from Minnesota to Greeley. I live with friends in an apartment. I will live here until I graduate. After I graduate high school, I will go to college.

52

Tales

Zamzam Ahmed

I was born in Somalia.

One of my memories from my country is the
people.
This memory made me feel happy because the
people is good.

While there, l ate chicken.
I drank juice.
I slept with my sister.
I played with my friends.
And I studied English and math.

I left my home country because l left
because my family moved to the USA.
Once in the United States moved with
my family.

Now that l am in Colorado I don't like it
because of the snow and the cold.

I would like my teachers to know it's hard to
learn English.

My name is Zamzam

"I am" poems

53

The Industrial Revolution
A Time of Change

When you hear the term *revolution*, you might think about a drastic change in a government or political system. But the Industrial Revolution in America was an economic revolution. It started in the 1800s and lasted into the 1900s. It changed the way people worked. It also changed the way that products were made. Historians divide this time period into two stages: the First Industrial Revolution (1800 to 1850) and the Second Industrial Revolution (1850 to 1915). The advances that occurred during the first stage were stepping-stones for the changes that came about during the second stage.

A Time of Innovation

During the First Industrial Revolution, the U.S. Patent Office gave out 62,000 **patents** for new inventions. During the Second Industrial Revolution, it issued more than 500,000 patents. The pace of change increased dramatically during the second stage. Because of many new inventions, things that were once made by hand could be now be made in factories. New factory machines were run by water power or steam power, and no longer powered by people in small workshops. These factories made it possible to make goods faster and cheaper than ever before.

The Civil War was a turning point in these major changes in America. Advances in manufacturing, transportation, and communication before 1860 were just the beginning of the expansion of those industries after the war. The United States was just becoming an industrial power, but after the war, things really took off.

Patent: an official document that gives protection for an invention. Owning a patent gives an inventor the right to stop someone else from making, using, or selling their invention without their permission.

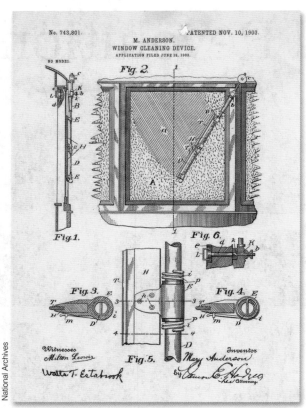

Mary Anderson's patent for a "window cleaning device" (windshield wipers).

Shift to Factories and Cities

Before the Civil War, most Americans lived and worked on farms. But after the war, they began moving into cities to work in factories. Manufacturing began to be a much bigger part of American life. Between 1860 and 1870, the number of factories in America increased by 80%. The time it took to do certain jobs was greatly reduced, thanks to new machines. Huge power looms in textile mills now made cloth. It no longer had to be made on hand looms. Steamboats and railroads changed transportation. Advances in the design of machinery and tools, like steel plows, made it easier to grow and harvest crops. Farmers could now grow more food with less work.

The invention of the cotton gin made removing seeds from cotton easier, and farmers increased production to make a larger profit. It didn't make it easier to grow cotton, nor did it make it easier to harvest; these tasks remained unchanged. Cotton farmers enslaved more people, especially women and children, to do the backbreaking work of growing and harvesting cotton—all for the pursuit of profit.

Toolkit Texts: Short Nonfiction for American History, Industrial Age and Immigration, by Stephanie Harvey and Anne Goudvis, ©2021 (Portsmouth, NH: Heinemann).

Factories, like these in Chicago, were built along waterways because goods could be shipped by water.

Workers: Library of Congress, 3g11947. Cotton plant: ©sframe/Fotolia.

In 1900, a group of Black American men, women, and children (above)— some holding baskets containing cotton—stand in a cotton field. Before the cotton gin was invented, cotton seeds had to be separated from the fiber by hand, a difficult and painful job. Left: A cotton plant.

National Child Labor Committee collection, Library of Congress, 04484

Many children, like this child working in a basket factory in 1908, worked long hours in dangerous conditions. There were few limits on child labor during this time, and in some places, the rule was "the younger, the better."

Unexpected Consequences

The Industrial Revolution had a lasting impact on all people, but not all classes benefited equally. Those who could take advantage of the better jobs or professions, or those who were lucky enough to be business owners, were able to enjoy comfort, privilege, and leisure in many ways. Factory and farm workers were exploited. They frequently had to work long hours in factories that were unsafe and often dangerous. Many of the workers who operated the machines and built the new roads and railroads lost their lives. Children worked in places like coal mines and mills. Wages were very low, and even with an entire family working, it was hard to earn a decent living. Millions of

©Kent Knudson/PhotoLink/Photodisc/Getty Images

Fossil fuels like oil and coal are found in the Earth's crust and contain carbon and hydrogen, which can be burned for energy. Factories produced large amounts of goods more quickly and cheaply, but also polluted the air and water.

immigrants also came to the United States from other countries to work, often facing discrimination. Cities became crowded. People often lived in cramped, unhealthy conditions, and they lacked services such as garbage collection, public parks, and care for their children.

As factories and cities grew, the environment was negatively affected. **Fossil fuels** powered the Industrial Revolution. Factories powered by coal spewed smog and soot into the air and dumped chemicals directly into rivers and streams, resulting in increased air and water pollution. Natural resources, like coal, oil, and lumber, were used up instead of conserved. There are laws now that limit pollution, but the effects of past pollution remain. Earth's average temperature has risen since the Industrial Revolution began, in part because of the use of fossil fuels. Problems linked to climate change include extreme weather and rising sea levels. To this day, fossil fuels continue to be a driver of both global warming and climate change.

Timeline

1791 Samuel Slater builds the first thread-spinning mill in the United States

1793 Eli Whitney patents the cotton gin based on experiments he and Catharine Greene completed; Samuel Slater builds the first successful water-powered textile mill in Rhode Island

1807 Robert Fulton designs a steam engine to power a boat

1809 The United States stops trade with Britian, so U.S. textile mills produce more cloth

1812 War of 1812 stops European imports, so U.S. factories produce more goods

1807

Library of Congress, 03982

May be reproduced for classroom use. *Toolkit Texts: Short Nonfiction for American History, Industrial Age and Immigration*, by Stephanie Harvey and Anne Goudvis, ©2021 (Portsmouth, NH: Heinemann).

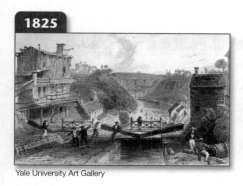

1825 Erie Canal is completed in New York

1830 Congress enacts the Indian Removal Act

1831 Cyrus McCormick invents the mechanical reaper; the first railroad in the United States to use a steam engine pulls freight and passenger cars

1834 National Trades' Union is started

1835 Lucy Larcom goes to work in a Massachusetts mill

1837 John Deere invents the first steel plow

1844 Samuel B. Morse invents the telegraph

1846 Elias Howe develops a sewing machine

1860 Pony Express moves mail cross country

1861–1865 Civil War

1869 Knights of Labor forms; Colored National Labor Union is started; Transcontinental Railroad is completed

1872 Elijah McCoy develops an automatic lubricator that allows trains to run for long periods of time without stopping and saves time and money

1876 Alexander Graham Bell patents the telephone with drawings drafted by Lewis Latimer

1877 Nez Perce Chief Joseph surrenders to the U.S. government; Great Railroad Strike occurs; Thomas Edison files a patent for the phonograph

1880 Thomas Edison develops an electric light bulb; John D. Rockefeller's Standard Oil owns 90% of oil refineries in the United States

1881 Lewis Latimer patents a carbon filament for the incandescent light bulb, which made electric lighting practical and affordable

1882 Chinese Exclusion Act is passed; Pearl Street Station in Manhattan was the first central power plant in the United States

1884 First skyscraper is built in Chicago

1886 American Federation of Labor forms; Haymarket Riot occurs

1892 Carnegie Steel Company is the largest U.S. steelmaker; Homestead Strike occurs

1894 Pullman Strike occurs

1897 First subway is completed in Boston

1903 Wright Brothers complete the first successful airplane flight

1906 Upton Sinclair shocks readers with his book *The Jungle*; Pure Food and Drug Act enacted

1913 Henry Ford sets up the first assembly line to manufacture cars

1914–1918 World War I; United States joins in 1917

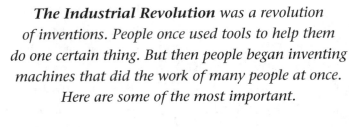

The Industrial Revolution was a revolution of inventions. People once used tools to help them do one certain thing. But then people began inventing machines that did the work of many people at once. Here are some of the most important.

INVENTING A REVOLUTION

James Watt as a boy, as he notices the force of steam in the family kettle.

THE STEAM ENGINE (1765)

James Watt gets credit for the steam engine. James Newcomen actually invented it, but Watt made big improvements to it. His steam engine was smaller. It also used less coal to run and provided much more power. Thanks to Watt's improvements, steam engines could be used to power machines in factories. Before steam engines, factories used water from rivers and canals for power. The water flowed alongside mill buildings and turned huge water wheels. Water wheels were eventually replaced by turbines that were even better at powering the mill's machines. Steam engines meant factories no longer had to depend on water power. Now they didn't need to be close to a river. Mills could be built anywhere.

Steam engine

May be reproduced for classroom use. *Toolkit Texts: Short Nonfiction for American History, Industrial Age and Immigration,* by Stephanie Harvey and Anne Goudvis, ©2021 (Portsmouth, NH: Heinemann).

Eli Whitney

Cotton gin

THE COTTON GIN (1793)

It used to take one person working a whole day to remove the seeds from a single pound of cotton. Then Eli Whitney invented his cotton gin. The gin could remove the seeds from 50 pounds of cotton in the same amount of time as it took a worker to gin one pound by hand. It showed just how much labor could be saved by using machines.

After the invention of the cotton gin, many Southern farmers switched to growing cotton. The cotton gin made growing cotton more profitable for plantation owners. Yet it saved labor for only one task—removing the seeds from cotton. It didn't make it easier to grow cotton or easier to harvest it. In fact, it involved back-breaking labor to grow and harvest cotton on a large scale. Plantation owners bought more en-slaved people so they could plant more cotton to sell. The cotton gin expanded cotton production and slavery. By the 1830s, cotton became the South's most important cash crop and greatly expanded the region's slave labor economy.

FAST FACT

This portrait of Eli Whitney (above) was painted by American artist and inventor Samuel Morse, best known for inventing the telegraph.

John Kay

Division of Cultural and Community Life, National Museum of American History, Smithsonian Institution

Flying shuttle

THE FLYING SHUTTLE (1733) AND THE SPINNING JENNY (1770)

Two inventions changed how quickly cloth could be made. John Kay invented a flying shuttle. This mechanical shuttle quickly passed thread back and forth through a loom. It worked faster than human hands could. It also meant that people could now weave cloth that was wider than their arms could reach. Next, James Hargreaves invented the Spinning Jenny. This machine spun cotton or wool into thread. One person sitting at a spinning wheel could make only a single thread at a time. But with the Jenny, one worker could spin eight threads at once. Hargreaves named his invention after his daughter.

Spinning Jenny

May be reproduced for classroom use. *Toolkit Texts: Short Nonfiction for American History, Industrial Age and Immigration,* by Stephanie Harvey and Anne Goudvis, ©2021 (Portsmouth, NH: Heinemann).

Hearing Opportunity Knock

Library of Congress, 25503

Peace Brings Economic Opportunity

After four long and bloody years, the Civil War finally came to an end in the spring of 1865. While it nearly destroyed the nation, it also created opportunities. Individuals in the North who manufactured arms, clothing, and supplies for the opposing armies became wealthy.

Many of these men looked for new opportunities to invest their money. At the time, the federal government had not yet established rules that regulated businesses. So a person who was willing to take great risks might also see enormous profits.

Railroads Move the Nation

In addition, the United States was shifting from being an agricultural nation to becoming an industrial nation. Railways were an important part of this process. They opened up access to the West and new areas for farming, ranching, mining, and land development. They moved people and goods across the

John D. Rockefeller became one of the biggest captains (or "kings") of industry in the 19th century.

By Peter Barnes, *Cobblestone*, ©2014 by Carus Publishing Company. Reproduced with permission.

nation in greater numbers and at higher speeds than ever before. Stops along routes became the sites of bustling towns and cities. Many fortunes were made on railroads.

But railroads were extremely expensive to construct. They required large amounts of labor and materials. Just one mile of railroad track might cost $20,000 to build.

This led to a whole new way of accumulating wealth. Individuals who were willing to take risks began their empires by dealing with the financing of railroads, not the actual building of railroads. The financial district in New York City, known as Wall Street, played an important role in the growth of big business during this period.

New Industries Boom

Other major industries, such as steel, coal, and oil, grew dramatically as railroads moved goods quickly from New York to California. New and growing businesses also benefited from advanced manufacturing techniques. Powerful machines performed tasks 5 to 10 times faster than humans had ever been able to do before. Some factories ran 24 hours a day and 7 days a week to deliver maximum production. Fierce competition led many businesses to increase efficiency.

Some business leaders fought competition by merging their resources, which forced smaller entrepreneurs out of the market. Bigger companies had more money to spend on research, advertising, and production.

Few Regulations on Businesses

By the late 1880s, Americans started complaining about **trusts** and **monopolies**. Many citizens thought it was unfair that giant corporations were able to force smaller companies out of business. Congress passed the Sherman Anti-Trust Act of 1890 "to protect trade and commerce against unlawful restraints and monopolies." But the law's vagueness left interpretation up to the courts. The courts tended to side with big businesses. The act was only slightly successful at preventing monopolies and curbing the greed of America's wealthiest industrialists at the turn of the 20th century.

Captains of Industry

Wealthy businessmen defended themselves against their critics. They claimed that they built things that benefited the nation. Steelmaker Andrew Carnegie argued that competition brought quality goods at cheap prices to all Americans. Cornelius "Commodore" Vanderbilt claimed that the millions he had earned on his railroad investments were "worth three times as much to the people of the United States."

Trusts are combinations of firms or businesses created for the purpose of controlling prices and reducing competition in an industry.

Monopolies are created when one group has exclusive control over the means of making and selling a product or service.

Library of Congress, 25747

To some Americans, wealthy industrialists put on a show
of giving their money away as a chance to improve their public images.
This cartoon's message to Andrew Carnegie and John D. Rockefeller
suggests that they give to worthy causes that really
needed help, such as hospitals for the poor.

A **precedent** is something that is established first, that has never happened before, and that can be used as an example in similar later circumstances.

Philanthropic means organized to provide charitable assistance to help humankind.

Carnegie, Vanderbilt, and other major 19th-century industrialists set a **precedent** for the 20th century: free markets offered opportunity for great profits. Today, however, government rules and regulations have been put in place to limit modern corporations and prevent monopolies.

And yet, like the original captains of industry, modern corporations, such as Coca-Cola, Walmart, and Microsoft, often play leading roles in the effort to fund important **philanthropic** foundations.

Historians have difficulty in determining how these people should be remembered. As one biographer wrote when describing John D. Rockefeller, "His good side was every bit as good as his bad side was bad."

CAPTAINS OF INDUSTRY
OR ROBBER BARONS?

During the Industrial Revolution from 1870 to 1915, the United States underwent impressive economic growth. Much of this growth was due to railroads—which now spanned from coast to coast—as well as steel mills and the coal mining industry. Big business boomed, and the economic explosion included many kinds of factories.

During this time of industrial growth and **innovation**, wealthy industrialists created their fortunes through business dealings in oil, steel, cotton, textile, and tobacco industries, railroads, and banks. They've been referred to as either robber barons or captains of industry depending on one's point of view and experience. Both can be defined as business **magnates**—people with great power, influence, and wealth. They had the power and means to create opportunities and jobs for the many people. But some paid little attention to workers' rights, allowed poor working conditions, and paid low wages to workers.

The term *robber baron* is considered a negative term. Robber barons typically used unethical business practices to eliminate their competition and develop

In 1869, the Transcontinental Railroad (above) was completed, marking a transportation milestone that revolutionized travel and industry in the United States.

Innovation:
a new method, idea, or product

Magnate:
a wealthy and influential person, especially in business

May be reproduced for classroom use. *Toolkit Texts: Short Nonfiction for American History, Industrial Age and Immigration*, by Stephanie Harvey and Anne Goudvis, ©2021 (Portsmouth, NH: Heinemann).

Monopoly:
having complete control over an industry with no competition

Philanthropist:
a person who seeks to improve the lives of others, especially by donating money to good causes like the arts, education, and medical research

Competitor:
one selling similar goods or services in the same market as another

a **monopoly** in their industry. Often, they had little empathy for workers and were motivated only to expand their own wealth.

Although captains of industry sometimes engaged in illegal business practices, they were often **philanthropists**. They used some of their great wealth in a way that would benefit society by providing more jobs and increasing productivity.

Whether one viewed them as captains of industry or robber barons, these individuals had a huge impact on America's development. With technology booming and immigrants coming to the United States seeking better opportunities for themselves and their families, these businesspeople left a mark on the United States.

John D. Rockefeller

Born in 1837, John D. Rockefeller became one of the richest people in the world as the founder of the Standard Oil Company. He invested in oil refineries, iron ore and gold mines, natural gas, and other ventures, creating thousands of jobs and incomes for those families. The wealth of John D Rockefeller was vastly more than even the richest people of today. Rockefeller bought out his **competitors**, sometimes forcing them out of business, so he had little competition. Without any competitors, he was able to charge any price he wanted for his products. Standard Oil controlled about 90% of the oil refineries and pipelines in the United States by the early part of the 1880s. Rockefeller was charged by the U.S. government with creating a monopoly, which was an illegal business practice. In 1911, the U.S. Supreme Court ordered him to break up Standard Oil Company into several separate companies. The Supreme Court decision made it possible for other businesses to compete with Rockefeller.

Although historians have criticized Rockefeller for his illegal business practices, Rockefeller was a philanthropist whose charitable efforts made a giant

Burning oil wells, like this one in Pennsylvania (right), were one reason that oil towns collapsed in the mid-1800s. In the 1860s, John D. Rockefeller (far right) established the Standard Oil Company during the oil boom. Rockefeller's investments in railroads and refineries would make him one of America's richest men.

Much of the steel used in the United States came from steel mills owned by Andrew Carnegie. New ways of processing steel made it stronger. As a result, skyscrapers could be built in major cities.

In this political cartoon from 1902, the artist celebrates Carnegie's generosity with the caption: "Andrew Carnegie makes all the other millionaires look like 'thirty cents.'"

May be reproduced for classroom use. *Toolkit Texts: Short Nonfiction for American History, Industrial Age and Immigration,* by Stephanie Harvey and Anne Goudvis, ©2021 (Portsmouth, NH: Heinemann).

impact. Over the course of his life, he donated great amounts of money to causes, especially for medical research and education. Today the Rockefeller Foundation continues to support charitable causes around the world.

ANDREW CARNEGIE

Born to a poor Scottish family, Andrew Carnegie and his parents immigrated to the United States when he was 13. He built his fortune by investing in the steel industry and became the owner of Carnegie Steel Company, which by 1889 was the largest steel company in the world. Not only was Carnegie smart when it came to the science behind steel making, he was always looking for cheaper and better ways of managing businesses and people. He owned coal and iron mines, ships, and railroads so he could control costs involved in making and transporting steel. His business practices made him unpopular with the workers in his steel mills. They were often were required to work long days for low wages and face unsafe or even dangerous working conditions.

At the same time, many Americans benefited from Carnegie's ideas, which made steel that was inexpensive and reliable. Steel structures were stronger and safer, and steel mills provided many jobs in the steel industry. In his efforts to contribute to society, Carnegie was also known to be an active philanthropist. He established the Carnegie Endowment for International Peace, the New York Public Library, and other libraries in many towns throughout the United States.

J.P. MORGAN

John Pierpont Morgan was a banker and business investor from a wealthy family. He modernized American banking practices and made them more efficient. He invested in Thomas Edison, the inventor of the light bulb, and the Edison Electricity Company, which made him even wealthier. He formed the banking company J.P. Morgan & Company, and as a banker, gained control of half of the country's railroads and many other companies.

J.P. Morgan

14

Library of Congress, 3g06404

In this political cartoon titled "The Helping Hand," J.P. Morgan is helping Uncle Sam row a boat. In the early 1900s, J.P. Morgan used his great wealth and power to help the United States government during times of economic crisis, but he gained control over the markets and increased his personal wealth.

Morgan engaged in some unethical practices to create a monopoly and control the banking industry. He also slashed the size of his workforce and his workers' pay to maximize his profits. Workers' wages were low and working conditions for employees were poor.

Some of his actions did benefit the United States and society. For example, his wealth was so vast that he was able to help bail out the federal government twice during an economic crisis, first in 1895 and again in 1907.

HENRY FORD

Automaker Henry Ford was a captain of industry who is considered to have treated his workers well. He believed that well-paid workers would be happier and more efficient. He paid auto workers $5 a day, which was twice as much as other auto manufacturers paid. With these higher wages, workers were able to afford to afford a car. During a time when workers were required to work 10 hours a day, 6 days a week, Ford scheduled his workers for 8-hour days, 5 days a week.

Ford was known to be generous with his wealth in terms of charitable contributions. He donated personal funds to many organizations including the Henry Ford Hospital for people who could not afford the cost of their medical care. Today, the Ford Foundation continues with a mission to reduce poverty and injustice, strengthen democratic values, and advance human achievement.

©Photo Researchers/Science History Images/Alamy

Library of Congress, 3c11278

Workers in factories owned by Henry Ford (right) made large numbers of cars in shorter periods of time as a result of assembly lines (left).

Ida Takes Aim

Ida M. Tarbell (above) wanted to explore Standard Oil's rise in the oil industry.

A **muckraker** is someone who searches for and exposes misconduct in public life. During the 1890s to 1920s, journalists who exposed established institutions and leaders as corrupt were called muckrakers.

When Ida M. Tarbell's mother warned her not to play in puddles, she was not talking about mud puddles. She meant the pools of black oil gushing from the oil well by their front door. In 1860, three-year-old Ida lived near Oil Creek in western Pennsylvania. Oil had recently been discovered in the area.

Hoping to make a profit, Ida's father started a small oil company. His business prospered for a number of years. Then John D. Rockefeller formed a group of oil producers into a trust and called it Standard Oil Company. The trust's enormous size and power allowed it to sell its oil for less. It forced smaller companies out of business. Ida's father's company was one of those.

Searching for the Truth

When Ida grew up, she became a famous **muckraking** writer for McClure's Magazine. Remembering how Standard Oil had crushed her father's business, she decided to uncover the story behind the company's success. By 1900, Standard Oil was the largest trust in the country. Many people discouraged Tarbell from exposing the secrets of the powerful monopoly.

But Tarbell planned to present a fair and accurate picture of the company. How could Standard Oil object to that? For two years, she interviewed people and searched through piles of documents and testimony. Some important papers had been destroyed or hidden, but Tarbell did not give up until she had all the facts.

Exposing Unfair Practices

Tarbell learned that Standard Oil had used unfair and dishonest practices to expand its business. For example, Standard Oil arranged illegally with the railroads to get cheaper delivery rates. Also, when other companies shipped oil, the railroads passed on part of the payment, called a refund, to Standard Oil. These advantages allowed the trust to set its prices so low that smaller companies could not compete for long and were forced to go out of business. Standard Oil even used spies: It paid railroad employees to report the scheduled shipping dates of other oil producers. Standard Oil then forced the railroads to stop those shipments.

In November 1902, Tarbell's first article appeared in McClure's. Eventually, 19 installments of "The History of the Standard Oil Company" ran in the magazine. In 1904, the articles were published as a two-volume book.

Tarbell's research revealed how John D. Rockefeller (below) became a giant in the business by using unfair practices to gain an advantage over smaller businesses.

A KANSAS DAVID IN THE FIELD.

Library of Congress, 25939

Taking a Stand

Tarbell was surprised at the backlash caused by her articles. She said, "I was willing that [Standard Oil] should combine and grow as big and wealthy as [it] could but only by legitimate means. But [the company] had never played fair, and that ruined [its] greatness for me." She called for the American people to take a stand against greed and dishonesty.

Tarbell's revelations made Standard Oil the focus of state and federal government investigations. In 1911, the U.S. Supreme Court ordered Standard Oil to break up into smaller companies. Independent oil businesses would no longer have to struggle against powerful oil trusts.

Tarbell and the other investigative journalists of that era played important roles. They drew attention to the problems confronting American society in the early 20th century. Instead of writing about big, complex economic issues, they focused on a single industry, city, or person. Thanks to their efforts, the public became informed and aware about issues that were real and personal. Armed with well-researched information, the concerned public then demanded changes.

UNIONS IN TOUGH TIMES

May be reproduced for classroom use. *Toolkit Texts: Short Nonfiction for American History, Industrial Age and Immigration,* by Stephanie Harvey and Anne Goudvis, ©2021 (Portsmouth, NH: Heinemann).

In July 1894, rioting workers set fire to 600 freight cars in the Chicago rail yards during the Pullman strike. Federal troops fired shots into the crowds of striking workers, killing some workers.

Labor union: an organization of workers formed to improve wages, benefits, and working conditions

Collective bargaining: the process of negotiation between employers and a group of employees to improve wages and working conditions

Strike: a refusal to work in an attempt to make their employer meet their demands

The **labor union** movement in the United States grew out of workers' need to protect their rights. A union is a group of people who join together to share and pursue a common purpose. Organized labor unions in industries and businesses fought for better wages, reasonable hours, and safer working conditions.

Unions formed in cities all over the United States in the 1800s. In 1833, several unions joined together in New York City with the goal of improving the lives of workers in various businesses. By the late 1800s, railroad workers, coal miners, mill and textile workers, and agricultural workers were members of unions. Union members try to bargain with their employers, who own or manage the companies, to gain higher wages, reduce their long hours, and provide safe working conditions. This is called **collective bargaining**. When bosses refuse workers' demands, workers often go on **strike**.

Following are a few important events in the labor movement during the Industrial Revolution.

1894: PULLMAN PALACE RAILCAR COMPANY

The Pullman Strike was a nationwide railroad strike that lasted for three months. The strike and boycott shut down much of the nation's freight and passenger trains west of Michigan. The conflict began in Chicago, when nearly 4,000 factory employees of the Pullman Company began a strike after George Pullman lowered wages, eliminated jobs, and increased the number of hours required of the workers at his factories. At the same time, he refused to lower rents in his company town or prices in his company store. This **boycott** grew and became one of the most serious labor revolts in American history, involving both the Pullman workers and eventually the American Railway Union. Railroad traffic was halted, and President Grover Cleveland called in the U.S. Army to stop the strikers from obstructing the trains. Violence broke out in many cities, and the strike ended. A total of 30 workers were killed in riots. Many Americans were appalled by the conflict this strike represented between the rich and poor.

The events of the Pullman Strike led to a deepening awareness that there was a labor issue in America. As a result, reformers began searching for a new way to protect public interest in the face of competing worker and business-owner interests.

> **Boycott:** to refuse to buy, use, or participate in something as a form of protest

---

1900–1902: COAL STRIKES

Coal miners struck in 1900 and 1902 in Pennsylvania. Miners successfully bargained for higher wages and shorter hours. President Theodore Roosevelt intervened in the strike to keep the flow of coal going to heat factories, homes, and businesses.

Breaker boys (right), sometimes as young as 8 years old, worked in unsafe conditions picking out rocks from loads of coal that came up from the mines.

LAD FELL TO DEATH IN BIG COAL CHUTE

Dennis McKee Dead and Arthur Allbecker Had Leg Burned In the Lee Mines.

Falling into a chute at the Chauncey colliery of the George S. Lee Coal Company at Avondale, this afternoon, Dennis McKee, aged 13, of West Nanticoke, was smothered to death and Arthur Allbecker, aged 15, had both of his legs burned and injured. Dr. Biel, of Plymouth, was summoned and dressed the burns of the injured boy.

He was removed to his home at Avondale.

Both boys were employed as breaker boys, and going too close to the chutes fell in. Fellow workmen rushed to their assistance and soon had them out of the chutes. When taken out McKee was found to be dead. His remains were removed to his home at West Nanticoke. Allbecker will recover.

Newspaper headlines, like this one from 1911 (left), captured the stories of terror and tragedy that often occurred from unsafe working conditions.

Labor Day originated as a holiday when New York City labor unions sought to bring attention to the fight for workers' rights with marches and parades. Soon labor parades began in other cities around the country. We still celebrate Labor Day every September as a tribute to the hard work and accomplishments of all American workers.

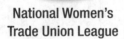

National Women's Trade Union League

1903: WOMEN'S TRADE UNION LEAGUE

The Women's Trade Union League was formed in 1903 by working women and social reformers who were fighting for better working conditions and wages for women. The organization provided financial help as well as training for women. It also fought against child labor and tried to make factories safer for workers.

Workers at a Ford factory in Michigan receive their ballot to vote on union representation as government officials and labor leaders look on.

1935: NATIONAL LABOR RELATIONS ACT

Congress enacted the National Labor Relations Act ("NLRA") in 1935 to protect the rights of employees. This act guarantees the right of employees to organize into unions, engage in collective bargaining, and take collective action such as strikes.

1938: FAIR LABOR STANDARDS ACT

The Fair Labor Standards Act of 1938 was created to establish a minimum wage and overtime pay when people work over forty hours a week. It also prohibits most employment of minors in "oppressive child labor." The act was designed to protect the educational opportunities of young people and prohibit their employment in jobs that are harmful to their health and safety. FLSA restricts the hours that youth under 16 years of age can work and lists hazardous occupations too dangerous for young workers to perform.

This 5-year-old child and other children picked cranberries in a Massachusetts bog in 1911. By 1910, the number of children working had grown to 2 million. The National Industrial Recovery Act and the Fair Labor Standards Act of 1938 reduced the number of working children, and for the first time, set a minimum wage and limited the number of hours that children could work.

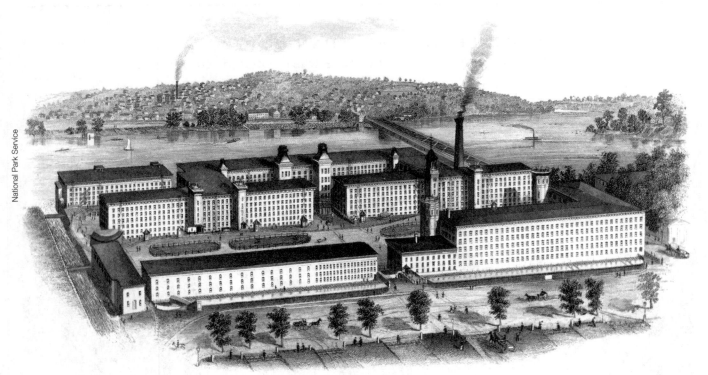

Boott Cotton Mills, Lowell, Massachusetts

STRIKES IN THE MILLS

DURING THIS TIME, many adults objected to the long hours, low pay, and dangerous conditions in the factories. In 1834, women in the Lowell textile mills in Massachusetts went on strike to protest a wage cut. They refused to work in an attempt to make their employer meet their demands. A few days later, most of the women had returned to work at lower wages. The strike had failed.

Two years later, the women went on strike again. This time, it was to protest an increase in the rent they had to pay at the company's boarding houses. During this time period, business owners often provided boarding houses for young female workers to stay in, but workers had to pay rent. One of the striking workers stood outside and gave a speech proclaiming how they had to resist the rent increase. This was considered shocking. At this time, women typically did not give speeches in public. About 2,500 workers walked off the job. Not enough workers remained to run all of the machinery. The strike continued for months. Eventually, the company agreed to not to increase the rent.

> **Did You Know?**
>
> In the 1830s, mill women made an average of $2.25 a week.
>
> Men averaged $6.75 a week.
>
> Children earned as little as 30 to 50 cents a week.

In the 1840s, many people who worked in mills in New England wanted to reduce the workday from 12 hours to 10 hours. They were not successful in changing this policy in Massachusetts at first. It was New Hampshire that became the first state to pass a law making the workday 10 hours long.

Industrial workers became used to standing up for themselves and making their beliefs known. Many began working to reform society on a larger scale. Some New England industrial workers, particularly women, became involved in the movement to end slavery. Others worked to secure greater rights for women, such as the right to vote. The Industrial Revolution had brought workers off farms and into mills. In their new environment, many workers began to speak up about the changing world.

©Hulton Archive/Getty Images

Harriet Jane Hanson Robinson worked as a child in a cotton mill in Lowell, Massachusetts. At the age of 11, she participated in an 1836 strike for better worker treatment. As an adult, Harriet organized the National Woman Suffrage Association of Massachusetts, fighting for the right to vote and equal citizenship for women.

National Park Service

American artist Winslow Homer depicted "the bobbin girl" who spent long hours wrapping thread around an empty bobbin, and then loading the bobbins into shuttles on the looms.

Model T
A Car for the Masses

"I will build a car for the great multitude. It will be large enough for the family, but small enough for the individual to run and care for. It will be constructed of the best materials, by the best men to be hired, after the simplest designs that modern engineering can devise. But it will be low in price that no man making a good salary will be unable to own one— and enjoy with his family the blessing of hours of pleasure in God's great open spaces."

— HENRY FORD

1915 Ford Model T

Today, going from New York to California is easy. Travelers can cover the 3,000 miles by plane, train, or automobile. At the beginning of the 20th century, however, the United States was mostly an agricultural nation. Traveling anywhere was difficult. People lived and worked on isolated farms and properties, largely cut off from all but their closest neighbors. Workdays lasted from sunup to sundown and left little time for socializing or playing.

For local transportation, people relied on horses and buggies, horse-drawn carriages, their own feet, or bicycles, which had become a popular fad in the last decades of the 1800s. Imagine just how far you would get if you had to walk to and from a destination in one day—while still getting your work done before you left! And roads consisted of worn dirt paths, not the well-maintained highways and paved local roads we have today.

An Affordable Automobile

All that began to change with Henry Ford's dream to create an affordable, reliable car. After years of tinkering and testing—and working his way through the alphabet—Ford introduced his Model T in 1908. Before the Model T, cars were expensive and of little use to rural, working-class Americans, owing to the poor condition of most country roads. But with its improved traction and better clearance, the Model T could handle those rough dirt roads. Ford's sturdy cars could lighten the workload, too. They could haul tools and

Henry Ford's idea for an assembly line allowed him to mass-produce an inexpensive, basic model car for Americans.

equipment, hay, and produce, for example, and they began replacing draft horses on farms.

Other manufacturers scoffed at Ford's idea to create an affordable automobile. Determined to build his cars efficiently, Ford had his cars built on an assembly line, which moved a car under construction along a path while stationary workers added parts along the way. As the cost of making the Model T dropped, Ford's sales sky-rocketed because more Americans could afford to buy his low-priced automobiles.

A New Way of Life

In a way, the Model T represented freedom. For the first time, Americans were not restricted to working close to their homes. They could run short errands. They could enjoy afternoon visits. The Model T changed the way Americans lived, worked, and played by making traveling safe, easy, and inexpensive.

More than 100 years have passed since Ford introduced his Model T. His dream started a fascination with cars that exists to this day in the United States.

Factory workers on the assembly line install upholstery for the seats in the body of the Model T. A sack of stuffing lies on the floor.

By Kelly Poltrack, Cobblestone, ©2009 by Carus Publishing Company. Reproduced with permission.

©surajet.I/Shutterstock

Our lives are full of amazing inventions!
Yet we often take for granted how things are created—
or it doesn't occur to us that there was ever a time
when certain things did not exist.

BRILLIANT BREAKTHROUGHS

American inventions have come about in different ways. Some of these creations came after years of hard work. Others were the result of experiments by different people, all contributing to the final concept. Still other ideas were almost accidental. They all have at least one thing in common, however: these inventions have changed our lives forever.

As you read about these everyday items, consider what goes into the invention process. It might start with a simple idea and a questioning mind. The patience to observe things and study previous accomplishments is key. And the strength of character, or vision, to continue a project even when others do not support it is truly essential. What do you think? Is there an inventor inside you?

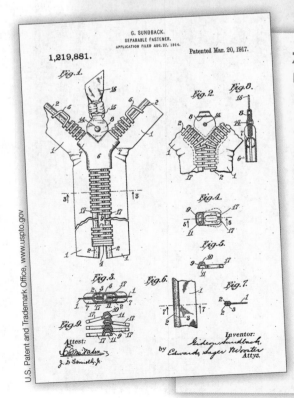

U.S. Patent and Trademark Office, www.uspto.gov

ZIPPER: JUST ZIP IT!

Elias Howe called it the "continuous clothing closure." Whitcomb Judson called it the "clasp-locker." **Gideon Sundback** called it the "hookless fastener" ("numbers 1 and 2"). These three Americans share credit for the evolution of the zipper. Its first incarnation in 1851 used string woven through eye clasps located on either side of two edges designed to come together. The wearer pulled the clasps tight with the string. The two sides, however, didn't always stay firmly together. Eventually, Sundback's 1914 idea to include a Y-shaped slider—through which two rows of teeth are staggered and then locked together—gave birth to a new way to open and close everything from suitcases to clothing to shoes. Still, the word *zipper* was not "invented" until 1923. The B.F. Goodrich Company first used the word to describe its line of rubber boots and shoe protectors, which included zippers to close them. Now it's not only a great American invention, it's also a great American word.

By Marcia Amidon Lusted. May be reproduced for classroom use. *Toolkit Texts: Short Nonfiction for American History, Industrial Age and Immigration*, by Stephanie Harvey and Anne Goudvis, ©2021 (Portsmouth, NH: Heinemann).

JEANS: LEAVE IT TO LEVI

Levi Strauss found success in San Francisco, California, but not in the way he expected. An immigrant from Bavaria, Strauss landed first in New York, where he learned the peddling trade from his two older brothers. After the California Gold Rush of 1849, Strauss headed west to open a dry goods store. He hoped to sell bolts of canvas for tents and wagon covers to the miners who still filled the area. But this enterprising young man quickly recognized a problem and a way to solve it. All the miners had one common difficulty: their clothes. The rugged outdoor life they endured caused their pants to tear or wear out long before they could be replaced. Strauss used his bolts of tent canvas to make a sturdier product for the miners.

He designed and sewed a pair of heavy-duty "waist overalls" especially geared to a miner's rough lifestyle. In the 1860s, he substituted denim, a softer material, for the canvas and dyed the material blue to camouflage stains. In 1873, he partnered with a Nevada tailor named Jacob Davis, and together they patented the process of affixing copper rivets to the jeans' pocket corners so that they would not tear when, hopefully, they filled with gold nuggets. Levi's pants became famous throughout California. By 1872, he was a millionaire, and today Levi's jeans are everywhere.

PATENT RIVETED CLOTHING

The Best in USE FOR

FARMERS, Mechanics AND MINERS!

LEVI STRAUSS & CO., SAN FRANCISCO, CAL.

ELECTRIC GUITAR: THE WIZARD OF WAUKESHA

Like many other ideas, the electric guitar owes its invention to more than one person. But although the instrument evolved over time, it would not be what it is today without **Les Paul**, who was born in 1915. Many rock, jazz, blues, and country musicians consider Paul the father of the electric guitar. As a teenager performing under the name "Red Hot Red," Paul played the harmonica and the guitar in his hometown of Waukesha, Wisconsin. To make sure his audience could hear him, he stuck a phonograph needle into his guitar and hooked his parents' radio speaker to a car battery and to the instrument. From this simple electronics experiment in 1929, Paul went on to build his first electric guitar from railroad-track wood. He sometimes gave his experimental guitars names, such as the "Log" and the "Clunker." Paul, the "Wizard of Waukesha," changed pop-music history.

Les Paul and Mary Ford
I JUST DON'T UNDERSTAND
and
PLAYING MAKE BELIEVE

Division of Cultural and Community Life, National Museum of American History, Smithsonian Institution

Dishwasher: No More Dishpan Hands

Sometimes the craziest reasons can spark an idea that has lasting benefits. Beginning in the late 1870s, **Josephine Cochran** of Illinois wanted an easy way to clean fine china. Cochran herself was not responsible for washing dishes, but the story goes that her servants, who did do the washing, kept chipping her china. To avoid too much rough handling during hand washing, she decided to make a "dish-washing machine." Cochran twisted wire into special racks made to fit her plates, cups, and saucers. The filled racks rested on a wheel inside a huge copper boiler. While a motor turned the wheel, hot soapy water sprayed up from the bottom of the boiler onto the dishes. Cochran showed off her "dishwasher," which she patented in 1886, at the 1893 Chicago World's Columbian Exposition to high praise. Today, dishwashers are considered standard kitchen appliances in many homes.

Portrait: ©New York Public Library/Science Source. Patent: National Archives.

Windshield Wipers: Rain, Rain, Go Away

The first cars were missing what we would consider some pretty important safety features, such as horns, seatbelts, roofs, and headlights. In fact, Henry Ford's first automobile, his 1896 Quadricycle, didn't have any brakes! At the start of the 20th century, however, when cars were still new, they were used mostly for recreation on nice-weather days. It was only as automobiles became more numerous on the roads and could finally reach speeds of over 30 miles per hour that they needed additional features to make the roadways safe. **Mary Anderson** is credited with the idea for a hand-operated window-cleaning arm to brush away rain, sleet, and snow. A crank inside the car moved a rubber blade on a swinging arm back and forth across the windshield. Anderson patented her idea in 1903. She could not find a company willing to invest in it, however, so she let her patent lapse. Then, in the 1920s, newer, faster, closed-bodied automobiles included automatic wipers. This basic idea to make driving safe in all kinds of weather is now a standard feature on all cars—as are seatbelts, horns, and headlights!

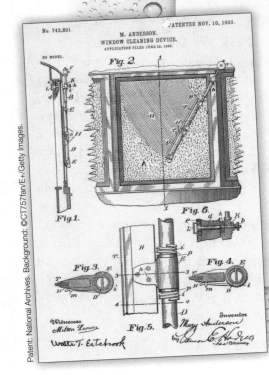

Patent: National Archives. Background: ©CT757fan/E+/Getty Images.

By Marcia Amidon Lusted. May be reproduced for classroom use. *Toolkit Texts: Short Nonfiction for American History, Industrial Age and Immigration,* by Stephanie Harvey and Anne Goudvis, ©2021 (Portsmouth, NH: Heinemann).

By Marcia Amidon Lusted. May be reproduced for classroom use. *Toolkit Texts: Short Nonfiction for American History, Industrial Age and Immigration*, by Stephanie Harvey and Anne Goudvis, ©2021 (Portsmouth, NH: Heinemann).

AN IMPROVED TRAFFIC SIGNAL: BETWEEN STOP AND GO

In 1922, inventor **Garrett Morgan** witnessed a traffic accident at a busy Cleveland, Ohio intersection. At that time, traffic lights only had two positions: red for stop and green for go. Drivers had no time to react when a green signal suddenly became red, and on Cleveland's crowded streets, this led to many serious and often deadly collisions. After seeing one of these accidents, Morgan had an idea to create a third signal, one that would give traffic time to clear an intersection before other cars entered it. Morgan invented a new traffic signal arrangement, a t-shaped pole with the three signal lights attached to it. At night, or when traffic was light, the signals could be adjusted so that drivers drove through intersections after pausing. This automated warning signal, which he patented in 1923, led to today's three-position traffic light. Morgan sold his invention to the General Electric company, and today all traffic lights have red, green, and yellow, making streets and intersections safer for everyone.

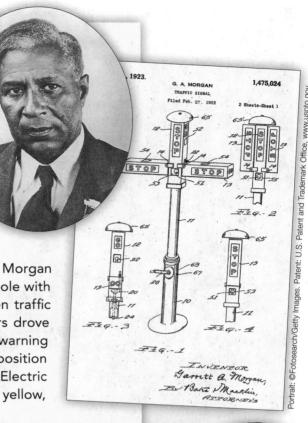

Portrait: ©Fotosearch/Getty Images. Patent: U.S. Patent and Trademark Office, www.uspto.gov.

LET THERE BE LIGHT: INSIDE THE LIGHT BULB

Most people believe that Thomas Edison invented the incandescent light bulb. But he couldn't have made it work as well without the contribution of an inventor named **Lewis Latimer**. In 1881, Latimer invented a carbon filament, which is the small glowing strand within a light bulb. Edison had used a paper filament, which burned out very quickly. Latimer's carbon filament lasted much longer, making electric lighting cheaper and more affordable for everyone. Latimer also invented an efficient manufacturing process for his carbon filament, as well as the familiar threaded socket that light bulbs screw into, although his socket was originally made of wood. But Latimer did not just work on light bulbs. He was skilled at mechanical drawing and electrical engineering, and drafted the drawings that Alexander Graham Bell used to patent his invention of the telephone.

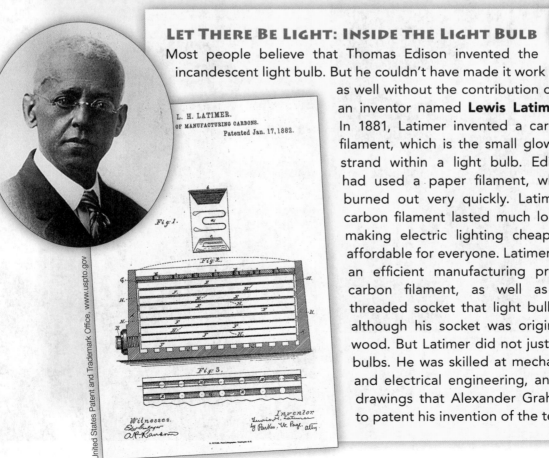

United States Patent and Trademark Office, www.uspto.gov.

Portrait: ©Edison Natl. Historic Site, NPS/U.S. Dept. of the Interior. Bulb: ©Brand X Pictures/Getty Images.

Awesome Inventions

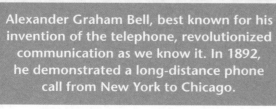

Ingenuity: inventive skill and cleverness

Nineteenth-century America witnessed remarkable changes. In less than 100 years, the country was transformed from a young, mostly rural and agricultural society into a strong urban and industrial nation. Americans from all walks of life helped fuel this dramatic change through thousands and thousands of inventions. Using imagination and **ingenuity**, they took ideas and turned them into practical products. From the big—electricity and telephones—to the small—safety pins and measuring spoons—these inventions all were created

How often do you talk or text with your friends on the phone? Can you imagine how life would be different without it?

Alexander Graham Bell, best known for his invention of the telephone, revolutionized communication as we know it. In 1892, he demonstrated a long-distance phone call from New York to Chicago.

May be reproduced for classroom use. *Toolkit Texts: Short Nonfiction for American History, Industrial Age and Immigration*, by Stephanie Harvey and Anne Goudvis, ©2021 (Portsmouth, NH: Heinemann).

in the 1800s. Some inventions, like the basic manual can opener, have remained virtually unchanged. Other creations, such as the record player, soon may be seen only in museums because newer inventions, like the CD player or MP3, have improved upon it and replaced it.

Inventing is often a process. Sometimes an idea sparks the creation of a related invention or an improvement on an original item. For example, the invention of the telegraph by Samuel F.B. Morse in 1844 gave birth to a variety of other ideas connected to the concept of sound and its ability to travel—from Alexander Graham Bell's telephone in 1876 and the radio at the turn of the 20th century, right up to cell phones at the turn of the 21st century.

Inventions are protected by the U.S. government. According to the Constitution, "Congress shall have the power . . . to promote the progress of science and useful arts, by securing for limited times to authors and inventors the exclusive right to their respective writings and discoveries." America's original Patent Office was started in 1802 when the country still was finding its way as a new nation. The Founders anticipated the importance of recognizing and protecting some people's creative contributions. During these early American years, many Americans were inventive; however, women and people of color were often discriminated against and unable to obtain to patents. These barriers did not stop their inventive spirit. Many people were inventing and contributing to the country's transition into a land of innovation.

Today, we take many of these early inventions for granted. Sometimes it is important to stop and look around in order to appreciate just how much we have been impacted by some nineteenth-century inventions.

1890 Candlestick phone

1910 Rotary-dial phone

1960s Push-button phone

1980s Cordless phone

1990s Mobile phone

2010s Smartphone

2015 Watch phone

Timeline of the Telephone

The telephone has gone through many changes over the years. This timeline charts just a few of these extraordinary leaps of innovation. The dates reflect the time when each phone was commonly used.

INVENTIONS THAT BRING MUSIC TO OUR EARS

The Personal Music Player

Thomas Edison was world-renowned for his inventions, including the phonograph featured in the portrait above. Although Edison patented the phonograph in 1877, earning himself the title of the "Wizard of Menlo Park," eleven years passed before he achieved clear sound quality to make it usable for the public.

Indentation: a cut or notch in the surface of something

Do you love to listen to music? Some kids like to listen to their favorite songs when they are hanging out with friends, practicing sports, or even studying. It is hard to imagine life without a soundtrack. But the way we listen to music has changed dramatically over the last 100 years.

All the way back in the late 1800s, Thomas Edison made an exciting discovery while working on a recorder for telegraph signals. He realized that **indentations** produced sound when a needle moved over them. So he created the phonograph, the first machine to record and play sound back. The first musical recordings were produced on small wax phonograph cylinders. They were amazing, but they were also bulky and could only hold two minutes of music.

Phonograph cylinders eventually gave way to flat discs made of vinyl or plastic that had sound grooves etched into them. These discs, called long-playing ("LP") records, could hold almost 45 minutes of music. Of course, you had to be careful with them. They were easy to scratch and would warp easily if they got too hot.

In the mid-1960s, the 8-track tape became popular. It took off because it was the first format you could easily take along in the car with you. An 8-track tape deck became popular in many vehicles. Unfortunately, the 8-track tapes became less popular and were largely forgotten when cassette tapes grew in popularity in the late 1970s and early 1980s.

Cassettes were hugely popular because they could hold about an hour's worth of music. They were also smaller and thus even more portable. Many people also bought blank cassette tapes and recorded their favorite songs from the radio onto them. They could also make their own custom mix tapes of favorite songs.

Cassettes remained popular for many years until digital music took over with the invention of the compact disc (CD). CDs could hold even more music—over 80 minutes. CDs were also very portable and durable.

CDs became less common in the early 2000s when people started downloading music. They could find their favorite music online and download it to an MP3 player. This device got its name from the type of files it stored—MP3s. Some people today still use MP3 players. Many people also store music on their phones. When they're ready to listen, they just connect their earbuds and press play.

Digital music files are much easier to store than 8-tracks, cassettes, or CDs. For example, a 120-gigabyte MP3 player holds over 280 hours of music! You'd have to carry around over 2,000 compact discs for that much music! It's about the same as 3,000 cassette tapes or 4,000 8-track tapes. That would require over 28,000 vinyl records!

However, many people today don't download or buy music at all. Instead, they stream their favorite music from online services. Spotify, Pandora, Tidal, Apple Music, and others allow music lovers to play music from any device. Most of these services have a free account option, but some charge a small fee. Today, streaming is the most common way to listen to music.

Many changes have taken place in music formats over the years. It can be fun to wonder what the next 10 years will bring. In another 10 years, how will you be listening to your favorite music? Will you still be streaming music on a smartphone? Or will there be something even smaller and more fantastic ahead?

Edison, Tesla, and the Battle of the Currents

May be reproduced for classroom use. *Toolkit Texts: Short Nonfiction for American History, Industrial Age and Immigration*, by Stephanie Harvey and Anne Goudvis, ©2021 (Portsmouth, NH: Heinemann).

Should electricity be AC or DC?

From the 1890s through 1906, Nikola Tesla spent a great deal of his time and fortune developing an invention that transmitted electricity without wires. In this 1901 photograph, Tesla sits next to his "magnifying transmitter," which generated millions of volts of wireless lightning.

That sounds like a simple question. But amazingly, determining the answer to this scientific question would spark a furious feud between two of the greatest inventors of the 19th century's Electrical Age: Nikola Tesla and Thomas Edison. These scientific squabblers actually started out regarding each other with great respect. Tesla, a gifted Serbian engineer, came to Manhattan in 1884 to meet Thomas Edison, the inventor of the light bulb, about whom he'd read so much. Edison, a once-failing student, had risen to become one of the most famous and accomplished inventors of the day, even described in newspapers as the greatest genius of the modern age. During his most inventive years (1876–1883), Edison conducted experiments at his Menlo Park, New Jersey, laboratory—an "inventions factory"—where he surrounded himself with talented workers. But in 1884 he was back in New York, and when the two met, Edison was so impressed with Tesla that he hired him on the spot.

Failed Friendship

For a time the two inventors worked together, designing generators and other electrical devices for Edison's new electric company. But their early friendship dissolved—some say in a dispute over money. Tesla claimed that Edison had promised him a bonus if he could make the company's dynamos work more efficiently—but then claimed he'd only been joking after Tesla succeeded. Edison's friends claimed that Tesla was at fault: He was too interested in his own ideas for machines that were not compatible with the Edison system. Whatever happened, the two men began to quarrel. Finally, Tesla quit, vowing to start a business of his own.

Odd Couple

In truth, the friction between Edison and Tesla may have started simply because the two men were really opposites in every way. While Edison was self-taught and "street smart," Tesla was scholarly and bookish. Edison liked to work with his hands, but Tesla preferred to "think out" ideas in his head.

More Tesla/Edison Inventions That Changed the World

Talk about a grudge match! The rivalry between these two geniuses became a contest to invent the Modern Age. Just check out some of their remarkable innovations:

Thomas Edison

Motion pictures Film has come a long way since Edison's invention of the kinetograph, an early motion picture camera, in 1892. He also developed 35 mm film, created the first "special effects," and made the first "talkie" (a motion picture with sound) in 1912!

Phonograph Today, it's Britney on CD, but in 1877, Edison built the first phonograph that played a record made from tin foil. His improved version is shown at left.

Mimeograph machine The granddaddy of every computer printer. Can you believe it was invented by Edison in 1875?

The stock ticker Twenty-three-year-old Thomas Edison made his early fortune by inventing "the machine that made Wall Street" in 1870.

Nikola Tesla

Neon lights Created by Tesla in 1891. By the way, he invented fluorescent light bulbs, too.

Radio Tesla sent the first "wireless" transmission in 1893. By 1900, he could detect waves from space, a process called radio astronomy today.

Robotics Tesla built a submarine in 1893 that carried no crew, and was propelled, steered, and submerged electronically by remote control.

Guided missiles First invented by Tesla in 1912. And, just to be on the safe side, he devised an advanced missile defense system in 1934.

More "Current" Events

To invent with Thomas Edison, visit the Edison Historic Site at www.nps.gov/edis/home.htm.

Then see Tesla's lab at www.teslascience.org.

Thomas Edison   Nikola Tesla

By Nick D'Alto, *Odyssey,* ©2002 by Carus Publishing Company. Reproduced with permission.

35

Edison experimented by a process of trial-and-error; Tesla, by working out long calculations. The two men were even physical opposites: Edison was short and portly; Tesla was tall and handsome. In every way, Tesla and Edison were technology's "Odd Couple."

AC vs. DC

It's no surprise, then, that these two inventors also held opposite views about electric current. Edison favored direct current. "DC" is simple to operate, but it can travel only for short distances, requiring power stations every few blocks. Tesla had developed a new system, called "polyphase alternating current," or "AC" for short.

In just a few years, Tesla's alternating current would revolutionize the world. His AC power plants would even harness Niagara Falls to bring electric power to cities many miles away.

But Edison continued to use DC, and he tried to convince the public that AC was dangerous. He argued that houses wired to AC current might catch fire, and warned people against walking near AC street poles.

Tesla, in turn, deprecated all of Edison's work. "If Thomas Edison had to find a needle in a haystack," Tesla once scoffed, "he would examine each straw instead of finding a smarter way."

Race of Progress

Rivals usually just fight it out. But these two geniuses turned their feud into a "race of progress." When Edison created a new kind of telephone, Tesla built the most powerful steam engine in the world. Edison invented the prefabricated house, but Tesla designed vacuum tubes that would pave the way for television. Edison amazed the public with the first movie studio; Tesla designed a machine that produced showers of artificial lightning. For the rest of their lives, Edison—the "Wizard of Menlo Park," as he was often referred to—would duel with Tesla—the "Master of Lightning" and creator of the **tesla coil**—to see which man was the world's greatest inventor.

> **Tesla coil:** a machine invented by Tesla in 1891 that makes lightning bolts. It is used to produce high-voltage, low-current, high-frequency alternating-current electricity.

Never-Ending Feud

The one thing these two geniuses could never invent was a way to end their feud. In 1910, Tesla developed an advanced turbine that could have helped Edison's firm. But the two men didn't trust each other, and the invention was never used.

When newspapers reported that Edison and Tesla had been nominated as co-recipients of the Nobel Prize in Physics, there was even talk that they might both decline it, rather than accept the award together. (In fact, we'll never know: The award committee selected two other scientists instead.)

So who finally won the "shocking" battle between Tesla and Edison? Some say that Tesla won, because we use his AC system today. Others say that Edison won; he collected more patents, earned more money, and became more famous. In fact, historians and biographers are still quarreling over which of these inventors made the greatest innovations. So in a way, the feud between Tesla and Edison is still going on!

Both were extraordinary innovators; they simply approached technology in opposite ways. Edison liked simple, practical ideas. As an amazing example, he built the first phonograph in just a few days, and had a commercial model ready for sale a few weeks later! In contrast, Tesla thought more about the future. Some of his experiments from the 1890s actually helped modern engineers invent the cell phone. Of course, technology depends on both short-term and long-term thinking. So you could say that these geniuses were both winners—in their own way.

Today, when you turn on Thomas Edison's fantastic invention, the light bulb, Nikola Tesla's remarkable AC power makes the bulb glow. Two great ideas, from two great inventors—this time working together. What a brilliant idea!

> ## AC or DC?
> ### An Electrifying Difference
>
> Flashlights work on DC; their current runs one way—from the battery to the bulb and back. But your house runs on AC; its current actually changes directions 60 times or cycles every second (sometimes called "60 hertz").
>
> Why is AC better for powering a city? One key is that AC can travel over thin copper wires. DC requires thicker wires, which cost much more.

The word *inventor* may conjure images of men like Thomas Edison and Alexander Graham Bell, but the history of women inventors is as long as that of male inventors.

Inventive Minds:
Women Inventors

The Lemelson Center for the Study of Invention and Innovation, located at the Smithsonian National Museum of American History, explores the role of invention and innovation in the United States, particularly its historical context, and how that history relates to current events.

Inventive Minds is a changing exhibition gallery that introduces museum visitors to the stories of American inventors. Through first-person videos, photographs, and artifacts, visitors to Inventive Minds learn about the traits that successful inventors share—insatiable curiosity, keen problem-solving skills, tenacity, and flexibility in the face of failure—and explore the creative spirit of American invention.

From September 2018 through December 2019, the Inventive Minds gallery featured a selection of stories illustrating the creativity of women inventors over more than a century. To learn more and view videos and photos, visit: https://invention.si.edu/inventive-minds-women-inventors.

The following stories illustrate the creativity of women inventors over more than a century. While these women are from different time periods and have developed different types of inventions, they share the traits of other successful inventors: insatiable curiosity, keen problem-solving skills, tenacity, and flexibility in the face of failure.

Dr. Patricia Bath • Eye surgeon and inventor

For Dr. Patricia Bath, an eye surgeon and a professor of **ophthalmology**, her greatest joy was inventing a treatment to help the blind see. She has been a trailblazer for women and Black Americans in the medical profession and was the first Black American woman doctor to receive a medical patent.

Dr. Bath has been an activist fighting for better healthcare for Black Americans for many years. In 1968 she organized her fellow medical students at Howard University to provide healthcare for the

Ophthalmology: the branch of medicine that studies and treats eyes and eye disorders

37

Poor People's Campaign. But that was just the beginning.

She changed the lives of millions of people by inventing a laser treatment for cataracts. Cataracts, often experienced by older people, form in the lens of the eye, and can cause blurry vision or even blindness. Usually people have to have eye surgery to remove cataracts, but Bath figured out a way to make the surgery faster, easier, and more accurate by using lasers. It took her nearly five years to complete the research on this amazing new advancement but eventually she received a patent for it.

Bath urged young people to follow their own career interests, to give back to their communities, and to believe in the power of their own ideas. "Believe in the power of truth," she told them. "Do not allow your mind to be imprisoned by majority thinking. Remember that the limits of science are not the limits of imagination."

Theresa Dankovich • Safe drinking water

We take safe drinking water for granted and barely even think about where our water comes from. But in a 2019 report, UNICEF and the World Health Organization estimate that about two billion people around the world do not have access to safe drinking water. This means that they often get their water from ponds, rivers, or wells that do not have clean, safe water. This makes people more likely to get illnesses or diseases from unsafe or unsanitary water. Inventor Theresa Dankovich noticed this problem and talked to people in countries around the world to figure out a solution. She invented a fairly simple germ-killing water filter that is made of thick paper. It has tiny silver particles that kill disease-causing bacteria and viruses. To make sure people would have plenty of filters, she developed a filter that cleans 20 liters of water for 20 cents, or 1 penny a liter. The filters are affordable, lightweight, and do not require heat, electricity, or a pump. "I saw an opportunity to simply listen to the people and to deliver designs that fit with the culture," says Ms. Dankovich. Her ability to listen, combined with her ingenuity, has made a big difference in the lives and health of people around the world.

Grace Hopper • Computer scientist and programmer

When World War II began, Grace Murray Hopper (1906–1992) was a mathematics professor teaching at Vassar College. She joined the U.S. Navy in 1943 and applied her math skills to writing computer code for the Mark I, a new electromechanical calculator at Harvard's Cruft Laboratory. Hopper was one of the first woman programmers. She believed that a programming language based on English was possible. Her compiler converted English terms into machine code understood by computers. In her lifelong computing career, she pioneered ways to make communication between humans and computers more user-friendly.

Grace Hopper was the longest serving female officer in the U.S. Navy and was honored when she retired at almost 80 years of age. She summed up her work with these words: "It's much easier for most people to write an English statement than it is to use symbols," she explained. "So I decided data processors ought to be able to write their programs in English, and the computers would translate them into machine code."

Grace Murray Hopper Collection, Archives Center, National Museum of American History, Smithsonian Institution

Colombian-born inventor Amy Prieto has spent her career researching fast-charging, long-lasting, and green rechargeable batteries. She joined the Colorado State University (CSU) chemistry department because of the culture of collaboration there, with an openness to sharing resources and knowledge that she believes is crucial to her work.

Prieto founded her company, Prieto Battery, to take the innovative battery from research to prototype to a product that can be used by many people. In addition, Prieto's battery contains none of the toxic or flammable liquid components found in traditional batteries. Prieto is working to develop a process that is cost competitive and friendly to the environment. This includes water-based manufacturing using citric acid (a common natural preservative) and a standard electroplating process.

May be reproduced for classroom use. *Toolkit Texts: Short Nonfiction for American History, Industrial Age and Immigration,* by Stephanie Harvey and Anne Goudvis, ©2021 (Portsmouth, NH: Heinemann).

A Woman in a Machine Shop

Smithsonian National Museum of American History. Pravel, Gambrell, Hewitt, Kirk, Kimball, and Dodge. ID #1980.0004.01

"**M**attie, will you make a new sled for us?" the boys called out as they ran home through the fresh New Hampshire snow.

Margaret sighed. Then she smiled and went to find her toolbox and some wood. She was not yet 15 that winter day in 1853, but the sleds, kites, and other playthings that she made for her brothers were the envy of all the kids in town.

Margaret like working with jackknives and pieces of wood. When she grew up, she said, "Dolls never possessed any charms for me. I couldn't see the sense of coddling bits of porcelain with senseless faces."

Inventing for Safety

Margaret E. Knight was born in York, Maine, in 1838. Her family moved to Manchester, New Hampshire, when she was young, and she and her brothers all worked in the cotton mills as children. When she was 12, Margaret saw a mill worker injured by a steel-tipped shuttle that fell from a loom. Shocked by the accident, she invented a safety mechanism to keep shuttles from flying loose. That mechanical device—her first invention— was so practical that it was soon adopted by all the cotton mills.

By the late 1860s, Knight was working for Columbia Paper Bag Company in Springfield, Massachusetts. There she operated machines that made the flat, envelope-shaped bags that were used at the time. A number of people tried to improve these machines so that they would

A model (above) of the paper bag machine that sparked a legal debate.

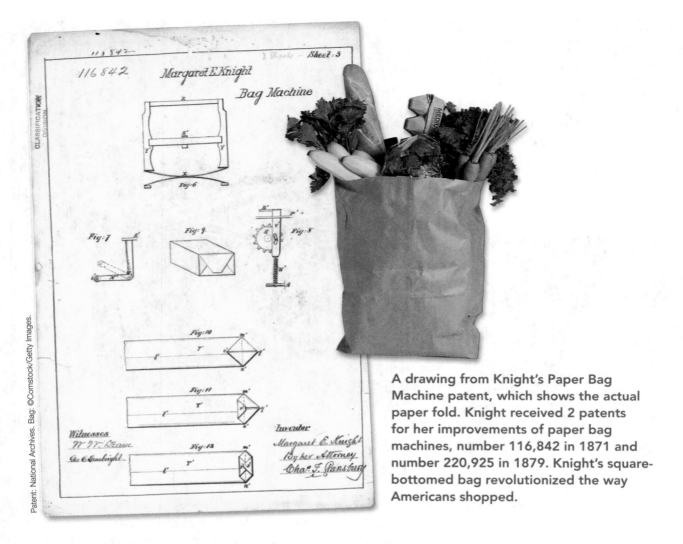

A drawing from Knight's Paper Bag Machine patent, which shows the actual paper fold. Knight received 2 patents for her improvements of paper bag machines, number 116,842 in 1871 and number 220,925 in 1879. Knight's square-bottomed bag revolutionized the way Americans shopped.

May be reproduced for classroom use. *Toolkit Texts: Short Nonfiction for American History, Industrial Age and Immigration*, by Stephanie Harvey and Anne Goudvis, ©2021 (Portsmouth, NH: Heinemann).

automatically make square bottomed, self-standing bags—like our present-day grocery bags—without having to cut, fold, and paste them by hand. No one had been able to make such a machine.

Innovating for Improvement

Knight studied the machines at the factory during the day and made numerous drawings and models at night in the boarding house where she lived. In 1867, she wrote in her diary, "I've been to work all this evening trying the clock work arrangement for making the square bottoms. It works well so far, so good. Have done enough for one day."

She completed a wooden model and made thousands of trial bags in the factory. When she was sure the machine was in working order, she hired a machinist to make an iron model so that she could register it at the U.S. Patent Office in Washington, D.C.

Before Knight had time to apply for a patent, however, she heard that a man names Charles F. Annan had just received a patent for a nearly identical machine. She discovered that Annan had been spying on the machinist who was making her model and that he had copied it and hurried to have it patented in his name.

When Knight died at the age of 76 on October 12, 1914, she held patents for 22 inventions.

Establishing Her Rightful Patent

Knight was furious. She hired an attorney, and armed with witnesses, documents, drawings, early models of her machine, and even her personal diaries, she fought for her rights to the patent. And she won!

Knight continued to broaden her mechanical skills. While most women inventors of the time patented devices for the home, she was truly "a lady in a machine-shop," as the *Woman's Journal* called her in 1872. She worked long hours in her "experiment rooms" in Boston. In the next 20 years, Knight patented machines for the paper bag, rubber, and shoe industries. By 1900, she was designing engines for the new automobile industry.

When Knight died at the age of 76 on October 12, 1914, she held patents for 22 inventions and had assigned patents for an estimated 60 more to her financial backers and employers. One newspaper caller her a "woman Edison." As a professional inventor, Knight might have considered that a great accomplishment.

Two more pages from Knight's patent for the Paper Bag Machine

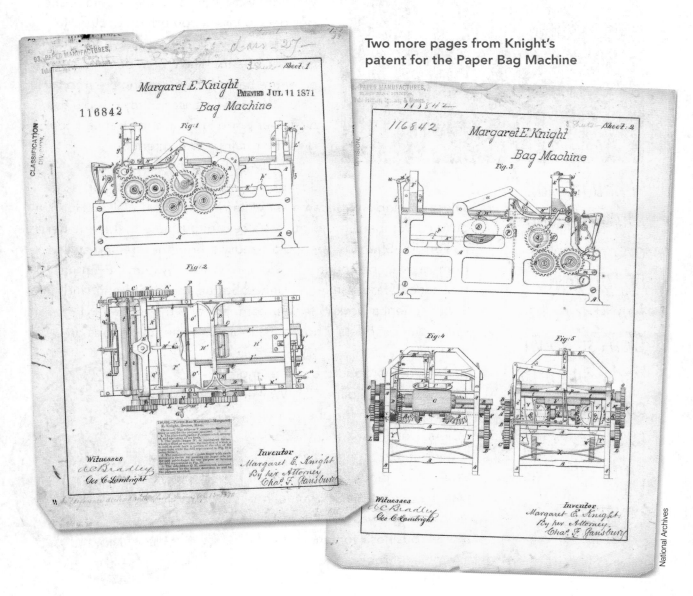

National Archives

Images ©Collection of the Smithsonian National Museum of African American History and Culture. Top: Gift of A'Lelia Bundles/Madam Walker Family Archives. Bottom: Gift from Dawn Simon Spears and Alvin Spears, Sr. Object number 2011.159.6

Madam C.J. Walker

Sarah Breedlove, an inventor and entrepreneur, was the first Black American woman millionaire. Born in 1867, just two years after the Civil War ended, she made her fortune through a series of inventions, all of which helped Black Americans care for their hair.

Breedlove worked at a few different jobs before deciding to begin creating hair products. She had tried a variety of products to treat her own hair loss, but when they did not solve the problem, she decided to invent something better. Her most famous invention was "Wonderful Hair Grower" cream. The cream became part of an entire hair care system she created to help "the great masses of my people to take a greater pride in their appearance and to give their hair proper attention."

In 1906, Sarah married Charles Joseph Walker, a newspaper advertising salesman, and she became known as Madam C.J. Walker. Her hair product company grew into a successful business that made her a millionaire. She also opened a beauty school that trained stylists from all over the country to use her "Walker System." Eventually, thousands of people in the United States, the Caribbean, and South America worked for her company and made their living selling her products. Thousands more used her inventions on their hair.

"I had to make my own living and my own opportunity. But I made it! Don't sit down and wait for the opportunities to come. Get up and make them."

As her products became more widely used, Madam C.J. Walker began using her fortune to help others, including many Black organizations and schools. When she died in 1919, she was the richest Black woman in America and was considered a model businesswoman, activist, and philanthropist.

May be reproduced for classroom use. *Toolkit Texts: Short Nonfiction for American History, Industrial Age and Immigration*, by Stephanie Harvey and Anne Goudvis, ©2021 (Portsmouth, NH: Heinemann).

AN AMERICAN TRIUMPH

Library of Congress, 03206

Building the Brooklyn Bridge, 1871

The cold, bitter winter of 1866–67 reminded the citizens of Brooklyn why they so desperately wanted a bridge constructed over the East River to connect them with New York City. Once again, the East River was frozen, leaving them no easy way to get to the city to either work or play. It took less time, it was said, to go from the state capital of Albany to New York City by train (at least 4 hours) than to go from Brooklyn to New York City by carriage when the river was frozen. This time, the political leaders of Brooklyn determined, the dream would not be denied.

Nothing like it had ever been tried on such a large scale. It would be the longest suspension bridge in the world, stretching over a mile from end to end. It would include an elevated pedestrian walkway and two twin towers that would dwarf everything in the surrounding skyline.

The bridge's designer, John Roebling, died in a freak accident as he was surveying the location of the bridge's Brooklyn tower in 1869 and the task of turning his design into reality fell to his son, Washington.

After the untimely death of his father, Washington A. Roebling became the chief engineer of the Brooklyn Bridge on August 3, 1869. "Here I was,

32 years old," Roebling wrote, "suddenly in charge of the most stupendous engineering structure of the age." John A. Roebling's design called for two towers rising offshore from New York and Brooklyn. They would support four giant steel cables, anchored onto land at each end. The middle bridge clearance would be 135 feet over the East River. Now all Washington had to do was build it.

From the Bottom Up

Construction began in 1870, with Roebling overseeing the building of two giant **caissons** to support the two towers at each end of the bridge. The caissons were large, upside-down wooden boxes with no bottoms. Their bottom footprint was as big as half a city block. They were towed into position and sunk on the river bottom. Compressed air was then pumped into the chambers to keep water from rushing in. Workers, called "sand hogs," climbed into the caissons through special shafts. Their job was to dig away at the mud and rock in the bottom of the East River until the caissons rested on firm bedrock. Once the workers reached the bedrock, the caissons were filled with concrete, which provided a sturdy foundation to support the bridges' two stone towers.

"Inside the caisson everything wore an unreal, weird appearance," wrote Master Mechanic E.F. Farrington. Barely nine feet separated the earthen floor from the ceiling. Candles and gas-powered **limelights** cast an eerie glow. The warm pressurized air often made pulses race and hindered speech. Many workers developed caisson disease. The risk of fire was also great. Eventually, they reached solid bedrock, the digging stopped, and the caissons were filled with concrete, thus becoming the foundation for the bridge.

Most laborers inside the caissons and on the rest of the bridge were immigrants. The majority were Irish. Others were Italians and Germans, along with some Chinese and Black Americans. The work was dangerous and difficult, yet people needed the jobs. The average daily wage for the bridge laborers was $2.50, a decent rate compared to what immigrants might otherwise get.

Working with hammers and shovels, workers dug out slimy mud and rocks. A mechanized **clamshell**

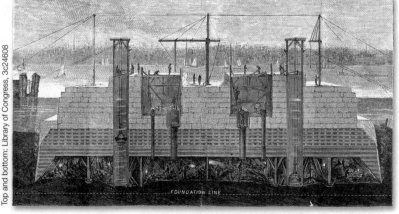

These views of the work being done on and within the caissons reveal a truly labor-intensive project.

Caisson comes from the French word, *caisse*, which means "box" or "chest."

Limelights are lamps that use calcium oxide.

A **clamshell** refers to a device that opens on two sides to scoop up material.

May be reproduced for classroom use. *Toolkit Texts: Short Nonfiction for American History, Industrial Age and Immigration*, by Stephanie Harvey and Anne Goudvis, ©2021 (Portsmouth, NH: Heinemann).

By Kathiann M. Kowalski, *Cobblestone*, ©2010 by Carus Publishing Company. Reproduced with permission.

lifted the material up and out. Small dynamite blasts broke up large boulders, but laborers did most of the work by hand. Meanwhile, above, workers began building the tower's foundation, slowly sinking the whole structure deeper and deeper as they laid heavy pieces of limestone on top of the caisson.

A fire in the Brooklyn caisson on December 1, 1870, stopped work for several months. But on March 11, 1871, the Brooklyn caisson finally sat on bedrock, 44 feet 6 inches below water level. Pumps began filling the caisson with concrete.

On the New York side, test **borings** showed that bedrock sat 106 feet below water level. The deeper the workers dug in the caisson, the more people became sick. Several men died from caisson disease. Meanwhile, the compacted sand became harder and harder. Reaching bedrock could take another year. Roebling feared that dozens more workers would die.

Roebling made a decision: On May 18, 1872, digging in the New York caisson stopped at 78 feet 6 inches below water level. To this day, the New York tower of the Brooklyn Bridge rests on hard-packed sand.

> **Borings**, or core samples, show different soils found as a tube drills down through the earth.

Top: Seated on a swing, Master Mechanic E.F. Farrington became the first person to cross on the initial wire rope connecting the two towers. **Bottom:** Large sections of the cities were cleared so the land approaches to the bridge could be built.

Library of Congress, 3c02102

High above the river on boatswain's chairs, workers lashed, or tied together, the stays of the bridge.

Tall Towers

One by one, steam **derricks** lifted huge granite blocks onto the concrete-filled caisson foundations. Dizzying heights and chilling winds were constant dangers as the towers grew. Three men fell and died. Falling stones and other accidents killed at least four more. Nonetheless, work pressed on until both towers, with their beautiful Gothic arches, were finished by July 1876. When completed, the tops of the towers stood roughly 276 feet 6 inches above water level. In the time before skyscrapers, when most buildings in New York were only two or three stories, this was simply astounding.

Derricks are machines designed to lift and move heavy objects.

May be reproduced for classroom use. *Toolkit Texts: Short Nonfiction for American History, Industrial Age and Immigration*, by Stephanie Harvey and Anne Goudvis, ©2021 (Portsmouth, NH: Heinemann).

©Ann Ronan Pictures/Print Collector/Getty Images

The four main cables actually consisted of many strands of wire wrapped together.

By Kathiann M. Kowalski, *Cobblestone*, ©2010 by Carus Publishing Company. Reproduced with permission.

This aerial view from the New York tower shows the bridge's pedestrian walkway in the center, with trolley tracks on either side and outer lanes for carriages and other vehicles.

Library of Congress, 00182

Meanwhile, workers built the 60,000-ton anchorages. Rising nearly 90 feet high, these structures would anchor the four massive cables on wrought-iron plates and then be covered in masonry. Their weight would counterbalance the four 1.7 million-pound cables, plus the bridge deck and traffic.

Cables and Suspenders

Workers had to build the bridge cables in place. Sailors were hired to do the job because they were familiar with the tall riggings of ships. To spectators below, the men looked like busy spiders. To hoist workers up, Roebling designed an endless wire rope, like a giant clothesline on pulleys.

Making huge steel cables above the river was an enormous challenge. "All four cables are made simultaneously," Roebling wrote. Each 16-inch-thick cable consisted of more than 5,000 wires.

When the main cable work ended, workers hung smaller vertical cables, or suspenders. They connected the cables to steel beams for the road deck. Diagonal cables would later stretch out from each tower for added stability.

Road Building

Workers had already begun building the two road approaches on land for the bridge. Now the bridge needed its 85-foot-wide deck. Two lanes of road traffic and one lane for trolleys would cross in each direction. An elevated walkway in the middle would carry foot traffic.

Roebling was not planning for trains to use the bridge, but he added extra steel to the floor for stability, just in case. While heavy trains never did cross, subway trolleys did. And the Brooklyn Bridge stayed strong enough for automobiles as they became popular in the following decades.

The Brooklyn Bridge opened on May 24, 1883, after 13 years of construction and a final price tag of $15 million. It had required endless hours of hard labor and resulted in more than 20 deaths and countless injuries. Finally, though, the bridge linked Brooklyn and New York. As Brooklyn mayor Seth Low said, "It is distinctly an American triumph."

Building the Brooklyn Bridge, by Frank Harris

First-person account of Frank Harris, construction worker on the Brooklyn Bridge

Frank Harris arrived in New York City from his native Ireland in 1871. The fifteen-year-old moved into a Brooklyn boarding house where a fellow resident, Mike, told him of jobs paying five dollars a day for working in the Brooklyn Bridge caissons. Frank tells the story of when he and Mike went to the construction site:

Library of Congress, 6a19661

Brooklyn Bridge, 1896

"Next morning Mike took me to Brooklyn Bridge soon after five o'clock to see the contractor; he wanted to engage Mike at once but shook his head over me. 'Give me a trial,' I pleaded; 'you'll see I'll make good.' After a pause, 'O.K.,' he said; 'four shifts have gone down already underhanded: you may try.'

When we went into the 'air-lock' and they turned on one air-lock after another of compressed air, the men put their hands to their ears and I soon imitated them, for the pain was very acute. Indeed, the drums of the ears are often driven in and burst if the compressed air is brought in too quickly. I found that the best way of meeting the pressure was to keep swallowing air and forcing it up into the middle ear, where it acted as an air-pad on the innerside of the drum.

When the air was fully compressed, the door of the air-lock opened at a touch and we all went down to work with pick and shovel on the gravelly bottom. My headache soon became acute. The six of us were working naked to the waist in a small iron chamber with a temperature of about 80 degrees Fahrenheit: in five minutes the sweat was pouring from us, and all the while we were standing in icy water that was only kept from rising by the terrific air pressure. No wonder the headaches were blinding. The men

May be reproduced for classroom use. *Toolkit Texts: Short Nonfiction for American History, Industrial Age and Immigration,* by Stephanie Harvey and Anne Goudvis, ©2021 (Portsmouth, NH: Heinemann).

didn't work for more than ten minutes at a time, but I plugged on steadily, resolved to prove myself and get constant employment; only one man, a Swede named Anderson, worked at all as hard.

[I was] advised to leave at the end of a month: it was too unhealthy: above all, I mustn't drink and should spend all my spare time in the open. After two hours' work down below, we went up into the air-lock room to get gradually 'decompressed,' the pressure of air in our veins having to be brought down gradually to the usual air pressure. The men began to put on their clothes and passed round a bottle of schnapps; but though I was soon as cold as a wet rat and felt depressed and weak to boot, I would not touch the liquor. In the shed above I took a cupful of hot cocoa with Anderson, which stopped the shivering, and I was soon able to face the afternoon's ordeal.

For three or four days things went fairly well with me, but on the fifth day or sixth we came on a spring of water, or 'gusher,' and were wet to the waist before the air pressure could be increased to cope with it. As a consequence, a dreadful pain shot through both my ears: I put my hands to them tight and sat still for little while. Fortunately, the shift was almost over and Anderson came with me to the horse-car. 'You'd better knock off,' he said. 'I've known 'em go deaf from it.'

He was kindness itself to me, as indeed were all the others."

Excerpted from: *My Life and Loves* by Frank Harris. Privately Printed, Paris. 1922.

The Jon B. Lovelace Collection of California Photographs in Carol M. Highsmith's America Project, Library of Congress, Prints and Photographs Division, 20585

The Golden Gate Bridge

When California's magnificent Golden Gate Bridge was completed on May 27, 1937, it became the longest suspension bridge in the world. Chief Engineer Joseph P. Strauss wrote a poem, "The Mighty Task Is Done," celebrating the end of four years of construction. The Golden Gate Bridge extends almost 9,000 feet with a tower-to-tower span of 4,200 feet. The bridge links the city of San Francisco to Marin County.

While most bridges are painted steel gray to protect them from corrosion, the Golden Gate Bridge was painted orange to help it blend in with its natural setting. The color matches the red-orange tones of the rocks and hills around San Francisco Bay. The Golden Gate Bridge is one of the most beautiful and most photographed bridges in the world.

By Marcia Amidon Lusted. May be reproduced for classroom use. *Toolkit Texts: Short Nonfiction for American History, Industrial Age and Immigration*, by Stephanie Harvey and Anne Goudvis, ©2021 (Portsmouth, NH: Heinemann).

A New Industrial Revolution

Highly trained engineers (above) are needed to build and code robots.

History might make it seem that the Industrial Revolution is something that happened once and is over. But there are experts in technology and manufacturing who believe that human society is now in a fourth industrial revolution! The first revolution, which happened between 1750 and 1820, was about **mechanizing** factories with water and steam power. These factories relied on fossil fuels. The second, which began after 1870, was characterized by the new use of electricity to produce power. In the third, starting in the 1950s, industry began using digital electronics and information technology to automate production. Each one of these revolutions changed how people worked and lived. The fourth industrial revolution, which has already started, will bring together everything from the first three. It will affect almost every industry, all over the world. It will also keep changing our everyday lives.

Ford automobiles were different than earlier cars because they were built in factories using conveyor belts to move the parts quickly.

The Age of Automation

The biggest changes in industry and manufacturing today are happening because of **automation**. Automation is not new. Factories have been using different kinds of automation for decades. One of the first uses of automation in a factory happened in 1913. Henry Ford had a factory that built some of the first cars that were affordable. Workers used to move from car to car, doing all the jobs needed to build each car. This meant that it took a long time to finish a car. Ford designed an assembly line system where the unfinished cars moved along on **conveyor belts**. Each worker specialized in one specific job. They stood in one place while the cars came to them. Every worker did the same job over and over again. This made it possible to build more cars more quickly.

Telling Machines What to Do

Later technology included machines that could be controlled by instructions using a punch card. A punch card was made of thick paper, with holes punched through it to create a code that a machine could read. Later machines were controlled by computers. Computer instructions told a machine exactly what process to perform. If it had to make a cut in a piece of metal, it could be given instructions to do it perfectly and precisely. Today, these machines are called Computer Numerical Control, or CNC, machines. They are also used to create engineering drawings, and for assembling electronics. This computer communicates with all the smaller machines used for certain parts of a manufacturing process.

Background: ©Alexey Lisovoy/Shutterstock. Top: Library of Congress, 4627992.

By Marcia Amidon Lusted. May be reproduced for classroom use. *Toolkit Texts: Short Nonfiction for American History, Industrial Age and Immigration*, by Stephanie Harvey and Anne Goudvis, ©2021 (Portsmouth, NH: Heinemann).

By Marcia Amidon Lusted. May be reproduced for classroom use. *Toolkit Texts: Short Nonfiction for American History, Industrial Age and Immigration*, by Stephanie Harvey and Anne Goudvis, ©2021 (Portsmouth, NH: Heinemann).

General Motors began building cars with the Unimate robotic arm in 1961.

Robots to the Rescue

Another way that manufacturing has changed is because of robots. The first robot to work in a factory was called Unimate. It started building cars for General Motors in 1961. Unimate was basically a giant arm. It was used to do jobs that were difficult or dangerous for humans. These jobs included lifting heavy objects, welding metal pieces together, or pouring **molten** metal into a mold. Factories learned that using robots could speed up production. But industrial robots must be programmed by humans. They are best at doing jobs that don't require decision-making or creativity. Humans are still needed to do those jobs. However, robots have started replacing more and more workers. It can cause problems when these workers can't find new jobs.

The use of robots in factories is growing and expanding. As robots become smarter, engineers see a future where they work along with human workers. The humans will be teaching the robots how to do certain work tasks. This also makes human workers more valuable. There's even a term for the idea that robots will complement human workers, not replace them. It's called "cobotics."

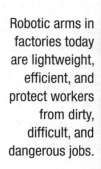

Robotic arms in factories today are lightweight, efficient, and protect workers from dirty, difficult, and dangerous jobs.

A Technology Revolution

Robots are not the only technology that industry is learning to use. Technologies like **artificial intelligence (AI)**, **robotics**, **3-D printing**, **nanotechnology**, and **biotechnology** are all becoming part of the manufacturing process. 3-D printing cuts down on waste and can speed up production. Nanotechnology can be used to make manufacturing computers faster, with better memory. It can also be used to make some products better, like making clothing that will adjust from hotter to cooler depending on the wearer. Engineers, designers, and architects are also combining these technologies in new ways. Technology is making communication and transportation faster and easier. This saves time, money, and energy.

The fourth industrial revolution has already started. Factories can combine computers, **digital technology**, robotics, and artificial intelligence, and use them with their human workers. This makes factories safer, faster, and less wasteful. Will there be a fifth industrial revolution? No one knows what amazing technology the future will bring. But it's likely that it will keep changing everything about human lives, including industry.

In the near future, delivery drones, like this unmanned aerial vehicle, will be used to transport packages or deliver food.

Glossary

3-D printing: the process of making three dimensional solid objects from a digital file

Artificial intelligence: the ability of a robot or computer to imitate human intelligence

Automation: using automatic equipment to produce something in a factory

Biotechnology: the process of genetically engineering living organisms to create new commercial products

Cobotics: a robot designed and built to work with humans

Conveyor belt: a band of rubber or fabric that constantly moves and carries items from one place to another

Digital technology: the branch of science and engineering that creates and uses digital or computerized devices

Mechanizing: to start using machines, technology, or digital devices to do something

Molten: something that has been made into a liquid because of extreme heat

Nanotechnology: using extremely small things, like atoms and molecules, to build very small devices

By Marcia Amidon Lusted. May be reproduced for classroom use. *Toolkit Texts: Short Nonfiction for American History, Industrial Age and Immigration,* by Stephanie Harvey and Anne Goudvis, ©2021 (Portsmouth, NH: Heinemann).

SHATTERING the Glass Ceiling!

In the 20th century, John D. Rockefeller, Andrew Carnegie, and J.P. Morgan created fortunes in oil, steel, and banking. How do the captains of industry in the 21st century differ from those in the early 20th century? What was missing then? Women, for one thing! In the early 1900s, women industrialists were nowhere to be found. In 2020, however, the number of women running large companies hit a record high of 37. But that still means only 7.4% of large American corporations are run by women. And since women make up slightly more than 50% of the population, we have a long way to go!

One barrier to women's advancement is known as the "Glass Ceiling." The glass ceiling **metaphor** describes invisible barriers ("glass") through which women can see higher level positions in the company but cannot reach them, regardless of their talent, education, or hard work. For many generations, this barrier has kept white men in charge of corporations and kept women out of positions of leadership.

With the Glass Ceiling Act of 1991, Congress created the Glass Ceiling Commission to study and make recommendations on ways to eliminate barriers and increase opportunities for women to advance in business. The report made suggestions on how to improve the workplace for women by reducing gender discrimination, the unequal treatment of an individual or group based on their gender. Legislative changes help women make progress, but it is a slow process.

Evidence suggests that putting women in leadership roles is good for women and good for business. A 2019 study by a leading business research group found that companies led by women **CEOs** often were more successful than companies led by male CEOs. The study also showed that corporate **boards of directors** with more women directors were often more successful companies. Read about several women CEOs who have shattered the glass ceiling by leading large corporations and making great contributions in business.

Mary Teresa Barra

Mary Teresa Barra is the chairwoman and CEO of the General Motors Company. An electrical engineer by training, she is the first female CEO of a major global automaker. For several years, she ranked number one on Fortune's Most Powerful Women's list. She grew up in humble surroundings near the GM factory in Detroit where her father

©2017 Santa Fabio

Mary Barra (left) and Girls Who Code Founder and CEO Reshma Saujani

worked for 39 years. She started working at GM at the age of 18, inspecting fenders and hoods to pay for her college tuition. Under Mary Barra's direction, General Motors partnered with a nonprofit, Girls Who Code, to increase access to computer science education for girls through after-school activities that teach computer science skills. "Becoming an engineer paved the way for my career," said Barra. "It's one of the reasons I am passionate about promoting STEM [science, technology, engineering and math] education to students everywhere."

A **metaphor** is a figure of speech that compares two things that are not alike but do have something in common.

A **CEO** is a chief executive officer, the highest-ranking person in a company.

The **board of directors** is an elected group of individuals that represent shareholders and advises senior executives. The board sets policies and guides a corporation's management.

Ursula Burns

As CEO of Xerox from 2009 until 2017, **Ursula Burns** was the first Black woman to become CEO of a Fortune 500 Company. She has been listed by Forbes magazine as one

Ursula Burns

of the 100 most powerful women in the world. She was raised in a low-income housing project in New York city by a single mom who immigrated to the United States from Panama. Ursula excelled in school and earned a master's degree in chemical engineering. In 2009, President Barack Obama appointed her to direct the White House National STEM program, which she led for seven years. In 2016, she was on a list of Hilary Clinton's potential candidates for vice president. She currently serves on the boards of Exxon/Mobile and Uber and is a founding director of Change the Equation, which focuses on improving the United States' education system in STEM.

Indra Nooyi

Indra Nooyi was the 5th CEO in the history of PepsiCo, and both the first woman and the first Indian American to lead the company. Born in Tamil Nadu, India, Nooyi has been a role model

Indra Nooyi

for women in business and is ranked among the world's 100 most powerful women. In 2018, she was named one of the "Best CEOs in the World" by *CEOWORLD* magazine and currently serves on a number of corporate boards. In April of 2020 during the COVID-19 crisis, Nooyi and her husband, Raj, donated 187,000 Scholastic books to schools in Connecticut as part of Partnership for Connecticut's Learn from Home initiative.

Susan Wojcicki

Susan Wojcicki, known as "the queen of the very small screen," has been the CEO of YouTube since 2014. A cofounder of Google, Susan grew up with her family on the Stanford University campus where her father was a physics professor. She started her first business at the age of 11, selling homemade spice ropes (braided yarn with spices attached) door to door. It was surprisingly successful, which spurred her on to later **entrepreneurship**. Wojcicki has been a champion for numerous causes, including the advocating for Syrian refugees, ending gender discrimination at technology companies, promoting paid family leave, getting girls interested in computer science, and prioritizing coding in schools.

In a 2016 interview, she stated, "I believe in new ideas and their ability to change the future."

Anne, Janet, and Susan Wojcicki

Anne E. Wojcicki

Anne E. Wojcicki, the youngest of the three talented Wojcicki sisters, is the cofounder and CEO of 23andMe, a genetic testing service that provides customers with information about their health and ancestry. 23andMe offers a testing kit that enables a person to mail a sample of their saliva and discover where their ancestors (relatives from the past) came from, and whether they are more likely to develop certain diseases, based on their genetic makeup. In 2015, 23andMe began offering tests authorized by the Food and Drug Administration for Alzheimer's and Parkinson's disease, as well as other medical conditions. Wojcicki is one of the technology leaders who funds The Breakthrough Prize in Life Sciences, a scientific award given to researchers who make advances toward understanding living systems and extending human life. She has said, "I don't want to just live to be a hundred, I want to be healthy at a hundred."

> An **entrepreneur** is a person who creates a new business.

May be reproduced for classroom use. *Toolkit Texts: Short Nonfiction for American History, Industrial Age and Immigration*, by Stephanie Harvey and Anne Goudvis, ©2021 (Portsmouth, NH: Heinemann).

TECHNOLOGY CHALLENGES

During this first half of the 21st century, we find ourselves caught in a high-speed train blur of time and technology unlike anything we have ever seen. Our fast-paced, rapidly improving technology brings remarkable benefits, and also comes with new and complicated challenges from the perils of screen time, to privacy issues, to automation and job loss.

Doctors recommend balancing screen time with other activities and making sure to finish your schoolwork and get enough sleep each day.

SCREENS: HOW MUCH TIME IS TOO MUCH?

Too often in classrooms across the United States, kids are scattered around the room alone, devices in hand, eyes focused on bright screens, thumbs filling in bubbles and blanks at warp speed. A rising backlash is reflected in headlines across the United States: "Silicon Valley Parents Are Raising Their Kids Tech Free," "Fed Up Parents Say Get Kids Off the Screens," "Parents Petition Schools to Limit iPad Use," "Kids Look Like Zombies," etc. And these come from the very places that developed digital devices. More than half of K–12 teachers now have a one-to-one student-to-device ratio in their classrooms. Add to this the amount of time kids spend on screens outside of school and it's hard not to be concerned. Studies of reading comprehension find that readers understand more when they read on paper than on screens. Other studies have shown that too much time on screens can lead to kids having fewer friends, showing more distracted behavior, and becoming anxious and depressed. Doctors, teachers, and parents are concerned. What can we do?

IS PRIVACY OVER?

Have you ever been online and seen the perfect book or video game pop up on the screen without asking for them? It seems like magic. Ads on Facebook reveal exactly what you want. Google tells us how long it will take to drive to work even though we haven't turned on the GPS. If Alexa is plugged in, Amazon listens to what we are saying even when we haven't woken her up. This is known as tracking. Each time we open an app or go to a website, companies like Amazon, Google, and Facebook track every move we make. The more time we spend online, the more they know about us and the less secure we become.

Many people are concerned that some companies have tracked and gathered so much information about us that we no longer have privacy. And yet we still have the right to privacy. How will we protect it?

A federal law, the Children's Online Privacy Protection Act (COPPA), helps protect kids younger than 13 when they're online. It's designed to keep anyone from getting a child's personal information without a parent knowing about it and agreeing to it first.

ROBOTS, AUTOMATION, AND JOB LOSS

Artificial intelligence is already here in a big way. Alexa, Siri, and driverless cars are all part of daily life. Robots continue to get faster, smarter, and cheaper. In a 2019 report, Oxford Economics estimates that robots will replace approximately 20 million jobs by 2030 with 8.5% of the global workforce losing their jobs to automation. The United States is expected to lose 1.5 million jobs to automation (use of machines or technology to create products without humans) by 2030. The effects of these job losses will fall most heavily on communities already experiencing low incomes and poverty. This is a worrisome trend considering the problems of income inequality that we already face in the United States and around the world. How will we fix it?

A robotics engineer designs robots and robotic systems that are able to perform jobs that are dangerous, dirty, or too difficult for humans.

Although technology brings many great advances to society, these issues represent just some of the technology challenges facing us in the 21st century. We are left with the question: *How will we address these challenges going forward?* Only time will tell.

Health experts warn that video games are taking over our lives.

Hooked On Games

Playing video games can be a fun way to unwind or spend time with friends. In schools, teachers use games like Minecraft to sharpen students' thinking, encourage teamwork, and spur the imagination.

But for some players, gaming has become an unhealthy habit. Late at night, they are glued to a screen. Schoolwork suffers. The video-game world feels like a friendlier place than the real one.

Mental health experts have taken notice. In June, the World Health Organization (WHO) added gaming disorder to its list of diseases and health conditions. According to WHO, the disorder can be diagnosed if gaming has damaged a person's relationships with family and friends and if it has affected his or her daily activities. To meet this diagnosis, the behavior and its effects have to be apparent for at least a year.

Not all experts agree with WHO's decision to call excessive gaming a disorder. They say people hooked on video games may be suffering other mental health problems that should be treated first.

Others think WHO made the right call. Psychiatrist Clifford Sussman specializes in gaming addiction. He says kids often have feelings of anxiety and loneliness. They get angry when a parent pries them from a device. "It becomes a self-destructive activity," Sussman says.

Taking Back Control

What makes video games addictive? They provide instant gratification. Playing activates the reward center of the brain. After a while, the brain becomes desensitized to pleasure. You feel bored without a controller in your hand, so you play even more.

One key to a healthy gaming is to track how long you play. Sussman recommends taking at least an hour-long break after every hour of play. That gives the brain time to recover.

Teachers can help you too, by keeping an eye on students' behavior. "Schools may be an excellent place for screening for gaming disorder," says psychologist Kimberly Young. She would like to see teachers trained to spot signs of addiction.

Young gamers who think they might have a problem should seek help from an adult. Sussman suggests you first answer a simple question: "Are you in control, or is the game in control?"

How the Industrial Revolution AFFECTS YOU

You weren't alive during the Industrial Revolution, but it affects you today. Here's how.

MORE FOR LESS

Before the Industrial Revolution, many goods were in short supply. Prices were often high. People might get one or two new outfits per year because clothing took a long time to make by hand. Factories drove many hand weavers and other skilled craftspeople out of business. But more products became available. And they often cost less.

❏ **How many new clothes did you get last year?**

GADGETS GALORE!

Your alarm buzzes. You get dressed. You grab breakfast in your modern kitchen. Before the Industrial Revolution, most goods were handmade. Machines were more simple. Now machines makes almost everything we use, all day long.

❏ **Count how many things you used today that were made in a factory.**

OFF TO WORK

Farmers generally worked right where they lived. After the Industrial Revolution, men, women, and children often worked away from home in factories. Work days often lasted 12 hours or longer. Many children who worked had no time for school. Workers finally objected to the long hours, poor pay, and bad conditions. Now laws limit the length of work days. They say how much workers should be paid. They also limit how much kids can work, and where.

❑ **Ask your mom, dad, or guardian about the length of their work day.**

GETTING AROUND

Factories, mines, and mills needed a way to get raw materials and ship out products. Steamboats, trains, and other types of transportation made it faster and easier.

❑ **List the different kinds of transportation you've used to travel in the last year.**

BE ON TIME

Factories paid workers for the time they spent doing their job. Paying attention to time is still a big part of our culture. Many days have set schedules. Your school and family require you to be on time.

❑ **Figure out how long your school day is. What happens if you are late?**

Globe: ©arquiplay77/Adobe Stock. Background: ©GeoPappas/Adobe Stock.

FROM FARMS TO CITIES

Before the Industrial Revolution, most people lived on farms. They grew, made, or traded for almost everything that they needed. The growth of factories changed all that. Today, most people live in cities or suburbs. And your family probably buys most of their food and clothing from a store.

❑ **Does your family buy any food or other products from local farms?**

SAFETY FIRST!

Factory work was dangerous during the Industrial Revolution. Cotton dust, coal dust, sharp objects, and moving machinery were just a few hazards. The government finally made workplace safety laws.

❑ **Talk with your family about safety rules at their jobs.**

Photo: ©Radius Images/Alamy. Background: ©NataLT/Shutterstock.

YOUR WORLD

Coal, oil, and other fossil fuels powered the Industrial Revolution. Factories often polluted the air, land, and water. There are now laws to limit pollution. But effects of past pollution remain. And fossil fuel use continues. Earth's average temperature has risen since the Industrial Revolution began. This is mostly due to the use of fossil fuels. Problems linked to climate change include extreme weather events and rising sea levels.

❑ **How can you reduce your energy use?**

Photo: ©Vladimir salman/Shutterstock. Background: ©Houghton Mifflin Harcourt.

May be reproduced for classroom use. *Toolkit Texts: Short Nonfiction for American History, Industrial Age and Immigration,* by Stephanie Harvey and Anne Goudvis, ©2021 (Portsmouth, NH: Heinemann).

Imagine gloves that can bridge the language barrier between those who use sign language and those who don't know how to sign.

Brett Eloff/Royal Academy of Engineering

Roy Allela Inventor of Sign-IO Gloves

Roy Allela (above right) and his Sign-IO glove, along with his coworker Chelmis Muthoni, Chief Operating Officer of Sign-IO.

Roy Allela, a 25-year-old software engineer and inventor from Kenya, is creating gloves that will make communication easier for people who are hearing impaired, deaf, or speech impaired. He recently invented a pair of gloves that allows people who use sign language to communicate with hearing people. A hearing or speech impaired person puts the Sign-IO gloves on their hands and, amazingly, the "smart" gloves translate sign language into speech that you can hear. The gloves have special flex sensors that connect to Bluetooth through an app that Allela invented.

Allela was inspired to invent the gloves because his family had trouble communicating with his six-year-old niece who was born deaf. His niece uses the gloves now and can communicate with hearing people without a translator. "My niece wears the gloves, pairs them to her phone or mine, then starts signing and I'm able to understand what she's saying," says Allela.

This exciting invention will be available to the public by the end of 2024. Allela's goal is to place at least two pairs of gloves in every special needs school in Kenya. He believes they could be used to help the 34 million children worldwide who suffer disabling hearing loss.

Kids Can Invent Solutions

Toolkit Texts: Short Nonfiction for American History, Industrial Age and Immigration, by Stephanie Harvey and Anne Goudvis, ©2021 (Portsmouth, NH: Heinemann). May be reproduced for classroom use.

The team was invited to Washington D.C., where the National Museum of American History put their prototype on display. It will stay there until next year's winners are selected.

A **gutter** is a trough on the edge of a roof to catch rainwater.

Paige Blair has always loved to build and create. With her mom, she started a Lego robotics team with other kids from Springfield, Missouri. Paige, Eli Carter, Jack Ireland, and Brayden Lauderbaugh, aged nine to ten years old, began meeting to build Lego robots. Then the team, called Coding Hex, learned about a creative challenge called the Spark!Lab Dr. InBae Yoon Invent It Challenge. The challenge invites young people around the world to identify a real-world problem and solve it. They have fun and help change the world for the better!

The challenge began in January 2018—a quick turnaround for the Coding Hex team. That year, the challenge was to solve a natural disaster problem. "We decided to work on hurricanes and flooded areas," said Brayden. "For our robotics challenge, we had to solve a problem involving water. Someone suggested using **gutters**, and it went from there," said Paige. "We saw what was happening in Florida and Puerto Rico during the hurricanes and wanted to invent something that would help. We saw that the biggest need was energy and clean water. Our invention provides both," said Eli.

The kids worked on their invention for several months before submitting it. When the winners were announced in May, they won in their age group! Their invention is called the FilTurbine Guttering System. Simply put, it filters rainwater and creates electricity. Rainwater goes into a guttering downspout. The water turns the **turbine**, creating electricity. The electricity is stored in a battery pack for temporary energy. The water continues into an underground **cistern** that stores it until it can be filtered for drinking. A hand pump provides access to the water.

The Invent It Challenge encourages kids to reuse or recycle materials as much as possible. For their prototype, the kids used a variety of materials. An old window screen served as the mesh at the top to keep large debris out of the gutter. The next piece of the prototype was an actual piece of a gutter. A parent supplied a hydropower kit for the turbine. For the filter and container, the team bought a Brita water filter system. And they kept it all together with lots of duct tape! The team shared some thoughts about the inventing process.

> A **turbine** is a machine or mechanical device that extracts energy from the flow of a liquid.
>
> A **cistern** is a tank or a receptacle for catching and storing rainwater.

How did you get interested in inventing?

Paige: I have just always liked making new solutions to problems.

Eli: I took **STEAM** classes at my local library. (**STEAM** stands for Science, Technology, Engineering, Art, and Mathematics.)

Jack: I got interested in inventing when I used to play with Legos a lot.

Brayden: I watched videos on inventing, and I was inspired.

How did your team work together?

Eli: We work well together. Everyone takes turns and listens to one another.

Jack: We did lots of team-building activities to work on teamwork.

Jack, Brayden, Paige, and Eli pose with their FilTurbine Guttering System invention.

What do you like about inventing?

Paige: Making the **prototype** and watching it work.

Jack: The feeling of success when you finally finish.

> A **prototype** is a first model of something.

Any advice for other kid inventors?

Paige: Make sure to have fun. If it's not fun, it won't be your best work.

Eli: Be creative with everything and put extra effort into the Tweak It step.

Jack: Keep trying and never give up.

Brayden: Talk with one another.

Erika Blair also shared some thoughts about being the team leader to this talented group of kids. Her favorite thing was "watching them make discoveries and keep trying whenever something didn't go quite to plan. They take what they have learned through research and turn it into a tangible creation that can make a difference."

Blair shared, "They really shined while working on the Invent It Challenge. I hope they will draw on this experience when they face challenges throughout life. Instead of seeing a problem and feeling defeated, I hope they can see a problem and know that they are capable of figuring out a solution."

Courtesy of Sherri Carter

ANOTHER SUCCESSFUL INVENTION

The Coding Hex team entered the Invent It Challenge again in 2020.
We asked the team about this experience and their award-winning invention.
Congratulations, kids!

"Each year, our inventions were inspired by someone we knew who was affected by that year's challenge theme. The theme of 2020 Invent It Challenge was increasing access to healthy foods for everyone, everywhere, every day. The Green Grocery Bus was inspired by one of the team member's aunt who has to rely on others for transportation to and from the grocery store. Our invention helps with that by transporting people on a solar powered bus that has special features to hold groceries. We even made an app that shows the bus schedule and routes.

"After we come up with our idea, we practice the Engineering Design Process. This process includes researching the problem and existing solutions, talking with experts, designing and building a prototype, and marketing our idea by creating a commercial for our invention. We enjoy the 'sell it' step the most because we can express our team's creativity by making a commercial for our invention."

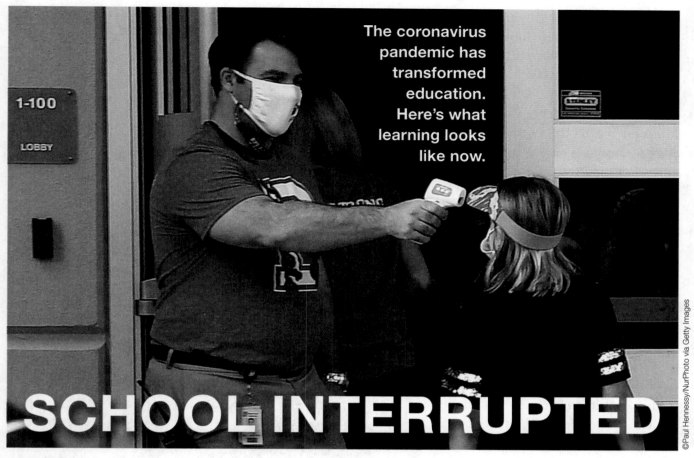

The coronavirus pandemic has transformed education. Here's what learning looks like now.

SCHOOL INTERRUPTED

A principal checks a student's temperature on the first day of school at Baldwin Park Elementary School in Orlando, Florida, on August 21, 2020. Face masks and temperature checks are required for all students who attend school in person in Florida.

Esteban Tarango, twelve, was excited to make new friends when he started middle school this year in Tempe, Arizona. Instead, his school year kicked off in front of a computer screen.

"I'm honestly kind of sad," Esteban said. "I feel like I'm missing out."

The back-to-school experience has been upended for students everywhere. That's because of the coronavirus pandemic. As of mid-July, school closures had affected more than a billion students worldwide. That's according to United Nations secretary-general António Guterres. In an August 4, 2020, video message, he said the pandemic "has led to the largest disruption of education ever."

In the United States, many schools have reopened with remote learning only. But some schools have brought students back into the classroom. Others are offering a mix of online and in-person instruction.

Life at school today looks very different. Schools are sanitizing often. Temperature checks are common. There are many new rules to follow.

"We'll have to wear a mask," Mia Westerman explained. She's a sixth-grade student in Clarksburg, West Virginia. "We'll have to social distance," she added. "And we're not allowed to change classes or eat in the cafeteria."

The Big Picture

COVID-19 was first discovered in 2019. It's the disease caused by the new coronavirus. Recent studies show young people are less likely to get seriously sick from the virus. But kids can spread the virus to others. Staying home is one way to slow the spread of the disease.

Decisions about how and when to reopen schools are being made on a case-by-case basis. They're constantly reevaluated by local officials and leaders. The virus is so new that our understanding of it is always changing. Plus, it is better controlled in some parts of the country than in others.

"It depends on where you are," Dr. Anthony Fauci said, when asked if kids should be back in classrooms. Fauci is the nation's top infectious disease expert. He spoke with the *Washington Post*, in a July 24, 2020, interview. "We live in a very large country," Fauci added.

No Easy Solution

Should kids be learning virtually or in the classroom? There's no easy answer to this question.

In-person learning would help the economy. It would allow some parents to go back to work. Even so, remote learning is the safest option in many places for now.

New measures are in place to promote social distancing in a school lunch room in Milford, Massachusetts, on September 11, 2020.

A teacher wearing a face mask walks around the classroom during a lesson at an elementary school in San Francisco, California, on October 5, 2020. Students who are attending school from home can be seen on the monitor at the back of the classroom.

But learning away from teachers and classmates is difficult. The isolation is having an effect on kids' mental health.

The pandemic has also created greater inequalities. Kids who rely on school for some of their meals might not have enough to eat. And some students don't have access to computers or reliable Internet at home. They're having a harder time getting their work done.

There's so much uncertainty in the world right now. But one thing is for sure: you and your classmates are part of history. Years from now, kids will learn about the coronavirus pandemic. They'll be curious about your experience. And they'll see you and your classmates as incredibly resilient.

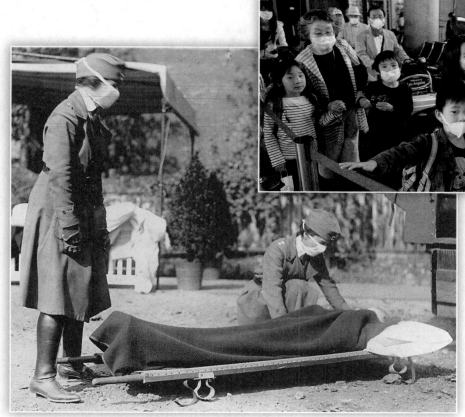

©MARK RALSTON/AFP via Getty Images

A family (above) wears face masks for protection from swine flu as they arrive at the Los Angeles airport in California in 2009.

Two Red Cross nurses (left) tend to a patient on a stretcher during the 1918 flu pandemic.

Library of Congress, 3c26995

THE HISTORY OF PANDEMICS

**This isn't the first time that disease has spread around the globe.
How do past pandemics from history compare to the COVID-19 health crisis?**

The new coronavirus pandemic is historic. But this isn't the first time a virus has sickened people around the globe. Pandemics have happened throughout history.

The most recent pandemic started just over a decade ago, in 2009, with the outbreak of a new kind of H1N1 flu called the Swine flu. The illness most likely started in North America, and it quickly spread around the world.

Swine flu wasn't nearly as deadly as the coronavirus. This made it easier to control. Governments did not have to issue stay-at-home orders like we are seeing today. By late 2009, vaccines were available to prevent people from becoming sick.

A Look Back

In 1918, a pandemic hit, caused by a new kind of flu called the Spanish flu. (The disease didn't actually start in Spain, but newspapers there were among the first to report on it. So people started calling it the Spanish flu, and the name stuck.)

Experts believe that one third of the world's population was infected with the disease. Many historians have compared it to the new coronavirus. "They're similar in the way they infect people," historian John Barry explains. "They're similar in the way they spread." Both affect a person's lungs, and they can both spread easily.

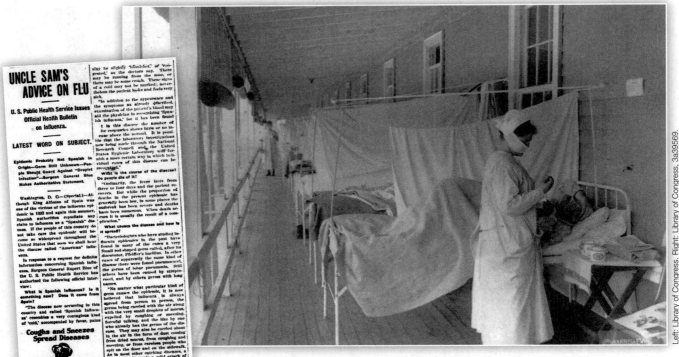

A nurse (above) takes a patient's pulse at a hospital in Washington, D.C., during the 1918 flu pandemic.

Left: Library of Congress. Right: Library of Congress, 3a39569.

Stopping the Spread

During the Spanish flu pandemic, the United States put in place restrictions similar to those we're seeing today. People were asked to wear face masks and encouraged to wash their hands. Officials limited large gatherings and ordered people to quarantine themselves.

"Quarantine is centuries and centuries old," says Katherine Foss, an author and professor who has studied pandemics throughout history. "It's the number one practice that is used to stop an outbreak. And it works even when scientists don't know what is making people sick."

Science has come a long way since 1918. Back then, doctors didn't even have microscopes that were powerful enough to let them see the viruses that cause pandemics. Today, scientists and doctors have advanced technology to help them battle the new coronavirus. "But since we're dealing with a brand-new virus that nobody has ever seen before, it still takes time to develop vaccines and treatments using modern medicine," Barry says. "In the meantime, the only thing left to fight it with are public-health measures like quarantine."

Barry says that although there have been many pandemics throughout history, kids should understand that this one is unusually severe.

"This is something you're going to remember for the rest of your life," he says. "This is not ordinary. This is a special time that requires special courage. You have an opportunity to rise to greatness. Social distancing matters, and it saves lives."

Living History

Foss encourages everyone to keep a journal during this time. Future historians will look to these accounts to learn what it was like to live through this pandemic.

Young people, especially, should record their experience, Foss says. These stories often go untold in history books. "It's important that when we look back later on, we can understand what it was like to be young during this time," she says. "Your stories about finding joy in times of crisis—those are stories we want told for centuries."

Quarantine Is Lifted

Pullman Herald, *November 15, 1918*

Between the spring of 1918 and the spring of 1919, a highly contagious and fatal influenza, called the Spanish flu, swept the country in three waves, devastating entire communities. Many historians believe that the Spanish flu is similar to COVID-19. They both affect people's lungs and can spread when an infected person coughs or sneezes. During the 1918 epidemic, like today, people were asked to wear face masks and wash their hands. Officials limited large gatherings and asked people to stay home. In this article from the Pullman Herald *dated November 15, 1918, the city health official of Pullman, Washington informs the community that the quarantine is over, but everyone needs to be remain cautious to keep the virus from spreading.*

The ban is off, yet the danger is not over, and I kindly ask every one to join in a campaign to keep this influenza under submission. . . . Just as surely, it will get you . . . if you give it a chance.

There will be services at the various churches Sunday, but if you are not feeling well stay at home for your own protection as well as that of others.

The schools will open on Monday. Watch your children carefully and if they are not well by all means keep them home.

Theaters, lodges and pool rooms will also begin operation Monday and we hope within the next few weeks to see Pullman the same busy, happy little city she was before this awful epidemic struck us.

J.L. GILLELAND,
City Health Officer

Excerpted from: The *Pullman Herald* Newspaper. Pullman, WA. November 15, 1918.

Born to Invent

Bishop's Great Idea

SOME KIDS are born inventors, creating cool things and coming up with interesting ideas. And some kids, like Bishop Curry Jr., from Texas, come up with ideas so great that they deserve a lot of attention.

Bishop, who is now in middle school, came up with a great idea when he was in fifth grade. A baby whose family lived just down the road from him died after being left in a hot car for four hours. "There was like a car death and then like a month later there was another one, and then [after] the third one it kind of popped into my head," Bishop said. His idea was to invent a car seat for babies with an alarm that would go off and alert the parents if the baby was left alone in a hot car. The seat would also be equipped with a system for cooling the child

By Marcia Amidon Lusted. May be reproduced for classroom use. *Toolkit Texts: Short Nonfiction for American History, Industrial Age and Immigration*, by Stephanie Harvey and Anne Goudvis, ©2021 (Portsmouth, NH: Heinemann).

down until they were rescued. Bishop even thought about having the seat link with the car's air conditioning system, so that it could turn it on automatically.

Bishop's dad thought the idea was worth getting attention. He mentioned it to the Toyota Company, where he works, and Toyota sent them both to the Toyota Technical Center in Detroit to witness car safety crash texts. Bishop was also invited to attend the Center for Child Injury Prevention Conference, where he spoke with the director of engineering for a child safety company called Evenflo.

To protect Bishop's idea, he and his father created a GoFundMe campaign to raise the $20,000 to patent the car seat idea. They raised the money in just one year, and now they're creating drawing and scale models as the next step to finding someone to manufacture the car seat. Bishop is working with a California company that links inventors to manufacturers. When he was asked about how he'd feel when he sees his idea become a real car seat, Bishop said, "I'd be like, 'What?' I'd probably pinch myself to see if I was dreaming."

By Marcia Amidon Lusted. May be reproduced for classroom use. *Toolkit Texts: Short Nonfiction for American History, Industrial Age and Immigration*, by Stephanie Harvey and Anne Goudvis, ©2021 (Portsmouth, NH: Heinemann).

Help Wanted Ads
and Spotlight on Child Labor

Make Tracks

Strong men needed to lay railroad tracks from coast to coast. Must be able to lift and place heavy wooden ties and metal rails. Bolters will spike them into place. Tents and meals provided.

Geniuses Needed

If you love to tinker and can turn ideas into products, we need you! Inventors will work at the Invention Factory, in Menlo Park, New Jersey, to create machines to make the world an easier place for everyone.

If you saw these ads in the newspaper during the Industrial Revolution, which job would you apply for?

Work from Home

Immigrant stay-at-home mother, make some extra money! Keep your kids home from school to help you pick walnut meats, finish seams, or sew on buttons. No cleanliness inspections required.

Seeking Iron Workers

Start at age 9 or 10 for this lifelong job. If you like it hot, you can work 12–14 hour days. You'll bring loads of ore to the furnaces or pour boiling liquid metal. Bonus: free soot facials.

Dig Black Gold

Calling all men and boys to the coal mines!
Pick, shovel, and blow up rocks
to fill coal cars underground.
Young breaker boys needed to
separate coal from rocks.
Work 10-hour days,
six days a week.

Luddites **Buddies**

If you're a weaver who is
unemployed, because a machine
took your job, then join us!
Men, grab your mask and hammer!
Help break into factories to
smash the weaving machines.

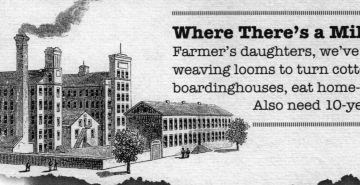

Where There's a Mill, There's a Way

Farmer's daughters, we've got jobs for you! Run the loud
weaving looms to turn cotton into cloth. Stay in the company's
boardinghouses, eat home-cooked meals, and attend classes.
Also need 10-year-old doffers to change the bobbins.

Child Labor

In the 1900s, **Luddites** were weavers and textile workers who objected to the use of mechanical looms and knitting frames. Most were trained artisans who had spent years learning their craft, and they feared that unskilled machine operators were robbing them of their livelihood.

These "wanted ads" for a job during the Industrial Revolution are not real, of course. But they capture many of the harsh realities about what many child laborers faced 100 years ago. Back then, some children began working at the age of five.

Not all children worked and some children worked to earn spending money during this time. But in the early 1900s, two million American children were working children. These children came from all backgrounds and races. One thing that they all had in common was poverty. These children worked because they needed to help their families. At an age as young as five, a child was expected to help with farm work and other household chores.

Some children worked in factories from a young age. These boys in a textile mill were so small they had to climb up on the spinning frame to mend the broken threads and put back the empty bobbins.

The farming lifestyle required lots of hard work, whether it was planting crops, feeding chickens, or mending fences. Many children also worked outside of their home or family farm—in textile or other factories, in coal mines, on street corners selling newspapers or vegetables. Some children worked in fields planting and harvesting cotton and other crops. Wherever they labored— in homes, factories, mines, or fields—they didn't have time to play or to go to school.

Around the turn of the 20th century, some individuals and **labor unions** began to take notice of the situation. They were horrified by the physical and moral dangers that child laborers faced. They argued that long hours of work deprived children of an education and ended their chance for a better future. They believed that children were the most vulnerable members of society and that the country had a responsibility to keep them safe. Historically, children had been viewed as little versions of adults, so the idea of offering them protection was new.

Compulsory Education

The effort to change attitudes about child labor in the United States was helped by a push to make education **compulsory**, which means children were required by law to attend school. Many believed that attendance at school would prevent children from being overworked in factories. In 1852, Massachusetts was the first state to **mandate** elementary school education for its residents. The 1852 law required every city and town to offer elementary school, focusing on grammar and basic arithmetic. More than 60 years later, Mississippi became the last state to do so. By 1918, all 50 states had passed laws that required children ranging in age for 5 years old to 14 years old to

Labor unions: an organization of workers formed to improve wages, benefits, and working conditions

Compulsory: required

Mandate: to officially require something

May be reproduced for classroom use. *Toolkit Texts: Short Nonfiction for American History, Industrial Age and Immigration*, by Stephanie Harvey and Anne Goudvis, ©2021 (Portsmouth, NH: Heinemann).

be educated through public or private schools.

Mandatory education made it harder—but not impossible—for employers to hire underage children. States in the South were less likely to enforce compulsory education laws. In fact, Alabama temporarily repealed its compulsory education law in response to pressure from a large textile company in the state. Many children worked in the textile industry and the industry depended on them.

In 1938, after several failed attempts, the federal government passed its first national child labor law. The Fair Labor Standards Act established a minimum age of 14 for employment and stated the number of hours children could work.

Today, most children can get a job after they turn 14 years old. By law these jobs cannot put teenagers in danger. Their employers have to limit the hours worked in a week and pay teenagers a fair wage. Although children continue to labor around the world in dangerous conditions, the United States has come a long way in the past 100 years.

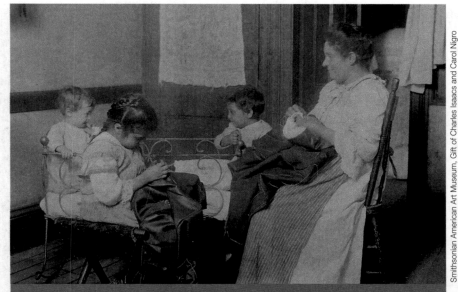

Some children helped their parents at home, cutting cloth, sewing clothes, or making artificial flowers. The wages earned by children were badly needed in some families to survive.

With children working long hours in factories, in mines, and on farms, there was little time left for school. But by 1900, 31 states had laws requiring students to attend school from age 8 to 14.

In Colonial times, a master might take on an apprentice to get help in his workshop and to pass on his craft.

WORKING DAYS
CHILD LABOR IN AMERICAN HISTORY

"Childhood should be a time for young people to be **nurtured** and allowed to play and learn."

"Childhood should be a time for young people to work to keep them out of trouble and to build character and discipline."

Which of the above two statements sounds better to you? Historically, children did not have much say in the matter. The idea that childhood should be a special time when boys and girls are cared for and allowed to play and learn is relatively new. Instead, most American children's days were filled with work.

Nurtured means helped to grow, develop, or mature.

May be reproduced for classroom use. *Toolkit Texts: Short Nonfiction for American History, Industrial Age and Immigration,* by Stephanie Harvey and Anne Goudvis, ©2021 (Portsmouth, NH: Heinemann).

By Barbara Bair, Lee Ann Potter, and Stephen Wesson, *Cobblestone,* ©2017 by Carus Publishing Company. Reproduced with permission.

Chores, Trades, and Work

Beginning at early ages, Native American children were taught useful skills to help their communities and prepare them for adulthood. When Europeans first came to live in North America, those children also kept busy by helping their families survive. Even the youngest children were assigned chores, such as gathering firewood, collecting eggs, or pulling weeds in the garden. Around the age of ten years old, colonial children often became apprentices. They learned a trade by living and training with someone who was an expert in a certain field. Boys were taught, for example, to become blacksmiths, ironworkers, and **sawyers**. Most girls were not expected to work outside of the homes, but some girls learned to be **milliners** or seamstresses.

Some children did not have any family to support them until they became old enough to live independently. They might sign a contract to work as an **indentured servant** for a certain number of years. Some indentured servants were paid for their labor, but most children simply were provided food and a place to live for the duration of their service.

By the mid-1800s, the **Industrial Revolution** began to shift how Americans lived and worked. People left behind family farms to live in towns or cities. Cities became centers for factories and industries, in which many laborers were needed to mass-produce goods and materials. Children filled some of the demand for workers. Girls left their homes on farms to live in boardinghouses and work in textile mills. Young boys followed fathers and older brothers into the coal mines.

Sawyers are people employed in sawing wood.

Milliners are people who make, design, or trim hats.

An **indentured servant** is a person who works as a laborer for a number of years to repay a debt.

The **Industrial Revolution** was a period of rapid growth in manufacturing, when machine-made products replaced handmade products.

After moving from farms to cities in the late 1800s, workers were exposed to air polluted by "modern" industries.

Poor Working Conditions

Mills and mines were dangerous places to work. The dust and dirt caused lung diseases. High-speed machines and underground work put children at risk of accidents. Canneries, where food was packaged into cans, resulted in cuts and infections. Glass factories exposed workers to high temperatures, cramped spaces, and broken glass, which led to burns, cuts, and other injuries. Labor unions and organizations tried to address some of the worst conditions, but their efforts were difficult to enforce across different states and industries.

In addition to undergoing a period of rapid industrialization, the United States also absorbed more than one million new immigrants between 1880 and 1910. Most immigrants settled in crowded tenement neighborhoods in the nation's cities. There, industries, factories, and packing plants offered newcomers employment close to the places where they lived.

In 1880, the U.S. **Census** reported that more than 1 million children under the age of 16 years old—or one out of six children—worked for money. Even more children worked who were not officially counted.

> A **census** is a count of the nation's population, which is done every 10 years.

Immigrant Families

Some immigrant children helped their parents in their apartments. The work, called "piecework," involved sewing clothes, making hats, rolling cigars, and fashioning artificial flowers and other small items. For each item that the family produced, it was paid a set price. That situation meant that even the youngest children were expected to help add to the total pieces created by a family to help pay the rent

Workers found the heavy, thick dust in coal mines difficult to see through and impossible to avoid breathing into their lungs.

National Child Labor Committee collection, Library of Congress, Prints and Photographs Division, 01127

May be reproduced for classroom use. *Toolkit Texts: Short Nonfiction for American History; Industrial Age and Immigration*, by Stephanie Harvey and Anne Goudvis, ©2021 (Portsmouth, NH: Heinemann).

Library of Congress, 04305

When the three eldest Cottone children— Joseph, 14 years old; Rosie, 7 years old; and Andrew, 10 years old—all helped their mother finish garments, the family made about $2 a week—if there was plenty of work. The two babies were not expected to help.

or buy food. If they worked outside their homes, the workplaces were referred to as "sweatshops" because unsafe numbers of people crowded together in them and were exposed to unhealthy conditions with little ventilation, poor lighting, and many fire hazards.

Young girls not yet old enough to work in factories or mills were hired out to do laundry or scrub floors in other people's houses. Young boys worked as newsboys distributing newspapers, as bootblacks shining shoes, or as messengers delivering telegrams. Outside of cities, children of all ages worked in fields, handpicking and gathering crops. No matter what the job, it often took priority over school. For families who needed to bring in more money, work was more important than school.

Protection for Children

The status of young workers concerned some Americans. A period of widespread social and political reform, knows as the Progressive Era (1890–1920), energized some activists who made child labor their cause. They were motivated by the belief that society and the federal government had to do more to protect the nation's children. Reformers, including settlement house founder Jane Addams, factory inspector Florence Kelley, and journalist Jacob Riis, became champions for children. They

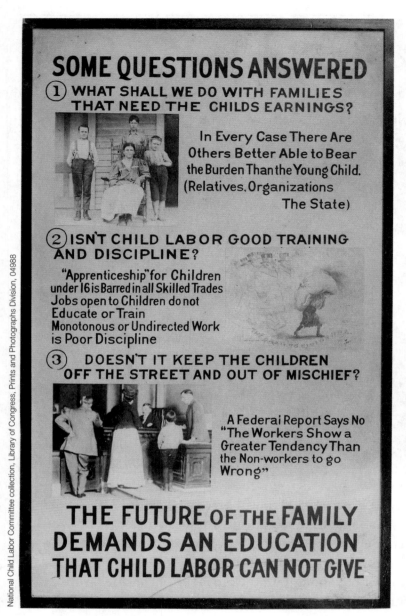

SOME QUESTIONS ANSWERED

1. **WHAT SHALL WE DO WITH FAMILIES THAT NEED THE CHILDS EARNINGS?**

   In Every Case There Are Others Better Able to Bear the Burden Than the Young Child. (Relatives, Organizations The State)

2. **ISN'T CHILD LABOR GOOD TRAINING AND DISCIPLINE?**

   "Apprenticeship" for Children under 16 is Barred in all Skilled Trades Jobs open to Children do not Educate or Train Monotonous or Undirected Work is Poor Discipline

3. **DOESN'T IT KEEP THE CHILDREN OFF THE STREET AND OUT OF MISCHIEF?**

   A Federal Report Says No "The Workers Show a Greater Tendency Than the Non-workers to go Wrong"

THE FUTURE OF THE FAMILY DEMANDS AN EDUCATION THAT CHILD LABOR CAN NOT GIVE

People who hoped to change Americans' attitudes about child labor created posters and exhibits to encourage support for reforms.

National Child Labor Committee collection, Library of Congress, Prints and Photographs Division, 04988

pointed out the importance of safe living and working environments. They also suggested other improvements for children, such as public parks to play in and the chance to go to school for at least part of the year.

Efforts to help working children took a variety of forms. Some groups created kindergartens and educated parents about the importance of early childhood development. Other reformers organized settlement houses and provided after-school and daycare programs for the children of working mothers. Some groups organized summer camps as a way for city kids to experience life in the country. Still other people worked to enact local laws and national policies that would officially address the dangerous conditions that young people faced working in textile mills, canneries, factories, fields, mines, and other places.

Attitudes toward child labor started to change in the 20th century as reformers increased efforts to pass local and state laws. The National Child Labor Committee (NCLC), formed in 1904, had a major role in bringing about the change.

The NCLC exposed employers that violated state child labor laws. It pressed for better laws that would limit the hours that young people could work and demanded that workplace surroundings become safer. Laws began to regulate what employers were allowed to do. States also passed laws that required children to attend school—at least part of the time.

After several attempts, a federal law regulating the employment of children passed in 1938. Today, both federal and state laws are in place to protect young workers and give them an opportunity to go to school and experience their childhoods before entering the workforce as adults.

Fast Fact

Some working families opposed the efforts of reformers because the parents needed the money that their children earned.

May be reproduced for classroom use. *Toolkit Texts: Short Nonfiction for American History, Industrial Age and Immigration,* by Stephanie Harvey and Anne Goudvis, ©2021 (Portsmouth, NH: Heinemann).

Girls who worked as spinners walked up and down the long aisles, brushing lint from the machines and watching the whirling spools for breaks in the thread. When a break occurred, they had to mend it quickly by tying the ends together.

Textile: cloth or woven fabric

Cotton gin: a machine that separates the cotton seed from the cotton fiber

Mill Girls
Harriet Hanson's Story

By 1835, Lowell, Massachusetts had become the center of the **textile** manufacturing in the United States. In Lowell's textile mills, raw cotton was turned into finished cloth. This raw cotton was planted and harvested in the Southern states. The invention of the **cotton gin** made growing cotton more profitable for cotton farmers and also expanded slavery. More enslaved people were exploited and forced to work as the cotton industry grew. Many of them were women and children who did the backbreaking work of growing and harvesting cotton. Raw cotton was then shipped to Northern states to be woven into fabric in textile factories.

Girls and women like Harriet Jane Hanson played important roles in these new factories. The stories they told in their dairies, letters, and other writing tell us much about their daily life and factory work during the Industrial Revolution.

Long hours.
Low pay.
Dangerous conditions.
Working in a textile mill wasn't easy.

Twelve-year-old Selina worked as a spinner in a cotton mill in Texas. She earned one dollar a day. Like other families, her mother and older sister also worked in the mill.

Who Was Harriet Jane Hanson?

Harriet Jane Hanson was born in Boston in 1825. She was a poor carpenter's daughter. Harriet was only six when her father died. Her aunt suggested that her family move to the fast-growing city of Lowell. Harriet's mother found work as a boardinghouse keeper. Lowell had hundreds of boarding-houses. Most mill girls lived in these large houses. Many came from farms across New England and didn't have family to live with.

Factory Work

The textile mills of Lowell were booming by 1835. The mills needed more workers. Many of the workers hired for Lowell's mills were children. Ten-year-old Harriet got a mill job in 1836. What were her days like? Harriet described her experiences in her book *Loom and Spindle*.

"I worked first in the spinning-room as a 'doffer.' The doffers were the very youngest girls, whose work was to doff, or take off, the full bobbins, and replace them with the empty ones.

"I can see myself now, racing down the alley, between the spinning frames, carrying in front of me a bobbin-box bigger than I was."

Spinning frames were the machines that spun cotton into thread. The bobbins were spools that held the thread. Doffers had to be sharp and quick.

Boott Cotton Mills at Lowell, Massachusetts

May be reproduced for classroom use. *Toolkit Texts: Short Nonfiction for American History, Industrial Age and Immigration*, by Stephanie Harvey and Anne Goudvis, ©2021 (Portsmouth, NH: Heinemann).

Many young women were drawn to Lowell by the opportunity to be independent, to study, and to learn. When they arrived, they found a vibrant intellectual culture. Many workers read voraciously in Lowell's city library and classrooms.

After all, no spinning frame ever stopped for long. Did Harriet ever have time to play? Sometimes. Overseers sometimes let the doffers play in the mill yard when they weren't working. But others did not show these young workers very much kindness.

Like many mill girls, Harriet felt proud to help her family by earning money. She earned two dollars a week as a doffer. Mill girls of Harriet's time worked from about 5:00 a.m. to 7:00 p.m., depending on the season. They only had half-hour breaks for breakfast and dinner. Harriet later said that these long hours were "the greatest hardship in the lives of these children."

Mill girls did many different jobs. Some ran large machines that carded (combed) the fibers so they weren't tangled before spinning. Others spun the fibers into thread while still others pulled threads through the loom's harnesses. On a different floor of the mill, mill girls tended machines that wove the threads together to make cloth.

In textile factories, children were hired because their nimble fingers and small hands could replace the bobbins or clear jams on machines more easily than larger adult hands. Children were also preferred because they were small and could easily fit between machines and into tight spaces. Factory owners could pay children less money than adults, and kids were less likely to go on strike or question rules or punishment.

Harriet Hanson's story is not unique. But it shows what life was like for factory workers. Factories could be drafty and cold or hot and humid inside. Dust and lint often filled the air. Home was a boardinghouse where dozens of other people lived. The ringing of bells ruled their day. But many mill girls loved the independence of working away from home. Without them, America's textile mills would never have been as productive as they were.

LETTERS FROM A MILL GIRL

May be reproduced for classroom use. *Toolkit Texts: Short Nonfiction for American History, Industrial Age and Immigration,* by Stephanie Harvey and Anne Goudvis, ©2021 (Portsmouth, NH: Heinemann).

Lowell, Massachusetts, on the Merrimack River, was founded in the 1820s as a textile manufacturing center. Powered by the river's 30-foot waterfall, the great mills housed thousands of machines that processed raw cotton into thread and then wove the thread into cloth.

Mill owners needed many workers to operate those machines, but they didn't want to pay too much for labor. They found the perfect labor force—mostly teenage girls and young women from the farms of New England. Life on farms had given girls and women experience in cloth production. They saw mill work as a way to help their families by sending money home as well as an opportunity to earn a little money of their own.

To help attract female workers, mill owners built boardinghouses near the mills. A respectable older woman called the boardinghouse keeper ran the house. She monitored the girls' activities and was required to report any bad behavior to mill management.

Work at the mills was tightly managed and monotonous. The girls signed a contract that bound them to follow the company's rules and to work 6 days a week, 12 to 14 hours a day, for at least 1 year. They were on their feet all day.

In the engaging letters that follow, Grace, a fictional character, moves from a farm to work in a textile mill. The story she shares is based on the actual experiences of mill girls.

Lowell, Massachusetts
September 21, 1835

Dear Mama,

I am arrived in Lowell at last. My, what a lot I have to tell you!

The journey here seemed mighty long. Bumping along in the wagon and then the train, I couldn't help but think how every mile was carrying me farther away from home.

Cousin Abigail met me at the depot. I knew her by her red hair—just like Papa's. She took me straight to her boardinghouse, so I only got a quick peek at the town. How I longed to stop and just stare at it all! The streets are lined with building after building, all crowded and close together. And so many people and horses and carriages hurrying here, there, and everywhere. It's so noisy and busy and bright.

Our boardinghouse is built of red brick. It is three stories tall, and our unit is joined to others on both sides. Thirty-six girls live here, four girls and two beds to a room. Abigail is in a room with older girls. I share a bed with a girl named Anne, who is fourteen—just my age! She is nice and quiet. A cheery, younger girl named Mary and a fourth girl, Susan, complete our room. I shouldn't say it, but Susan is a bit stuck-up. Anne whispered to me that it's because we're new girls and Susan has been here for five months. We are all crammed in like hens in the chicken coop. We have a single pitcher and basin for washing up.

At the spinning machine

Mrs. Chase keeps the house. There are such a lot of rules! We must be ever so quiet coming into the house and hang up our bonnets, shawls, and coats in the entry. We must never be rude or loud. And we must all be in bed by 10 o'clock.

I must say they feed us plenty. Yesterday's noon dinner was codfish hash and apple pie and warm biscuits and hot coffee.

One nice surprise is there are some books here we can borrow. I know Papa used to think me too bookish for a farm girl but, oh, Mama, I am so eager to read them.

Well, I had better stop. It's almost bedtime, and tomorrow I go to the mill to see about getting a position.

Your loving Grace

By Cynthia Overbeck Bix, *Cobblestone*, ©2017 by Carus Publishing Company. Reproduced with permission.

October 1, 1835

Dear Mama,

I am a real mill girl! Perhaps Papa is looking down from heaven right now to see his girl doing her part for the family. Do you think so?

Cousin Abigail took me to the Boott Cotton Mill to see about work. The mill is a collection of great brick buildings with high walls all around. The buildings are five stories, with row upon row of windows, staring down like stern eyes. I was almost afraid to go in. But I plucked up my courage and spoke to the overseer. And, glory be, I am to be a spinner, and start on Monday! Isn't that fine?

I own I'm a little scared to begin.

*Your loving
Grace*

Walking the line, looking for broken threads

By Cynthia Overbeck Bix, *Cobblestone,* ©2017 by Carus Publishing Company. Reproduced with permission.

November 7, 1835

Dear Mama,

Forgive me for not writing sooner. This is the first chance I have had.

I don't mean to complain, but—oh! my fingers are sore and my feet are so swollen.

Let me tell you about my days. At 4:30 in the morning, the factory tower bell wakes us with a loud clanging. Such a scrambling goes on in our room. We must all be dressed and at the factory by 5 o'clock sharp or risk being locked out and losing our day's wages.

In the spinning room are rows and rows of big machines with huge, leather driving belts, all running at top speeds. You have never heard such a terrible, loud clatter in all your life. We have to holler to hear each other talk. It never lets up all day long.

All the windows are shut tight. It's so stuffy—a fine cotton dust flies everywhere. It makes me sneeze and gets in my hair something awful. It gets hot, too. By the end of the shift, my dress is all wet down the back.

My job is to tend the spinning machines that wind thread onto rows and rows of tall bobbins. I tend eight sides. One side includes long rows of many bobbins, and you'd be amazed at how fast they spin! All day, I walk up and down on the lookout for broken threads. I must tie them together quickly so as not to stop the machine too long. The overseer keeps a sharp eye on all of us.

When the bell rings at 7 o'clock, we stop work. We hurry back to the boardinghouse, eat breakfast, and then it's back to the factory by 7:30. We do it all again for our noon dinner. After that, I am at my machines until closing time at 7 o'clock in the evening. We make our way home in the dark. By then we are all so tired, we're like to drop. Last night at supper, little Mary fell asleep right at the table!

Mama, enclosed you will find my first month's wages. I earned 14 dollars. They took out 5 dollars for my room and board, and I kept 50 cents for myself as you told me to. I hope the 8 dollars and a half will help.

I write this after church. I know you will be pleased to hear that we all follow the company rule and attend every Sunday. It is our only day off.

Your loving Grace

Walking into town

By Cynthia Overbeck Bix, *Cobblestone,* ©2017 by Carus Publishing Company. Reproduced with permission.

November 30, 1835

Dear Mama,

Yesterday, Anne and I walked into town for the first time. Oh, how I wish you could see it! On Merrimack Street, there is store after store. And all with glass windows in their fronts, filled with such pretty things! They have such beautiful woolen shawls. I wished with all my heart I could buy one for you, Mama. But they cost 3 dollars—almost a whole week's earnings. Also I saw the sweetest pair of fur cuffs. They'd make my old coat look fine, but of course I didn't buy them.

Anne has invited me to be part of her literary society. She says the girls write stories and then read them to the group. I am excited to join them.

But I miss home so very much. Here it's all noise and clatter and bustle. I haven't got a moment to myself. I miss our brook under the trees and long to hear the birds singing.

I fear the winter ahead will seem dreadfully long. But spring will follow, and soon after that I hope I can come home to visit for a day. Until then, I hope my earnings are helping.

Your loving Grace

LOWELL OFFERING

January, 1845.

"The worm on the earth
May look up to the star."

A REPOSITORY.
OF ORIGINAL ARTICLES, WRITTEN BY
"FACTORY GIRLS."

LOWELL: MISSES CURTIS & FARLEY.
BOSTON: JORDAN, SWIFT & WILEY,
121 Washington Street.
1845.

The girls who worked in the mills created book clubs and published journals such as the *Lowell Offering*, which provided a literary outlet for the girls with stories about life in the mills.

By Marcia Amidon Lusted. May be reproduced for classroom use. *Toolkit Texts: Short Nonfiction for American History, Industrial Age and Immigration*, by Stephanie Harvey and Anne Goudvis, ©2021 (Portsmouth, NH: Heinemann).

The Fire Danced on the Machines

"I saw flames on the outside of the windows shooting up. The flames were climbing up from the 8th floor. I was scared and it seemed to me that even before I could move, everybody in the shop started to scream and holler. The girls at the machines began to climb up on the machine tables maybe because it was that they were frightened or maybe they thought they could run to the elevator doors on top of the machines. The aisles were narrow and blocked by the chairs and baskets. They began to fall in the fire."

These are the words of Celia Walker, who was working at the Triangle Shirtwaist Factory as an examiner on March 25, 1911. It was her job to check the work of the other young women who sewed shirtwaists—a kind of blouse or shirt popular with women at that time—to make sure that it had been done correctly. The company, which occupied three floors in a building in New York City, was what is known as a **sweatshop**. More than a hundred young women worked there, most of them immigrants and

Sweatshop: a factory where workers are employed at very low wages for long hours and under poor conditions

Fire hoses sprayed water on the upper floors of the Asch Building that housed the Triangle Shirtwaist Company during the tragic fire.

The fire department arrived quickly but was unable to stop the flames. Here, firefighters look for victims.

just teenagers, sewing for 12 hours a day, every day, for just $15 a week. On that March day, a Saturday, there were 600 workers at the Triangle Factory. Over one hundred of them would die that day.

The Triangle Shirtwaist Factory was owned by Max Blanck and Isaac Harris, two men who already had a history of owning garment factories that mysteriously burned down. Most of the fires took before working hours, most likely so that the men could collect insurance. In 1911, there were also no precautions taken to prevent fires, and no regulations that were enforced to make sure that workers were safe. At the Triangle Factory building, Blanck and Harris refused to install a sprinkler system to put out fires. The only elevator could hold just 12 people at a time, and the door at the bottom of one of the two stairwells was locked during working hours. The other stairwell's door opened inward, making it a trap if a large number of people crowded up against it. The building's fire escape was so narrow that only one person could use it at a time.

The fire began in a rag bin. With so much fabric, dust, and other materials crowded in such a small area, the fire began to spread immediately. Anna Pidone, a forewoman, remembered, "The fire danced on the [sewing] machines." The aisles were blocked by crates of finished blouses and bolts of cloth, making it difficult for the workers to reach the fire escape, the stairwells, or the elevator. Rose Indursky, whose job it was to sew sleeves into blouses, remembered:

"When I went out into the hall staircase I bent down and looked downstairs and I could see the fire come up. In the shop the girls were running around with their hair burning. First I ran into the dressing room with the machinist and some of the others. Then the walls in the dressing room began to smoke. We ran back into the shop; girls were lying on the floor, fainted, and people were stepping on them. Some of the other girls were trying to climb over the machines. I remember the machinist ran to the window and he smashed it to let the smoke that was choking us go out. Instead, the flames rushed in. I stood at the window; across the street people were hollering "don't jump, don't jump." I turned around and ran to the hall staircase door. My hair was smoldering—my clothes were torn. I put my two hands on my smoldering hair and ran up the stairs. I went into the 10th floor. Nobody was there except one man . . . and he hollered to me, can you come to the roof, can you come to the roof. My life was saved on account of [him]."

The manager tried to use the firehose to put out the flames, but it was rotted and the valve was rusted shut. As the flames increased, many first tried to get to the elevator, but it could only make four trips up and down before the heat and flames made it break down. Sarah Friedman, who was working on the 9th floor of the factory, tried to escape the flames that way:

"The elevator had made several trips. I knew this was the last one but it was so loaded that the car started to go down. The door was not closed. Suddenly I was holding to the sides of the door looking down the elevator shaft with girls screaming and pushing behind me. It was the old style elevator—cable elevator—to make it go down, you pulled the cable from the floor up. That cable was at the side of the elevator shaft. I reached out and grabbed it. I remember sliding all the way down. I was the first one to slide down the shaft. I ended up on top of the elevator and then I lost consciousness. Others must have

Newspapers detailed the devastating fire and the trial that followed. Though factory owners were acquitted of any responsibility, the tragedy led to major labor law reforms in New York.

landed on top of me. When the rescue workers came to the shaft they pulled me out and laid me out on the street. I had a broken leg, broken arm. My skull had been injured. One of my hands had been burned. . . ."

In desperation, many girls simply jumped out of the 8th and 9th floor windows. The fire department's ladders could only reach seven stories up, so they stretched out nets to catch the girls, but these quickly ripped. Bodies piled up on the sidewalk. Other workers fled to the roof of the building, where they were able to climb onto adjoining buildings. Ethel Monick, a lace cutter working on the 8th floor, managed to reach the street. She told a journalist, "There were 150 girls up there who will never get out." She was right. In just 18 minutes, it was over. One hundred forty-six people had died.

On April 5, 1911, the International Ladies Garment Workers Union led a march on New York's 5th Avenue to protest the conditions that had led to the tragedy at the Triangle Shirtwaist factory. Eighty thousand people attended. But despite the evidence that the owners had been negligent, a grand jury did not indict them for manslaughter. However, the women who died at the Triangle Factory did inspire the passage of the Sullivan-Hoey Fire Prevention Law, which required all New York factories to install sprinkler systems. It also brought public attention to the working conditions in sweatshop factories, and led to other reforms. It is still remembered as one of the worst incidents in American industrial history.

A DAY IN THE COAL MINES

May be reproduced for classroom use. *Toolkit Texts: Short Nonfiction for American History, Industrial Age and Immigration,* by Stephanie Harvey and Anne Goudvis, ©2021 (Portsmouth, NH: Heinemann).

Do you ever wish that you didn't have to go to school? Not if you had been born during the Industrial Revolution. You might have thought that going to school was a treat.

Kids as young as five years old worked in factories, mills, and coal mines. Many of these kids wanted to learn to read and write. But they had to work long hours to help support their families. "I want to learn but I can't when I work all the time," said twelve-year-old Furman Owens. Furman started work when he was just eight years old.

Kids often worked twelve or more hours a day, every day. Workplaces could be dangerous. Children were sometimes injured or even killed in accidents. Others became sick from breathing in harmful fumes. Many of these hardworking kids never had a chance to go to school or even play. There was no recess time in the factories or mines!

A young worker (above) carries a bundle of wood pieces for slowing down moving cars. A 12-year-old boy (below) pushes a heavy coal car.

Both adults and children worked in coal mines. Everyone needed coal. It provided fuel for ships, trains, machines, factories, and homes all across the country. Jobs in coal mines were easy to find. But the work was difficult and often very hazardous.

Imagine yourself working as a coal miner for a day. Your day lasts for ten to twelve hours. It starts with a long trip underground in an open elevator called a "cage." You and the other workers wear caps with headlamps. These lamps are often the only light in the cold, dark mineshafts.

Coal: ©PhotoLink/Photodisc/Getty Images.

Young boys (left) opened and closed the doors for coal cars.

Library of Congress, NCLC collection. Top: 01111. Bottom left: 01057. Bottom right: 01132.

A "nipper" opens a ventilation door in a coal mine (above left). Breaker boys (above right) removed rocks from crushed coal.

Since you are one of the youngest miners, you might work as a "nipper." Nippers are the door keepers of the mine. Your job is to open and close the mineshaft doors for the coal cars. You spend long hours sitting alone in the dark, listening for the approaching cars.

If you are a fast runner, you might be a "spragger" instead. Spraggers run alongside the moving coal cars. They slow them down by jabbing a thick piece of wood, called a sprag, into the wheels. The fast moving, heavy mine cars often crush or run over spraggers.

Groundwater seeps into the mineshaft. A pump helps keep the tunnel from flooding, but you still work all day in knee-deep water and mud. At other times it is dry and dusty. Coal dust gets into your eyes, nose, and mouth. It also collects in your lungs. It can cause something called black lung disease. This illness makes it hard to breathe. Many miners cough all day while they work.

Now imagine working as a coal miner. You will work today, tomorrow, and every day after that. A life like that makes going to school sound like fun!

BREAKER BOYS
"I Could Not Do That Work and Live"

Photographer Lewis Hine took some of his most haunting photos in the dark tunnels and dirty breaker rooms in the nation's coal mines. The faces of the boys, some as young as eight years old, were often black with soot.

The coal mine's whistle blew as the "breaker boys," most of them between the ages of eight and twelve (but some as young as five or six) went to work, scrambling in just as the sun began to rise. They climbed onto wooden boards perched over the conveyor belts and chutes that carried the coal, and settled in for a ten-hour work day. As soon as the coal began moving into the room, it raised clouds of black coal dust, which immediately covered the boys. The air was black with swirling coal dust, so thick that it was difficult to see, and some boys wore headlamps. Long iron chutes clanked and clattered as they delivered raw coal onto the breaker floors, and the machinery made a deafening grinding noise. It was too noisy to talk, and hard to breathe.

This was a common scene in the coal mines during the early part of the twentieth century. After raw coal was mined from beneath the surface, it had to be broken into smaller pieces and sorted into uniform sizes. It also had to be cleaned of impurities like slate, rocks, soil, clay, and other debris. Some boys broke the large chunks of coal, and others sorted and cleaned it. These

By Marcia Amidon Lusted. May be reproduced for classroom use. *Toolkit Texts: Short Nonfiction for American History, Industrial Age and Immigration*, by Stephanie Harvey and Anne Goudvis, ©2021 (Portsmouth, NH: Heinemann).

Breaker boys worked in a room that was extremely hot in the summer and bitterly cold in the winter. The air was hazy with coal dust. A breaker boy's hands became cracked and sore from sorting the coal, which was as sharp as broken glass.

Library of Congress, NCLC collection, 01133

boys sat on their wooden boards arranged in rows, and as the coal moved past them, they bent over and picked out as much unwanted material as they could. Once the coal had moved past all the breaker boys, it was funneled into clean coal bins.

Young boys were hired because they would work for as little as 40 or 50 cents a day, much less than adults. Many of them came from immigrant families who desperately needed the extra income, so these boys worked six days a week. Few ever attended school, and most never learned to read or write.

Joseph Miliauskas, whose family had emigrated to the Pennsylvania coal mines from Lithuania in 1900, worked as a breaker boy:

Library of Congress, NCLC collection, 01076

Trapper boys sat on a bench in front of a heavy wooden door, opening it when the coal car came through, and then closing it quickly to keep air from blowing through the mine and lowering the temperature. It was a lonely job, and trapper boys sat in total darkness for nine or ten hours a day.

"The boss was behind us with a broom, and if he caught you slipping up and letting some slate come down, boy, you'd get it in the back with a broom. . . . [My] second day [on the job] my fingers were all cut up and bleeding. I asked the boss if I could go home and he hit me with the broom and said, "Stay there." Twelve o'clock came and the whistle blew. I took my dinner pail out

and went home . . . and said to my mother, "Mom, I'm not going back to work anymore. My fingers are all bloody." "Oh, yes you are," she said. So I stayed home that afternoon and then went back. [After] you're there two or three weeks, your fingers get hardened up. No more blood. You get used to it."

Hazardous Work

Breaker boys were not allowed to wear gloves so that they could better pick up pieces of material. Bloody fingers from sharp pieces of slate were only one hazard. Scraping their fingertips over the top of the coal and rock also made them bloody. This condition, called blood fingertips, lasted until their fingers toughened up, and the breaker boys learned that urinating on their fingers would make them toughen faster. Because the coal was washed to help remove the impurities, the interaction of the coal and the water created sulfuric acid that burned fingers and hands. Other hazards included getting feet, arms, hands, and legs caught in the gears of machinery and amputated. Some boys were even crushed in the machinery, but their bodies wouldn't be retrieved until the end of the day when the work stopped. Boys could also be crushed or smothered by loads of coal rushing down the chutes. Breathing coal dust all day caused conditions like asthma and black lung disease, which made the lungs turn black from coal particles and caused chronic bronchitis. These conditions often lasted for their entire lifetimes. Long hours spent bent over the coal chutes led to permanently curved spines, and the loud noise of machinery could result in hearing loss.

The work was difficult and tedious, and many grown men could not have done it. In 1905, a journalist named John Spargo tried to do a day's work as a breaker boy in a Pennsylvania mine. He only managed to last a half hour, writing, "I tried to pick out the pieces of slate from the hurrying stream of coal, often missing them; my hands were bruised and cut in a few minutes; I was covered from head to foot with coal dust and for many hours afterwards I was spitting out some of the small particles of [coal] I had swallowed. I could not do that work and live."

Breaker boys worked long hours, sunrise to sunset, in terrible conditions, and yet they still found time for fun. Joseph Miliauskas remembered eating lunch as quickly as possible:

"We ate our sandwiches in no time, then started playing tag. We knew every hole in that breaker, and we'd hide and go through

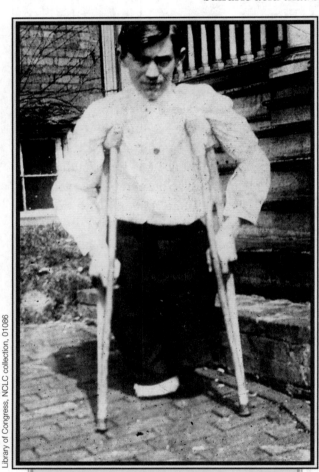

As they moved among the machinery, some boys lost their feet, hands, arms, or legs if they became caught under conveyor belts or in gears. This boy's legs were cut off by a motor car in a coal mine in West Virginia when he was 14 years old.

By Marcia Amidon Lusted. May be reproduced for classroom use. *Toolkit Texts: Short Nonfiction for American History, Industrial Age and Immigration*, by Stephanie Harvey and Anne Goudvis, ©2021 (Portsmouth, NH: Heinemann).

These mine workers in Pennsylvania hauled heavy carts full of coal to the shaft of the mine.

in complete darkness. We'd go over the machinery and around it. You get to know it because everything stops during lunch hour. We got to know it like a bunch of rats."

Breaker Boy Activism

Breaker boys were also known for their activism. They often protested their working conditions by going on strike or joining labor unions. These strikes shut down the entire mine and the boys would be beaten by their supervisors until they returned to work. Sometimes their own fathers, desperate not to lose wages during a strike, would help the bosses beat these boys.

Improvements in mining technology, such as using machines and water to remove impurities, gradually eliminated the need for breaker boys by 1920. But in addition to technology, it was a growing public awareness of child labor that helped get young boys out of these hazardous jobs. When photographer Lewis Hine photographed breaker boys at work, his powerful images brought public attention to their working conditions and forced new child labor laws. But it wasn't until 1938 that the Fair Labor Statistics Act was passed, prohibiting children younger than 14 from working at all, and prohibiting anyone under the age of 18 from working in a hazardous area.

Breaker boys helped bring about these changes, but until laws were passed and enforced, tens of thousands of boys were working in mines every year. When they outgrew their breaker jobs, many moved into other jobs there, working there for the rest of their lives in the dark and dust of the coal mines.

Champions for Reform

Jane Addams

Ellen Gates Starr

Imagine that instead of going to school 7 hours a day, 5 days a week, 9 months a year, you went to work 14 hours a day, 6 days a week, 12 months a year. In the late 1800s, some **reformers** grew concerned about the negative impact that working under such conditions had on working-class and poor children. Those children did not go to school, and they did not have much time to play. Reformers brought the issue of how children were **exploited** to the government's attention. They also rolled up their sleeves and made change happen.

> **Reform** means to make changes to an institution or practice to improve it.
>
> **Exploited** means to benefit unfairly from the work of someone, typically by overworking or underpaying them.

Jane Addams and Ellen Gates Starr

In 1889, Jane Addams and Ellen Gates Starr opened one of the first settlement houses in the United States. They found and fixed up a house in a poor, immigrant neighborhood in Chicago. Addams and Starr called their settlement house Hull House. College-educated individuals like them made a commitment to live and work in the house and in the community to improve the daily lives of those who lived around them. They took a particular interest in children. They believed children should

The library at the Henry Street Settlement House in New York City was put to good use by the community it served in 1910.

Library of Congress. Addams: 3a01940. Starr: George Grantham Bain Collection, 23460. Library: NCLC collection, 04575.

Library of Congress, 07713

Mary Harris "Mother" Jones (center) leads her "army" of striking textile workers as they set out on their march from Philadelphia to New York.

Settlement houses were important reform institutions in the early 20th century. Most were large buildings in crowded immigrant neighborhoods, where settlement workers lived, provided services for neighbors, and sought to end poverty.

have fresh air, time to play, and safe places to play—not dark alleys or busy city streets. Toward that goal, they helped create city parks and playgrounds.

Addams, Starr, and others who lived in Hull House believed children should have the opportunity to grow up healthy and to go to school. They offered courses on how to prepare healthful meals and provided childcare. They also ran after-school and summer-school programs for children of immigrant families and working mothers. They helped the mothers who came to Hull House to find jobs that paid a fair wage, so that young children and their families would not have to work.

Mother Jones

Another reformer, Mary Harris Jones, was referred to as "the most dangerous woman in America" by the district attorney of West Virginia for stirring up 20,000 "contented" miners to "lay down their tools and walk out." Jones was only five feet tall, but she motivated men, women, and children to action with her passionate calls to improve the lives of working families. She earned the nickname "Mother" Jones because she showed so much concern for working families and working children.

Jones became famous by speaking out on behalf of people who worked in mines, on railroads, or in textile mills. She supported their right to join organizations called labor unions. At the time, individual workers had almost no way to change a difficult and unsafe work situation. By joining together in unions, however, workers had some power to negotiate with the owners for better treatment, shorter workdays, and higher wages. Jones's efforts to change how workers were treated sometimes resulted in her arrest and imprisonment.

In July 1903, Jones organized a famous event called the "March of the Mill Children." She believed that child labor had to be regulated or abolished, especially in textile mills. Jones led a large group of child workers and their parents on a nearly 100-mile walk from Philadelphia to New York. Jones even went to President Theodore Roosevelt's home in Oyster Bay outside New York City to try to get him to discuss child labor laws. Her courage and willingness to take a stand got people's attention and made a difference.

Lillian Wald and Florence Kelley

Two other settlement house supporters, Lillian D. Wald and Florence Kelley, also looked to Roosevelt as a force for change. In 1905, they asked the president to make children a priority. They wanted the U.S. government to establish an office at the national level that would be charged with looking out for the interests and welfare of children and families. Kelley previously had served as an inspector of factories in Chicago, where she checked to see if factory owners obeyed Illinois laws to protect child workers. That experience had made her aware of the problems children faced.

Wald and Kelley's idea, a Children's Bureau, was not created right away. In 1904, however, an organization called the National Child Labor Committee (NCLC) had formed. It grew out of a large meeting that took place in New York's Carnegie Hall. It brought together many people who had been working to create or enforce laws to protecting child workers. Three years later, the U.S. Congress gave the NCLC a charter, or official approval. Wald, Kelley, and Addams all became directors of the NCLC. With the NCLC's support, the goal of a Children's Bureau was realized in 1912.

Julia Lathrop and Grace Abbott

Two women who worked at Hull House, Julia Lathrop and Grace Abbott, became the first leaders of the new bureau. Lathrop was the first woman to head a government bureau in the United States. Abbott was in charge of the part of the bureau that

Lillian D. Wald

Florence Kelley

May be reproduced for classroom use. *Toolkit Texts: Short Nonfiction for American History, Industrial Age and Immigration*, by Stephanie Harvey and Anne Goudvis, ©2021 (Portsmouth, NH: Heinemann).

Julia Lathrop

Grace Abbott

protected child workers. She fought for a special act of Congress that would make it a crime to sell items made by child workers from one state to another. Called the Keating-Owen Child Labor Act, it became a law in 1916. People who profited from the work of children protested. So did some families who needed the money that their children earned. In 1917, the U.S. Supreme Court decided that the Keating-Owen Child Labor Act was unconstitutional, so it was no longer enforced.

The Children's Bureau still exists today. Although it originally was part of the Department of Commerce and Labor, today it is part of the Department of Health and Human Services. The Children's Bureau oversees issues related to the general health and well-being of the nation's children and families. The bureau organized a national Conference on Children and Youth. The conferences brought together people to share ideas of ways to support and improve the lives of children, particularly those who are the most vulnerable or neglected.

Behind the Lens

Jacob Riis was one of the many urban reformers who helped expose the awful conditions endured by children. Riis was 21 years old when he immigrated to the United States from Denmark in 1870. He initially found work as a carpenter, but he also experienced times of poverty and hunger when he was unemployed. He became famous as a writer and lecturer. His writing and his photographs of conditions he saw in New York City were published in a best-selling book, *How the Other Half Lives* in 1890, followed by *Children of the Poor* in 1892. After reading *How the Other Half Lives*, future U.S. president Theodore Roosevelt, at that time New York's police commissioner, introduced himself to Riis. The two men became good friends.

Jacob Riis

Riis was determined to make the middle and upper classes of New York society see how their poorest neighbors lived. His books described life in the slums and tenements of New York. It also focused on child laborers. One of the children Riis wrote about was named Katie. When Riis asked Katie what she did, she replied, "I scrubs." The daughter of Irish immigrants, Katie was nine years old when she described for Riis her work as a scullery maid and housekeeper. To see a picture Katie and to find out more about Jacob Riis and the working children he photographed, check out the Library of Congress's website at www.loc.gov/exhibits/jacob-riis/.

An Excerpt from *The Autobiography of Mother Jones*

In the late 1800s, newspapers called Mary Harris "Mother" Jones "the most dangerous woman in America." Why? This firebrand championed workers' rights, exposing how mill and factory owners made money off their less fortunate laborers. These laborers often included children, who toiled for long hours for little pay, instead of going to school. In July of 1903, Mother Jones organized a protest march to publicize the terrible working conditions children experienced. Some 200 adults and dozens of children joined her in a march from Philadelphia to New York City—which ended with the group's unsuccessful attempt to meet with President Theodore "Teddy" Roosevelt at his home in Oyster Bay, New York. While the marchers were furious that their efforts were ignored, Mother Jones knew their protest had brought the country's attention to the plight of working children. In the next several years, several states (including New York, New Jersey and Pennsylvania) passed laws against child labor.

George Grantham Bain Collection, Library of Congress, 19170

Mother Jones at New York City Hall in 1915

Chapter X:
The March of the Mill Children

The Liberty Bell that a century ago rang out for freedom against tyranny was touring the country and crowds were coming to see it everywhere. That gave me an idea. These little children were striking for some of the freedom that childhood ought to have, and I decided that the children and I would go on a tour.

I asked some of the parents if they would let me have their little boys and girls for a week or ten days, promising to bring them back safe and sound. They consented. A man named Sweeny was marshal

May be reproduced for classroom use. *Toolkit Texts: Short Nonfiction for American History, Industrial Age and Immigration*, by Stephanie Harvey and Anne Goudvis, ©2021 (Portsmouth, NH: Heinemann).

for our "army." A few men and women went with me to help with the children. They were on strike and I thought, they might well have a little recreation.

The children carried knapsacks on their backs in which was a knife and fork, a tin cup and plate. We took along a wash boiler in which to cook the food on the road. One little fellow had a drum and another had a fife. That was our band. We carried banners that said, "We want more schools and less hospitals." "We want time to play." "Prosperity is here. Where is ours?"

We started from Philadelphia where we held a great mass meeting. I decided to go with the children to see President Roosevelt to ask him to have Congress pass a law prohibiting the exploitation of childhood. I thought that President Roosevelt might see these mill children and compare them with his own little ones who were spending the summer on the seashore at Oyster Bay.

The children were very happy, having plenty to eat, taking baths in the brooks and rivers every day. I thought when the strike is over and they go back to the mills, they will never have another holiday like this. All along the line of march the farmers drove out to meet us with wagon loads of fruit and vegetables. Their wives brought the children clothes and money. The trainmen would stop their trains and give us free rides.

Marshal Sweeny and I would go ahead to the towns and arrange sleeping quarters for the children, and secure meeting halls. As we marched on, it grew terribly hot. There was no rain and the roads were heavy with dust. From time to time we had to send some of the children back to their homes. They were too weak to stand the march.

Everywhere we had meetings, showing up with living children, the horrors of child labor.

We marched down to Oyster Bay but the president refused to see us and he would not answer my letters. But our march had done its work. We had drawn the attention of the nation to the crime of child labor. [While the children eventually had to go back to work], not long afterward the Pennsylvania legislature passed a child labor law that sent thousands of children home from the mills and kept thousands of others from entering the factory until they were fourteen years of age.

"Mother" Jones Writes Again

"Mother" Jones to-day wrote to the President as follows:
New York, July 30, 1903
The Hon. Theodore Roosevelt, President, USA

Your Excellency—
Twice before have I written to you in requesting an audience that I might lay my mission before you and have your advice on a matter which bears upon the welfare of the whole nation. I speak for the emancipation from mills and factories of the hundreds of thousands of young children who are yielding up their lives for the commercial supremacy of the nation. Failing to receive a reply to either of the letters, I yesterday, sent to Oyster Bay, taking with me three of these children that they might plead with you personally.

Secretary Barnes informed us that before we might hope for an interview, we must first lay the whole matter before you in a letter. He assured me of its delivery to you personally, and also that it would receive your attention.

I have espoused the cause of the laboring class in general and of suffering childhood in particular. For what affects the child must ultimately affect the adult. It was for them that our march of principle was begun. We sought to bring the attention of the public upon these little ones, so that ultimately sentiment would be aroused and the children freed from the workshops and sent to school. I know of no question of today that demands graver attention from those who have at heart the perpetuation of this Republic.

The child of today is the man or woman of tomorrow: the one the citizen and the other the mother of still future citizens. I ask Mr. President, what kind of citizen will be the child who toils twelve hours a day in an unsanitary atmosphere stunted mentally and physically, and surrounded with immoral influence? Denied education, he cannot assume the true duties of citizenship, and enfeebled physically and mentally, he falls a ready victim to the perverting influences which the present economic conditions have created.

I grant you, Mr. President, that there are State laws which should regulate these matters, but results have proven that they are inadequate. In my little band are three boys, the oldest

11 years old, who have worked in mills a year or more without interference from the authorities. All efforts to bring about reform have failed.

I have been moved to this crusade, Mr. President, because of actual experience in the mills. I have seen little children without the first rudiments of education and no prospect of acquiring any. I have seen other children with hands, fingers, and other parts of their tiny bodies mutilated because of their childish ignorance of machinery. I feel that no nation can be truly great while such conditions exist without attempted remedy.

It is to be hoped that our crusade will stir up a general sentiment on behalf of enslaved childhood, and secure the enforcement of the present laws.

But that is not sufficient.

As this is not alone a question of the separate States, but of the whole Republic, we come to you as the chief representative of the nation.

I believe that Federal laws should be passed governing this evil and including a penalty for the violation. Surely, Mr. President, if this is practicable—and I believe you will agree that it is—you can advise me of the necessary steps to pursue

I have with me three boys who have walked a hundred miles, serving as living proof of what I say. You can see and talk with them, Mr. President, if you are interested. If you decide to see these children, I will bring them before you at any time you may set. Secretary Barnes has assured me of an early reply and this should be sent care of the Ashland Hotel, New York City.

Very truly yours,
Mother Jones

Editor's Note: *President Roosevelt did not meet with the marchers, as his personal secretary blocked a meeting and said any requests should be made in writing to the President. Mother Jones wrote several letters to Roosevelt, but she never received a response.*

Excerpted from: *The Autobiography of Mother Jones* by Mother Jones, 1837–1930, Edited by Mary Field Parton, 1878–1969, Chicago: Charles H. Kerr & Company, 1925.

Lewis Hine:
What the Camera Captured

In glass factories, "carrying-in" boys carried molten glass from the furnace to the bottle makers, then back to the furnace again. The floor was spattered with broken glass, making cuts common. Many boys suffered from heat exhaustion.

Lewis Wickes Hine knew that a picture could tell a powerful story. He also had great compassion for families living in poverty and working to build a better future. Hine's earliest photos were of families at the Ellis Island immigration station from 1904 to 1909. Hine admired them for trying to make their dreams come true. In his photographs, Hine recorded the hope and fear he saw expressed by many immigrants.

He cared especially about the children. Hine published some of his photographs. About that time, an organization called the National Child Labor Committee (NCLC) was investigating child labor conditions. In workplaces that were hazardous and unhealthy, children worked long hours at exhausting jobs and were paid almost nothing. The committee believed that if the public could see children doing adult work in horrid conditions, surely it would take notice. In 1908, the NCLC hired Hine to photograph children at work. Over the years, Hine took thousands of photographs for the NCLC, which distributed Hine's photographs in pamphlets, magazines, and newspapers. Hine dedicated his art to helping America's children—to telling their stories and freeing them from abusive labor conditions.

Pin boys worked in bowling alleys all night, setting the bowling pins.

Library of Congress, 04636

Hine's work got the public's attention. His revealing photographs played a major role in child labor reform, since for many people, seeing was believing. In 1938, the Fair Labor Standards Act banned oppressive child labor, set a minimum hourly wage (24 cents), and established a maximum workweek (44 hours).

While he probably is most famous for his photographs of children at work, Hine also took photographs of the American Red Cross's relief efforts during World War I and the building of the Empire State Building. He also worked for the Works Progress Administration to document industry and employment during the Great Depression.

These photographs are part of the collection of the NCLC and are attributed to Lewis W. Hine. From 1908 to 1924, Hine worked for the NCLC, traveling throughout the country. He photographed children working at a variety of jobs from fields to factories and sweatshops. He hoped that when his photographs were shared with a wide audience, more Americans would demand social reform.

Hine often noted names, ages, addresses, tasks, hours, and wages of the individuals he photographed. The captions are based on the information collected by Hine when he visited the workplace.

Library of Congress, 04050

This 11-year-old newsboy sold newspapers all day on the streets of Newark, New Jersey. Some of the newsboys had been selling newspapers on street corners since they were six or seven years old.

This young girl sold baskets in the city, waiting for customers until dark. She had been on the corner since the early morning with her sister and friend who helped her.

This 12-year-old boy worked as a bootblack, shining shoes with his homemade shoeshine kit for hours every day.

These girls picked berries for hours every day. Then berry carriers, like these girls, hauled 60 pounds of berries from the fields to the sheds.

May be reproduced for classroom use. *Toolkit Texts: Short Nonfiction for American History, Industrial Age and Immigration*, by Stephanie Harvey and Anne Goudvis, ©2021 (Portsmouth, NH: Heinemann).

Library of Congress, 00599

This family rented 20 acres of a cotton farm in Oklahoma. The children aged
5 and 6 years old picked 20 to 25 pounds of cotton a day with their parents.
The 3-year-old child was also learning to pick cotton.
The family members were sharecroppers who had to give ¼ of the cotton
and ⅓ of the corn that they grew to the landowner to rent the land.

The hot air in textile
mills and factories
was full of lint, and
the whirring machines
were deafening.
Children often worked
barefoot to make it
easier to climb onto
the huge machines
to change spools or
bobbins. Forced to
work quickly, children
often caught their
fingers in the
machinery.

Library of Congress, 02119

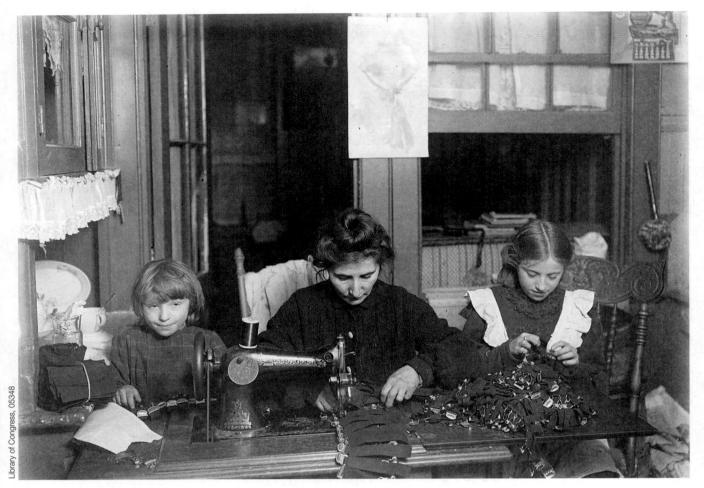

Whole families toiled in crowded tenements in temperatures that were stifling in the summer and bitter cold in the winter. This mother and her 2 young daughters, age 13 and 7, were paid pennies to sew women's clothes.

At canneries along the seacoast, children as young as 3 years old stood all day in sheds shucking oysters or peeling shrimp. During canning season, families worked from 3:00 or 4:00 a.m. until late afternoon. Children constantly cut their hands on the sharp knives used to crack oyster shells.

Excerpt from Lewis Hines' Report

Child Labor in the Canning Industry of Maryland. July 1909.

Millions of American children worked in agriculture and industry in the early 20th century. In 1904, progressive reformers founded the National Child Labor Committee (NCLC). The NCLC hired Lewis Hine to photograph children working in fields, factories, mines, and city streets to raise awareness of the abuses of child labor. His photos and reports, produced between 1908 and 1924, fueled public opinion and inspired Congress to enact national child labor legislation. Below is an excerpt from his 1909 report on children working in the canning industry.

In the canning industries of Baltimore, as is the case in similar establishments elsewhere, children are permitted to work for long hours, even though they may be very young. Incredibly small are the fingers that work along with those of the rest of the family, and if the child is too small to sit up, it is held in the lap of the worker or stowed away in boxes near at hand. . . .

There are several dangers connected with this work [in the fruit and vegetable canning factories] when children do it. On every hand, one can see little tots toting boxes or pans full of beans, berries, or tomatoes, and it is self-evident that the work is too hard. There are machines which no young person should be working around. Unguarded belts, wheels, cogs and the like are a menace to careless children.

In the fields convenient to Baltimore [Maryland] . . . , children are employed as a matter of course. The living conditions in the shacks they occupy are not only harmful in physical ways, but the total lack of privacy where several families live in one room is extremely bad. There is little rest for the children in these crowded shacks.

[He then tells the story of one family. . . .]

John Meishell . . . went to work with his wife and five children at oyster shucking (for Peerless Oyster Co.) at Bay St. Louis,

Mississippi during the winter of 1907–08. The children were then 1, 3, 6, 8 and 9 years of age. The baby had to be cared for in the shed where they worked because the company permitted no one to stay at home to care for it. The three year old helped some. The rest worked regularly. They were routed out of bed by their boss at 3 a.m. and worked until about 4 p.m. They say that the children had to work in order to give the family a living wage. . . . the most the father made was $6.00 a week. Their transportation [was] paid and they had free rent (in shacks where they were huddled like sheep). They bought supplies and food of the Company Store where exorbitant prices were charged for poor food. . . . they were cheated in the weighing and measuring of oysters [that they shucked] and fired on various pretexts [the company made up excuses to fire them].

[In the spring], they returned to Baltimore with no money ahead. The children had absolutely no schooling. One of them said she was kept back two grades and is now in the 4th grade although [she is] eleven years old.

Respectfully submitted,
Lewis Hine
July 10, 1909

Hines visited seafood canneries in many states. Many canneries employed entire families like this one who shucked, packed, and steamed oysters. To his horror, he found that kids who worked in canning sheds were even younger than those in cotton mills.

Excerpted from: *Child Labor in the Canning Industry of Maryland* by Lewis W. Hine. Personal Letter written July, 1909.

May be reproduced for classroom use. *Toolkit Texts: Short Nonfiction for American History, Industrial Age and Immigration,* by Stephanie Harvey and Anne Goudvis, ©2021 (Portsmouth, NH: Heinemann).

Kids Fight Back!

MOST PEOPLE DON'T THINK MUCH about the roles that kids have played in history. Children were a large part of the work force during the Industrial Revolution. By 1900, over two million children under age 16 had worked in terrible conditions. They worked in the textile mills, coal mines, and factories. They made clothing, shoes, and glass. In the beginning, there were no laws or regulations to protect children who worked in these places. Employers could also get away with paying children much less than adult workers.

Workplaces could be dangerous. The hours were long. Children worked with huge, heavy machines. They sometimes suffered severe injuries. Children working during the early days of the Industrial Revolution usually had to stop going to school. It was the only way to keep their jobs.

For all these reasons, many children actively protested. They were part of the labor movement, too. They fought for better working conditions, higher pay, and fewer hours. Young female mill workers in Lowell, Massachusetts went on strike in 1836. They were protesting a reduction in their wages. Eventually they asked people to sign petitions to support their cause. They also created the Lowell Female Labor Reform Association. It was the first women's labor union in the United States.

By Jill Silos-Rooney, *Appleseeds*, ©2014 by Carus Publishing Company. Reproduced with permission.

Many young workers were badly injured on the job. Neil Gallagher (right) lost his leg when it was crushed between two coal cars.

Kids also fought back against unfair working conditions in New York City. Newspaper boys went on strike there in 1899. These "newsies" fought back when newspaper owners Joseph Pulitzer and William Randolph Hearst raised the price of papers. Newsies had to first buy the papers that they sold to the public. Higher newspaper prices made it harder for newsies to make money. The owners also refused to buy back any unsold papers. Louis Ballat was a 14-year-old newsie. He was known as "Kid Blink" because he was blind in one eye. He rallied the other newsboys and they went on strike. They even closed down the Brooklyn Bridge! They were brutally attacked. But the newsboys did get the owners to buy back any unsold papers. This way the newsies didn't lose money.

Children who worked in factories refused to accept poor conditions. They fought the business owners. They helped win more workers' rights, better pay, and better work conditions.

A CHILD LABOR REVOLUTION

NEWSPAPERS IN THE MINING REGION TELL OF THE NEW LAW'S RESULTS

(For further information address Pennsylvania Child Labor Association, 1338 Real Estate Trust Building, Philadelphia)

Dunmore School Board Forced to Act by Increased Attendance Made by Working Out of New Labor Law

THE SCRANTON REPUBLICAN, TUESDA

New Child Labor Law Sends Many Youths Back to School

PROF. GEORGE HOWELL

CHILD LABOR LAW CROWDING SOME SCHOOL HOUSES

FEW MINORS ASK FOR CERTIFICATES

NEW CHILD LABOR LAW CAUSES A BIG INCREASE IN SCHOOL ATTENDANCE

Mine Accidents

Extra! Extra! Newsboys Strike!

May be reproduced for classroom use. *Toolkit Texts: Short Nonfiction for American History, Industrial Age and Immigration,* by Stephanie Harvey and Anne Goudvis, ©2021 (Portsmouth, NH: Heinemann).

A large group of newsboys (above) gathered together on a street in New York City in 1908. Most of the newsboys in large cities came from poor immigrant families and sold papers in the afternoons and evenings, after their school finished.

Kid Blink, a teenage boy small for his age and blind in one eye, buttoned his shirt and brushed back his hair as he took the stage. Five thousand newsboys inside and outside New Irving Hall in lower Manhattan roared in approval. Kid raised his hands, a signal for silence. He said, "You know me, boys!"

"You bet we do," they responded.

"What we want is to stick together like glue. Am I right?"

"Yes, yes!" replied the crowd.

He scratched his head and said, "Ain't that 10 cents worth as much to us as it is to Hearst and Pulitzer, who are millionaires? If they can't spare it, how can we?"

"Soak 'em, Kid!"

"Soak nothing. I'm trying to figure it out, how 10 cents on 100 papers can mean more to a millionaire than it does to newsboys, and I can't see it." Kid went on to ask for no violence even though he himself had toppled newspaper wagons the night before. He said the boys needed to stick together. They could do it, if they worked together.

The newly formed Newsboys' Union had called for the rally, bringing together the striking "newsies" and organizations and local officials who supported them. Policemen stood outside, but they showed sympathy for the boys.

By Barbara Krasner, *Cobblestone,* ©2017 by Carus Publishing Company. Reproduced with permission.

Newsboys were typically between the ages of eight and 15 years old. They paid up front for newspapers—50 cents for 100 papers. They then sold them for a penny each, earning a nickel for every ten papers they sold. They stood on city street corners in the evenings and on weekends in all kinds of weather and shouted out headlines to try to get people to stop and buy a paper. Sometimes they made up headlines when the news was slow. They often remained out on the street until late at night. If they didn't sell their stack of papers, they didn't make any money. In fact, they sometimes lost money. For boys who were homeless or who helped support families, the pennies they made as newsboys were critical.

In the spring of 1898, newspaper **moguls** William Randolph Hearst, owner of the *New York Journal*, and Joseph Pulitzer, owner of the *New York World*, decided on a new strategy to increase their circulations. **Sensationalist** coverage of the Spanish–American War in Cuba had resulted in an increased demand for newspapers, which were the only source for news and information. The publishers raised their prices to the newboys to 60 cents for 100 papers. While the war was on, it was easy to sell newspapers. But the war ended after less than four months, in August 1898. Nearly a year later, the demand for newspapers had dropped, but the newsboys still paid 60 cents per 100 for the *Journal* and the *World* papers.

The newsies decided to take a stand. If Hearst and Pulitzer did not return the cost of a stack of papers to 50 cents, the boys threatened to boycott the two papers. Undaunted, Hearst and Pulitzer refused. Equally determined, the newsboys struck the companies, beginning on July 21, 1899.

In addition to Kid Blink, other newsboys as well as local officials spoke at the rally on July 25. Former New York assemblyman Philip Wissig shared his experience selling newspapers in 1860. He told the crowd that he was proud of their spirit and their fight to be treated fairly. Dave Simons, the teenage president of the Newsboys' Union, read a list of resolutions. He asked newspaper advertisers and dealers for their help with the strike and urged them to boycott the two papers. He asked them not to buy the *World* or *Journal* until terms

Moguls are rich or powerful people.

Sensationalist means something that is intended to arouse strong reaction or interest.

Background: ©picsfive/Adobe Stock

National Child Labor Committee collection, Library of Congress, Prints and Photographs Division, 03651

could be reached. He asked advertisers to take their business elsewhere and encouraged New Yorkers to get their news from other sources. The *Sun*, the *Telegram*, and the *Daily News* all gave newsboys a working wage. The resolutions were adopted with cheered approval.

Demonstrations took place throughout the city. Small groups of strikers roamed the streets to prevent the sale of the two boycotted newspapers. Unsold and shredded copies of the evening editions of the *World* and the *Journal* ended up in the streets. The newsboys marched across the Brooklyn Bridge, shutting down traffic. The strike also spread to communities in New Jersey and New York's Westchester County.

The publishing companies put out a call for men to sell the papers during the strike. The men who were hired were offered two dollars a day and given instructions to wait for newspapers to be delivered to them at designated locations. But the striking newsboys learned of the plans. They threatened the **scabs** and tore up the papers upon delivery. The hired men defended themselves and used sticks and fists to beat the boys, but few of the men remained on the job to sell the papers.

By July 27, the newspapers reported that the newsboys were weakening. Kid Blink and Simons were accused of betraying the cause. Reports spread of each boy receiving $400 to break up the strike. The newsboys called a meeting. Simons showed up and offered his pockets to be checked for money. The newsboys found nothing and cleared him of the charges. He resigned as president but was elected treasurer of the union. Kid Blink did not attend the meeting.

In the end, thousands of working boys won a victory against two powerful publishers. Newsboys had handled as much as 60% of the papers' sales. The print runs of the newspapers dropped to almost one third of their pre-strike runs, falling from 360,000 to 125,000 newspapers. The battle had pitted kids against adults, the powerless against the powerful, the poor against the rich, the workers against the owners. The two-week strike did not reduce the price that the newsboys paid, but it did resolve the issue of the unsold papers. The publishers agreed to buy them back.

The story is that Kid Blink was spotted in City Hall Park wearing a new suit of clothes and thumbing a wad of money. He never made newspaper headlines again.

Scabs are people who will work while others are on strike.

Background: ©picsfive/Adobe Stock

By Barbara Krasner, *Cobblestone*, ©2017 by Carus Publishing Company. Reproduced with permission.

Child Labor

It's the LAW

Lewis Hine took this photo of children arriving at a factory at 6:00 p.m. to work the night shift on a cold, dark December night. When they went home the next morning after working twelve hours, they were all drenched by a heavy, cold rain.

Industry is the production of goods or related services within an economy.

Loopholes are ways of avoiding a burden by using a gap or an ambiguity in a rule or law.

By 1910, about two million children under the age of 15 worked in **industry**, according to National Archives and Records Administration data. Some states had started passing child labor laws in the 19th century. Yet other states still allowed children to toil in textile mills, factories, and mines for 60 or more hours per week. Laws also had **loopholes**. Some parents lied about their children's age because the family needed the children to work to survive. Employers often found ways to claim that they didn't know the true ages of their young workers.

School attendance laws were likewise not strictly enforced. A 1907 Alabama law said children aged 12 to 16 years must attend school for at least eight weeks per year. But school certificates weren't required.

Laws in Northern states were generally more protective of children than those in the South. However, companies competed across state lines. Since child labor was cheap, companies looked for ways to remain competitive and resist or avoid stricter requirements. They might relocate businesses from Northern to Southern locations.

The Push for Federal Law

The National Child Labor Committee (NCLC) began pushing for a national law soon after its founding in 1904. Its leaders couldn't get President Theodore Roosevelt to back a child labor ban introduced by Indiana senator Albert Beveridge in 1906. But, with the president's support, Congress did

Commerce is the exchange of goods and services for money, usually on a large scale and requiring transportation across great distances.

Exempt means free from an obligation or duty.

order a large-scale study of child workers by the Bureau of Labor. A 1912 law also set up the Children's Bureau to report on "all matters pertaining to the welfare of children." The newly formed Department of Labor assumed those agencies' work and some other responsibilities in 1913.

In 1916, Congress passed the Keating–Owen Child Labor Act. The law banned interstate sales of anything from factories or mines that used child labor. In 1918, the U.S. Supreme Court held the law unconstitutional. If Congress could interfere in local matters by forbidding the movement of harmless goods across state lines, "all freedom of **commerce** will be at an end," wrote Justice William Day.

Reformers didn't give up. The 1919 Child Labor Tax Act put a 10% tax on profits of companies that employed children. That law was held unconstitutional in 1922. Congress passed a proposed constitutional amendment in 1924, but not enough states supported it. A cotton industry law limited child labor under the National Industrial Recovery Act of 1933. But then that law was also held unconstitutional.

Finally, in 1938, Congress passed and President Franklin D. Roosevelt signed the Fair Labor Standards Act. The law restricted child labor with terms similar to the 1916 law. When the Supreme Court ruled on the law in 1941, though, a majority of the justices were now Roosevelt's appointees, and the Court upheld the law. After the act became law, children under 14 years old could not work in most jobs. And minimum age requirements, limits on hours, and minimum wage requirements became basic national protections for most teenage workers.

Loopholes Remain

The new law didn't cover all jobs. Various "street trades" were allowed, such as newspaper sales and door-to-door peddling. Child actors or performers were **exempt**, as were children who worked for their parents. So, additional garment industry bans were needed to deal with home-based sweatshops.

Changes over time adjusted the minimum wage and altered some details. For example, rule changes in the 1990s allowed teenagers under 16 to work at sports events, no matter how late games go. Other proposals to relax or tighten child labor laws come before Congress periodically.

The biggest loopholes for child labor today are in agriculture. "There's no minimum age for a child to be hired on a small farm with parental permission. And a child can work from age 12 on any size farm with parental permission," says Zama Coursen-Neff. She heads the children's rights division of Human Rights Watch, a nonprofit group headquartered in New York.

Designed to Protect

Generally speaking (and not including agricultural jobs or jobs in which children work for their parents), U.S. federal law says that a child must be 14 years old to work in nonhazardous jobs. A child under 16 years old is not allowed to work during school hours. When school is in session, a child employee can only work 18 hours per week, 3 hours per day. When school is out of session, a child employee can work 40 hours a week, 8 hours per day. In the summer, the workday cannot start before 7:00 a.m., and it must end by 9:00 p.m.

©Images Ideas/Jupiterimages/Getty Images

Mr. Smith (center), an overseer in a South Carolina mill, refused to allow his children to work there. He said cotton mill owners in the South got around the child labor law by allowing a young child to help an older sister or brother, and the name of the small child was kept off the company's books.

Photo: National Child Labor Committee collection, Library of Congress, 01409. Background (sky): ©Traveller Martin/Shutterstock.

Farm work can be dangerous. Kids working with crops can be exposed to pesticides. Children on tobacco farms can also absorb poisonous nicotine. Also, kids on farms sometimes run machinery or equipment that they wouldn't normally be able to use in other industries.

Child farm workers can also "work for unlimited hours outside of school," Coursen-Neff says. Many are exhausted from toiling both before and after school. Children who move from place to place, such as **migrant workers**, miss out on more schooling. "The kids who work in the fields should have the same protections as all other kids," Coursen-Neff observes.

Migrant workers are temporary farm workers who travel from place to place, depending on which crops are being planted or harvested at particular times in different areas.

A Worldwide Issue

Child labor is also an international problem. About 168 million children between the ages of 5 and 17 years old work, reports the International Labour Organization (ILO). The children are often from poor families, and many work instead of going to school. More than 50% of children work in the field of agriculture. Children also make products sold in today's global economy, such as carpets and clothing. The work is often hazardous for children, particularly mining, where unhealthy conditions and the use of explosives increase the chance of serious injury.

The United States has made big strides in dealing with child labor. But more can be done—both at home and abroad. "We have to do the best we can for our kids," says Coursen-Neff.

Did You Know?

Child Labor Today • The majority of child laborers around the world today work in agricultural fields, such as farming, hunting, fishing, or forestry.

"Fair Trade" products follow guidelines that certify or identify them as items that are made and produced without using child labor.

The International Labour Organization, based in Switzerland, has designated June 12 as the annual World Day Against Child Labor. It was first celebrated in 2002.

Child Labor in Recent Times: *Voices from the Fields*

In 1993, S. Beth Atkin published Voices from the Fields: Children of Migrant Farmworkers Tell Their Stories. *She interviewed farm workers and their children, as well as young workers themselves. They shared their life experiences and their aspirations and dreams for the future.*

Atkin began the chapter, "Working in La Fresa," with this background information about migrant farmworkers and their families.

In the early 1990s, 20% of people picking crops and working in agriculture were under eighteen years of age. Agriculture was the only industry in the U.S. that legally employed children under the age of sixteen. Because families needed the money and parents had no one at home to take care of their children, young children worked beside their parents picking crops, arranging strawberries in a box or tying up packages of vegetables. If children are under the legal age limits (ten for strawberries and potatoes and twelve for all other crops), they are not considered to be working but "helping out."

Nine-year-old Jose Luis Rios lives with his large extended family in a small house in Los Lomas, CA. All of his relatives work in the fields, including his brothers and sisters. Here is his story in his own words:

"My name is Jose Luis Rios and I am in third grade. I have nine brothers and sisters. We live with our parents and aunt and uncle and cousins in Los Lomas. All my relatives that I can think of work in the fields.

My parents work in la fresa [the strawberries] and la mora [the raspberries] and my mom sometimes packs mushrooms. During the week, they leave in the morning around six o'clock. I go help them, mostly on weekends. I help pick the strawberries and put them in boxes.

My parents can't always find work. Usually there is work in the summer, so then I help my father every day in the fields. I have to pull up the grass around the strawberries and I pick. I have to bend over. I bend over for a long time. When I work in the fields with my father, I eat strawberries and he gives me *frijoles* [beans] sometimes when we stop to eat. We rest and then we go back to work.

[With my cousins], we play tag in the fields. My brothers work in the fields but not usually my sisters. They go to school. Rogelio, my little brother who is two, comes to the fields, but he just plays. He doesn't make any trouble.

When I work in the fields I don't get paid. I don't want them to pay me . . . they pay my parents for what I pick. I like that my parents get paid because then they buy me toy cars and trucks or maybe a bicycle.

Sometimes I'm tired in school on Mondays because I worked on the weekend. I like coming to school better than working in the fields. I go to school on the bus at seven-thirty. I like going to school to learn because then you know things. The people who haven't gone to school, they work in the fields.

I'm trying to learn English at school, but I like to speak Spanish because I'm understood better. I have more friends that speak Spanish than English. My parents tell me to study English, but I like studying the Native Americans best because they wrote, they did drawing, and they hunted buffaloes. I like the Mayans. They made houses so the water couldn't get in when it rained. In school I like to write, too. I write about the birds because they are pretty and they fly. And I like to write about sheep and animals and also the Ninja Turtles."

Excerpted from: *Voices from the Fields: Children of Migrant Farmworkers Tell Their Stories* by S. Beth Atkin. Boston, MA: Little Brown and Company. 1993.

Back Where I Started

Vito de la Cruz

When Vito de la Cruz was a kid, he lived in San Benito, Texas, a town of about 24,000 people at the absolute southern tip of Texas—just a stone's throw away from the Mexican state Tamaulipas. Almost 90% of the people in San Benito were of Hispanic or Latino descent, and the average income was less than half the American average.

In the summers, his family traveled from Texas to North Dakota, stopping along the way to pick crops as they ripened from South to North. The money they made working the fields during the summer would last them the rest of the year.

Vito started working the fields when he was five. He remembers it as "equal parts hardship and poverty." But he also remembers the togetherness. The family traveled together, worked together, and cooked together. He came to think of the other migrant workers as extended family, as well.

Vito's aunts and uncles were all US citizens, but many of the people in the extended family of migrant workers were not. Vito remembers working a tomato field as a 13-year-old when green vans filled with immigration officers rolled in. "People started stampeding. To this day I can smell the dirt

Fast Fact

The U.S. Constitution protects the basic human rights of undocumented immigrants working and living in the United States.

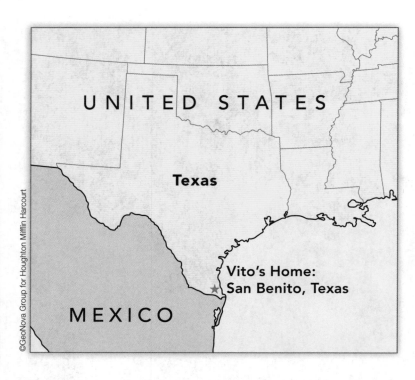

and the fear," he said. "I could hear the noise the batons made as the border patrol beat them over the heads and on their bodies."

Vito's uncle grabbed his shoulder and told him not to run—they were safe because of their citizenship. The immigration officers passed by him, herding undocumented workers into a ditch where the workers were handcuffed and dragged away. Vito knew that what happened that day wasn't the way things should be.

"Laws should be enforced; folks who violate [the laws] should be apprehended and prosecuted—but there is a dignity that sometimes gets forgotten, a human dignity that gets trampled on," he said.

For Vito, the ability to stand up for basic human dignity started with him getting an education. Vito had learned how to work hard in the fields and he applied the same work ethic at high school. His sister, Nena, pushed him to work even harder. She has been the first member of her family to graduate from high school. Even while taking care of Vito, Nena went to college. Vito wanted to go to college too. He wanted to learn about the laws that protect basic human rights, regardless of a person's nationality.

"So I went to Yale," he said. Yale University only accepts about 6% of students who apply—and that's 6% of people who have the guts to apply! If you want to be a lawyer, it's one of the top three undergraduate schools in the country. Vito's hard work had taken him a long way since his days in the fields. After graduating from Yale, he went even further, moving west across the entire United States to Berkeley, California, where he went to law school. And after he graduated from law school, he started using what he learned to help migrant workers.

"After law school, I wanted to go back where I started," he said. Vito took a job working as a staff attorney for the California Rural Legal Assistance program. He worked primarily in the areas of employment discrimination, farm labor issues, and migrant worker housing, health, and education issues. After a journey that started with injustice and was built with hard work, Vito could now help ensure that people who worked hard under a searing sun—the people who had been his extended family— would be treated with the dignity they deserved.

Find Out More

Learn more about the law and how it affects you at lawforkids.org.

May be reproduced for classroom use. *Toolkit Texts: Short Nonfiction for American History, Industrial Age and Immigration*, by Stephanie Harvey and Anne Goudvis, ©2021 (Portsmouth, NH: Heinemann).

CHOCOLATE FROM CHILDREN

Have you had some chocolate recently? Most Americans eat about 12 pounds of it each year! But many people don't know that children in West Africa pick most of the world's cocoa beans. (Cocoa is the main ingredient in chocolate.) People who buy chocolate are becoming more and more worried about child labor.

Imagine this. Ten-year-old Sametta lives in Côte d'Ivoire (or Ivory Coast), a country in West Africa. She wakes up at 4:00 a.m., eats millet porridge, and then walks two miles to her family's cocoa bean field. For the next 12 hours, she picks cocoa pods and then breaks them open. She scoops out the 30 to 50 seeds, or "beans," that are inside the pods. (About 400 beans are needed to make a pound of chocolate.) Sametta does not have time to go to school. Her family needs her to work in order for them to survive. Her health is also at risk. The cocoa pods are sprayed with poisonous pesticides. So Sametta uses a knife with a long, sharp blade when she works so that she does not have to touch the pods.

This is not a story from long ago. This is happening right now. Every day in Ivory Coast, Ghana, Nigeria, and Cameroon, about 300,000 children pick cocoa beans that will be sold to big chocolate companies. Most of the children work on their families' farms. They need to sell every bean to make money for their families to survive. School is out of the question. Worse, some children are forced to work without pay. They sleep in dirty rooms, work 12-hour days, are fed very little, and are sometimes treated harshly.

Why is this happening? The reason is money. Extremely poor countries send children to work in other countries where cocoa beans grow. In exchange, their government is paid. Also, families who own the cocoa bean farms are very poor. They depend on growing and selling cocoa beans to survive. Without help from their children, the farmers would not be able to buy food. Big chocolate companies pay farmers a very low price for their cocoa beans. Most farmers earn only between $30 and $100 a year—total.

DANGERS OF CHILD LABOR IN COCOA

2 million children are engaged in hazardous work on cocoa farms in Côte d'Ivoire and Ghana. More than half report being injured by their work. Dangerous conditions on these farms that may impact children's health, access to education and future livelihoods include:

Spraying pesticides

Lifting heavy loads

Burning fields

Using sharp tools

Learn what DOL is doing to combat child labor in cocoa: dol.gov/ilab

In 2001, the U.S. government created an international agreement with major chocolate companies. It said that chocolate companies should help eliminate child slavery and child labor by July 2005. So far, however, the agreement has not ended child labor.

Still, there is hope, as organizations around the world work to eliminate child labor. For example, a group of farms in Africa and South America are called Fair Trade Certified. Companies that buy cocoa beans from these farmers sign an agreement. They promise to pay the farmers a Fair Trade price. This is enough for them to buy food and clothing for their families and send their children to school. There are about 45,000 farmers in this program. Any chocolate made from these farmers' beans is labeled Fair Trade.

The Rainforest Alliance is also working hard to tackle child labor and rural poverty in West Africa. Partnering with local communities in Côte d'Ivoire and Ghana, they train cocoa farmers in growing practices that can help protect soils, waterways, and wildlife—while also increasing cocoa yields and improving incomes. The Rainforest Alliance also works closely with farmers, parents, and local organizations such as teachers' groups to monitor and prevent child labor and take concrete steps to help ensure children go to school. Cocoa grown on farms that meet strict standards designed to protect the environment and ensure the well-being of farm workers and their families can earn the Rainforest Alliance Certified seal.

You can help eliminate child labor too by looking for the Rainforest Alliance's green frog seal and the FairTrade trustmark when you shop for chocolate.

May be reproduced for classroom use. *Toolkit Texts: Short Nonfiction for American History, Industrial Age and Immigration*, by Stephanie Harvey and Anne Goudvis, ©2021 (Portsmouth, NH: Heinemann).

HARD AT WORK
WHO'S HELPING?

DO YOU EVER daydream about taking a day off from school? What if you never had the *opportunity* to go to school? Many children around the world work full time and can't go to school. It's a big problem, because when children have to work, they can't get an education. When they do not get an education, they are not able to find better jobs, and the cycle of child labor and poverty continues.

Recent estimates state that 98 million children around the world work in agriculture—on farms, in forests and forestry jobs, and in the fishing industry. Many children work on their family's farms, but helping out after school or in the summer is very different than kids who are forced to work because their families cannot survive otherwise.

When children work when they are too young, or when the work they do harms their health or prevents them from getting an education, we call this child labor. The number of children working around the world is declining, thanks to global awareness of this issue and the efforts of many individuals and groups who advocate for children.

Malala Yousafzai (above, left) and Kailash Satyarthi talk during a visit to the Norwegian Nobel Committee in December 2014.

Who is helping to solve the worldwide problem of children working rather than going to school?

MALALA YOUSAFZAI

Malala Yousafzai is a young woman who fights to ensure all girls receive twelve years of free, safe, quality education. As a child, her father ran a school for girls in their village in Pakistan. She loved school, but everything changed when the Taliban took control of the country. The Taliban is a militant group in parts of Pakistan and Afghanistan that does not want women and girls to be educated. Malala began to speak out about girls' right to learn, which made her a target. In 2012, Malala was shot in the head by a gunman who was angered by her campaign against the Taliban's ban on female education. After being shot, Yousafzai was flown to England for treatment and has lived there since. According to Malala, "It was then I knew I had a choice: I could live a quiet life or I could make the most of this new life I had been given. I determined to continue my fight until every girl could go to school."

Malala famously said, "One child, one teacher, one book and one pen can change the world." In her work, she tackles difficult problems like child poverty, knowing that many girls have to work and this prevents them from attending school and getting an education. Today, she travels to many countries to meet girls fighting against poverty, child marriage, and gender discrimination to go to school. With her father, she started the Malala Fund, a charity dedicated to giving every girl an opportunity to achieve a future she chooses. In 2014, Malala received the Nobel Peace Prize and became the youngest-ever Nobel Laureate.

KAILASH SATYARTHI

This Indian activist has gone to prison for his work against child labor. He even led a march through 103 countries to raise awareness of the plight of children forced to work. Satyarthi believes that the best way to end child labor is by giving children the right to an education. Along with girl's education advocate Malala Yousafzai, he won the Nobel Peace Prize in 2014 for his commitment to end child labor. Today, Mr. Satyarthi is leading the 100 Million campaign, which aims to inspire young people to stand up and act for their own rights and the rights of their peers. He works in many countries to end child labor and make sure children get an education.

> **NGO**
> (nongovernmental organization): a non-profit, citizen-based group with a specific social, environmental, or political mission

RAINFOREST ALLIANCE

This international **NGO** is working to convince countries around the world to pass laws that protect children from child labor. These laws require companies to find out if child workers are involved in the production of the goods they are selling. This is a complicated problem, and a number of European countries, including the Netherlands, are taking action. In May of 2019, the Dutch government passed a law that requires companies selling their products in the Netherlands to demonstrate that they are taking steps to prevent child labor. By taking such measures, countries can refuse to buy the products of companies who allow or enable child labor.

Dr. Anneke Fermont, Kyagalanyi Coffee Limited/Rainforest Alliance

Students from Erussi Primary School in Uganda, where Rainforest Alliance has worked with coffee growers to reduce child labor so kids can go to school.

Rainforest Alliance

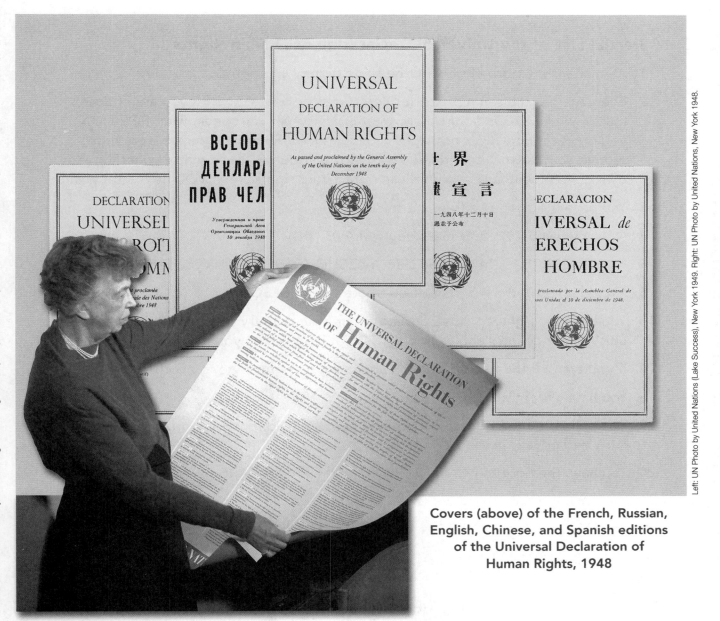

Covers (above) of the French, Russian, English, Chinese, and Spanish editions of the Universal Declaration of Human Rights, 1948

Mrs. Eleanor Roosevelt, former first lady of the United States and the chair of the UN Commission on Human Rights, holding a Declaration of Human Rights poster in November 1949.

UNITED NATIONS
UNIVERSAL DECLARATION OF HUMAN RIGHTS

Seventy-five years ago, after World War II, nations came together to create a **Universal Declaration of Human Rights.** Mary Robinson, former President of Ireland and the United Nations High Commissioner for Human Rights, says that this document "affirmed the 'inherent dignity' of all members of the human family." It spells out the rights we all have to food, safe water, health care, education, shelter, and much more.

Today, the United Nations and especially UNICEF (the United Nations Children's Fund) work around the world on behalf of these rights. A version of some of these rights, in young people's language, is included here.

A Partial List of the Universal Declaration of Human Rights

1 All humans are born FREE with the same dignity and rights.

2 Everyone has the same rights. It doesn't matter what GENDER you are. It doesn't matter what COLOR your skin is, what LANGUAGE you speak, what RELIGION you practice, how RICH or POOR you are, how DIFFERENT you are from those around you, or what country you come from. It doesn't even matter whether your own government agrees with these rights. Your rights are in YOU no matter what.

3 You have the right to a free and safe LIFE.

4 Nobody has the right to make you a SLAVE.

5 Nobody has the right to TORTURE you, BULLY you or punish you too severely.

6 Every human in the world must be treated as a PERSON.

13 You have the right to MOVE around within your country. You have the right to LEAVE your country and COME BACK to it if and when you want to.

14 If you aren't SAFE in your country, you have the right to go to another country.

15 You have the right to BELONG to a country.

23 All adults have the right to WORK and must be paid for their work and treated fairly and equally in the workplace.

24 You have the right to FOOD, SHELTER, and HEALTH CARE.

26 You have the right to go to SCHOOL for free.

28 You have the right to LIVE in a world where EVERYONE'S human rights are respected.

30 Your human rights are YOURS always. NOBODY can take them away.

Excerpted from *Every Human Has Rights: A Photographic Declaration for Kids*

May be reproduced for classroom use. *Toolkit Texts: Short Nonfiction for American History, Industrial Age and Immigration*, by Stephanie Harvey and Anne Goudvis, ©2021 (Portsmouth, NH: Heinemann).

Everyone deserves to live, go to school, and work with dignity, agency, and self-determination. As a global community, we can work together to promote the rights of all people.

Suvashis Mullick/Rainforest Alliance

Rise of the Tenement

Tenements: Library of Congress, 4a18586. Bricks: ©Photodisc/Getty Images.

A **tenement** is an overcrowded apartment building often located in a poor section of a city. In many big cities, neighborhoods were lined on both sides of the street with tenement buildings.

"I come from New York, the city of the **tenements**, where people are so crowded together that frequently twenty-four families are living on a lot no larger than 25 feet by 100; . . . in rooms which have no more light or ventilation than can sift into them through two other rooms that separate them from the outer air," said Robert W. DeForest. DeForest was chairman of the Tenement House Commission. This was part of his speech to the National Conference of Charities and Corrections in Atlanta, Georgia, in May 1903.

In its study, the commission found that more than two-thirds of New York City's 2 million inhabitants—that is, approximately 1.3 million people—were living in tenements. The city had only around 82,000 of such houses.

The size of the residential lots that DeForest mentioned was considered large in 1811. That was the year the initial plan for New York City was developed, and the lots were designed for single-family homes. However, the city's population grew from 96,000 in 1810 to more than 300,000 by 1840. Many of the new arrivals, including waves of Irish and German immigrants, needed homes quickly. Where would the city leaders put all these people?

This tenement family's kitchen has several uses. It is a workspace (the family is knitting to earn money), a kitchen and pantry (herbs and peppers are drying on twine in the back window) and a laundry room (clothes are hanging against the wall).

May be reproduced for classroom use. *Toolkit Texts: Short Nonfiction for American History, Industrial Age and Immigration*, by Stephanie Harvey and Anne Goudvis, ©2021 (Portsmouth, NH: Heinemann).

The First Tenement

Some historians believe that the first tenement appeared in 1833 on New York City's Water Street (today considered "downtown"). It was four stories high with one apartment on each floor. Every foot of space was precious in crowded cities, and thousands of people were looking for places to live. Because of the high cost of land and the building owners' desire to make money, many more tenement buildings were soon built in New York and other cities.

There were typically four different designs for a tenement in the first half of the 1800s. It could be a house with one apartment on each floor; a house with two apartments on each floor, sharing a common hallway; a house with three apartments on each floor—two in front and one in the rear, with a hallway between the front apartments leading to the rear; or a house with four apartments on each floor and a hallway running through the middle.

Conditions Deteriorate

Tenements were converted from those original single-family homes, and they were never intended to house that many people. **Landlords** thought of ways to fit many people into small spaces in order to collect as much rent as possible. By 1843, the Association for Improving the Conditions of the Poor described these buildings as "generally defective in size, arrangement, supplies of water, warmth, and ventilation; also the yards, sinks, and sewage are in bad conditions."

Disease became common among residents. "Tenement" and "crowded living conditions for the poor" became **synonymous**. The New York City health inspector believed laws governing landlords needed to be established to try

Landlords are those who own and rent land, buildings, or dwelling units.

Synonymous is having the same or similar meaning.

to prevent such horrible circumstances, as well as the spread of illnesses. However, as explosive growth in New York City continued, the state of its poorest inhabitants worsened. By 1850, the city's population reached more than half a million people. Tens of thousands of people, unable to find or afford housing, lived in cellar apartments. Stores and warehouses were converted hastily into tenements to accommodate immigrants from Europe and people moving from smaller American cities and rural areas.

A committee was appointed to look into the conditions of tenement houses. Its 1857 report stated, "In its beginning, the tenant house became a real blessing to that class of industrious poor whose small earnings limited their expenses." Obviously, the lack of reliable public transportation was another issue; working-class people needed to live close to where they were employed. Sometimes, tenement homes had to double as workplaces, especially in the clothing- and cigar-making industries.

Populations Grow

An increase in immigration from Europe between 1880 and 1924 only added to New York City's housing problems. A record year for immigration through **Ellis Island** came in 1907. An average of 3,000 people entered the United States each day that year. Many moved right into New York's already overcrowded tenements. By 1914, the Lower East Side—only about 1% of the city's total land—housed one-sixth of the city's population!

New York City was not the only **urban** area with tenements. Baltimore (Maryland), Boston (Massachusetts), Buffalo (New York), Chicago (Illinois), and Philadelphia (Pennsylvania) had tenements also, for many of the same reasons and with many of the same problems. In 1881, Chicago's health commissioner issued a report that spoke of the "great and rapid influx of population," which caused "a dangerous overcrowding in all the poorer districts."

Whether residences or workplaces or both, tenements became a distinctive way of life for many city dwellers in the late 19th and early 20th century.

Ellis Island was the main U.S. immigration station from 1892 to 1943.

Urban relates to the characteristics of a city.

The large tub in the center of this photo of a typical tenement kitchen was used to wash laundry as well as bathe small children.

By Barbara Krasner-Khait, *Cobblestone,* ©2004 by Carus Publishing Company. Reproduced with permission.

The Pros and Cons of Tenement Life

Pros

Closeness to work: Tenement residents had a difficult time finding dependable public transportation to bring them to their workplaces. Living and working close together made life easier.

Friendship and support: Immigrants from the same home country often lived in the same neighborhoods and found support in social organizations. These associations offered help in finding jobs and places to live, as well as support when family members became sick. Immigrants whose native language was not English had to overcome a language barrier. Living near people of the same background helped them cope with the uncertainties that came from leaving their homelands and, eventually, helped them to ease into their new life in the United States.

Entertainment: **Nickelodeons** and dance halls offered nearby, inexpensive ways to have fun and relax. The beach and amusement park at **Coney Island** were a popular place to hang out. Swimming in neighborhood pools and floating in New York's East River also provided social outlets. Taking strolls to see store windows and riding the trolley provided entertainment, too.

> **Nickelodeons** were early movie theaters that charged five cents for admission.
>
> **Coney Island** is a Brooklyn neighborhood on the river famous for its boardwalk and entertainment.

Enjoying inexpensive movies at theaters was one of the pleasures of city life.

Cons

Disease and poor sanitation: A resident of New York's Lower East Side between 1883 and 1900 said he never saw a bathtub in any of the 14 buildings in which he lived. City inspectors paid a visit to the tenements only when a complaint was made. Cities didn't employ sanitation workers, so this created unsanitary living conditions and overflowing garbage in the streets. These unsanitary conditions led to illness and death among tenement residents.

Lack of outside air and ventilation: Prior to 1879, rooms in tenements were not required by law to have access to outside air. Very little fresh air or light entered the rooms. That meant that residents had to endure sweltering heat during the summer.

Darkness: One social worker nearly tripped over children sleeping in a tenement's hallway because there was no lighting at night. Eventually, building owners were forced to install lights near the stairs.

Fire hazards: Wooden staircases, few windows, and overcrowding in some tenements led to tragedy when a fire started and residents were unable to escape.

> **Ventilation** is the circulation of fresh air.

The large amounts of garbage that collected in the streets made the city unsanitary.

Collection of the Tenement Museum, Courtesy of the Confino Family

Greenhorn No More
Victoria's Story

Editor's Note: *Visitors to the Lower East Side Tenement Museum in New York City can meet Victoria Confino (portrayed by a costumed interpreter). In the early 1900s, Victoria actually resided in the building. The museum staff has compiled her story through research and interviews of Confino family descendants. Following is a description, in what might have been her own words, of Victoria's environment.*

Upon hearing a knock at the door, 14-year-old Victoria cautiously opens it. It is a friend from the neighborhood, bringing some **greenhorns**. They recently arrived in New York and are in need of some advice. Victoria invites them in and offers to help them in any way she can.

Victoria asks where her visitors are from, after showing them to the parlor. "Ireland," replies one member of the group.

Greenhorns are recent immigrants unfamiliar with the ways or customs of a place.

The Confino family (above) emigrated from Kastoria (present-day Greece) to New York in 1913. In this photo of the family taken just after they arrived in the United States, young Victoria stands on the right. Today, Victoria's story comes to life through a costumed interpreter at the Lower East Side Tenement Museum.

By Meg Chorlian, *Cobblestone,* ©2004 by Carus Publishing Company. Reproduced with permission.

Victoria lived in this building at 97 Orchard Street, which is now the Lower East Side Tenement Museum.

"Oh, yes," says Victoria. "We have had many Irish families in this neighborhood. Welcome to America." She continues by explaining, "I am from Kastoria, in the Ottoman Empire. My family came to this country three years ago in 1913. I live here with my parents and six brothers. Two cousins also were boarding with us for a time."

One of the newcomers looks bewildered as he gazes around the small room. "Where do you all sleep?" he asks.

"Two sleep here," says Victoria, indicating a bed in the room. "Some sleep on these chairs all pulled together in a row, and some sleep on the floor here. I sleep on a **manta** on the kitchen floor. My parents sleep in the bedroom with the baby."

"Where are your parents now?" asks one of the children shyly.

"My father is at work at his apron and dress factory. I work there, too. My mother is visiting a neighbor with my baby brother."

"You work?" asks the same child.

"Yes," replies Victoria. "Most children here work. Every penny counts to buy food for the family or to pay the rent. I would rather be in school, but my parents took me out of school so I could pull threads in the factory. I used to attend Public School 65, just a few blocks away. But for me, it was a little difficult because I could not speak any English when my family arrived in America. We speak **Ladino** in our home. Back in Kastoria, girls are not allowed to go to school at all, so I tried not to be too embarrassed when I was placed in the second-grade class here."

Victoria pauses, then says, "Would you like to see the rest of the apartment?" The visitors stand up and follow her into the kitchen, the room through which they entered the apartment.

Victoria points out the laundry tub to the immigrants. Showing them a bar of soap and an **agitator**, Victoria explains how her family members wash their clothes against a washboard and then hang them to dry on rope strung across the kitchen. She also points to the cookstove, which burns coal and is the family's source of heat.

She moves out of the way so the group can see the only other room in the apartment, a small bedroom. Underneath the bed is a **chamber pot**. Victoria explains that chamber pots stowed under beds are used at night. They are emptied in the morning into a privy—basically, a closet-like structure built over a hole

> A **manta** is a thick Turkish carpet.
>
> **Ladino** is a Judeo-Spanish language spoken by Sephardic (those who lived in Spain and Portugal during the Middle Ages) Jews.
>
> An **agitator** is a machine that shakes or stirs laundry.
>
> A **chamber pot** is a pot or vessel used in a bedroom as a toilet.

The museum recreated the homes of families who lived on the Lower East Side, like the Confino family. This kitchen also served as the laundry room and gathering place in the tiny apartment.

Staff at the Lower East Side Tenement Museum were able to get a copy of Victoria's P.S. 65 elementary school report card.

Photographs in the Carol M. Highsmith Archive, Library of Congress, 13285

Collection of the Tenement Museum, Courtesy of the Confino Family

Water closets are rooms containing toilets and sometimes washbowls or sinks.

A **Victrola** is a phonograph machine or record player.

Baklava is a Turkish or Greek dessert made of paper-thin layers of pastry, chopped nuts, and honey.

in the ground—in the backyard of a building. While there are two **water closets** out in the hall, "there also are four apartments on a floor. With at least five people living in each apartment, it is better to be prepared."

As they all return to the parlor, another visiting child asks, "What do you do for fun?"

Victoria smiles and indicates the **Victrola**. She winds it up and invites the child to dance with her to the *Blue Danube Waltz*. After a few minutes, they are laughing and out of breath.

"When there is time to play, there are always games going on outside," explains Victoria. "There are lots of children in this neighborhood. You often can find a game of jump rope, ball, potsy [hopscotch], or hide-and-seek to join. But for me, there is work at the factory and then work at home, too. I watch my younger brothers and help my mother prepare the meals and keep the rooms clean.

"It is hard sometimes. I want to be an American. But our life in Kastoria was very different. We had a fine, big house. Aunts and uncles and cousins lived with us, and there was plenty of room. We had a grocery store, and our family owned a vineyard. We lived near a beautiful lake."

Then, Victoria shares more about her families story. "But then wars were starting in our part of the world, and my parents feared that my brother Joseph would be drafted into the Turkish army. Too, there was the fire that destroyed our house. And, my older sister, Allegra, got married and moved here. So coming to America seemed like the best thing to do. We were able to keep the family together."

Victoria looks at the new immigrants sympathetically. "You must have similar stories. I would like very much to hear them, but right now I must go. My father will be expecting me at the factory. Please come again. We can talk while we share some delicious Turkish coffee and **baklava** that I will make for you. Good-bye—it was very nice to meet you. Thank you for visiting." And she waves as her new friends file out the door.

THE PROMISED LAND

In towns throughout the South, Black American families were heading north to start a new life in the city. Black American artist Jacob Lawrence told the story of their experiences in a series of paintings called The Migration Series.

Between 1910 and 1940, close to two million Black Americans left the South for the cities of the North and West. Just prior to this period, 90% of all Black American people lived in the South, and 75% of them (approximately eight million people) lived in rural areas. By 1960, however, the majority of Black American people had become urban dwellers. Why did this migration take place?

The first clue can be found in an 1865 speech to the Massachusetts Anti-Slavery Society by Frederick Douglass, the most influential speaker for Black rights in the 1800s. Douglass asked: "What does the black man want?—immediate, unconditional, and universal" first-class citizenship in every state of the Union. Douglass then reminded his audience that freedom meant more than removing shackles from men, women, and children. Douglass argued that freedom had to include the "right to choose one's own employment." It also had to include the right to vote and to participate fully in local, state, and national government.

POLITICAL AND SOCIAL INJUSTICE

For a few exciting years after the Civil War officially ended in 1865, Douglass and other Black Americans rushed to exercise political freedoms won through the Fourteenth Amendment to the United States Constitution, which declared that people born in America were citizens

May be reproduced for classroom use. Toolkit Texts: Short Nonfiction for American History, Industrial Age and Immigration, by Stephanie Harvey and Anne Goudvis, ©2021 (Portsmouth, NH: Heinemann).

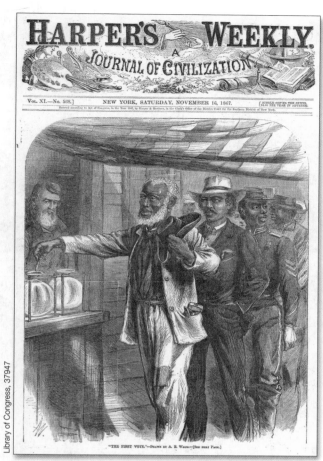

Black Americans voted for the first time in 1867. This engraving in a contemporary magazine shows an elderly Black artisan casting his vote, followed by a businessman and a soldier.

This late 1800s cartoon depicts the Ku Klux Klan (K.K.K.) and another secret semi-military society, the White League, banding together to destroy freedom and equality for Blacks.

of the United States. Even though the war was officially over, Black people continued to be treated unfairly and brutally. In most cases, white Southerners initiated violence against former enslaved people who challenged labor contracts, attempted to leave plantations, tried to purchase land, or sent their children to school.

In 1866, the Klu Klux Klan was founded in Tennessee. Its members—including ex-slaveholders, businessmen, and white politicians—were determined to restore white supremacy throughout the South. Klan members intimidated and committed acts of violence against Black people. The Klan did not target only Black politicians. It also went after Black American people who had learned to read and write, who owned land, or attempted to stand up against racial injustice.

Laws that had been passed to address racial injustices, such as the Civil Rights Act of 1875, were overturned. Most of the political and civil rights won by Black legislators and activists after the Civil War were taken away. Several Southern states wrote white supremacists constitutions that excluded Black men from voting. Following **Reconstruction**, all Black men who had won seats in state legislatures were voted out of office. Between 1901 and 1928, there was no Black representation in the U.S. Congress. Other injustices imposed even deeper pain.

> **Reconstruction** refers to the process and the time period, after the Civil War, of reorganizing the Southern states that had seceded and reestablishing them in the Union.

SHARECROPPING

By the end of 1800s, most Black Americans in the South worked on the land raising cotton and were exploited as sharecroppers. Most received no wages. "Payment" came in the form of shares of the crop. When landowners provided seed, tools, fertilizers, and mules or oxen to plow the land, Black farmers received approximately one-third of the crop. Often, however, Black farmers were cheated out of their fair share.

In the early 1900s, farming went from bad to worse. The boll weevil, a beetle that attacks the bolls or seeds in cotton plants, destroyed cotton crops throughout the South. Severe floods added to the problems and, as a result, sharecroppers fell deeper into debt to the landlords.

RACIAL VIOLENCE AND UNFAIR LAWS

Most Southern communities had become a very hostile environment for Black people. Some white Southerners used racial intimidation and violence to ensure white racial supremacy. Even more brutal, Black people were terrorized by the threat of murder by racial mobs. This lawless killing was called **lynching**. Between the years 1890 and 1920, thousands of Black men were murdered by mobs.

Jim Crow laws were shameful laws that separated Black citizens from white citizens. With Black Americans removed from politics, white people who resented Black progress enacted these laws designed to control and dominate Black people. One of the first places where Black people were segregated from whites was in transportation,

A thirteen-year old sharecropper boy harvests cotton in Georgia.

May be reproduced for classroom use. *Toolkit Texts: Short Nonfiction for American History, Industrial Age and Immigration,* by Stephanie Harvey and Anne Goudvis, ©2021 (Portsmouth, NH: Heinemann).

Lynching refers to killing without due process of law, especially to hang by a mob.

The term *Jim Crow* comes from a variety show where a white man blackened his face with charcoal and ridiculed Black people.

In 1896 Supreme Court ruled that "separate but equal" facilities for blacks and whites was constitutional. Yet, school facilities for Black Americans were run down and poorly kept and the teachers were paid half the salaries of white teachers.

©MPI/Archive Photos/Getty Images

A family leaving Florida to start a new life in the North.

particularly on trains. By the late 1800s, Jim Crow laws restricted Black men, women, and children from parks, shops, restaurants, streetcars, hospitals, beaches, schools, and libraries. In 1896, the U.S. Supreme Court upheld Jim Crow segregation laws in Louisiana with the famous *Plessy v. Ferguson* case. It stated that separate facilities for Black and white people were permissible if they were equal. This separate-but-equal doctrine denied Black people equal treatment under the law (one of the guarantees of the 14th Amendment). Soon "white" and "colored" signs appeared in railroad stations, restrooms, theaters, auditoriums, and over drinking fountains. Jim Crow laws even reached the extremes of maintaining a separate Bible for Black and white witnesses in courtrooms and separate burial grounds.

By the early 1900s, such injustices had destroyed the majority of rights for which Frederick Douglass and his peers had fought so hard. Nevertheless, the dream of democracy still lived in the hearts and minds of Black Americans. As Jim Crow laws and the threat of violence against Black Americans continued, some began to migrate to the cities. The reason: cities offered more opportunity for men and women to shape their own destinies through Black American religious, fraternal, and women's organizations.

LAND OF HOPE AND FREEDOM

Black Americans also left the South to follow the promise of freedom that lay in the mythic land north of the Ohio River. The North was called "the Promised Land," drawing imagery from the Bible as a place of hope, freedom, and economic opportunity. The journey north was also an escape from the "land of Egypt" (that is, the South) with its lynchings, unequal rights, and economic exploitation. Migrants described crossing the Ohio River as crossing the River Jordan. These biblical images were well known to all Black Americans in the days after the Civil War, when hopes were high for greater equality, justice, and opportunity.

When the Promised Land beckoned, many of the migrants who answered the call recorded their experiences in reports, articles, and letters to the communities they left behind. These accounts help us understand what is must have been like to move hundreds of miles to a new home and a new way of life.

May be reproduced for classroom use. *Toolkit Texts: Short Nonfiction for American History, Industrial Age and Immigration,* by Stephanie Harvey and Anne Goudvis, ©2021 (Portsmouth, NH: Heinemann).

Letters Home

Newly arrived in Chicago (above), Black American men, women, and children pose together with suitcases and luggage.

Migrants are people who move from one place to another, especially in order to find work or better living conditions.

When the Rev. R.H. Harmon arrived in Chicago with his wife and 28 members of his congregation from Harrisburg, Mississippi, he told a *Defender* reporter, "I am working at my trade. I have saved enough to bring my wife and four children and some of my congregation. We are here for keeps. They say that we are fools to leave the warm country, and how our people are dying in the East. Well, I for one am glad that they had the privilege of dying a natural death there. That is much better than the rope and torch. I will take my chance with the Northern winter."

Migrants were eager to let folks back home know how their new lives were taking shape. They wrote about their cities, their well-paying jobs, housing, and churches. One Chicago woman wrote to her church sister, "The weather and everything else was a surprise to me when I came. I got here in time to attend one of the greatest revivals in the history of my life—over 500 people joined the church. . . . The people are rushing here by the thousands, and I know if you come and rent a big house you can get all the roomers you want . . . I am quite busy. I work for the same company. We get $1.50 a day, and we pack so many sausages we don't have much time to play but it is a matter of a dollar with me and I feel that God made the path I am walking therein."

Positive Changes

Some explained how good they felt about their decision to migrate north. A Mississippi fellow wrote home on November 13, 1917, from Chicago, "I should have been here 20 years ago. I just begin to feel like a man. It's a great deal of pleasure in knowing that you have got some privilege. My children are going to the same school with whites, and I don't have to 'umble to no one. I have registered—Will vote the next election and there isn't any 'yes sir' and 'no sir'—it's all yes and no and Sam and Bill."

Another migrant said in 1919, "If I had the money I would go South and dig up my fathers' and my mothers' bones and bring them up to this country [Philadelphia]. I am forty-nine years old and these six weeks I have spent here are the first weeks in my life of peace and comfort."

Bittersweet Emotions

Homesickness for old friends and the church, however, was a frequent subject in letters home. For example, in May 1917, a man new to Akron,

New York's Harlem became a bustling center of activity, especially during the Harlem Renaissance.

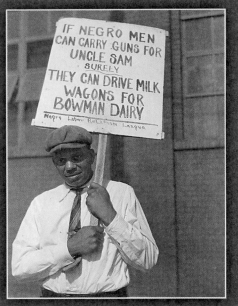

Library of Congress, 8a33115 (left) and 8c19566 (right)

In Chicago, Illinois in 1941, these picketers protested discrimination.

Ohio, wrote, "I work like a man. I am making good. I never liked a place like I do here except home . . . the people are coming from the south every week the colored people are making good they are the best workers. The Baptist Church is over crowded with Baptist from Ala and Ga. 10 and 12 join each Sunday."

For many, getting used to this new life would take some time. Writer Richard Wright, who moved to Chicago in 1927, wrote about his first impressions: "My expectations were modest. I wanted only a job . . . It was strange to pause before a crowded newsstand and buy a newspaper without having to wait until a white man was served. And yet, because everything was so new, I began to grow tense again, although it was a different sort of tension than I had known before." He then wrote about the city's towering buildings and the icy weather and wondered whether he had made the right move. "I was seized by doubt. But going back was impossible. I had fled a known terror, and perhaps I could cope with this unknown terror that lay ahead."

Library of Congress, 8d03731

Many of the migrants who came to Chicago between 1910 and 1930 started businesses. One was the "Perfect Eat" shop. Its owner, Ernest Morris, can be seen standing in the rear.

May be reproduced for classroom use. *Toolkit Texts: Short Nonfiction for American History, Industrial Age and Immigration,* by Stephanie Harvey and Anne Goudvis, ©2021 (Portsmouth, NH: Heinemann).

JACOB LAWRENCE'S
The Migration Series

Do you like to draw? Tell stories? Read about the past? Observe your world? The renowned Black American artist Jacob Lawrence did. Born in 1917 in Atlantic City, New Jersey, Lawrence moved to Harlem in New York City when he was 13. As a young artist in the 1930s, Lawrence felt the stories of Black Americans were invisible to most Americans and used his paintings as one means of telling others these stories.

Lawrence had often listened to his family talk about their experiences migrating north and, as a teenager in Harlem, he knew young migrant children who were struggling to adjust to the new city lifestyle.

Drawing from these experiences, Lawrence was inspired to create The Migration Series in 1940–1941. Because he felt that one painting would not be enough to tell all the stories, he painted 60 different pictures that fit together as a series. He also wrote captions for each. As the basic theme for the first 30 panels, Lawrence painted some of the reasons why people left the South. For the second half of the series, he turned his attention to the migrants' new life in the North.

In 1942, two museums purchased Lawrence's The Migration Series. The odd-numbered panels went to The Phillips Collection in Washington, D.C., and the even numbered ones to the Museum of Modern Art in New York City.

Panel No. 11: "Food had doubled in price because of the war." Lawrence vividly expressed the food shortage by focusing on a young child with large eyes watching his mother prepare food in a sparsely furnished room with no toys and a single candle for light. To make the painting more interesting and persuasive, Lawrence used such simple shapes as rectangles and triangles and only a few colors–red, yellow, turquoise, and brown. The effect on the viewer is dramatic. Your eyes might zoom from the red of the mother's dress to the bright yellow of the candle flame to the child's large eyes.

Panel 47: This painting depicts one of the many disappointments migrants faced: "As the migrant population grew, good housing became scarce. Workers were forced to live in overcrowded and dilapidated [run down] tenement houses." Can you count how many people Lawrence painted sleeping together in this one tiny room? How do you think it would feel to sleep here every night?

For more information about the artist
and The Migration Series,
go online to visit
"Jacob Lawrence, Over the Line"
at the Phillips Collection website at:
www.phillipscollection.org.

Renaissance refers to any revival of art, literature, or learning similar to the Renaissance, the great revival of art, literature, and learning in Europe in the 14th, 15th, and 16th centuries.

*When **Langston Hughes** (right) first went to Harlem as a young college student in 1921, he found a neighborhood, a city, and a people in the middle of exciting social change. Within a few years, this special period had been given the name the **Harlem Renaissance**. By that time, Hughes was not just a spectator, but one of the people who had helped make the renaissance happen.*

From The New York Public Library, 1216447

HARLEM RENAISSANCE

From The New York Public Library, 56805976

A neighborhood in the Northern part of New York City, Harlem was originally a wealthy area with families who were mostly white. With the construction of the new subway system in the early 1900s, the area was, for the first time, connected to the city's downtown section. The result was an increase in building in Harlem. As housing became more available, many Black families, including those with jobs in other parts of the city, began moving into Harlem's beautiful brownstone homes. Soon, the area became a popular neighborhood for

Selma Burke, pictured here with a sculpture of Booker T. Washington, was a sculptor who received national recognition for her portrait of Franklin Delano Roosevelt, which was the model for his image on the dime. In the 1920s, Burke became one of the few Black women to achieve fame during the Harlem Renaissance. Burke was committed to teaching others and founded art schools in New York City and Pittsburgh.

May be reproduced for classroom use. *Toolkit Texts: Short Nonfiction for American History, Industrial Age and Immigration,* by Stephanie Harvey and Anne Goudvis, ©2021 (Portsmouth, NH: Heinemann).

In the 1920s and 1930s, Lenox Avenue was one of Harlem's busiest and most vibrant streets.

New York's growing Black middle and upper-middle class, many of whom had just recently moved to New York from the South, the Midwest, and the Caribbean.

ARRIVING IN HARLEM

About 100,000 Black Americans moved to Harlem in the 1920s. By 1930, two-thirds of all Black people in New York City lived in the neighborhood. All were looking to take advantage of the economic opportunities the city had to offer. Never before had there been such a concentrated community of Black Americans, many of them well educated, with professional jobs. Most of the people who chose to move to Harlem came looking for a change and were ready to promote change by working together.

It is no surprise that people soon began to think of this period in Harlem as a renaissance. New ideas were changing people's attitudes. Black soldiers who had fought in World War I (1914–1918) were asking why, after fighting for their country, they were still subjected to segregation, prejudice, and unfair treatment at home. Many other Black

Corporal Lawrence McVey, Sr., was a member of the 369th United States Infantry, nicknamed the "Harlem Hellfighters." The 369th Regiment was the first Black regiment of troops to reach the battlefields of World War I. Due to racial tension within the U.S. Army, the 369th Regiment was assigned to the French Army. At the end of their service in WWI in February 1919, the regiment had spent 191 days in combat, the longest of any American regiment.

In appreciation for their actions in WWI, the 369th Regiment was awarded the Croix de Guerre medal by the French government for acts of bravery in conflicts against the enemy.

Americans agreed this was an important question for which there was no good answer. Black leaders, including W.E.B. Du Bois and Marcus Garvey, often spoke to large audiences in Harlem about the problems Black people faced in America and the need for them to be proud of themselves and other Black people's accomplishments.

CREATIVITY THRIVES

Organizations such as the National Association for the Advancement of Colored People (NAACP), the National Urban League, Garvey's Universal Negro Improvement Association, and the Brotherhood of Sleeping Car Porters and Maids were founded in Harlem. All allowed people to work together to solve many of the social problems Black Americans faced. At the same time, Black artists were beginning to think deeply about how Black people could create literature, art, and music that acknowledged their place in American culture, but still reflected their Black, Southern, or even African roots. Harlem became known as a creative space where museums, theaters, clubs, publications, and writers' groups all helped Black artists to flourish. As a result, it soon became a magnet for creative people.

Hughes and other artists soon found themselves at the center of a larger debate that scholars, political leaders, and other Black Americans in Harlem were already having: What did it mean to be Black in America? A most exciting effect of this new artistic freedom Black Americans were finding in Harlem was that they could now finally tell their own stories and paint their own portraits. But what should that story and picture look like?

Marcus Garvey

Should it be the story of the most successful members of Harlem society, those who were some of the wealthiest and best-educated Black people in America? This group was sometimes called the "Talented Tenth," meaning they represented the top 10% of Black Americans. For some, the "Talented Tenth" was the image of Black America because they were the best positive examples of Black culture for both whites and other Black people to see. There were also those who argued that the story of Black America should really be the story of the millions of Black Americans who had not experienced the same opportunities for educational and financial success. These people included the sharecroppers, domestics, and other poorer, less educated Black Americans living in rural areas and inner cities across America.

Some people thought Black Americans could tell their story best by retelling the story of slavery. Others thought they could do so by painting a picture of Africa, a place unfamiliar to most Americans, both black and white, but imagined as an exotic, primitive place. Which would be the best picture of Black America? Would artists have to choose? The artists of the Harlem Renaissance believed they did not. By putting all of these images together in new ways, they helped define the "New Negro" for the rest of the world.

Scenes from Harlem in the late 1920s:

Top: Children at play in the streets.

Middle: Women at work in a doll factory.

Bottom: The community in Harlem welcomed home Black soldiers after World War I with joy.

May be reproduced for classroom use. *Toolkit Texts: Short Nonfiction for American History, Industrial Age and Immigration,* by Stephanie Harvey and Anne Goudvis, ©2021 (Portsmouth, NH: Heinemann).

By Lisa Clayton Robinson, *Footsteps,* ©2009 by Carus Publishing Company. Reproduced with permission.

By Marcia Amidon Lusted. May be reproduced for classroom use. *Toolkit Texts: Short Nonfiction for American History, Industrial Age and Immigration*, by Stephanie Harvey and Anne Goudvis, ©2021 (Portsmouth, NH: Heinemann).

American poet and writer Langston Hughes stands on the steps in front of his house in Harlem, New York, in June 1958.

WHO'S WHO IN THE HARLEM RENAISSANCE

It was the early part of the 20th century, and in the Harlem neighborhood of New York City, an explosion was taking place. It wasn't a physical explosion. It was an exciting explosion of music, art, literature, theater, and politics, and it was the start of a golden age for Black Americans. Harlem had seen a population boom as Black Americans from the South came North as part of the Great Migration, looking for work, and Harlem was one of the most popular destinations. Here they created and preserved a unique culture. This golden age came to be known as the Harlem Renaissance, and it would pave the way for the Civil Rights movement of the 1960s.

Many famous musicians, writers, actors, artists, and thinkers found their voices during the Harlem Renaissance. As author Nikki Grimes said, "African American artists of the period were, in large measure, breaking out of the constrictions white society had set for them. They were claiming and remaking their own images, and doing so in bold and striking ways." Here are the stories of some of them.

Library of Congress, George Grantham Bain Collection, 3a03567

"A people without the knowledge of their past history, origin and culture is like a tree without roots."

MARCUS GARVEY 1887–1940

Marcus Garvey came to Harlem from Jamaica, and in 1918 he began publishing an influential newspaper called *Negro World*. But Garvey is best known for founding the Universal Negro Improvement Association, or UNIA. This group campaigned for "separate but equal" status for everyone of African descent, and its goal was to establish Black states in places all over the world. With almost a million members, the UNIA was the first Black national movement in the United States, with chapters all over the world. UNIA believed in supporting Black-owned businesses, and together with Garvey, founded a shipping company, the Black Star Line. It established trade between America, the Caribbean, South and Central America, Canada, and Africa. Marcus Garvey was a controversial figure. Some considered his views to be too extreme. However, his messages of pride, dignity, and African American identity would inspire many people during the Civil Rights movement.

DUKE ELLINGTON 1899–1974

Duke Ellington was born in Washington, D.C. His father was a butler in a wealthy household and was said to have sometimes worked in the White House, as well. Ellington first wanted to be a painter, but in his teens he became interested in music and taught himself to play the piano. In 1923 he moved to New York and started his own band. They played regularly at the Cotton Club, a Harlem nightclub where Black musicians performed for white audiences. It was opened for white patrons who wanted to experience Black culture without actually having to socialize with Black people. Over his lifetime, Ellington composed thousands of songs. His band and his music created one of the most complex and distinctive jazz sounds in American music, and yet it was also extremely popular. Ellington is well known for the jazz tune "Take the A Train," about a subway line in New York City. The song was written by Ellington's collaborator, Billy Strayhorn.

Collection of the Smithsonian National Museum of African American History and Culture

"Art is dangerous. It is one of the attractions: when it ceases to be dangerous you don't want it."

By Marcia Amidon Lusted. May be reproduced for classroom use. *Toolkit Texts: Short Nonfiction for American History, Industrial Age and Immigration*, by Stephanie Harvey and Anne Goudvis. ©2021 (Portsmouth, NH: Heinemann).

By Marcia Amidon Lusted. May be reproduced for classroom use. *Toolkit Texts: Short Nonfiction for American History, Industrial Age and Immigration*, by Stephanie Harvey and Anne Goudvis, ©2021 (Portsmouth, NH: Heinemann).

LOUIS ARMSTRONG 1901–1971

Louis Armstrong was a jazz musician who played the trumpet. He was often called "Satchmo" by his fans, and he was a founding father of jazz music and an influence on music in general. Armstrong was born in one of the poorest areas of New Orleans. By age 7, he was already playing the trumpet. He moved to Chicago, and eventually to Harlem, where he played with many jazz bands and orchestras. He also had a deep voice and a style of jazz singing called "scat" singing, where the voice imitates an instrument using wordless syllables or nonsense words. It was often said that Armstrong used his voice like an instrument and his instrument like a singer's voice. Armstrong toured the world and became a celebrity, serving as "Ambassador Satch," and spreading good will for America. But he will always be remembered for helping to make jazz a uniquely American music.

Armstrong: New York World-Telegram and the Sun Newspaper Photograph Collection, Library of Congress, 3c18976. Trumpet: Collection of the Smithsonian National Museum of African American History and Culture.

Louis Armstrong's trumpet is now part of the Smithsonian Institution's collection.

"Do you dig me when I say, 'I have a right to blow my top over injustice?'"

ZORA NEALE HURSTON 1891–1960

Zora Neale Hurston, writer and anthropologist, was born in Eatonville, Florida, the first incorporated all-Black city in the United States. At 16, she joined a traveling theater company and moved to New York, where she went to college. As an anthropologist, she studied Black folklore and culture in the South. She also helped start a literary magazine called *FIRE!!*, which explored the Black American experience during the Harlem Renaissance in a realistic and modern way. Hurston went on to write novels, the most famous of them being *Their Eyes Were Watching God*, which is still widely read today.

"There are years that ask questions and years that answer."

Library of Congress, Prints & Photographs Division, Carl Van Vechten Collection, 5a52142

JOSEPHINE BAKER 1906–1975

Josephine Baker was born in St Louis, Missouri, but she achieved her greatest fame in France. She lived in poverty as a child but learned to sing and dance and eventually moved to New York to perform on Broadway. She moved to France in the 1920s and became a very popular entertainer there. The French were obsessed with American culture and jazz, and Baker made an impression on them by performing one dance onstage wearing only a feather skirt. During World War II she was a member of the French Resistance, working against the Nazi regime. She returned to the United States after the war, and during the 1950s and 1960s, she fought racism and segregation. In 1963, she participated in the March on Washington with Dr. Martin Luther King Jr. After a lifetime of dealing with racism in the United States, she was greeted with a standing ovation when she performed at Carnegie Hall in 1973.

"I have walked into the palaces of kings and queens and into the houses of presidents. And much more. But I could not walk into a hotel in America and get a cup of coffee, and that made me mad."

LANGSTON HUGHES 1902–1967

Langston Hughes was a writer of poems, novels, plays, and newspaper columns. He was one of the most important people of the Harlem Renaissance. He was born in Joplin, Missouri, but first explored Harlem as a college student. When he was working as a busboy in a New York City hotel in 1925, Hughes gave poet Rachel Lindsay three of his poems. The next day, newspapers reported that Lindsay had "discovered" a Black busboy poet, bringing attention to Hughes' writing. Hughes helped launch the magazine *FIRE!!* All of his writing focused on the Black experience. His books of poetry and his novels often explored racial justice and politics. They are still read and treasured today.

"We younger Negro artists who create now intend to express our individual dark-skinned selves without fear or shame. If white people are pleased we are glad. If they are not, it doesn't matter. We know we are beautiful. And ugly too."

By Marcia Amidon Lusted. May be reproduced for classroom use. *Toolkit Texts: Short Nonfiction for American History, Industrial Age and Immigration*, by Stephanie Harvey and Anne Goudvis, ©2021 (Portsmouth, NH: Heinemann).

Dreams

Langston Hughes
1902–1967

Hold fast to dreams
For if dreams die
Life is a broken-winged bird
That cannot fly.

Hold fast to dreams
For when dreams go
Life is a barren field
Frozen with snow.

Migration's Legacy

Without question, the Great Migration reshaped America. The activities of Black American migrants shifted the color line in America and set in motion a process that reached its peak in the Civil Rights movement of the 1950s.

Library of Congress, 8d19397

Richard Wright

Although the Great Migration affected all aspects of American life, one of the more important areas—and one of the more difficult to measure—is the degree to which migration altered "Black identity." Widely known Black American author Richard Wright wrote about the discrimination and violence suffered by Black Americans in the South and North. He went on to become one of the most famous writers of the 20th century. Wright referred to this area as the Black sense of place within American democracy.

Early Life

Wright was born in rural Mississippi and suffered under Jim Crow laws until he moved—first to Memphis, Tennessee, and then to Chicago in the 1920s. In his autobiography, *Black Boy*, Wright explained the many ways these laws tried to silence his humanity, and especially how they tried to keep him in what the white South called his "place." Wright recalled that he was taught to calculate and "exercise a great deal of **ingenuity** to keep out of trouble" by pretending to know his "place." "Well, I had never felt my 'place,' or, rather, my deepest instincts had always made me reject the 'place' to which the white South had assigned me. It had never occurred to me that I was in any way an inferior being." Moreover, the white South said it not only knew Wright's "place" but

Ingenuity means being clever, creative, or inventive.

May be reproduced for classroom use. *Toolkit Texts: Short Nonfiction for American History, Industrial Age and Immigration,* by Stephanie Harvey and Anne Goudvis, ©2021 (Portsmouth, NH: Heinemann).

Harlem in the 1930s: School's out, and the weather's too warm to stay indoors. Families watch over kids as they play with friends outside.

also who he was. Wright, on the other hand, did not believe that white South knew who he was—but then neither did he.

In order to find himself, Wright felt he had to go north to free himself from the suffocation of the Southern social system. For Wright, as for all migrants, the move opened up opportunities in jobs that few Black American people had held previously, as well as gave him a chance to realize his potential as a human being. That was the good news.

He soon grew anxious again, as a new color line held him back from full participation in Black Chicago. Although Wright and his generation of migrants may have been dismayed with the "invisible" color line they confronted up North, they were not deterred from seeking their goal—full citizenship rights.

Fighting for Democracy for All

At the time, World War I was raging, and the country's intent was to make the world safe for democracy. This goal served to reinforce the migrants' goal. Black Americans not only migrated north during World War I, but they also fought in World War I. Their hope, as labor activist A. Philip Randolph said, was to make the world safe for democracy and to make Georgia safe for Black Americans.

From The New York Public Library, 1228871

The Universal Negro Improvement Association (UNIA), founded by Marcus Garvey, organized this parade in Harlem in 1920.

Gradually, a new leadership arose. The activism, dreams, and aggressiveness of the new migrants were such a departure from the behavior and expectations of the "Old Guard" leaders within the Black community that the new arrivals were called "New Negros" or the "New Crowd." They rallied behind the cry of social activist W.E.B. Du Bois, who announced after the end of World War I: "Make way for Democracy! We saved it in France, and by the Great Jehovah, we will save it in the United States of America, or know the reasons why." The New Negro was hailed as a role model for the Black community. As a result, many leaders of the 1920s New Negro Movement planted seeds that bore fruit during the Civil Rights movement of the 1950s.

The Great Migration unleashed a new spirit, a new confidence that changed the daily existence of all Black American people and the political, economic, and cultural life of America. Because the New Negro did not back down, Black Americans gained entrance to new jobs in industry and helped forge a partnership between Black and white labor. They also shaped the content of a new American culture with the introduction of great literature during the **Harlem Renaissance**.

©E. Elcha/Anthony Barboza/Archive Pictures/Getty Images

Cabaret singer and dancer Florence Mills became an international star. She was known for her delicate voice, vibrant stage presence, and wide-eyed beauty.

> **Harlem Renaissance** refers to the literary and artistic movement centered in Harlem in New York City during the 1920s and 30s.

May be reproduced for classroom use. *Toolkit Texts: Short Nonfiction for American History, Industrial Age and Immigration,* by Stephanie Harvey and Anne Goudvis, ©2021 (Portsmouth, NH: Heinemann).

May be reproduced for classroom use. *Toolkit Texts: Short Nonfiction for American History, Industrial Age and Immigration*, by Stephanie Harvey and Anne Goudvis, ©2021 (Portsmouth, NH: Heinemann).

We Are Americans:
"Escaping the South in 1924"

Mildred Arnold was part of the Great Migration. She came to Newark, New Jersey, from the South in 1924 when she was ten years old. The first leg of her journey was from the small town of North, South Carolina, to the city of Columbia, where a train could take her north. At the time, Southern communities often tried to prevent African Americans from leaving so they would not lose their cheap labor.

"My daddy had to leave North at night. He had to get somebody with a horse and buggy to drive him to Columbia. But the next morning the man who drove him had to be back so they wouldn't know what [he] did that night. He had to be back the next morning to go to work just like he hadn't been anyplace.

[Several months later my daddy] sent my mother some money and she got us all ready. It was just before the Fourth of July holiday. . . . There was a lady in Columbia who was like the underground railroad, like things you read about. Her place was a stopping off place. . . . When you got to Columbia, you could lay over at her place until you could get out; she would put you up.

So my mother came up to the station that Saturday morning; we were all dressed. Not too much baggage. The baggage was gone; our clothes were gone. They were taken the night before. . . . We had just enough like we were going up to Columbia for the day.

We children were on the platform; I was the oldest. We didn't talk to anyone because you didn't want to let the white people know what was going on. You didn't dare. All my mother wanted to do was to get that train so she could get to Columbia. So we had to be very quiet. . . .

[Finally the family reached New York City.] My father and uncle met us at the Pennsylvania Railroad Station and brought us up here to Newton Street [in Newark, New Jersey], right across from the Newton Street School. We came on the trolley. . . . Oh Lord, to come up South Orange Avenue on that trolley car, that was something. I never rode on a trolley before; I had never even seen a trolley. I was saying to myself, 'What is this? We can ride like this?'. . . . Everything was amazing. . . . You had a lot of gaslights in Newark. When they came on in the nighttime . . . the streets lit up. We had never seen anything like that. Down South, when the sun went down there was only darkness."

Excerpted from:
We Are Americans: Voices of the Immigrant Experience by Thomas Hoobler and Dorothy Hoobler. New York, NY: Scholastic. 2003.

Excerpt from

THE GREAT MIGRATION
JOURNEY TO THE NORTH

Toolkit Texts: Short Nonfiction for American History, Industrial Age and Immigration, by Stephanie Harvey and Anne Goudvis, ©2021 (Portsmouth, NH: Heinemann).

Between 1915 and 1930, more than a million African Americans left their homes in the South, the southern part of the United States, and moved to the North. This moved was named the "Great Migration."

In the South, members of the Ku Klux Klan were attacking African Americans, making it unsafe for them to live there. There were "White Only" signs on water fountains, in lunchrooms, and other places, meaning that only white people could use them. Many African Americans could not find jobs in the areas where they lived. For all of these reasons, African Americans, in large numbers, began to move away.

When they reached the North, they found that it was far from perfect. They had not escaped racial discrimination. Even so, things were better, and most people stayed in their new cities and worked hard to earn a living and take care of their children.

In August of 1929, when I was three months old, my father took the train northward from our home in Parmele, North Carolina, to Washington, D.C. My parents had heard from relatives and friends who had already moved to Washington how much better life was for them. Although Washington was not quite in the North, many North Carolinians and other southerners settled there.

My father found a job and a place for us to live. A month later, after he had saved enough money for train fare, he sent it to us, so that my mother, my brother, and I could join him. I was too little to know it then, but I had become a part of the Great Migration.

—Eloise Greenfield

Eloise Greenfield is an American children's book author and poet famous for her descriptive, rhythmic writing style and positive portrayal of the Black American experience.

MY FAMILY:

Parmele, North Carolina.
Nice town. Not many jobs, though,
in 1929. Not enough work
for Daddy, a man with a wife
and two children.
Some people were moving north.
Mama and Daddy read about it,
heard about it, from cousins
and friends. "Come north," they said.
"Come to Washington, D.C."
August. Mama and Daddy
wait at the station for Daddy's train.
Sad to separate, even for a little while.
Maybe longer. Who knows?
They say goodbye, but Mama
doesn't cry. Yet. She walks
the road home, alone. Sits on the
porch and lets the tears fall.

One long month and the money
comes. Train ticket money.
Daddy's found a job and a place
for us to live. "All aboard!"
the conductor calls. Not an easy trip
for Mama. Two babies to care for.
Me, four months old, my
big brother, Wilbur, eighteen
months. A long ride, and then,
"Wash-ing-ton!" the conductor
Calls. We're home.

We are one family
among the many thousands.
Mama and Daddy leaving home,
coming to the city, with their
hopes and courage,
their dreams and their children,
to make a better life.

MUDDY WATERS
AND THE BLUES

Blues: a type of music that includes a wide range of emotions and musical styles that was started in the South in the 1870s by Black Americans

THE BLUES AND THE GREAT MIGRATION

Between the 1920s and the 1940s, hundreds of thousands of Black Americans left their homes in the rural South in search of job opportunities, better living conditions, and increased racial justice. During this "Great Migration," as it came to be known, large numbers of Black people settled in cities such as Memphis, Tennessee, and Chicago, Illinois. As Black people moved to these and other urban centers, they brought the music of the Delta with them. This music was called the **blues**. Memphis was the first stop on the road north. Here, the mixing of cultures from various areas produced a more rhythmic music that used the harmonica, horns, and pianos.

A NEW MUSICAL SOUND

In Chicago, the use of electricity changed the blues forever. In cities, musicians could not rely on a simple acoustic guitar to carry the music over noisy audiences. During the 1940s and 1950s, Chicago blues musicians made the blues more modern by amplifying their instruments and using microphones. One of these musical pioneers was singer-guitarist Muddy Waters. He combined popular swinging rhythms with Delta slide guitar and powerful vocals to create a groundbreaking record in 1948.

Muddy Waters' cutting-edge sound was immediately popular in cities. Performing live, the Muddy Waters band created a new musical sound that would become a model for much of the popular music of the next 50 years. Muddy's influence changed the face of the blues and shaped the music that would become known as rock and roll.

MUDDY'S EARLY LIFE

McKinley Morganfield (later known as Muddy Waters) was born on April 4, 1915, in the Mississippi delta. As a child and young adult, he endured the hard life of a **sharecropper**. In the rural South, sharecropping was an exploitative arrangement for many Black families. Farmers who rented land to grow crops often ended up owing their landlord for seeds, tools, and other supplies. They were rarely able to earn enough money to buy their own land or improve their situation. His grandmother nicknamed him Muddy when he was a young boy and the kids at school added Waters. He began to use his childhood nickname as his stage name, Muddy Waters. Muddy's father, Ollie Morganfield, was also a talented musician and guitarist. In the South of 1943, racism was a way of life. Muddy left Mississippi and made his way to Chicago, where he made his name as a blues musician. During the day he worked odd jobs and at night he played the blues.

AN INTERNATIONAL STAR

By 1950, Muddy was making records and was famous all over the United States. "Rollin' Stone," one of his singles, became so popular that it went on to influence the name of the major music magazine. "The Rolling Stones" became one of the most famous rock bands of all time. Muddy Waters went on to become an international star. By the end of his lifetime, Muddy Waters had won six **Grammy Awards**, as well as countless other honors. In 1987, he was inducted into the Rock and Roll Hall of Fame.

To listen to blues songs and learn more about the blues music, visit teachrock.org.

Sharecropper:
a farmer who rents a small plot of land and gives part of his crop to the landowner

Grammy Award:
an award presented to musicians to recognize achievements in the music industry, such as song or album of the year

AN INTERVIEW WITH MUDDY WATERS

"GOT A RIGHT TO SING THE BLUES"

As told to Alfred Duckett
Excerpted from the *Chicago Defender*, March 26, 1955

"In my lifetime, I've seen a lot of progress and a lot of Southerners getting to learn to appreciate my people as human beings. . . . I'm not up on a platform preaching, I make my living recording blues which sell to millions of people all over the country . . . and singing in nightclubs which fortunately for me, are usually jammed with people who want to hear my music.

"In boyhood, I always had an ear for the blues. I loved the blues. I guess I was born with two things—trouble and love for the blues. . . . My daddy played a guitar in his day. But a good buddy of mine . . . taught me the guitar after I'd been fooling around with a harmonica. [I began writing songs] and people down home liked and appreciated my music. They understood it.

"[When I moved to Chicago] . . . I didn't intend to give up my determination to play the blues. People began to listen to the blues, they began to realize that these blues expressed their own feelings when they were low or discouraged. . . . The way to defeat [these feelings] is to look [them] straight in the eye. That's what I was doing when I sang my blues."

Four Themes of
Immigration

A melting pot. A mosaic. A salad bowl. Those are some ways to describe the United States as a nation of immigrants. But is that really true? What if we thought about immigration in a very different way? Instead, we could say . . .

- Some of us were already here.
- Some of us were forced to come here.
- Some of us were caught up or incorporated into the United States as borders changed.
- Some of us came here voluntarily.

An exhibit at the Smithsonian's National Museum of American History, One Nation, Many Voices, offers an exciting new take on immigration and migration in our history. This exhibit challenges us to think beyond immigration as it occurred in the 19th and early 20th centuries. The exhibit begins much earlier in our history, with the indigenous people who were here first. Then we look at how the movements of people across and within our nation's boundaries shaped the history of our country.

Some of us were already here.

A short history of how people who were already here were displaced and their traditional way of life changed forever.

Diverse groups of Native peoples speaking about 500 languages lived in what is now the United States when Columbus arrived (around 1500). They had lived on the North American continent for thousands of years. While no one knows for sure, historians estimate that from 50 to 75 million people lived on the continent around

Cliff Palace, Mesa Verde's largest cliff dwelling, is where the Ancestral Pueblo people made their home for over 700 years, from 600 to 1300.

1500. Beginning in the 1500s and into the 1600s, according to Smithsonian historians, "hundreds of thousands of Europeans and Africans [came] to the North American continent, where Native peoples had lived for millennia. . . . What happened next was a profound unsettling of long-established societies." Disease, brought by Europeans coming to North America, swept through Native populations that lacked **immunity**, killing a large percentage of the **indigenous** population. What followed for the Native Americans on the continent was a long

struggle to hold onto their lands, traditions, and languages. Sometimes Native people, like the Pueblo, resisted those who were moving into their tribal nations. Sometimes Native nations, like the Cherokee and other Southeastern groups, **assimilated** to the people and cultures intent on building settlements and farming on their traditional lands. It's a story of conflict and change, as those who were here first encountered people and events that would forever alter their cultures, languages, and way of life. But one thing remains. The original inhabitants are still here: Today, about three million American citizens are members of 574 Native nations.

Recording Events Through Native American Ledger Art

Traditional artists of the Plains nations used images to record important knowledge and events, painting narratives on tipis, buffalo robes, shields, and other objects. Using new materials brought by European colonists trading and coming to live on the plains, Native artists used ledger and accounting books to document their side of the

In this drawing from a ledger book, a Kiowa warrior is coming down from his lookout hill. He carries a pair of field glasses, possibly acquired through trading, which he used to discover the cavalry unit riding nearby. The Kiowa tribesmen welcome the scout back to camp.

Immunity: being able to resist a disease

Indigenous: those who lived in a country or a region at the time when people of different cultures or ethnic origins arrived. They are also known as Native people.

Assimilate: to gradually change a person or group's language and culture from their home country and adopt the language and practices of another group

May be reproduced for classroom use. *Toolkit Texts: Short Nonfiction for American History, Industrial Age and Immigration*, by Stephanie Harvey and Anne Goudvis, ©2021 (Portsmouth, NH: Heinemann).

Black Hawk (Makataimesbekiakiak—Sauk)

story of the conflicts that occurred over land, as well as other aspects of life from the mid-1800s through the early 1900s.

The Words of Black Hawk, Chief of the Sauk and Fox Indians: Land Cannot Be Sold

Many tribal leaders spoke out and fought against what was happening to their people. Black Hawk, Chief of the Sauk and Fox Indians, led a resistance movement in the Northwest Territory that became known as the Black Hawk War of 1832. Black Hawk's goal was to keep European colonists from settling on the traditional lands of the Sauk people. Chief Black Hawk's words illustrate his beliefs that the land belongs to those who lived on it and cared for it. These beliefs differed from those held by European colonists.

"My reason teaches me that Land cannot be sold. The Great Spirit gave it to his children to live upon, and cultivate as far as is necessary for their subsistence, and so long as they occupy and cultivate it, they have the right to the soil. . . . Nothing can be sold but such things as can be carried away."

The Trail of Tears

As the number of European colonists increased in the 1700s, both the U.S. government and the new arrivals forced Native American tribes off their lands east of the Mississippi River. Sometimes these newcomers purchased the land. Other times, federal legislation and treaties, which were often broken by government authorities, forced Native peoples to give up their land.

In one of the most tragic examples of Native American displacement, the **Indian Removal Act** of 1830 signed by then President Andrew Jackson, decreed that Native people in the Southern regions be removed and resettled on land west of the Mississippi River. This land was considered the "American desert," far less suitable for farming and grazing animals than the nations' ancestral lands in the South. The Choctaw people were the first to be removed from their lands in 1831–33.

In 1838, army troops began rounding up the Cherokees, removing them from their homes and forcing them to walk almost 1,200 miles from Georgia to Oklahoma. The sick, the young, and the elderly rode in wagons, while the others trudged on foot through winter weather. Hunger, exposure, and disease took their toll. This terrible forced migration became known as the *Trail of Tears*. Tragically, 4,000 Cherokees, about one quarter of the population, died on the journey.

Broken Promises

By the late 1800s, even those Native peoples who lived west of the Mississippi came into conflict with the growing presence of permanent European Americans. In many parts of the West, traditional hunting and farming lands were taken from Native peoples as a result of unfair treaties or government orders. Most of the bison that they had relied on for food (meat), tools (bones), and shelter and clothing (hides) were killed. Some nations, such as the

> **Indian Removal Act:** a U.S. government law that systematically removed independent Native nations from their ancestral lands in the South, including the Chickasaw, Choctaw, Muskogee-Creek, Seminole, and Cherokee people

The Cherokee people suffered on the Trail of Tears, which took its name from the Cherokee phrase Nunna daul Tsuny, meaning "The Trail Where They Cried."

Sioux and the Apaches, fought back and resisted efforts by the U.S. government to take their land and force them onto **reservations**. But they ultimately were no match for the U.S. Army. Unable to save their land or their way of life through negotiation or battle, most tribes found themselves forced to live on reservations by the end of the 1800s.

We Are Still Here

In the United States today, there are 574 Native nations. Across the United States in recent years, Native peoples from many tribes have fought to protect sacred sites on their ancestral lands. Here we share an example of how members of one sovereign nation are reclaiming their land and their traditional way of life.

> **Reservation:** area of land set aside for use by Native American tribes by the U.S. government to make way for European settlement. Today, Native peoples living on reservations have the right to govern themselves and to maintain their cultural traditions.

Snoqualmie Tribe. In the hills east of Seattle, Washington, the members of the Snoqualmie Tribe prayed, collected signatures, and appealed to Congress to stop construction of new houses and a convention center to preserve the land they hold sacred, including a towering waterfall.

In November 2019, Snoqualmie tribal leaders stood by the roaring waterfall and announced that they had finally succeeded in acquiring and conserving the land where their ancestors were buried. "We have reclaimed our most sacred and traditional land," said Snoqualmie Tribal Chairman Robert de los Angeles. "We have taken another step toward healing the desecration of this area." In March 2020, the tribe also won a court ruling that returned additional Native lands to the tribe that were promised in a broken treaty with the U.S. government many years ago. This will expand the reservation lands and restore the tribe's right to govern the land as a sovereign nation.

Tribal members have lived in the Northwest region since time immemorial. Long before explorers came to the Pacific Northwest, tribe

May be reproduced for classroom use. *Toolkit Texts: Short Nonfiction for American History, Industrial Age and Immigration,* by Stephanie Harvey and Anne Goudvis, ©2021 (Portsmouth, NH: Heinemann).

Carol M. Highsmith Archive, Library of Congress, Prints and Photographs Division, [50924]

Members of the Snoqualmie tribe believe that mist rising from the Snoqualmie Falls, a 270-foot-high waterfall east of Seattle, lifts their prayers.

Gift of Joseph H. Hirshhorn to the Smithsonian Institution in 1966

Artifacts, like this bronze plaque from Benin, give us a window into the well-established cultures of West Africa. This plaque depicts members of the noble court with beaded necklaces and ornate hats.

members hunted deer and elk, fished for salmon, and gathered berries and wild plants for food and medicine. Today, members of the tribe live on the reservation and in surrounding communities. They are working to protect and preserve the environment of the Snoqualmie reservation and traditional tribal lands through stream habitat and water quality improvement projects, recycling, and energy conservation.

Some of us were forced to come here.

A short history of how enslaved people were forced to came to this continent, and how they migrated and moved once they were here.

For centuries, Africa was the home of many ancient and diverse cultures, with over 800 languages spread across the continent. Large West African kingdoms, such as Mali and Benin, in addition to large cities like Timbuktu, had plentiful resources coveted by Portuguese, Spanish, Dutch, and English companies that built trading posts along the coast. In the 1600s, Europeans colonists in the Americas looked to profit off of the land and resources by exploiting the Native people. At first, Europeans enslaved indigenous people living in both North and South America to work on farms and plantations. Beginning in 1619, West Africans were tragically captured and sold to British and European slave traders.

The Middle Passage

Most Africans arrived in the Americas, starting in 1619, as enslaved people. Captured in Africa, they were sold to British and European slave traders and brought on ships to many places in both North and South America, as well as the Caribbean islands. This destroyed the populations of West Africa and brought about vast changes to people and cultures across the Americas, Europe, and Africa. The terrifying sea voyage from Africa to the Americas was known as the **Middle Passage**. Estimates suggest that as many as two million captured Africans died on the journey,

> **The Middle Passage:** the sea journey undertaken by slave ships to transport enslaved people from West Africa across the Atlantic Ocean

©Ariadne Van Zandbergen/Alamy Stock Photo

Oppression: cruel and unjust treatment

Abolitionists: people who worked to end, or abolish, slavery

Plantation: a large farm that grows cotton, tobacco, coffee, or sugarcane where enslaved people were forced to do the work

The Cape Coast Castle, on the coast of Ghana, was where kidnapped and enslaved Africans were imprisoned before being sent on slave ships to the Americas.

before ever reaching the Americas. It's estimated that about 300,000 enslaved people were brought to the 13 colonies before 1776.

Resisting Oppression and Escaping

The life of an enslaved person was one of abuse, violence, and unending work. Many enslaved people risked everything, including their lives, to resist **oppression** by slave owners and escape.

The decision to escape presented an extremely difficult choice for enslaved people, as they often had to leave behind loved ones, who were sometimes punished in the place of the person who had fled. Beginning in the 1830s, the Underground Railroad emerged as a network of secret routes and safe houses that helped enslaved

people journey from one place to another on their way to some of the Northern states and Canada. The Underground Railroad had routes of escape, called *tracks*, safe houses along the way called *stations*, and runaways, called *passengers*. Those who assisted the escape, often **abolitionists**, were called *conductors*. Some conductors, like Harriet Tubman, had escaped from slavery. She became famous for guiding more than 300 enslaved people to freedom in the North and Canada.

The Second Middle Passage

As the U.S. government forced Native peoples to give up their traditional lands in the South (in what is now Alabama, Louisiana, and Mississippi as well as parts of Georgia), **plantation** owners

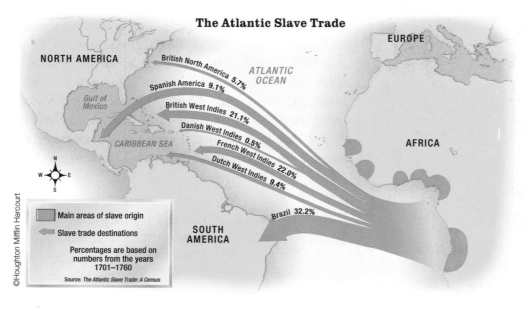

This map of the transatlantic slave trade illustrates the areas of West Africa from which enslaved people came, as well as the colonies and other parts of the Americas where they were taken.

May be reproduced for classroom use. *Toolkit Texts: Short Nonfiction for American History, Industrial Age and Immigration,* by Stephanie Harvey and Anne Goudvis, ©2021 (Portsmouth, NH: Heinemann).

Black communities and abolitionists protected people on their dangerous journeys, providing food, clothing, medical assistance, and even jobs.

©Paul Collins/www.collinsart.org

saw economic opportunity and moved in to start planting cotton. The Atlantic slave trade—importing people from Africa to the United States—had ended in 1808. Enslavers ruthlessly expanded the domestic slave trade by increasing the number of enslaved people. Entire families were sold by tobacco farmers in Virginia, Maryland, and the Carolinas to owners of cotton plantations in the Deep South, who were willing to pay a lot of money for enslaved people to harvest cotton. This led to what's been called the Second Middle Passage, or the internal slave trade. Living and working conditions were dramatically worse for enslaved people in the Deep South, and it was much more difficult to reconnect with other family members. From 1790 to 1860, one million enslaved African Americans were forced to migrate into the Deep South.

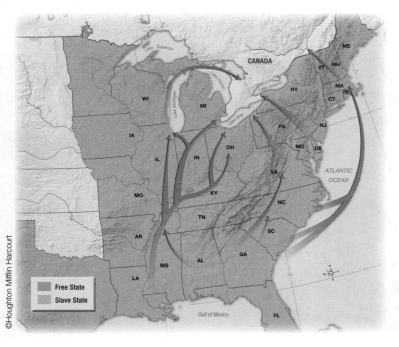

This map shows some of the major routes of the Underground Railroad.

The Homestead Act of 1862 helped create more than 372,000 farms and enabled Black Americans, such as the Shores family (above), to start new lives out West.

The Great Exodus: Exodusters

After the Civil War, the West beckoned to Black people, many of whom who were still working on plantations as **sharecroppers** in order to survive. In the spring of 1879, a mass migration of some 6,000 Black people from the South began heading for Kansas, Nebraska, and other parts of the West. Eventually, an estimated 15,000 to 20,000 Black people were persuaded to move west, mostly on foot but sometimes by boat up the Mississippi River. They became known as the Exodusters. They created communities such as Nicodemus, Kansas, and other towns where they were able to own their own land and escape the prejudice and racial violence of the South.

The Great Migration

Between 1910 and 1940, almost two million Black Americans left their homes in the Southern part of the United States, and moved to cities in the North and West. One of the largest internal migrations in U.S. history, this movement was called the *Great Migration*. In the South, Blacks faced overwhelming racial and economic discrimination.

Sharecropper: a farmer who rented a small plot of land and gave part of his crop to the landowner, but rarely earned enough money to buy his own land or improve his situation

Many of the Black men and women who came to Chicago between 1910 and 1930 started businesses and became entrepreneurs. The Perfect Eat Shop, a restaurant near South Park, is an example of a prosperous Black-owned business.

Library of Congress, 8d03731

May be reproduced for classroom use. *Toolkit Texts: Short Nonfiction for American History, Industrial Age and Immigration*, by Stephanie Harvey and Anne Goudvis, ©2021 (Portsmouth, NH: Heinemann).

The French and Spanish established colonies and missions on land where Native peoples lived and farmed. Many Native peoples resisted efforts to suppress their spiritual beliefs and practices. Yet many other Native Americans did find meaning in new Christian teachings. Across the continent, people sometimes joined new and old religious elements to create new beliefs.

Library of Congress, 18202

State, local, and federal laws enforced racial segregation in stores, restaurants, schools, libraries, buses, and other places. Many could not find jobs in the areas where they lived. For all of these reasons, Black people, in large numbers, began to move to cities outside the South for more opportunities.

When they reached Northern cities, Blacks still faced considerable prejudice and racial segregation. But they built new communities together, found work where they could earn a living and began new lives.

Some of us were caught up or incorporated into the United States as borders changed.

Many people came to live in the United States because they were caught up as borders moved.

Beginning in the 1500s, explorers from European countries like Spain and France, as well as England, came to seek their fortunes on the North American continent. Over many years, the Spanish started settlements in what is now Florida and Louisiana, the Southwest (Texas, New Mexico, Colorado), and California. The French claimed much of the middle of what is now the United States. Great Britain claimed the Oregon Territory in what is now the Northwest.

In 1803, the size of the United States almost doubled with the Louisiana Purchase. The U.S. government bought this region from France, and this encouraged

In less than 50 years, the United States grew from the Mississippi River to the Pacific Ocean, starting with the Louisiana Purchase and ending with the territories gained from Mexico.

©GeoSystems for Houghton Mifflin Harcourt

CANADA

49

British treaty line 1818

OREGON COUNTRY 1846

LOUISIANA PURCHASE 1803

MEXICAN CESSION 1848

UNITED STATES 1783

PACIFIC OCEAN

GADSDEN PURCHASE 1853

TEXAS ANNEXATION 1845

ATLANTIC OCEAN

MEXICO

Gulf of Mexico

FLORIDA 1819

177

Ceded: to give up or surrender land

Annexed: to add land or a territory so as to become a part of a country

Tejanos of Texas, **Nuevo Mexicanos** in New Mexico, and the **Californios** of Los Angeles were people of Latin American descent who arrived in Mexico hundreds of years ago. Most brought with them the cultural traditions from Spain and Mexico, spoke Spanish, and owned cattle ranches or large farms.

Mestizo: people of mixed European and indigenous ancestry

Photographer Dorothea Lange captured this image of a family from Mexico entering the United States at the immigration station in El Paso, Texas in 1938. Mexican immigrants and their descendants now make up a significant portion of the U.S. population and have become one of the most influential social and cultural groups in the country.

Americans to move even further west and south. In 1819, Spain **ceded** the Florida territory to the United States. Mexico had taken over much of California and other parts of the Southwest from the Spanish, land that it ceded to the United States after the Mexican–American War in 1848. And the independent territory of Texas was **annexed** to the United States and became a state in 1845.

The Southern Border

The United States and Mexico have shaped each other's borders, identities, and cultures over hundreds of years. The United States–Mexico border is often portrayed today as a place of political and ethnic divisions. Yet shared history, commerce, and labor contribute to the rich and dynamic culture along the nearly 2,000-mile border spanning California, Arizona, New Mexico, and Texas.

The United States and Mexico went to war in 1846 over the territory known as Texas, which was then a part of Mexico. In February 1848, a treaty was signed in a small Mexican town called La Villa de Guadalupe Hidalgo. Under the Treaty of Guadalupe Hidalgo, the two nations agreed that Mexico would give up more than half of its land in return for $15 million. This included areas now known as California, Texas, Nevada, Utah, and parts of Arizona, New Mexico, Colorado, and Wyoming. Now, seemingly overnight, 525,000 square miles, or about half of Mexico's territory, became part of the United States.

As a result, all of the people in these areas—including the **Tejanos** of Texas, **Nuevo Mexicanos** in New Mexico, and the **Californios** of Los Angeles, as well as Native people and **mestizo** people—found themselves in a new nation, even though they were on the same land they and their ancestors had lived on for generations. In this new reality, they would be living under leaders who didn't understand their faith, language, or cultures. In July 1849, the U.S. government announced that anyone still living in California or anywhere in the rest of the former Mexican territory would automatically become a U.S. citizen. What does it mean to become a citizen of a country that

Library of Congress, 8b20985

By the end of the 19th century, many Mexican Americans had been deprived of their land, and found themselves living in a hostile region. They created a new type of popular music—the *corrido*, or border ballad. These storytelling songs carried news of current events and popular legends around the border region. Passed from one singer to another, many of these songs survive to the present day.

has conquered you? What do you do when the border moves? Mexicans who had long been established in California struggled to retain their culture, property, and political influence as Americans set their sights on the territory.

Borderland Today

The land around the United States–Mexico border has been defined by interactions among many cultural groups, including Native peoples, Mexicans, European Americans, and migrants from around the globe. These roots influence the art, music, stories, architecture, and other aspects of the culture of those living on the border. It is an area where cultures and identities are created and blended. The borderlands show us that multiple stories of racial and ethnic difference make up America.

Some of us came here voluntarily.

*Many people came to live in the United States by choice
for many different reasons.*

People came to our nation for many different reasons. Some fled their home countries because their lives were endangered due to extreme poverty, war, religious persecution, and other difficult conditions. For some immigrants, leaving their homeland was a painful decision, but also one that offered the promise of better life. Others came because they saw economic and educational opportunities not available to them in their home countries. These opportunities and hope for a better future propelled countless immigrants to embark on journeys to these shores, often leaving loved ones behind in their home countries.

Throughout the rest of this resource, peoples' perspectives and experiences, as well as their challenges and successes, are told through their stories. But there is no one single story when it comes to immigration. In her talk "The Danger of a Single Story," Chimamanda Ngozi Adiche reminds us that inherent in the power of stories is a danger—the danger of knowing only one story about a people or culture. When many different voices are shared, there is a greater chance of understanding the issues surrounding immigration in the past, present, and future.

America is a place of many stories. Listen to and honor the stories of American history, as well as the stories in your neighborhood, school, and community today.

May be reproduced for classroom use. *Toolkit Texts: Short Nonfiction for American History, Industrial Age and Immigration*, by Stephanie Harvey and Anne Goudvis, ©2021 (Portsmouth, NH: Heinemann).

Four Themes of Immigration
Suggested Resources

In creating the *Many Voices, One Nation* exhibit at the Smithsonian's National Museum of American History, museum educators began by surveying how immigration is taught in schools. They found that the history of immigration, as it's frequently covered, is not the whole story. Often, the study of immigration begins in the mid-1800s, with first arrivals at Ellis Island, followed by waves of immigrants for years to come. But there are many other important migration stories that suggest a more accurate and inclusive way of thinking about the movements of people, cultures, and events over time in our history. We hope the brief overview you just read inspires you to dig deeper into these examples of displacement, enslavement, migration, and border changes.

In order to have a more expansive view of these four themes of immigration, we recommend the following resources.

The Smithsonian exhibit **Many Voices, One Nation** at the National Museum of American History, Washington, D.C., offers new perspectives and a more accurate and inclusive take on immigration and migration throughout American history.

www.americanhistory.si.edu/many-voices-exhibition

Becoming US is a new educational resource for middle and high school teachers and students to learn immigration and migration history from educators at the National Museum of American History.

https://americanhistory.si.edu/becoming-us/

The 1619 Project is an ongoing initiative from *The New York Times Magazine* that "aims to reframe American history, placing the consequences of slavery and the contributions of Black Americans at the very center of our national narrative."

https://www.nytimes.com/interactive/2019/08/14/magazine/1619-america-slavery.html

Re-imagining Migration, a project by University of California, Los Angeles, emphasizes culturally responsive pedagogy and how teachers can integrate this into their instruction. "Our mission is to ensure that all young people grow up understanding migration as a shared condition of our past, present, and future in order to develop the knowledge, empathy and mindsets that sustain inclusive and welcoming communities."

https://reimaginingmigration.org

Voyages: The Transatlantic Slave Trade Database is a free online database sponsored by the National Endowment for the Humanities that incorporates 40 years of archival research and brings together images, maps, voyage logs, and other records of about 35,000 transatlantic slave ship crossings.

https://www.neh.gov/news/voyages-the-transatlantic-slave-trade-database

Teaching Tolerance offers resources for both teachers and students to promote an accurate understanding of immigration history and current-day issues. Lessons help teachers address immigration myths, research changing demographics, and explore the value of a diverse society.

https://www.tolerance.org/topics/immigration

An Indigenous Peoples' History of the United States for Young People. 2019. Roxanne Dunbar-Ortiz, adapted by Jean Mendoza and Debbie Reese. Boston, MA: Beacon Press. "Dunbar-Ortiz reveals the roles that settler colonialism and the policies of American Indian genocide played in forming our national identity."

WAVES OF IMMIGRATION

The stories included here reflect the experiences of those who came voluntarily.

Immigrants arrived in waves, but they always arrived. In the early 1800s, they came because they could buy land cheaply. Later, during the Industrial Revolution, they came to work in factories. Economic growth led to many opportunities for jobs in industry as well as agriculture. People also left their home countries because of poverty, war, persecution, and other difficult conditions.

When we think about why immigration has ebbed and peaked over time, we ask four questions:

◆ Why did people come to the United States?
◆ Why did people leave their home countries?
◆ How did they make the journey?
◆ Will they be allowed in?

That fourth question—"Will they be allowed in?"—is one that is relevant today. And the answer to it, as you will see, has varied over the last 150 years. Until 1882—that's almost 100 years after the United States became independent—the answer was almost always "yes." The doors were wide open for those who could afford to pay for passage and food on a ship. And once they arrived in port, immigrants could count on walking off the ship into American life. Almost everyone was allowed in. Only those with contagious diseases, like yellow fever or smallpox, were held back in **quarantine** until they recovered.

Quarantine:
a place of isolation for people who arrived from another country and may have been sick or exposed to disease

May be reproduced for classroom use. *Toolkit Texts: Short Nonfiction for American History, Industrial Age and Immigration,* by Stephanie Harvey and Anne Goudvis, ©2021 (Portsmouth, NH: Heinemann).

Potato blight: a devastating disease that infected potatoes and ruined the potato crop in Ireland in the 1840s

RIPPLES THEN WAVES: FROM THE EARLY 1800S TO 1850

In the early 1800s, immigrants arrived at a slow and steady pace. Land owners made a profit by selling land to people who were able to buy it, move their families, and start farming. Open land wasn't available in their home countries. Most of the arrivals were from northern and western Europe, where it was possible to cross the Atlantic in as little as a month. The small sailing ships mostly carried cargo, but each one could carry some passengers. Most of the immigrants had some money, were Protestant, and could read and write.

All that changed in the 1840s, when a **potato blight** brought famine to Ireland and the first big wave of immigrants to the United States. Many Irish depended on potatoes as their main food. When the potato crop was ruined by disease, starvation and poverty pushed these mostly Catholic Irish to flee to the United States. In fact, one-half the population of Ireland came to America. New, faster ships could cross the Atlantic in just two weeks. These ships carried cargo and had accommodations for many passengers. The Irish couldn't afford the first- or second-class cabins. They traveled in dormitories below decks called steerage. In America, they landed on the East Coast and found jobs digging canals and building the railroads.

Another wave brought in Germans. They had been arriving since the 1830s, but economic hardships convinced many more to leave for the United States. Some came with money, and they headed west where they settled in cities like Milwaukee and St. Louis. Between 1845 and 1855, the wave carried a million Germans into the United States.

Meanwhile, on the West Coast, the discovery of gold tempted large numbers of people to come to California. When news of the gold rush reached China, the first of more than 300,000 Chinese men took the long trip across the Pacific Ocean to the United States. They hoped to make their fortunes in gold but miners who were already there wanted to protect their own jobs, so they pushed them out. Many Chinese then turned to working on the railroads.

Library of Congress, 3b10519

This photo illustrates the experience of immigrants traveling to the United States. In good weather, steerage passengers could leave their crowded quarters in the ship's hold for some light and air.

A NATIVIST MOVEMENT: THE 1840S AND BEYOND

The large numbers of Catholics from Ireland and Germany alarmed some Americans. Religious prejudice sparked a nativist movement that emerged in the Northeast and spread to other parts of the country. The **nativists** were American-born Protestants who wanted to keep people from other countries out of the United States. Working-class nativists thought the Irish were taking their jobs. They attacked Irish homes and churches

Nativists were opposed to immigration by any group of people who were born outside of the United States. Nativist beliefs were often grounded in both cultural and religious prejudices. Nativists believed they were the only true Americans and fought actively to keep other groups out of the United States.

Despite discrimination and violence, the Chinese population grew. In this photo, Chinese "children of high class" walk in San Francisco with their father. Chinese merchants and businessmen urged the state of California to provide education for their children.

in Philadelphia, New York, and Boston during riots in the 1840s. Nativists tried to make it harder for people to become citizens.

The Chinese also faced waves of prejudice and laws designed to keep them out. In 1882, the United States decided to stop Chinese laborers from entering the United States. It was the first time, but not the last, that the U.S. government decided to bar immigration from a specific racial group. Immigrants from other Asian countries, such as Japan, were also banned. By the early 1900s, immigration from Asia was effectively closed.

THE "NEW" IMMIGRATION:
ANOTHER BIG WAVE AFTER 1865

More immigrants continued to find opportunity in the United States during and after the Civil War (1860s and 1870s). They tended to be from the same places as mid-century immigrants, many coming from Germany and the Scandinavian countries of Denmark, Norway, and Sweden.

But then, starting in the 1880s, two things changed. First, the federal government took over control of immigration. Second, new groups of people came, in big numbers.

Here's what happened: For the very first time, Congress passed laws about who could or couldn't come in. They excluded the Chinese completely,

This 1918 postcard shows Ellis Island, opened in 1892 to process immigrants arriving in New York City.

Library of Congress, 4a31821

Lines of drying laundry hang from the windows of tenements in New York's Manhattan, about 1900.

and also denied entry to convicted criminals, people who were unlikely to be able to work, and those with any illnesses or diseases. In the 1890s, new federal immigration stations, like the one on Ellis Island, opened.

Meanwhile, the new arrivals came in great numbers. Between 1881 and 1924, an estimated 23 million people entered the United States, mostly from southern and eastern Europe. They came from places like Austria, Greece, Hungary, Italy, Poland, and Russia. Desperately poor, most people did not know how to read or write and spoke no English. Terrible conditions and **persecution** in their home countries, for both Catholic and Jewish people, pushed them to leave for the United States. They also came to the United States because of the promise of jobs in America's new industries like iron, steel, and mining, and by the huge construction boom in U.S. cities. And faster steamships, with larger steerage areas that could transport more people, made the trip shorter and cheaper. Few had the money to head inland, so they settled in cities, where poor housing and greedy landlords created overcrowded and unhealthy conditions.

RESTRICTING IMMIGRATION: QUOTAS IN THE 1920S

Once again, some Americans viewed the latest arrivals as second-rate and unable to **assimilate**. The newest immigrants also were willing to work in the lowest-paying jobs. Nativists accused them of taking jobs away from Americans. By 1910, nearly 15% of the U.S. population was foreign-born. World War I (1914–1918) only increased nativist fears. Many Americans believed that there were too many immigrants to assimilate into an American way of life and the government should keep them out. The nativist push to limit immigration returned.

In 1921 and 1924, Congress passed laws that restricted immigration sharply. Racial and ethnic **discrimination** was built into these laws. The National Origins

Persecution: unfair and cruel treatment because of race, religion, or political beliefs

Assimilate: to gradually change a person or group's language and culture from their home country and adopt the language and practices of another group

Discrimination: the unjust treatment of people, based on their race

Children and adults who had to work during the day attended night school to learn English, like this class held in Boston. Americans who feared that there were too many immigrants often did not realize how hard immigrants struggled to become American.

Quotas: a limit on the number of people who could come from each country each year

Act of 1924 marked the first time you could say there was "a line" to get into the country. People had to get visas and wait for their turn in the **quota**. The newly established Border Patrol began to monitor the nation's borders in part to prevent the flow of immigrants. Until this time, the country's shared borders with Canada and Mexico were open and unrestricted

ANOTHER WAVE: 1925–1965

Over the next 40 years, fewer people came to the United States. In fact, during the **Great Depression** in the 1930s, more people left the United States than entered it. By 1970, less than 5% of the population was foreign-born.

All of that changed on August 3, 1965, when President Lyndon B. Johnson signed the Immigration and Nationality Act of 1965 that abolished the quota system. Johnson said the quota system had "violated the basic principle of American democracy."

President Lyndon Johnson signs the 1965 immigration reform bill into law at the Statue of Liberty, with New York City in the background.

The **Great Depression** was a time when America's economy was not working. Many businesses and banks failed. During this time, many people were out of work, hungry, and homeless. It affected people both rich and poor, from all cultural backgrounds and all religions, in both urban and rural sections of the country. In the city, people would stand in long lines at soup kitchens to get a bite to eat. In the country, farmers struggled in the Midwest where a great drought turned the soil into dust, causing huge dust storms.

National Park Service

Like many early immigrants, modern immigrants come to America to seek a better life. These new citizens take the oath of citizenship after completing the naturalization process.

The new system welcomed larger numbers of immigrants from all over the world, not just from Europe. People would be admitted, President Johnson said, "on the basis of their skills and their close relationship to those already here." This meant that those who were skilled workers or had family in the United States were given preference over others.

RECENT IMMIGRATION:
FROM 1965 TO THE PRESENT

Today the United States is more diverse and multicultural than ever. One hundred years ago, nearly 90% of immigrants were from Europe. In the last two decades, immigration from Europe has dropped to about 10%, while arrivals from Asia (including China, India, Korea, and Vietnam) make up close to 30% and those from the Americas (including Mexico, Cuba, the Dominican Republic, and El Salvador) have grown to about 50%. In 2019, recent arrivals are more likely to come from Asia than anyplace else.

National Park Service

This woman from Somalia shows off her citizenship certificate with great pride.

187

Source: U.S. Census Bureau, 1850–2000 Decennial Census; 2010 American Community Survey.

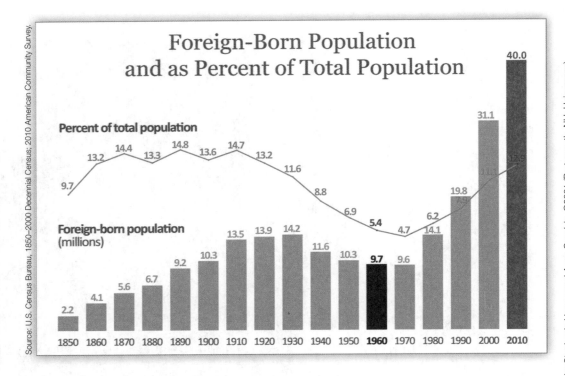

Foreign-Born Population and as Percent of Total Population

Percent of total population

9.7, 13.2, 14.4, 13.3, 14.8, 13.6, 14.7, 13.2, 11.6, 8.8, 6.9, 5.4, 4.7, 6.2, 11.7, 12.9

Foreign-born population (millions)

1850	1860	1870	1880	1890	1900	1910	1920	1930	1940	1950	**1960**	1970	1980	1990	2000	2010
2.2	4.1	5.6	6.7	9.2	10.3	13.5	13.9	14.2	11.6	10.3	**9.7**	9.6	14.1	19.8	31.1	40.0

May be reproduced for classroom use. *Toolkit Texts: Short Nonfiction for American History, Industrial Age and Immigration*, by Stephanie Harvey and Anne Goudvis, ©2021 (Portsmouth, NH: Heinemann).

Refugees: people who have been forced to leave their country in order to escape war, persecution, or natural disaster

At the same time, the issue of **refugees** seeking asylum and undocumented immigrants have become hot topics. In recent years, over 70 million people worldwide have been forced from their homes by conflict, persecution, or natural disasters. Some of them wish to enter the United States. An estimated 11 million people live in the country without documentation. The question for the future is: How will the United States address these issues?

International Rescue Committee Photo

After living in a refugee camp in Thailand for years, this family heads to a bus that will take them to the airport for the long trip to Salt Lake City. They are among the lucky few who were offered a chance to start a new life in the United States. Worldwide, just 1% of refugees are invited to resettle in a third country to rebuild their lives.

Library of Congress, Frances Benjamin Johnston Collection, 38995

Family Reunion
Ellis Island Experience

Editor's Note: While this is a fictional story, the following is based on facts about immigrants' experiences at Ellis Island and the photos are of real immigrants or scenes at Ellis Island.

Angelina's family endured a long journey to Ellis Island, like this group of women and children (above) coming from eastern Europe on deck of the *S.S. Amsterdam* around 1899.

Angelina Palmieri's heart pounded so hard, she thought it would leap from her chest. She was going to see Papa again!

Ten-year-old Angelina thought about Papa all the time—she missed him so much! But she also was nervous about seeing him after such a long time. Papa had not even met Angelina's youngest sister, Maria, who was born after he went to America.

Angelina's father had left the Palmieris' village of San Cataldo in Sicily, Italy, four years ago, when she was only six. He went to make a new life for his family in America, and now he was living with his brother in a place called Pittston, Pennsylvania. Papa's last letter contained tickets for Mama, Angelina, and her three sisters for a steamship voyage to New York. They had to travel in **steerage** because that was all Papa could afford.

Steerage is the section of the ship, usually near the bottom, that offers the cheapest passenger accommodations.

With as many of their belongings as they could stuff into suitcases, the Palmieri family took a seven-hour train ride to the port city of Palermo. There, they boarded the ship—called the *Sicilian Prince*—that would take them to America. Soon after their journey began, however, Angelina became sick with a fever and swollen glands along her neck.

She survived the 13-day voyage, and the *Sicilian Prince* pulled into New York Harbor on July 22, 1907. Its crew held back Angelina's family, as well as a large number of other passengers, but allowed some people to leave the ship.

"Why can't we get off like those people?" Angelina asked her mother.

"They might be Americans, or they might be passengers who traveled in **first or second class**. If you are new to America and traveled in steerage, like us, you have to go to Ellis Island first. They do not let just *anybody* into America."

Angelina began imagining the worst. What if she or Mama or her sisters were not allowed to enter this new country? Would she ever see them or Papa again?

The Palmieri family waited its turn to take the short ferry ride from the ship to Ellis Island. When Angelina, Mama, and the girls finally entered the Main Building at Ellis Island, all they could do was stare at the thousands of people. "How will Papa ever find us?" Angelina thought to herself.

First or second class is the most luxurious and expensive of accommodations.

Angelina and her sisters might have looked like these immigrant children who arrived at Ellis Island around 1915.

Fast Facts

The more official name for the great hall at Ellis Island was the registry room. The largest room in the main building, it was where immigrants went through their first round of questioning in the inspection process.

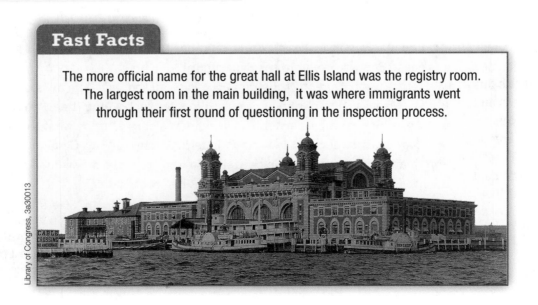

Library of Congress, George Grantham Bain Collection, 22287

Library of Congress, 3a30013

May be reproduced for classroom use. *Toolkit Texts: Short Nonfiction for American History, Industrial Age and Immigration,* by Stephanie Harvey and Anne Goudvis, ©2021 (Portsmouth, NH: Heinemann).

Waiting in line was a large part of the experience.
These immigrants sit and wait to be called for their final examination.

"Stay close together!" Mama said. Angelina, holding tightly to Maria's hand, could barely hear Mama above the tremendous noise in the building's baggage room. It was overwhelming to have so many different people speaking so many different languages all together in one area.

Officials in uniforms took papers out of Mama's hands. Someone attached a tag to Angelina's shoulder. She looked around and realized that everyone had on a tag that identified him or her by name, ship's name, and the page number of the ship's passenger list on which his or her name appeared. One official tried to take Angelina's luggage, but she resisted. She was not about to hand over her personal things, which included a special gift for Papa.

"Angelina, you must give them your satchel. You do not want to be carrying it with you all day." Mama pointed to a nearby mountain of luggage. "We will get it back before we leave, I promise."

With so many bags in the baggage room at Ellis Island, Angelina's worries about losing her satchel would not be unreasonable. Here, a child sits on his luggage while he waits.

By Barbara D. Krasner, *Cobblestone*, ©2006 by Carus Publishing Company. Reproduced with permission.

A doctor checks each immigrant for trachoma by folding back the upper eyelid (above left).

Reluctantly, Angelina let go of the satchel, and a worker ushered the Palmieri family toward a giant staircase. Prodded by officials and crowds of other immigrants, Angelina, Mama, and the girls walked up the stairs. At the top in the Great Hall, a doctor examined each member of the family as she walked toward him. The doctor spoke to Angelina, but she did not understand English.

"Tell him your name and walk a little for him," Mama instructed in Italian. "He wants to see if there is anything wrong with you." Angelina obeyed and then took her turn standing in front of more doctors, who were seated at a long table.

Another doctor approached Angelina with an instrument that looked like a buttonhook. Pulling her eyelid up, he checked to see if she had **trachoma**. The doctor also examined her nails and then her scalp for skin infections. Indications of any of these diseases were reasons for immigrants to be **detained** and subjected to more inspections—or worse, **deported**!

"X" Marks the Spot

Like many others who literally had "just gotten off the boat," Angelina feared being marked with chalk on her clothing. The immigrants knew that any labeling done in chalk was not a good sign. Sometimes a word, such as *hands*, *nails*, or *skin*, was written. More often, though, simple letters, like the following, spoke volumes about the wearer to immigration officials:

X = suspected mental defect
B = back
CT = trachoma
E = eyes
F = face
Ft = feet
H = heart
L = lameness
N = neck
Pg = pregnancy
Sc = scalp
S = senility

©Undrey/Shutterstock

Trachoma is a contagious eye disease that sometimes can cause blindness.

Detained means some immigrants were not allowed to leave Ellis Island, especially if they were ill.

Deported means some immigrants were sent back to their home country.

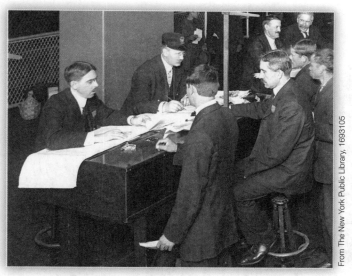

From The New York Public Library, 1693105

Like Angelina's mama, immigrants had to answer a barrage of questions about their background and their plans for life in America. Here, inspectors question travelers being registered in the Main Hall.

Although it took only a few minutes, to Angelina this process seemed to take hours. And there were so many questions! One wrong answer could send the whole family back to Sicily. Not understanding and afraid to respond, Angelina looked at Mama for reassurance.

When the doctor felt along the sides of Angelina's neck, she swallowed nervously, hoping her glands were no longer swollen. Then Angelina noticed a piece of chalk in the doctor's hand. She knew what chalk marks meant: detainment or deportation.

The doctor reached out to Angelina. She cringed and held her breath, but instead of a chalk mark on her coat, Angelina got a pat on the shoulder! She breathed a sigh of relief and smiled at him and Mama.

The legal inspection came next. Maria squirmed against Angelina as they waited in a long line until their ship number was called. Ever so slowly, the Palmieris moved along with others from the *Sicilian Prince*. Angelina's high-buttoned shoes pinched her toes, yet there was not even a bench on which to rest. She waved her shawl in front of her like a fan—it was growing very warm with all the people inside the building.

After several hours, the Palmieris approached the inspectors' desks at the back of the Great Hall. A man checked their tags and spoke to Mama in Italian. He asked a lot of questions: What is your name? Where were you born? Where are you going? Do you have relatives in America? Who paid for your passage? How much money do you have? Mama answered them all.

The inspector checked her responses against the information on the ship's manifest. He seemed to be satisfied.

One official handed "landing cards" to Mama, Angelina, and her sisters. Relieved and excited, they made their way back downstairs and collected their bags. As they walked out of the building, they spotted him: There was Papa, with his arms outstretched and his face beaming with joy!

In Greatest Numbers

Immigrants to America came from all over the world, including Cuba, China, India, Syria, Egypt, and Mexico. But most newcomers came from Europe between 1880 and 1920. Following is a list of those countries that had the greatest numbers of people coming to the United States:

Italy 4,600,000

Austro-Hungarian Empire 4,000,000
(Austria, Hungary, Czech Republic, Slovakia, Slovenia, Bosnia, Croatia, and parts of present-day Poland, Romania, Italy, Ukraine, Moldova, Serbia and Montenegro)

Russian Empire 3,300,000

German Empire 2,800,000

Britain 2,300,000

Canada 2,300,000

Ireland 1,700,000

Sweden 1,100,000

Photographs in the Carol M. Highsmith Archive, Library of Congress, Prints and Photographs Division, 14320

FROM EASTERN EUROPE TO AMERICA

Many Eastern European farmers (above) could not grow enough food to feed their families during the famine in the 1890s. Hundreds of thousands of people immigrated to the United States by 1910.

IN 1894, an 11-year-old girl named Maryashe Antin left her village of Plotzk, on the Dvina River in western Russia, to move to America. She wrote a narrative of her journey, beginning with her last days at home:

> "America" was in everybody's mouth. Business men talked of it over their accounts. . . . people who had relatives in the famous land went around reading their letters for the enlightenment of less fortunate folks; . . . old folks shook their sage heads over the evening fire, and prophesied no good for those who braved the terrors of the sea and the foreign goal beyond it;— all talked of it, but scarcely anybody knew one true fact about this magic land. . . ."

Maryashe's father had left for America three years earlier, hoping to rebuild his family's fortunes. On the day his family left to join him, carrying just a few possessions with them, Maryashe remembers that the entire village went to the railroad station to see them off. After 16 days, her family landed in Boston, where they saw her father waiting on the wharf:

> "To have crossed the ocean only to come within a few yards of him, unable to get nearer till all the fuss was over, was

dreadful enough. But to hear other passengers called who had no reason for hurry, while we were left among the last, was unendurable. Oh, it's our turn at last! We are questioned, examined, and [allowed to enter the country]! A rush over the planks on one side, over the ground on the other, six wild beings cling to each other, bound by a common bond of tender joy, and the long parting is at an end."

"TO AMERICA!"

Maryashe's story is just one of the many immigration stories that took place between 1880 and 1920 as over one million people, mostly Jewish, left the countries of Russia, Ukraine, Poland, Latvia, and Lithuania. Many of them had been forced to leave because of extreme prejudice and harsh treatment under the rule of the Russian czars, who were Russia's ruling emperors. Because of their religious beliefs, which were different from those of many Russians and Russia's rulers, Eastern European Jews had been separated from the rest of the population and forced to live in city ghettos or small villages called *shtetls*. It was difficult for them to make a living, and they were often attacked by non-Jews or by Russian officials. After Czar Alexander II was assassinated in 1881, the blame was placed on a Jewish group, and this brought a new wave of violence. Neighborhoods and villages where Jewish people lived were burned during organized attacks called **pogroms**, and many people were tragically slaughtered. After a meeting of a Jewish community in Kiev (now in Ukraine), a speaker proclaimed, "In America we shall find rest; the stars and stripes will wave over the true home of our people. To America, brethren! To America!"

> **Pogroms** are organized massacres of a minority group.

Many Jewish citizens had to flee at night, secretly, because the czar had passed a law, making immigration to a new country illegal. Avoiding Russian border guards, and often bribing people to help them, Jewish families arrived in western Europe. Then they boarded ships for America, often spending the long crossing crowded in the steerage class of huge ships.

Many Russian immigrants settled in New York City's Lower East Side, which became one of the most densely populated neighborhoods in the world. Russians contributed their diverse cultural traditions and devout faith to the communities where they settled.

George Grantham Bain Collection, Library of Congress, 3a38143

FLEEING FROM EASTERN EUROPE

Non-Jewish people were also fleeing Russia and Eastern Europe at the end of the 19th century and the beginning of the 20th. At that time, there were severe shortages of available land for farming, and many farmers and peasants could not grow enough food to survive. Because of the czar's ruling that ethnic Russians could not leave the country, only about 65,000 Russians had been able to leave by 1910. However, Ukrainians, Belarussians, Lithuanians, and Poles arrived at Ellis Island by the hundreds of thousands during that time.

In 1917, the imperial government of Russia was overthrown by socialist revolutionaries called Bolsheviks, starting a civil war. As the old Russia became a new communist country, the Soviet Union, many people were caught up in violence and property destruction, and about 30,000 Russians fled to the United States. By now, those fleeing Russia were not just farmers and peasants. Many of those leaving were professional people or prominent citizens, like aristocrats, professionals, and former imperial officials. Because they opposed the "red" (Communist) Soviet government, they were called "White Russians." Many of them were forced to work manual labor jobs for the first time in their lives. This led to stories of former princes working as waiters, and former generals driving taxis.

BECOMING AMERICAN

Between 1880 and 1924, when the U.S. Congress began to restrict immigration, it is estimated that as many as three million Eastern Europeans came to the United States. Unlike immigrants from other countries, who often came to the United States just to make money before returning to their homeland, many Jews would stay in New York City, to form close communities with others from their old villages or cities. By the early 1900s, one-third of the Jewish population of the United States lived in New York City. Eastern European immigrants, both Jewish and non-Jewish, brought their culture and their values to America with them, and many would go on to be some of America's most respected writers, musicians, actors, and businesspeople.

Igor Sikorsky, inventor of small aircrafts and helicopters, immigrated to the United States from Russia in 1919 and became a pioneer in aviation design and construction.

©Granger

By Marcia Amidon Lusted. May be reproduced for classroom use. *Toolkit Texts: Short Nonfiction for American History, Industrial Age and Immigration,* by Stephanie Harvey and Anne Goudvis, ©2021 (Portsmouth, NH: Heinemann).

By Marcia Amidon Lusted. May be reproduced for classroom use. *Toolkit Texts: Short Nonfiction for American History, Industrial Age and Immigration*, by Stephanie Harvey and Anne Goudvis, ©2021 (Portsmouth, NH: Heinemann).

An American Welcome

Mexican citizens on foot and in wagons cross the bridge into Mexico at Brownsville, Texas in 1911. For many Mexican immigrants, moving to the United States was not necessarily a one-time journey of permanent relocation. Since the distance was so short, Mexican citizens regularly crossed back and forth between the two countries.

Mexican Immigration in the 1800s and 1900s

Too often, immigration history seems to focus on people who came to New York or California from Europe, Asia, and other countries overseas. But during the late 1800s and the earliest years of the 1900s, many immigrants came to America from much closer to home. And America welcomed them.

Immigration from Mexico to the United States has ebbed and flowed since the state of Texas was annexed in 1845. In reality, it wasn't that Mexicans were crossing the border into the United States; the border actually crossed them. Their homes and communities became part of the United States. Eventually the new industries developing in the United States, such as agriculture and mining, attracted Mexican workers. And states like Texas, California, New Mexico, and Arizona needed plenty of workers to grow crops, work in mines, and build irrigation systems. The upheaval of the Mexican Revolution also convinced many Mexicans, especially refugees and political exiles, to seek safety in the United States. Many rural Mexicans simply wanted to find more stable lives and better jobs. As a result of all these factors, the number of legal immigrants to the United States from Mexico grew from about 20,000 in the 1910s to as many as 100,000 a year in the 1920s. El Paso, Texas served as the gateway for Mexican immigrants and became known as the Mexican Ellis Island.

At a time when many Americans saw immigrants from Europe and Asia as being less desirable in terms of education, literacy, and work ethic, Mexicans enjoyed a favored status.

Mexican migrant workers harvest peppers in California in 1936. American farmers needed Mexican laborers to harvest cotton, fruits, and vegetables.

When the Immigration Act of 1924 set quotas for how many immigrants would be allowed into the United States from each country, the limits did not apply to people from Mexico. Farmers argued that they would have no one to plant and harvest their crops without Mexican laborers. It also helped that many Mexican immigrants did not stay in the United States permanently. It was so easy to cross back and forth over the border that many spent periods of time working in the United States, then went back home to Mexico for a certain amount of time. Many workers left their families in Mexico and worked in the United States to support them. Pablo Mares, who came to the United States from Mexico because of the Mexican revolution, described his experience:

"The work is very heavy, but what is good is that one lives in peace. Here one is treated according to the way in which one behaves and one earns more than in Mexico. I have gone back to Mexico twice, but I have come back, for in addition to the fact that work is very scarce there, the wages are too low and one can hardly earn enough to eat. Here it is almost the same, but there are more comforts of life and one can buy many things cheaper and in payments."

A family of Mexican beet workers stands in front of their home in Rocky Ford, Colorado, 1915.

Throughout our nation's history, Mexican Americans have contributed to the music, architecture, literature, language, and food of the United States.

Mexican girls (top) sing and dance together in San Antonio, Texas, 1939.

Women (below) make tortillas by hand in a bake shop, San Antonio, Texas, 1939.

Not every Mexican immigrant was happy to be in the United States, despite the better opportunities for work. Elisa Silva, who came to Los Angeles at the age of 20, was honest about it:

"Of the customs of this country I only like the ones about work. In Mexico, the people are kinder than they are here. I shall never really like living this way, besides since I don't know English and believe that it won't be so easy for me to learn it, I don't believe I will ever be able to adjust myself to this country. Life, to be sure, is easier here because one can buy so many things on credit and cheaper than in Mexico. But I don't know what it is that I don't like."

Mexican immigration to the United States continued until the 1930s and the Great Depression. Suddenly a lack of jobs for Americans created negative feelings toward immigrant Mexican laborers, and many workers who had been welcomed just a decade before were now treated with hostility and often deported. The welcome mat for Mexican immigrants had been pulled in.

The Push and Pull of America

What could entice a person to leave his or her home, friends, and family; make a long, dangerous trip across the ocean; and begin a new life in a strange country? For some, coming to America was seen as a great adventure; for others, it was a frightening ordeal.

Immigration in the 19th Century

N o matter the reason, several factors went into making the difficult decision to move halfway around the world. Economic reasons spurred many to leave for America. Some of the earliest immigrants arrived in the United States during the mid-1840s when Europe was experiencing a severe **famine** due to crop failures (particularly Ireland's potato crop). For many northern Europeans, there was little land on which to farm or live, so they ended up in overcrowded conditions, faced with starvation.

> A **famine** is a major food shortage that often causes starvation.

Economic Opportunity

People dealing with high taxes and poverty, largely from eastern and southern Europe, were then part of a second wave of immigrants who began arriving in America during the late 1800s.

"[T]here was absolutely no chance for the common man to get ahead," one immigrant explained. Czech immigrant Charles Bartunek, who came to New York in 1914, stated, "We'd have meat about once a year. . . . Once in a while, Mother would buy one of those short bolognas, cut it up and everyone would get a little piece. I used to think, if [only] I could get enough of that to fill my stomach."

In this 1880 political cartoon, immigrants are welcomed into the "U.S. Ark of Refuge" as they flee war and upheaval in their native countries.

Toolkit Texts: Short Nonfiction for American History, Industrial Age and Immigration, by Stephanie Harvey and Anne Goudvis, ©2021 (Portsmouth, NH: Heinemann).

May be reproduced for classroom use.

Immigrants hoped to find the freedom and stability in America that they did not have in their homelands. The arrival at Ellis Island brought a range of emotion from joy to sorrow to members of this immigrant family in 1905.

Religious Freedom

Others came to America for religious reasons. In the latter part of the 19th century, a large number of Russian and eastern European Jews were being persecuted for their religious beliefs. Their homes were burned in **pogroms**, and people were killed or hurt in riots and other acts of violence. They yearned for the freedom to worship as they pleased without the fear of punishment.

Escape from Unrest

A third major reason people came to America was to escape war and unrest. Early immigrants were fleeing from the social upheaval caused by the **Industrial Revolution**. The working class, or common people, rebelled against unfair treatment by the wealthy upper class, or aristocrats, in the Russian Revolution. In Ireland, the poor were treated badly by rich landowners. And a 1910 revolution in Mexico caused 700,000 people to flee their homes in search of freedom.

Land of Opportunity

While many immigrants were pushed to leave behind the difficult conditions or circumstances in their native countries, they also were pulled by the possibility of a better life in America. Those who had **immigrated** earlier, such as family members or former neighbors, wrote letters to those in their native countries. They described the many opportunities in the United States and made life sound very inviting. After all, there was plenty of land to farm, and many jobs were available either building canals and railroads or in the factories of the growing cities. Immigrants to America could afford to live *and* send money back to their families in Europe.

Most importantly, America offered the kind of freedom—from famine, persecution, and war—that could not be found at home. Immigrants had what was termed "America fever." As they arrived in the United States, immigrants' spirits were high with expectations.

Pogroms are organized massacres of a minority group.

The **Industrial Revolution** was a period starting in the late 1700s and continuing through the 1800s when machine labor replaced many jobs done by skilled craftspeople.

To **immigrate** means to move into a new country to live.

May be reproduced for classroom use. *Toolkit Texts: Short Nonfiction for American History, Industrial Age and Immigration*, by Stephanie Harvey and Anne Goudvis, ©2021 (Portsmouth, NH: Heinemann).

Voyage of Hope
Voyage of Tears

Hope was the one guiding star that led millions of people to immigrate to America. But those people had to endure a lot even before they arrived on this country's shores. Their journey began when they said good-bye to their ancestral homes and set out—by train or wagon or on foot—for a seaside port and a ship that would take them to their new country.

By 1880, an Atlantic Ocean crossing on a steamship lasted 8 to 14 days—not bad, compared with the one- to three-month expeditions of the earlier sailing ships. Shipping lines actually competed for immigrating passengers, who were considered highly profitable, self-loading cargo. Some ships, for example, could hold more than 2,000 passengers in steerage. At 10 to 40 dollars per traveler, those ships could make a good profit carrying many people in the least expensive and least luxurious way.

Packed onto a ship's steerage deck (top), these immigrants have a long, crowded journey ahead of them. This grandmother's face (bottom) portrays the mixed emotions of hope and fear.

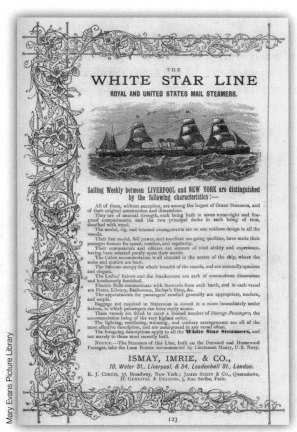

Mary Evans Picture Library

All over Europe, posters advertised passage to the United States. The White Star Line traveled between Liverpool, England, and New York City in the 1800s.

Waiting to Leave

When immigrants arrived at European port cities, such as Antwerp (Belgium), Liverpool (England), or Naples (Italy), to name just a few, they often had to wait up to two weeks for a ship that was departing for the United States. So, shipping companies made even more money by building hotels where travelers had to pay to stay while they waited. The Hamburg-Amerika Shipping Line maintained an entire village on the outskirts of Hamburg, Germany, that included two churches, a synagogue, and housing for 5,000 people.

Steamship companies required steerage passengers to take a bath, have their baggage disinfected, and be examined by doctors before boarding. The immigrants also answered questions—such as name, age, occupation, native country, and destination—for the ship's manifest. At the other end of the trip, immigration officials would use such information to verify and group the immigrants.

On Board the Ship

Once the ship was underway, first- and second-class passengers ate meals in a dining hall and enjoyed private cabins through which fresh sea breezes could blow. Steerage passengers, on the other hand, had food brought to them, as they traveled in the bottom levels of the ship where there was no privacy. "That hope to be in America was so great and so sunny, that it colored all the pain that we had during our trip," remembered Gertrude Yellin about her voyage in 1922.

Steerage passengers slept in narrow bunks, usually three beds across and two or three deep. Burlap-covered mattresses were filled with straw or seaweed. During fierce North Atlantic storms, all **hatches** were sealed to prevent water from getting in, making the already stuffy air below unbearable.

Byron Company (New York, N.Y.). Museum of the City of New York. 93.1.1.13374

Immigrants in steerage slept in iron-framed bunks built close together. The beds had thin canvas mattresses often filled with straw or seaweed.

> **Hatches** are the coverings for the openings on the deck of a ship.

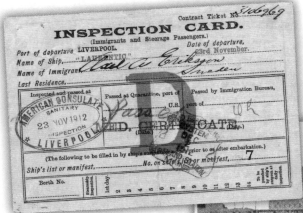

In 1912, the ship's doctor on the Laurentic inspected each immigrant every day. Steamship companies tried to introduce strict medical examinations, but often there were simply too many passengers for these rules to be enforced.

Looking tired and a little lost, a group of immigrants descend a barge's ramp to arrive at Ellis Island.

Top: Inspection Card Courtesy National Park Service, Museum Management Program and Statue of Liberty. STLI 21962. Photo by United States Public Health Service. Bottom: Library of Congress, 3a14957.

Illness and Seasickness

Some children died when contagious illnesses, such as measles, broke out onboard ship. Throughout their 1905 voyage, Fannie Kligerman's mother hid Fannie's infant sister in an apron, hoping the child would stay healthy. She did.

Outbreaks of seasickness also were common on every ship. Hundreds of passengers stayed in their beds through most of the ocean crossing. Bertha Devlin, who was seasick on her journey, recalled a particularly bad ocean crossing: "One night I prayed to God that [the boat] would go down . . . I was that sick. . . . And everybody else was the same way."

Onto Ellis Island

Immigrants often crowded on the deck of the ship at the end of the trip when the Statue of Liberty was sighted in New York Harbor. Steamships made their first stop at a pier on the mainland. There, the first- and second-class passengers were free to leave the ship, with little or no medical examination. Afterward, steerage passengers were crowded onto a barge or ferry, often with standing room only, and taken to Ellis Island. On

a busy day, immigrants might have to wait their turn to disembark, standing for several hours with no food or drink. The ordeal of the ocean voyage was over, but the unknowns of the Ellis Island examination process were just ahead.

A Note About Names

Contrary to some popular stories, Ellis Island immigration officials did not change the names of immigrants upon their arrival here in America. They used the ships' manifests—which were completed at the point of departure in Europe or elsewhere and not in the United States—to verify information during the inspection process. Many immigrants themselves probably changed or abbreviated their names to Americanize them or make them sound less foreign in their new home.

Toolkit Texts: Short Nonfiction for American History, Industrial Age and Immigration, by Stephanie Harvey and Anne Goudvis, ©2021 (Portsmouth, NH: Heinemann).

Background: ©airn/Shutterstock

Ellis Island Interviews: Immigrants Tell Their Stories in Their Own Words

Marge Glasgow immigrated to the United States from Scotland at age 15 in 1922.

"My whole idea was to get to the United States, and work, and help to bring my family. Eventually, each one would come, because there were many people migrating, so I was very insistent and of course, they were afraid to let me go at a young age. I had no relatives in America . . . but I thought I could work, get a job, and send money home to my parents.

I finally got my way. My mother got me a pretty outfit and I left home. My father and brother took me to the boat. I don't remember the name. It was a ten day journey. The journey over, I began to have regrets about leaving home. I was feeling very lonesome, sorry for myself, crying all the time . . . I was afraid of Ellis Island. I had heard stories that if they keep you at Ellis Island they go through your hair looking for bugs. My mother was always scaring me with that.

I remember the Great Hall, and the desks there with men. I don't know if they were doctors, judges or what, questioning the people you know. That's when I was very scared, to be all alone in the big building being questioned. So I was really crying hysterically and sobbing, so hard that the doctor came to me. They had doctors there examining everybody and one said 'Please, please don't cry so hard. We're trying to help you. We won't hurt you.'

[But then he said] "You have something in your eyes that we have to test [trachoma] and it will take ten days to test. It might be a disease. You'll be taken care of. Everything will be fine."

So I sort of calmed down, and then a nurse came and she took me. She put me to bed in a room next to her. The next morning everything was calm and nice. The nurse was still taking care of me. She took me outside and I looked at the boats and wondered "Will they let me into the United States, or will they send me back?" I wanted so much to live here in the United States.

Then after lunch, somebody came and brought me some flowers . . . I spent ten days there and every day was better than the last . . . they were extra kind because they felt sorry for me, I guess, that I was alone and coming to a country not knowing anyone. So my entrance to the United States was very pleasant. It was wonderful.

I had to be sixteen to work. I was too young. So my decision then was to go as a mother's helper. About two months later, my brother came. My sister came after that, and within a year, three more of my family came over, including my mother and father. I went to Ellis Island to meet them."

Ellis Island Interviews: Immigrants Tell Their Stories in Their Own Words

Betty Garoff immigrated to the United States from Russia at age 8 in 1921.

She came from Stansa Nigarela, a small village near Minsk, and grew up in a Jewish community during the turmoil of World War I. When she was eight years old, she saw her father for the first time in the Great Hall at Ellis Island.

"My father left for America in 1913, the year I was born, to avoid going to the service. My mother was pregnant with me when he left, so he never saw me until I arrived at Ellis Island.

It was really rough on us. During the war years, to make a living, my mother illegally sold salt. I don't know where she got it. That's how she supported us, my brother and me. I remember my grandfather, he lived on the farm. My grandmother died during the influenza (flu epidemic of 1918), I don't remember her at all.

I must have been about four or five years old when the family became separated. The soldiers had come and we were (forced to leave) the village entirely. Everyone went their own way. My brother and I were left behind. We got separated from my mother. Just Lou and I were together. We were very close. Lou was thirteen months older than me. We traveled during the night, and slept during the day hidden in barns, until a family who knew of my grandmother, they took in Lou and me as their grandchildren. They hid us. This particular Christian family took us in, and they really did save our lives.

When the soldiers came to look for us, we were hidden in a closet. She fed them [the soldiers] food and drinks until they were intoxicated. They didn't find us and they left. I can't remember how long we stayed. But it was after the war and the village was taken back. Everyone started coming home and then we found each other and we were able to go home to our village.

Many Jewish people faced persecution for their beliefs and culture. Some, like Betty and her brother, were helped by local Christian people, who disagreed with the unfair and often cruel treatment.

In 1921

My father requested for us to come to the United States. It was time. . . . We were in steerage of course. It was the three of us. My mother wouldn't leave us out of her sight. We slept in hammocks. Rows of hammocks. It wasn't private or luxurious. Mostly we ate hard-boiled eggs, raw potatoes and we got an occasional apple. Whatever you wore, whatever you had, was with you. We didn't have any luggage or anything like that.

We arrived in cold, cold weather. But we were all elated seeing the Statue of Liberty. It was a thrilling moment to know we had arrived and would soon be on land. At Ellis Island I remember the huge room where we were sitting and waiting to be called. People were leaving, some were staying. I was bewildered, I never saw that many people. . . .

Papa didn't come for us because we were the last ones left on the ship. . . . I was crying and telling my mother that I think we'll have to go back, Ma. Papa doesn't want us and we will have to return.

[At one point, people were looking for Betty, hysterical because she was nowhere to be found. Finally they met her father, he answered some questions, and the family was released.]

He dressed us all in American clothes, then he took us and registered us for school. . . . I spoke Yiddish. I'm sure the teacher didn't know Yiddish but (we all talked) until we could communicate. But I fit right in. My mother also went to school, she was really amazing. She went to school, she learned English, she was able to write a letter. She read the newspaper. She got her own citizen papers. I admired her for that."

Excerpted from: *Ellis Island Interviews: Immigrants Tell Their Stories in Their Own Words* by Peter M. Coan. New York, NY: Facts on File, Inc. 1997.

I Was Dreaming to Come to America: Memories from the Ellis Island Oral History Project

Lazarus Salamon immigrated to the United States from Hungary at age 16 in 1920.

"I feel like I had two lives. You plant something in the ground. It has its roots and then you transplant it where it stays permanently. That's what happened to me. You put an end . . . and forget about your childhood; I became a man here. All of a sudden, I started life new, amongst people whose language I didn't understand. . . . [It was a] different life; everything was different . . . but I never despaired, I was optimistic.

And this is the only country where you are not a stranger, because we are all strangers. It's only a matter of time of who got here first."

Excerpted from: *I Was Dreaming to Come to America: Memories from the Ellis Island Oral History Project* by Veronica Lawlor. New York, NY: Penguin Books. 1995.

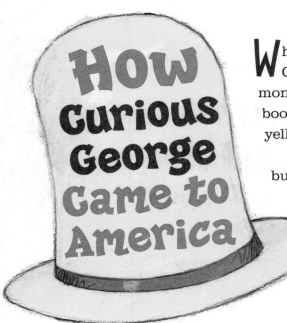

How Curious George Came to America

What do you think about when you hear the name Curious George? Do you think about a mischievous monkey who is always very curious? Do you think about books with bright yellow covers and a man with a big yellow hat?

Curious George, the story, was "born" in France, but its creators had an international background. Hans and Margret Rey, who created George, were both born in Germany. They first worked together when they lived in Brazil, where they later married. They spent their honeymoon in Paris, France, and liked it so much they decided to stay.

It was in Paris that the Reys began writing and illustrating books, and it was in Paris that Curious George was created. He first appeared in the Reys' book *Cecily G. and the Nine Monkeys*. Yes, he was one of the nine monkeys. Hans and Margret liked George so much they decided to write a whole story about his adventures. They called the book *Curious George*. They went on to write and illustrate six more Curious George books. Hans Rey once said, "Basically, I illustrate and Margret writes."

Illustrations by Kevin Menck

George is a very curious little monkey and is always getting into trouble. However, more than once, George got Hans and Margret out of trouble. Here's what happened: There was a war going on. The French police thought the Reys might be spies working for the German government. Officers arrested the couple, searched their belongings, and discovered their story about Curious George. The police decided that the creators of such a charming story could not possibly be spies. The police released Hans and Margret. Curious George saved the Reys from jail!

It wasn't long before Hans and Margret were in danger once again. It was 1940, and Adolf Hitler's German army was invading countries across Europe. The Reys knew they had to escape before Hitler's soldiers arrived in Paris. Hans, who was skilled at making gadgets, built two bicycles from spare parts. Then, early one morning in June, the Reys strapped their Curious George story to one of their bicycle racks. They grabbed their warm coats and a bit of food, and they were off.

Illustrations by Kevin Menck

Toolkit Texts: Short Nonfiction for American History, Industrial Age and Immigration, by Stephanie Harvey and Anne Goudvis, ©2021 (Portsmouth, NH: Heinemann).

When the German army invaded Paris, Hans and Margret were pedaling away. They were headed toward Spain, riding along the country roads of France. After four tiring days, the Reys and George reached the French border where they sold their bicycles and bought train tickets to cross Spain into Portugal. Weeks later, they boarded a ship and crossed the Atlantic Ocean to Brazil. Following a short visit there, the Reys sailed for America.

The Statue of Liberty welcomed Hans and Margret as they sailed into New York Harbor. Meanwhile, Curious George waited patiently in their baggage. The Reys settled into an apartment in New York. Within a week, they found a publisher who liked their story about a good little monkey who was always very curious. Curious George had finally come to America!

Hans Rey once said,

"Among children, we seem to be known best as the parents of Curious George. . . .
'I thought you were monkeys, too,' said a little boy who had been eager to meet us, disappointment written all over his face."

May be reproduced for classroom use.

Interview with

Louise Borden

Readers all over the world know and love Curious George, the little monkey whose curiosity gets him into, and out of, the most exciting situations. The dramatic history of his creators, Margret and H.A. Rey, was a mystery to many until author Louise Borden wrote *The Journey That Saved Curious George*.

In 1940, Hans and Margret Rey had to flee their home in Paris, France, as the German army advanced. They began their dangerous journey to freedom on bicycles, pedaling to southern France with their children's book manuscripts among their few possessions. One of these manuscripts went on to become *Curious George*, the tale of that inquisitive monkey who is one of the most enduring characters in children's literature.

Louise Borden has written 30 books for children, including fiction, nonfiction, historical fiction, and biography. Louise travels all over the world to research books about fascinating people and their adventures. We spoke with Louise about her own adventures writing this amazing story.

At the beginning of World War II, the German army invaded and took over many countries in Europe, including France.

Why did you write about the Reys and their journey during the war?

After reading a few lines in an autobiographical snippet of Margret and H.A. Rey that mentioned their flight from Paris on bicycles in June 1940, I was instantly drawn to their wartime adventure. I had studied this very time in history when millions of refugees were on the roads of France. When I began to ask people in the publishing world what they knew of the Reys' escape from the Nazi invasion, no one seemed to know the details of those harrowing days. The story felt incomplete. I wanted to know more. I wanted real images. I was curious, just like Reys' famous little monkey, George.

And so I began my own journey, a journey of research. Rich sources for my research were Margret and Hans Rey's personal papers at the de Grummond Children's Literature Collection at the University of Southern Mississippi. But after sifting

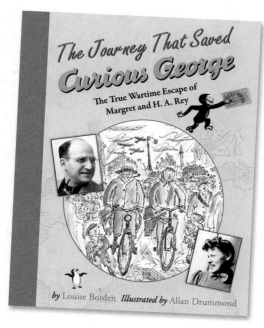

The Journey That Saved
Curious George
The True Wartime Escape of
Margret and H. A. Rey

by Louise Borden *Illustrated by* Allan Drummond

213

through hundreds of the Reys' letters, notebook pages, and photographs, and even after walking through Paris on various research trips, I still had questions without answers. How many kilometers did the Reys travel on those two bicycles? Which roads did they follow on their journey south? What happened to the belongings that they had to leave behind? What wartime dangers did they face?

Where did your questions and research take you?

Over several years, I had conversations in person or by phone with people who had known the Reys. I wrote letters and e-mailed people in Germany, England, Portugal, and France. And I traveled to some of the towns, cities, and addresses gleaned from the letters and work diaries that the Reys wrote during 1936–40, the years they lived in Paris. Each step of the way, I tried to focus on Margret and Hans before *Curious George* was published and brought them fame.

Dates, postmarks, travel papers, and expense records provided invaluable clues in French, English, German, and Portuguese. Newspaper interviews from the 1940s and 1950s gave me needed details. Slowly, piece by piece,

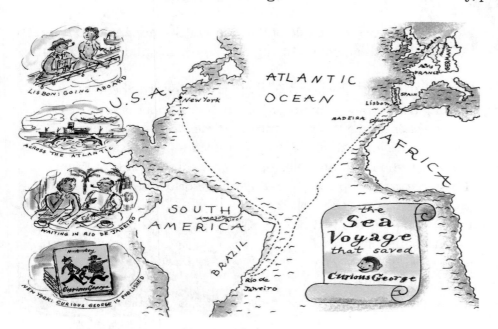

I began to stitch together the fabric of their story. And realized the importance of this wartime escape. Imagine our world *without* Curious George. In late June of 1940, German troops occupied France, and on July 23, the Reys left Portugal on the *Angola*. That

September, new laws required that all Jews in France had to be registered. Many were later deported to Hitler's death camps. Because Margret and Hans were Jewish, this might have happened to them as well.

The Journey That Saved Curious George is my way, as a writer, of becoming witness to part of Hans and Margret Rey's story. It is my way of honoring their creativity and their courage during a dark time in history for many countries in Europe. In our 21st century, whenever America has tough times and tragic events—such as terrorist attacks, or wars, or an unexpected pandemic—I think of how brave and resilient these two artists were . . . and this gives me my own courage and hope.

Library of Congress, 3g03659

NOT THOSE HUDDLED MASSES

The inscription on the base of the Statue of Liberty (quoted on the next page) proclaims an offer of opportunity to millions of immigrants who want to begin a new life in America. Most people who moved from northern and western Europe found this nation's doors wide open. Unfortunately, the same cannot be said for immigrants from other parts of the world.

Early in its history, the United States gladly received all immigrants in order to fuel the country's rapid economic growth. Most immigrants came from Great Britain, Germany, and Scandinavia (Norway, Sweden, Denmark, and the like). Although language and cultural differences existed, they shared similar Protestant faiths.

By the 1850s, though, this welcoming attitude began to change. The potato famine of the 1840s had brought Irish Catholics to America in record numbers. Many people wanted to put a stop to all immigration regardless of where people came from. **Nativists** were opposed to immigration by any group of people who were born outside of the United States. American-born Protestants who hoped to "protect" America from

In the editorial cartoon above, characters representing factory owners and politicians greet the immigrant as a source of labor and votes, while other characters, such as the craftsman and the middle-class citizen, are less enthusiastic. They fear their jobs and livelihoods will be taken away by the immigrant's arrival.

immigrants—in particular, the large numbers of Catholic arrivals in the 1840s. This movement did not slow down immigration at the time, but it reared its ugly head again in the 1890s.

Other immigrant groups also faced waves of prejudice. Thousands of Chinese men came to California in search of gold during and after the 1849 Gold Rush. The Chinese were prevented from working in the mines and instead began working on the railroads. To add insult to injury, in 1882, the United States passed the Chinese Exclusion Act, which forbade the entry of Chinese laborers into the country. This was the first group of immigrants to be excluded based on race.

Also in 1882, the first national immigration restriction policies were enacted because American lawmakers wanted to control who was allowed into the country. Also excluded were people who had criminal records, who had disabilities, or who had diseases.

" . . . GIVE ME YOUR TIRED, YOUR POOR, YOUR HUDDLED MASSES YEARNING TO BREATHE FREE . . . "

The 1890s brought other troubles as the United States faced an economic depression. Many Americans lost their jobs and blamed immigrants for these problems. At the same time, immigrants from southern and eastern Europe were coming to America in record numbers. The nativist push for immigration control returned.

World War I (1914–1918) only increased nativist fears. In 1917, the United States insisted that all immigrants over the age of 16 be able to read in their own languages. This meant that people who were **illiterate** were not allowed in.

Nativists were opposed to immigration by any group of people who were born outside of the United States.

Illiterate is being unable to read or write.

Quotas is the limit on the number of people that may be admitted to a nation.

But when literacy tests failed to slow immigration, **quotas** were put into place. And American lawmakers no longer tried to hide the fact that Italians, Hungarians, Poles, eastern European Jews, and Greeks were not welcome.

In 1924 the National Origins Act restricted immigration even further. Between 1892 and 1954, more than 12 million immigrants came through Ellis Island. But the U.S. door was not open to all.

May be reproduced for classroom use. Toolkit Texts: Short Nonfiction for American History, Industrial Age and Immigration, by Stephanie Harvey and Anne Goudvis, ©2021 (Portsmouth, NH: Heinemann).

Statue of Liberty

"The Statue of Liberty Enlightening the World" was a gift of friendship from the people of France to the United States and is recognized as a universal symbol of freedom and democracy. The Statue of Liberty was dedicated on October 28, 1886.

Between 1886 and 1924, almost 14 million immigrants entered the United States through New York. The Statue of Liberty was a reassuring sign that they had arrived in the land of their dreams. To these newcomers, the Statue's uplifted torch did not suggest "enlightenment" as the name suggests, but rather, "welcome."

Over time, Liberty became a symbol of hope to generations of immigrants. The opening of the immigrant processing station at Ellis Island in 1892 in the shadow of the Statue of Liberty solidified this association with hope and opportunity for immigrants. In addition, Emma Lazarus' poem "The New Colossus" vividly depicted the Statue of Liberty as offering refuge to new immigrants from the miseries of Europe. The poem received little attention at the time, but in 1903 was engraved on a bronze plaque and affixed to the base of the Statue.

THE GREAT BARTHOLDI STATUE.
LIBERTY ENLIGHTENING THE WORLD.
THE GIFT OF FRANCE TO THE AMERICAN PEOPLE.
ERECTED ON BEDLOE'S ISLAND. NEW YORK HARBOR.

The statue is of copper-bronzed, 148 ft in height, and is to be mounted on a stone pedestal 150 ft. high; making the extreme height 298 ft. The torch will display a powerful electric light, and the statue thus present by night as by day, an exceedingly grand and imposing appearance.

The New Colossus

By Emma Lazarus

Not like the brazen giant of Greek fame,
With conquering limbs astride from land to land;
Here at our sea-washed, sunset gates shall stand
A mighty woman with a torch, whose flame
Is the imprisoned lightning, and her name
Mother of Exiles. From her beacon-hand
Glows world-wide welcome; her mild eyes command
The air-bridged harbor that twin cities frame.
"Keep, ancient lands, your storied pomp!" cries she
With silent lips. "Give me your tired, your poor,
Your huddled masses yearning to breathe free,
The wretched refuse of your teeming shore.
Send these, the homeless, tempest-tost to me,
I lift my lamp beside the golden door!"

*Give me your tired,
your poor,
your huddled masses
yearning to breathe free . . .*

©zokru/iStock/Getty Images

The New Colossus sonnet by Emma Lazarus. November 2, 1883.

Emma Lazarus

EMMA LAZARUS was born on July 22, 1849, in New York City to a wealthy family who immigrated from Portugal to the United States. Lazarus was the poet who wrote "The New Colossus," the poem inscribed on a plaque on the base of the Statue of Liberty. Aside from writing, Lazarus was also involved in charitable work for refugees. She worked as an aide for Jewish immigrants who had been detained by immigration officials. She was deeply moved by the plight of the Russian Jews she met there and these experiences influenced her writing.

In 1883, Lazarus was asked to compose a sonnet for an art and literary auction to raise funds for a pedestal for the Statue of Liberty. The Statue of Liberty, which stands on an island in New York Harbor, was a gift from France to the United States to celebrate our county's free and democratic traditions. Lazarus, inspired by her own Sephardic Jewish heritage and her experiences working with refugees, wrote "The New Colossus" on November 2, 1883. After the auction, the sonnet appeared in Joseph Pulitzer's *New York World* as well as *The New York Times*. Lazarus died in New York City on November 19, 1887.

Lazarus' famous sonnet depicts the Statue of Liberty as the "Mother of Exiles," a symbol of immigration and opportunity, symbols associated with the Statue of Liberty today. It was not until 1901, 17 years after Lazarus' death, that Georgina Schuyler, a friend of hers, found a book containing the sonnet in a bookshop and organized a civic effort to resurrect the lost work. Her efforts paid off and in 1903, words from the sonnet were inscribed on a plaque and placed on the inner wall of the pedestal of the Statue of Liberty. Today, the plaque is on display inside the Statue's pedestal.

ENGRAVED BY T. JOHNSON.   PHOTOGRAPHED BY W. KURTZ.

May be reproduced for classroom use. *Toolkit Texts: Short Nonfiction for American History, Industrial Age and Immigration*, by Stephanie Harvey and Anne Goudvis, ©2021 (Portsmouth, NH: Heinemann).

Angel Island Immigration Station

Angel Island is the largest natural island in the San Francisco Bay. Beginning with the earliest inhabitants, the Coast Miwok, Angel Island was a seasonal hunting and gathering location for the local native tribes.

In 1905, Congress approved money to build an immigration center on Angel Island. From 1910 to 1940, the U.S. Immigration Station processed hundreds of thousands of immigrants arriving in San Francisco. The majority of immigrants came from China and Japan, but also from India, Russia, and the Philippines.

We needed to save the immigration station to remind us of the tough times some immigrants had coming to this country. They were treated shabbily, but they actually made this country a better place. We don't have exclusion laws anymore, but we could have them in an instant tomorrow. It could easily happen to some other group of people. That's why we need memorials like Angel Island, so that we will learn from our past and not repeat the same mistakes.

— Alexander Weiss
park ranger who found the poetry
on the walls of the immigration station

Angel Island has often been called the "Ellis Island of the West" because it was there that U.S. government officials decided who could enter the United States. But the two immigration centers were different in several ways. Twelve million immigrants came through Ellis Island in the 62 years it was open. Less than a half million people came through Angel Island during the 30 years it was open.

Most immigrants who passed through Ellis Island were accepted into the United States, and their stays at Ellis Island were short. Immigrants who were admitted through Angel Island passed through quickly if they were children of U.S. citizens. Some immigrants, however, were detained at Angel Island for long periods of time. They were treated differently because of strict immigration laws during this time.

In 1940, the administration building on Angel Island burned to the ground, and all applicants were moved to the mainland. During World War II, Japanese and German prisoners of war were detained at the Station before being sent to facilities farther inland. In 1954, the transition of Angel Island as a California State Park began. In the early 1960s, the final departure of the military allowed the rest of Angel Island to become park lands. Today, the station is open to the public as a museum—"a place for reflection and discovery of our shared history as a nation of immigrants."

Louie Share Kim

Library of Congress, 03059

©Sam Louie

Louie Share Kim, age 14

©Sam Louie

Louie Share Jung, paper father to Share Kim

Paper Son

Fourteen-year-old Louie Share Kim arrived at the Angel Island Immigration Station from Guangdong Province, China, in 1916. He had traveled alone on a journey that took nearly a month to cross the Pacific Ocean. He had little schooling, no job skills, and no place to live, and he did not speak any English. Yet his family pinned all their hopes on him to become a success in America. His father made sure he even looked American in his passport photograph by making him wear a suit and tie.

Two Fathers

But Louie Share Kim really had two fathers—or so it seemed. The Chinese Exclusion Act, in effect from 1882 to 1943, stopped all Chinese laborers from entering the United States. Only diplomats, merchants, students, teachers, visitors, and those claiming U.S. citizenship were able to enter from China. To get around the law, many immigrants from China claimed to be related to a U.S. citizen—on paper only.

Share Kim became a paper son of Louie Share Jung in America. A **paper son** was a person who immigrated from China using fake documentation of family ties in order to obtain U.S. citizenship. Share Jung was a U.S. citizen born in San Francisco who often traveled to China. Share Kim's father made arrangements to have Share Jung claim Share Kim as his son. The two families were very close friends. Share Jung had known Share Kim since birth.

Arriving in the United States

At Angel Island, officials detained Share Kim. They interrogated him and Share Jung. They asked question after question about their family history and their village's layout. Once satisfied with the answers, Share Kim was allowed to enter America. He received his Certificate of Identity, which stated he was admitted as the "son of a native."

When Share Kim was 20 years old, his real father wrote him a letter from China. "Dear Number One Son," the letter began, referring to Share Kim as the eldest son. "It is time to come home."

Share Kim's wife and children
were detained at Angel Island.

Now considered a "son of a native," Share Kim could visit his village in China and know that he would be readmitted into the United States. He arrived in China on a Tuesday. He was married on Saturday to a woman chosen by his parents and whom he had never seen before.

Bringing the Family

Share Kim returned to America to work. In 1924 and in 1929, he returned to China to visit his village and see his wife. They had two children. After each visit, Share Kim returned to the United States to work. Louie Share Kim was separated from his family for more than a decade. In 1935, he decided to bring his family to America. He and his wife offered a 12-year-old boy in the village the opportunity to go with them. They gave the boy the name John. John became their paper son.

Keeping Secrets

Some Chinese scholars estimate that 80% of Chinese in America had a paper son in their family history. Louie adds, "I knew as a child growing up that I was never to reveal to others that my father was a paper son for fear that we might all get deported.

"My parents never talked to me about their immigration experience," he says. "I never even knew they were detained at the Angel Island Immigration Station until after my mother passed away at the age of 98." Louie conducted research at the National Archives and Records Administration in San Bruno, California. He found a record of the interrogation of his mother and siblings during their detainment. The interview was 42 single-spaced typed pages. Louie says, "Many of my friends and relatives said their parents never talked about their immigration experience either. I suspect those experiences were painful, something they would rather forget."

Sam Louie shares his family's
story as a volunteer at the
Angel Island Immigration Station.

Toolkit Texts: Short Nonfiction for American History, Industrial Age and Immigration, by Stephanie Harvey and Anne Goudvis, ©2021 (Portsmouth, NH: Heinemann). May be reproduced for classroom use.

POETRY CARVED ON THE WALLS

ROOM No. 3

Chinese applicants made up 70% of the detained population at any time at Angel Island. They were subjected to tougher examinations, harsher interviews, and longer detentions than any other group. They endured it in the hope that they and their families might build new and better lives in the United States.

In 1940, a fire in the administration building shut down the immigration station after 30 years. It brought to a close one of the bitterest chapters in the history of immigration to America. After World War II (1939–1945), the remaining buildings on the site were abandoned and then marked for demolition. That order was never carried out, thanks to a California State Park ranger named Alexander Weiss, who noticed something interesting in 1970.

While Weiss was making his rounds on the island, his flashlight picked up Chinese calligraphy inscribed on the abandoned barracks building's walls. He informed his superiors of his discovery, but they shared neither his enthusiasm nor his belief that the writing on the walls held any significance. He then contacted a former professor at San Francisco State College, George Araki. Araki and San Francisco photographer Mak Takahashi traveled out to the island. Using floodlights, they photographed practically every inch of the barracks that bore writing before the building was scheduled to be destroyed.

They discovered that most of the calligraphy was poetry. Chinese men who had been detained in the building had carved poems into the walls. They captured their feelings about their ordeal and described the voyage to America, the longing for families back home, and the outrage and humiliation at the treatment they received.

The discovery occurred at a time of intense Asian American activism around issues of racial equality and social justice. It sparked community interest in the site. People lobbied not only for the demolition to be stopped but also for the site to be preserved. In 1976, the Angel Island Immigration Station Historical Advisory Committee, which later became the Angel Island Immigration Station Foundation (www.aiisf.org), helped raise $250,000 for the preservation of the building and the poetry. The barracks opened to the public in 1983.

Since then, community activists and descendants of detainees have worked to recover the immigration history of Angel Island. In 1997, the immigration station earned designation as a National Historic Landmark. Government sources contributed $30 million to preserve the poetry and restore the site as an immigration museum and symbol of America's history of racial exclusion.

More than 200 Chinese poems have been recovered and recorded. Most of the poems were unsigned, most likely for fear of punishment from the authorities. Many were written and carved by teenaged villagers. Those young men had no more than a grammar school education, but they knew how to express themselves in the classical forms of Chinese poetry. Using simple, direct language, the poems convey a strength of spirit. They also describe what it was like to be imprisoned on the island and chronicle the indignity and trauma that the U.S. immigration system imposed on one group of immigrants.

只可木屋拘留幾十天
所因墨例致牢連
可惜英雄無用武
奮擊何如燕來
從今遠別此樓中
各位鄉君眾歡同
莫道其間皆西式
囹如龕亦莫相嗤

The west wind ruffles my thin gauze clothing.

On the hill sits a tall building with a room of wooden planks.

I wish I could travel on a cloud far away, reunite with my wife and son.

When the moonlight shines on me alone, the night seems even longer.

At the head of the bed there is wine, and my heart is constantly drunk.

There is no flower beneath my pillow, and my dreams are not sweet.

To whom can I confide my innermost feelings?

I rely solely on close friends to relieve my loneliness.

This poem was found on the wall
of the barracks building.

The Jon B. Lovelace Collection of California Photographs in Carol M. Highsmith's America Project, Library of Congress, 25214.

Did You Know? The federal government uses a National Historic Landmark designation to recognize a site's national significance and protect its value as part of the nation's heritage. Only about 2,500 places, from all over the United States, have qualified for this program.

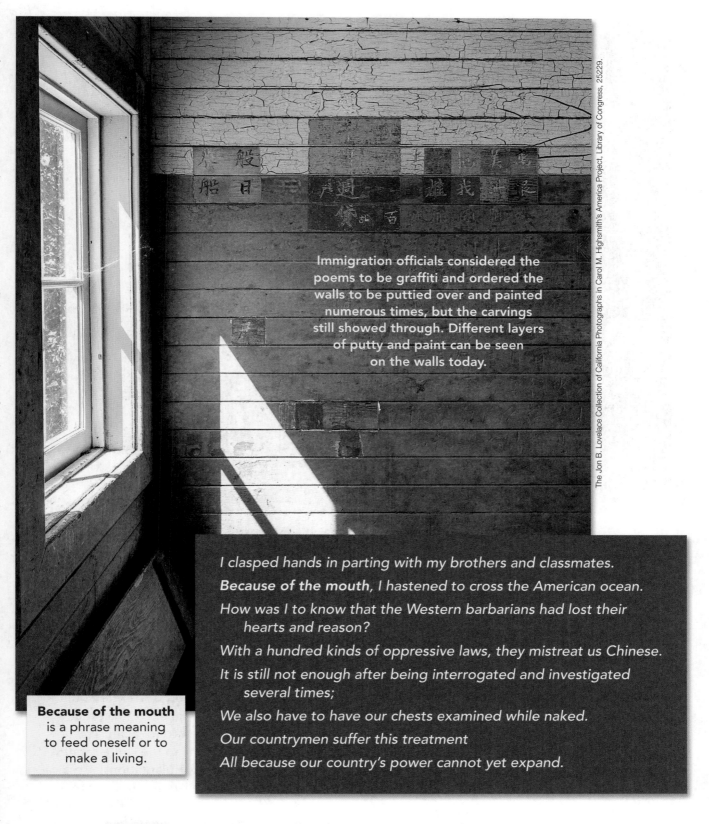

Immigration officials considered the poems to be graffiti and ordered the walls to be puttied over and painted numerous times, but the carvings still showed through. Different layers of putty and paint can be seen on the walls today.

The Jon B. Lovelace Collection of California Photographs in Carol M. Highsmith's America Project, Library of Congress, 25229.

I clasped hands in parting with my brothers and classmates.

Because of the mouth, I hastened to cross the American ocean.

How was I to know that the Western barbarians had lost their hearts and reason?

With a hundred kinds of oppressive laws, they mistreat us Chinese.

It is still not enough after being interrogated and investigated several times;

We also have to have our chests examined while naked.

Our countrymen suffer this treatment

All because our country's power cannot yet expand.

Because of the mouth is a phrase meaning to feed oneself or to make a living.

Want to learn more? The author of this article, Judy Yung, has co-edited a book with Him Mark Lai and Genny Lim on the subject of the poems. *Island: Poetry and History of Chinese Immigrants on Angel Island, 1910–1940* introduces readers to 135 poems that were found written or carved onto the walls at Angel Island.

Day of spacious dreams!
I sailed for America,
Overblown with hope.

—Ichiyo

In Search of Peace and Prosperity

Japanese Immigration

Japanese immigrants began their journey to the United States in search of peace and prosperity, leaving an unstable homeland for a life of hard work and the chance to provide a better future for their children and grandchildren. The Yamane family (above) immigrated from Japan at the turn of the century. Here three generations pose for a family portrait in Tacoma, Washington in 1918.

In the mid-1800s, Japan's economy was not working well and many people couldn't find jobs. Many fell into poverty. They left to earn money abroad as *dekasegi* (sojourners) living temporarily in another land. They went to other parts of Asia, South America, and North America. In the United States, they became first-generation Japanese Americans, or Issei.

The Japanese government carefully selected which workers got passports. Workers would leave only if they had a labor contract that guaranteed their safe return to Japan. The first people to immigrate to the United States worked on Hawaii's sugar plantations. A typical contract required these laborers to work for three years for the plantation owner, who paid their passage; gave them food, lodging, and medical care; and paid them about nine dollars a month—higher wages than they could have earned in Japan. Women laborers, who were less numerous than men, were paid less.

Japanese American women and men in Hawaii at the turn of the century. Hawaii was the first major destination for immigrants from Japan, and it was profoundly transformed by the Japanese presence.

Some Japanese workers came to the U.S. mainland as student laborers. Most student workers settled in San Francisco and, usually through the help of Christian missions, learned English, found work, and attended school.

Japanese laborers also were recruited for jobs in California, the Pacific Northwest, and Alaska. They were sent to work on railroads, sawmills, fish canneries, mines, and, most often, farms. Conditions in temporary farm camps often were terrible.

Japanese laborers fought for better working conditions even though most labor unions refused to let them join. In 1903, Japanese and Mexican sugar beet workers in California successfully banded together against local growers and labor contractors. Japanese grape pickers in California organized into unions briefly in 1908. The following year, Japanese laborers in Hawaii staged a successful strike against plantation owners.

Despite the difficulties these laborers faced—or perhaps because of them—self-sufficient Japanese communities developed, including businesses, newspapers, social organizations, and even baseball leagues. Some people saw these communities as exclusionary—as taking away "American" jobs while limiting contact with non-Japanese people. Others saw the Japanese

> The Japanese custom is to write a person's "last" name first. In this article, we have Americanized all names, with the "last" name following the "first."

Like other Japanese immigrants who hoped to build a new life in the United States, the Yamane family established a successful business, a small grocery store that sold Japanese and American products. The property was owned by the eldest son, Kazuo, who was born in the United States, was an American citizen, and could legally own land and property.

George Grantham Bain Collection, Library of Congress, 3a41751

Catalog ID: 2009.20.34, Washington State Historical Society, Tacoma (Wash.)

Some Japanese American men who immigrated to the Northwest worked in the forestry industry, harvesting lumber and building railroads. Other early immigrants to the Pacific coast worked in mining camps or fish canneries or opened general stores, restaurants, and small hotels.

Snoqualmie Valley Museum: Image PO.040.1357. Clark Kinsey Photo.

as excluded, shunned by the larger society. Some organizations promoted integration but with little success. Anti-Japanese hostilities flourished, particularly in California, where Japanese farm workers had purchased farms and were becoming prosperous.

Barred from gaining citizenship, people of Japanese descent were prohibited from buying land. Things got even worse in 1924 when the National Origins Act stopped people who would not be allowed to become citizens from even coming to the United States, in the first place.

By 1924, there were already 400,000 people of Japanese descent in the United States, including Hawaii. They had begun to think of themselves as *teiju* (settlers). But without the right to become citizens (which they would not get until 1952), they were no longer "overblown with hope" about life in America. The "only . . . hope left," wrote a Japanese newspaper, " . . . is the maturation of our American-born children." Finally in 1952, the Supreme Court ruled that the laws barring Japanese and other foreign-born residents from owning land were unconstitutional.

Illustration by Cheryl Jacobsen

Western U.S., Hawaii & Japan

From Japan to Hawaii to the U.S. mainland, Japanese immigrants logged more than six thousand miles across the Pacific Ocean on their journey to America.

The Immigration Act of 1952 allowed immigrants who had previously been barred from gaining citizenship to become "naturalized" (the granting of full citizenship to people of foreign birth).

May be reproduced for classroom use. *Toolkit Texts: Short Nonfiction for American History, Industrial Age and Immigration,* by Stephanie Harvey and Anne Goudvis, ©2021 (Portsmouth, NH: Heinemann).

Picture Brides

Between 1900 and 1920, about 22,000 Japanese women arrived in the United States. Some were married in a traditional ceremony in Japan with one important person absent—the groom. These women, known as "picture brides," met their husbands for the first time in America. The meeting often came as a shock.

Arranged marriages were customary in Japan, with the prospective couple exchanging photographs before they met. In the United States, **Issei** men met few eligible Japanese women and were forbidden to marry non-Japanese women. Some did not want to return to Japan for fear of being drafted into military service. Others could not afford the expense or the time to seek a bride in their homeland. So an Issei man wanting to marry sent a photograph of himself to a matchmaker in Japan, who found a suitable wife.

Before issuing a passport to a bride, the Japanese government required the prospective husband to show that he could support her and to list her name in his family's registry (a government document listing all family members) six months before the marriage. Brides had to pass a physical examination before they left Japan and when they arrived in the United States. Until 1917, when the United States recognized the Japanese marriage ceremony, the couple got married again in America.

Often the photographs the men sent home had been taken years earlier or were of someone else. The husband's house usually turned out to be, as one bride described, "one room, barren, with one wooden bed and a cook-stove—nothing else." Picture brides often worked in the fields or their husband's business and also took care of the house. They were expected to wear bulky Western clothes, constricting corsets, and toe-pinching shoes. Some women found their situations intolerable and left their husbands, but they did not return to Japan; that would have shamed their families.

Japan stopped issuing passports to picture brides as of March 1920. This further restricted the flow of Japanese immigrants to America. But the picture brides were already giving birth to a new generation of American-born Japanese called **Nisei**.

> **Issei:** people born in Japan who immigrated to another country
>
> **Nisei:** people of Japanese ancestry who are born in another country

Japanese American National Museum (Gift of Madeleine Sugimoto and Naomi Tagawa, 92.97.108)

In this painting by Japanese American painter Henry Sugimoto, Japanese women arrive in the United States to meet their new husbands. A woman in a blue kimono bows to an older man after disembarking a ship. Scenes from Japan and Mt. Fuji are in the background.

National Archives

Just as Ellis Island was the immigrant processing center of the East Coast, Angel Island was the immigration station on the West Coast. Here, a group of new wives of Issei and picture brides arrive in the United States around 1915.

May be reproduced for classroom use. *Toolkit Texts: Short Nonfiction for American History, Industrial Age and Immigration,* by Stephanie Harvey and Anne Goudvis, ©2021 (Portsmouth, NH: Heinemann).

Konoye Hirota's Journey Inspires Generations

Konoye Hirota immigrated to the United States from Japan in 1917.

By Judy Sakaki

Sonoma State University president Judy Sakaki gave the keynote address at the Nikkei Angel Island Pilgrimage at Angel Island State Park on October 13, 2018.

"This island . . . Angel Island . . .

It's where many of our ancestors first stepped into a new country . . . into a new way of life . . . and into a new world. And, because they did . . . many of us are here.

For many JA's or Japanese Americans, Angel Island marks the start of the experience of our family in the United States. Irrespective of where we were born, where we grew up, where we went to school or where we now work. . . . many of us are connected by the shared Angel Island experience of our grandparents, great grandparents or ancestors.

I was born and grew up in Oakland. As a young girl, I attended Japanese School on Saturdays and Sunday School at the Buddhist temple. In college, I enrolled in Japanese language classes and then in search of my roots, I decided to spend a summer in Japan. I took classes at Sophia University in Tokyo, and for the first time, I met cousins, aunts, uncles and other relatives in Fukuoka. I was an undergraduate searching for my roots and discovered so much.

I learned *Gaman*—enduring the seemingly unbearable with patience and dignity.

Gambatte—fight for it, do your best.

Shikata ga nai—it can't be helped.

I learned much from strong and caring women, my mother and my grandmothers.

Bachan means grandmother.

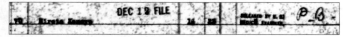

Konoye Hirota listed on a Japanese arrivals log from Angel Island in December 1917. Note the "P.B.," which stands for "Picture Bride." (Courtesy Ancestry.com)

My maternal **bachan**, Konoye Hirota, arrived here in 1917.

My paternal *bachan*, Shigeru Sakaki, arrived here in 1918 . . . exactly 100 years ago.

230

Both of my grandmothers were picture brides. After arriving here at Angel Island, my grandmothers married my grandfathers . . . men they did not know, and whom they had never met.

My *bachans'* stories are as inspiring to young people as their ancestors' stories are inspiring to me.

And especially in times like these . . .

. . . when many immigrant and minority communities in our country feel worried, and afraid . . .

. . . I believe that we share a responsibility to tell the stories . . .

. . . to remember the stories . . .

. . . and to *draw strength* from the stories we celebrate here today.

For me personally, the story of my maternal *bachan*, Konoye Hirota, never fails to fill me with hope . . . with perseverance . . . with admiration, with gratitude and with fortitude.

My *Bachan*

She was the younger sister who went to the boat dock to say goodbye to her older sister, her *o-ne-san*, who was about to sail for America as a picture bride.

But on the dock, her older sister grew afraid.

My *bachan's* older sister, her *ne-san*, decided just as the boat was about to leave the dock. . . . that she could not go to a country where she knew no one, and where she did not speak the language.

So the older sister urged her brave younger sister . . . my *bachan* . . . to go in her place.

My *bachan* was dutiful and did as she was asked. She took her older sister's suitcase . . . full of clothes that were not her own . . . and boarded the ship bound for San Francisco . . . clutching the picture of her husband-to-be, my ji-chan, grandpa. Masajiro Hirota.

To this day, I draw strength from the courage and optimism my *bachan* always kept alive.

All across the thousands of miles of the northern Pacific . . .

. . . for weeks . . .

. . . my *bachan* stayed strong.

She knew nothing about the country where she would live.

She knew nothing about the man she would marry.

She spoke no English . . . and she knew no other Japanese people in her new home.

From Konoye Hirota's "alien registration file," dated 1942. (Courtesy National Archives)

And yet, my *bachan* always remained optimistic . . .

. . . she stayed courageous . . .

. . . she stayed hopeful.

Her heart was always filled with gratitude.

In her new home, with her new husband, she raised five children.

In the war years, in the internment camp, facing racism and discrimination, she stayed positive . . . she stayed strong.

My *bachan* is my hero.

That is why, to this day, I think to myself:

'If my *bachan* could survive all *that* . . . and with her optimism intact . . . then I can survive anything, too.'

And that is also why I believe we share a responsibility to tell our family stories.

Mementos from the past, and memories from the past . . .

. . . the treasured items, and the feelings of strength and optimism, that the men and women who came before her carried with them on the ships from Japan . . .

. . . and through the years in the internment camps.

We are all here today because of the strength . . . the perseverance . . . and the optimism of the family members who walked here before us.

We carry their gaman and gambatte spirit.

We are all here today because of their courage . . . their hope . . . and their determination to live the lives that became the stories we celebrate today.

My heart is filled with gratitude for all who came here . . . to Angel Island.

Arigato.

Thank you so very much."

Judy's mother, grandparents, and uncle in the Topaz incarceration camp in Utah (Courtesy Judy Sakaki)

Judy Sakaki is president of Sonoma State University. After a distinguished career in the University of California and California State University systems, she became the first Japanese American woman in the nation to lead a four-year university or college on July 1, 2016.

To read more personal stories of immigrants to the Pacific Coast, visit https://www.immigrant-voices.aiisf.org/.

Angel Island
West Coast Stories

The majority of immigrants who passed through Angel Island Immigration Station in the early 20th century came from China and Japan, but a large number of groups also came from a few other nations.

A group of Russian immigrants sat on the deck of a ship in San Francisco Bay after surviving turbulent storms on the Pacific Ocean.

©Bettmann/Getty Images

A Russian Exodus

Before the turn of the 20th century, Russian Jews began fleeing to America to escape **pogroms** that persecuted them for their religion and faith. Then, World War I (1914–1918) devastated Europe. As Russians dealt with the aftermath of that conflict, the Bolshevik Revolution overthrew the royal Romanov family, and a civil war began. Life in the Russian Empire became extremely difficult, and many Russians tried to escape the situation. Most of the immigrants who came in the 1920s were from the upper class—aristocrats, former imperial officers, and educated professionals. Known as "White Russians," they did not support the "Red" Communist government that was emerging in the new Soviet Union. At first, the U.S. government welcomed the White Russians. But fears that communism was spreading in the United States led to greater restrictions.

Pogroms are organized persecutions of a minority group. The term was mainly used to describe attacks on Jewish people in Czarist Russia.

First Stop, Hawaii

In January 1903, about 100 mostly young Korean men arrived to Hawaii. At the time, the Hawaiian Islands were a U.S. territory. The men were recruited to work on the island's sugar plantations. Many of them were eager to leave Korea, which was struggling under the rise of Japanese military control. Faced with heavy taxes and food shortages, Korean farmers lost their land. Over the next two and a half years, more than 7,500 Koreans followed that initial group to Hawaii. Eventually, many of them continued on to the U.S. mainland for better job opportunities. The influx of Korean workers halted in 1908, after the United States and Japan reached the Gentlemen's Agreement, which restricted immigration from Japan and Korea. An exception was made for young Japanese and Korean women, who were either wives or "picture brides," coming between 1910 and 1924 to join their husbands. After Japan annexed Korea in 1910, many more Koreans fled their homeland for America.

A Temporary Welcome

In 1898, when the Philippines became a U.S. territory, Filipinos immigrated freely to the United States as U.S. nationals. The Philippines developed an export economy that sent its agricultural products overseas. Small family farms were unable to compete, so many young Filipinos left for America. Between 1906 and 1935, they headed to Hawaii to work on sugar and pineapple plantations. They also eventually found work as migrant laborers in California. In 1934, when the United States granted common-wealth status to the Philippines, the status of Filipino immigrants changed, and immigration from the Philippines was restricted to 50 people per year. That limit remained until Congress passed the immigration and Nationality Act in 1965.

Angel Island Immigration Station processed Korean immigrants arriving in San Francisco, but many early Korean immigrants came to Hawaii.

Many Filipino immigrants worked on farms and helped with harvests, like this field laborer in California in 1939.

NEIGHBORS
NORTH AND SOUTH

IT'S COMPLICATED. Throughout history, Mexico and the United States have had a complex relationship. "On the one hand, the two countries are close. But on the other hand, they're also distant because there are big, big differences," said Richard Miles. He's a former diplomat at the Center for Strategic & International Studies in Washington, D.C. Here's a look back and ahead.

LOOKING BACK

Even before the U.S. Border Patrol officially began in 1924, immigration officials patrolled the southern U.S. border. In 1904, officials worried about Chinese people coming into the United States through Mexico. Meanwhile, up to 16,000 Mexicans were working on U.S. railroads during the first decade of the 20th century. Hundreds of thousands more people moved north after a revolution broke out in Mexico in 1910.

Refugees are people who must leave their home country for their own safety and survival. This may be due to conflict, war, natural disaster, or economic hardship.

U.S. flag (top left): ©charnsitr/Shutterstock. Mexican flag (top right): ©Artgraphixel/Shutterstock. Photo (bottom): Library of Congress, George Grantham Bain Collection, 15424.

Refugees from the Mexican Revolution in the 1910s headed for Marfa, Texas.

Mexican workers helped build railroads in the southern United States.

Tensions grew between the two countries as political upheaval continued in Mexico. U.S. president Woodrow Wilson sent U.S. Marines to Veracruz in 1914. Mexico had wrongfully detained several U.S. soldiers. Wilson again sent troops in 1916 after Francisco "Pancho" Villa attacked Columbus, New Mexico. Things settled down a bit once Mexico adopted a new Constitution in 1917.

Mexicans were largely excluded from U.S. immigration **quotas** in the 1920s. Then the **Great Depression** began in 1929 and attitudes shifted. President Herbert Hoover announced a program of "American jobs for real Americans." The government **deported** up to 1.8 million people. Most of the deportees may have come from Mexico, but a number of the deportees were American citizens.

In 1933, President Franklin D. Roosevelt said America would be a "good neighbor." But relations grew tense when Mexico's government took over the nation's oil companies in 1938. U.S. companies had invested money in those companies. But Roosevelt

CANADA

UNITED STATES

MEXICO

ATLANTIC OCEAN

PACIFIC OCEAN

Gulf of Mexico

Caribbean Sea

N
W   E
S

©GeoNova Group for Houghton Mifflin Harcourt

Quotas are fixed numbers of people allowed into a country.

The Great Depression (1929–1939) was the United States' worst economic downturn.

Deported means removed from a country and sent back to one's home country.

didn't send troops. Mexico eventually paid millions of dollars to U.S. oil companies for properties it had taken. And the two countries fought on the same side in World War II (1939–1945).

Beginning in 1942, the Bracero program brought more than 4.5 million temporary workers from Mexico to the United States. Most of the workers found jobs on farms and for railroads. Yet, anti-immigrant feelings surged again as Americans came home from serving in World War II and then the Korean War (1950–1953). In 1954, President Dwight D. Eisenhower's administration began a program that deported more than 1 million people of Mexican descent.

After the Bracero program ended in 1964, the Mexican government built factories in border towns. The factories gave jobs to many people. And low wage rates attracted companies to Mexico. Companies imported raw materials from the United States. They sent finished goods back. Both countries benefited. Mexico made more money after offshore oil reserves were found in the Gulf of Mexico. However, its government borrowed heavily, so the national debt grew. And income inequality—the gap in income between rich and poor or middle-class people—was a serious problem in Mexico. The problem grew worse as **inflation** rose and oil prices fell.

Inflation also was a problem in the United States in the 1970s. Yet, Americans were still better off overall. "Any time you have two countries side by side in which there's a big difference in riches and wages, you're going to have people in the poorer country trying to migrate to the richer country for jobs," Miles said. The United States passed laws such as the Immigration Reform and Control Act in 1986, which tried to stop migration from Mexico.

Worries about drugs and crime have been another big issue. President Richard M. Nixon's administration announced a "war on drugs." It began beefing up border patrols and inspections. Money from the drug trade fueled corruption in Mexico. Crime and drugs remain serious concerns for both countries, although progress is being made.

> **Inflation** is an increase in prices accompanied by a fall in the value of money.

©David A. Litman/Shutterstock

Mexican laborers have filled agricultural jobs in the United States, working as seasonal field workers gathering and packaging fresh produce.

The border wall has become a controversial topic today as
the United States tries to find ways to curb immigration.

TODAY—AND THE FUTURE

In 1994, Mexico, Canada, and the United States entered into the North American Free Trade Agreement (NAFTA). That treaty allowed these countries to engage more openly and freely.

Mexico's economy improved under NAFTA, and many Mexican citizens have returned to Mexico. Immigration from Mexico to the United States has slowed. Today, most people who want to migrate across America's southern border are fleeing violence and poverty from other countries in Central America.

That situation presents tensions for the United States and Mexico. In 2017, President Donald J. Trump called for a "wall" along the border. Security experts say it wouldn't really secure the border. Trump has also expressed various anti-Mexican sentiments. Meanwhile, Mexican president Andrés Manuel López Obrador has expressed some anti-American feelings. "Neither Mexico nor its people are going to be the piñata of any foreign government," he said during his campaign in 2018.

Both countries have leaders whose political speeches are often **antagonistic**. Nonetheless, the United States and Mexico are making progress. Communication and cooperation take place at a variety of levels, Miles noted. Overall, that's good.

"The neat and special thing about our relationship with Mexico is it touches the daily lives of more U.S. citizens than any relationship in the world," former ambassador Earl Wade said in 2017. Yet, even with shared interests in trade, security, and culture, challenges remain. In January 2021, Joseph Biden became the 46th president of the United States. Citizens from both countries are waiting to see if the immigration policies with Mexico will change once again.

> **Antagonistic** means showing or feeling hostility or opposition to someone or something.

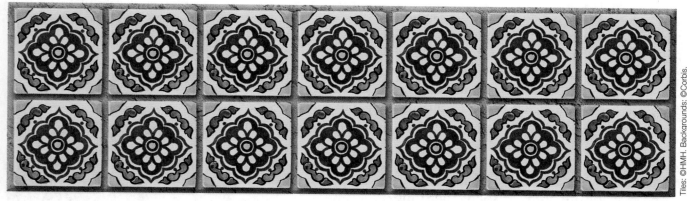

Celebrating Our Southwest Heritage
A Talk with Khristaan Villela

Khristaan Villela

The Southwestern United States was once part of Mexico. Before that, it spent centuries under Spanish colonial rule. And Native groups have lived in the area for thousands of years before that. These roots continue to influence the Southwest's art, music, stories, architecture, and other aspects of its culture.

To learn more, we talked with Khristaan Villela. He is executive director at the Museum of International Folk Art in Santa Fe, New Mexico. The museum's mission is to help visitors see folk art as a form of creative expression and as a way to find common bonds among people from different backgrounds. Villela also is the chair of Arts and Science for the New Mexico Department of Cultural Affairs. The Department of Cultural Affairs works to preserve the state's diverse cultural heritage.

What sets the Southwest apart from other parts of the United States when it comes to cultural influences?

The **demographics** of who lives in the Southwest are distinct from many parts of the United States. In addition to Anglo Americans, there are large populations of Native Americans, as well as Hispanic descendants of the Spanish colonial settlers. Plus there are people of Mexican descent who moved more recently to the Southwest.

> **Demographics** are statistical data related to a population.

How is the way the area sees its culture distinct from citizenship or national boundaries?

Both Mexico and the United States as modern nation-states are relatively recent additions to the map. So is the current international border. Hundreds of years of arts and culture and language predate Mexico here in the Southwest. There are rich inputs from Spain, and from indigenous people, as well as from Anglo American settlers. A lot of shared cultural aspects span the border.

What is an obvious way in which we see that cultural heritage?

Food brings people together. Enchiladas, tortillas, beans, and chili peppers are all food of Mexican origin. Lots of regional or local **cuisines** are ultimately related to Mexico. But they look different whether you're in Arizona or Southern California or Texas or Chicago. Cuisines are living traditions.

What's a less obvious example of the area's Hispanic heritage?

Cowboy culture in the Southwest largely comes from Mexican and earlier Spanish colonial ways of ranching.

Why is it important to preserve and learn about buildings and other sites that date back to the area's days of Spanish and then Mexican rule?

They're like time capsules. Buildings such as the Palace of the Governors in Santa Fe were built in the early 1600s. There probably were even some foundations that were laid before the Pilgrims landed [in what is now Massachusetts] in 1620. Those buildings are the legacy of the colonial period, of the struggles of the European powers in North America. They remind us also that the Spanish and the Mexicans were settlers here, just as the later Anglo Americans were. And the first people whose land this was, the Olmecs and Native American tribes, still live in the Southwest.

A traditional Mexican dish, enchiladas have become a familiar meal to many Americans.

Cuisines are styles of cooking.

What should people appreciate about the Southwest's artistic traditions?

[Before the United States claimed] the Southwest, the different Native tribes all had vibrant arts and cultural traditions. When the Spanish arrived in 1598, they brought a whole other group of arts and culture. Some interesting blending happened.

For example, famous Navajo weaving resulted from the introduction of Spanish sheep. There was the introduction of some European dyes. Silverwork also came from the Spanish. The Spanish taught the native Pueblo and Navajo people silver-working methods. So, you have parallel traditions.

The Palace of the Governors dates to 17th century, when the building served as the seat of Spain's New Mexico territory.

May be reproduced for classroom use. *Toolkit Texts: Short Nonfiction for American History, Industrial Age and Immigration,* by Stephanie Harvey and Anne Goudvis, ©2021 (Portsmouth, NH: Heinemann).

What should people appreciate about stories, music, and dance in the Southwest?

Some music and dance traditions in the Southwest can be traced all the way back to Spain via Mexico. Others can be traced back to Spain via Mexico with really significant variations. That's because they're being performed in a part of the world where there are large numbers of indigenous people, who also have traditions of music and dance and folklore. The traditions are mixing.

Visitors to Santa Fe can browse a Native American market, at which native craftspeople display and sell their work.

How do you see the area's cultural history as being relevant to current political discussions about the border?

Many people in the Southwest are not migrants to the United States. In some cases, their ancestors were living here before the U.S. government controlled the area. Some like to say that they didn't cross the border, the border crossed them. The U.S.–Mexican border was **porous** until the early 20th century. It's not a hard line, even today.

Los Comanches celebrates when Spanish and Pueblo people came together to protect New Mexican land from invading forces, often the Comanches. Performers re-enact the Comanche dances, drumming, and dancing door to door.

What do you love about your job?

My favorite things are seeing what the **curators** find that they would like to add to our collections. I also love when school groups come to our museum. Sometimes, it's the first time a child has been to a museum.

Porous describes something that is easy to pass through.

Curators at a museum make decisions about materials for a collection and how those materials are interpreted through exhibits.

Vendors: ©rawf8/Shutterstock.com. Background: ©Corbis.

Dancers: Library and Archives, Museum of International Folk Art. Background: ©Corbis.

Photos top and bottom: Courtesy of C.N. Le

C.N. Le (top) is a sociologist at the
University of Massachusetts.
He immigrated to the United States
with his family as a child (bottom left).

The **Vietnam War** (1959–1975) was
a conflict in which the United States
supported South Vietnam's anti-communist
government against communist-led North
Vietnam. South Vietnam's government fell
shortly after the last American troops left in
1975 and many people became refugees.

A **sociologist** studies groups, institutions,
and development in human society.

Recent Arrivals from Asian Countries

May be reproduced for classroom use. *Toolkit Texts: Short Nonfiction for American History, Industrial Age and Immigration,* by Stephanie Harvey and Anne Goudvis, ©2021 (Portsmouth, NH: Heinemann).

"Wow! I like this place," Liying Zheng thought
as she gazed out the airplane flying from Seattle,
Washington, to Portland, Oregon. "I'm going to stay
here as long as I can." Zheng arrived from China in
1991 to study information technology. After decades
of restricting citizens from leaving, China had just
recently begun letting more scholars study abroad.
Once earning her graduate degree, Zheng stayed in the
United States to work. Now Washington is her home.

C.N. Le's family came to California when he was
five years old. "We were refugees from (South) Vietnam
at the end of the **Vietnam War**," Le says. "We were
very fortunate to be able to come to the United States."
Today Le is a **sociologist** and heads the Asian American
studies program at the University of Massachusetts,
Amherst.

Zheng and Le are two of the United States' citizens
who have immigrated from Asian countries. Hailing
from about 20 countries, Asian Americans became
the country's largest immigrant group in 2011. By
2013, their share had grown to 41% of new arrivals,
the highest number of immigrants from Asia in U.S.
history.

That wasn't always the case. Thousands of Chinese
and Japanese workers came during the second half of
the 19th century to build railroads and work on farms.
Filipinos came after the United States acquired the
Philippines in 1898. But discriminatory laws limited
large-scale immigration until quotas ended in 1965.

Recent Pushes and Pulls

By 2018, China, India, the Philippines, Vietnam, and
Korea ranked among the top 10 countries of birth for
America's foreign-born population. "The consistent pull
factor (the reason people come) is the opportunities
that they have here," says Le.

Meanwhile, factors back home pushed immigrants to move abroad. Although the economies of India and the Philippines have been growing, for example, professional opportunities and good jobs were often limited. According to Jeanne Bartilova at the Migration Policy Institute in Washington, D.C., many immigrants from Asian countries can earn more money in the United States than in their country of origin.

Like Zheng, many people came as college students. Starting in the 1960s and 1970s, university programs, particularly, attracted students from India, Taiwan, and South Korea, notes Bartilova. "A large number of them stayed," she says.

A growing U.S. economy brought in skilled professionals, such as scientists, engineers, and business executives. An ever-increasing need for doctors and medical workers resulted in the need for medical personnel in this country. In 2018, immigrants from Asian countries were the largest group of foreign-born health care workers, and most were physicians, surgeons, and registered nurses.

Family ties drew many more immigrants from Asian countries to the United States. Some relatives had been long-time residents, and others came more recently as students or workers. Still others came as a result of American political and military involvement in the Philippines, Japan, Korea, and Vietnam. Once initial family members became permanent residents or citizens, they often brought more family members here.

Facing Challenges

Thriving in a new country isn't easy. Many new arrivals have sought support through familiar ethnic communities, such as local Chinatowns, Koreatowns, and Little Manilas.

"When you meet with people who speak the same language, there's one less hurdle," explains Zheng. "Also, sharing a similar cultural background makes it easier for people to understand you."

"These ethnic communities play a very valuable role in integrating newcomers into mainstream society," Le stresses. They build networks

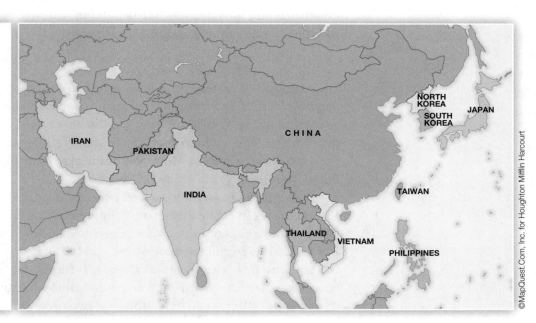

**Top 10
Origin Countries of
Asian Immigrants, 2018**
(in order of most to least)

China

India

The Philippines

Vietnam

Korea

Taiwan

Iran

Japan

Pakistan

Thailand

©MapQuest.Com, Inc. for Houghton Mifflin Harcourt

In 2009, people from Asian countries became the largest and fastest-growing group of foreign-born immigrants to the United States.

that connect people to society in helpful ways. Ethnic communities help people learn about job opportunities, schools for children, and more.

Researchers who study immigration note that the attitudes towards immigrants often change depending on economic conditions. Similar attitudes confronted European immigrants during the 19th and 20th centuries when immigrants were sometimes welcomed as workers and other times actively prohibited from coming. When the United States experiences a healthy economy with plenty of jobs and opportunities, immigration is not a controversial issue. But when there is an economic downturn and jobs become harder to find, there can be resentment towards immigrants for taking "American" jobs.

Contributing to Our Nation

Yet immigrants have often helped America's economy. "Immigrants make contributions all across the spectrum," says Le. They provide needed expertise, skills, and labor. They pay Social Security, income tax, and other taxes. They help to keep the economy humming by buying homes, products, and services. Moreover, immigrants bring innovative ideas and entrepreneurial spirit to the U.S. economy.

Immigrants from Asia, as well as from around the world, enrich the United States in other ways, too. "The more different cultures you know and the more exposure you have, the more knowledge you have," says Zheng. People from many countries add to the rich cultural diversity by introducing new ideas, perspectives, traditions, art, and food. The world becomes more interconnected as people share cultures and develop friendships with people from different backgrounds.

May be reproduced for classroom use. *Toolkit Texts: Short Nonfiction for American History, Industrial Age and Immigration*, by Stephanie Harvey and Anne Goudvis, ©2021 (Portsmouth, NH: Heinemann).

Building a Library of Books

An Interview with Kha Yang Xiong

Meet Dr. Kha Yang Xiong, teacher and author. When Kha was seven years old, her family immigrated to the United States. Today, Kha is a teacher helping children learn English and an author on a journey to create books about the Hmong people, culture, and language.

©2019

1 Tell us about the Hmong people and how they came to the United States.

Most of the Hmong in the world live in Asia. Millions of them live in China and Vietnam. They have been farmers for thousands of years, growing the food they need to survive. In addition to China and Vietnam, hundreds of thousands of Hmong live in Laos, Thailand, and the United States.

The Hmong people living in the United States immigrated as a result of the Vietnam War. Many Hmong people fled their native Laos at the end of the Vietnam War and spent years in **refugee camps** in Thailand. Eventually many Hmong families resettled in the United States.

2 What were your experiences as a child coming to the United States?

My earliest memories are when we lived in a refugee camp in Thailand. As a soldier in the Vietnam War, my father brought us to safety before he passed away. Life fenced in a tiny space with rationed food wasn't too bad. Like other happy children, we ran around in the dirt and played in the rivers freely. After four years living in the camps, my uncle brought us over to the states. We were dropped off in Little Rock, Arkansas.

> **Refugee camps** are temporary facilities built to provide protection and assistance to people who have been forced to flee due to conflict, violence, or persecution.
>
> **Persecution** is hostility and oppressive treatment because of race or political or religious beliefs.

Nav Vaj (center) is wearing typical Hmong clothes from Laos.

The Hmong people living in the United States are mainly from Laos and they immigrated to the United States as a result of the Vietnam War. During the Vietnam War, the Hmong were recruited by the Central Intelligence Agency (CIA) to fight alongside the United States. Hmong soldiers helped American soldiers navigate through the thick jungles of Laos. After the United States lost the war, Americans pulled out of Laos. This left the Hmong people in danger of being killed by the communist Laotians. As a result, the United States allowed Hmong **refugees** to immigrate to America. Although, it is estimated that over 30,000 Hmong people died in the Secret War of Laos.

7

Dr. Kha Yang Xiong tells the history of the Hmong people in her children's book.

My first day of school was a bit strange as I looked around my classroom. The other children had light skin and light hair. I was very different from these children. They called me names and pulled on their eyes to mimic my small eyes. I remember trying to hide my lunch from the other kids because it was different.

My mother spoke no English and she did not understand the American school system, so she was not involved in my education. When I got sick, I would write my own notes to excuse myself. As an immigrant Hmong child, my educational experiences were often confusing and lonely. Immersed into a culture, eventually I learned to speak English. When I gained my English skills, I also gained the roles and duties of an adult even though I was only a child. With my skills, I had to help translate for my mother at the store and many other places.

3 Why did you become a teacher and an author?

After high school, I was inspired to attend college. College meant working full-time and attending classes in the evenings and weekends so I could support my family. But with hard work, focus, dedication, and determination, I graduated from college. Then I received my master's degree. While I was working in the schools, I enjoyed helping students learn a new language. When I looked at them, I saw myself as a child facing the same kinds of challenges. I knew that not many people would understand their situation like I did. That was why I became a teacher.

After receiving my master's degree, I went further into graduate studies and earned my doctorate degree. I decided to study my own people because I was very concerned about the heritage language loss I saw with my own children and my brother. My brother had lost much of his Hmong language skills to the point where he could not communicate with our mother. Actually this is an issue not only in my own family; many children

May be reproduced for classroom use. *Toolkit Texts: Short Nonfiction for American History, Industrial Age and Immigration*, by Stephanie Harvey and Anne Goudvis, ©2021 (Portsmouth, NH: Heinemann).

of my friends and extended family are experiencing the same situation. They do not speak or understand the Hmong language. When children lose their heritage language, they lose a connection to their culture as well. This leads to detrimental impacts on an individual's identity and self-esteem. It also impacts a child's relationship with their parents and grandparents.

As a teacher, I am very aware of the negative impacts of losing one's language and culture. I am committed to helping my students maintain their language and cultural identity. When children know that their teachers value their experiences and cultural background, they are more connected to and engaged with their school community. In particular, I want to make sure that Hmong children will learn about their own people, their culture, and their history. Throughout all my years in school, not once did I see a book in my own language. I want to help the children remember who they are and how to maintain their heritage language.

I decided to make a library of books to teach about the Hmong people. There are few if any books written in the Hmong language for children. It is important to publish these so that children can learn to read, write, and speak Hmong. If young children can see books that reflect themselves, they will feel proud to be Hmong.

My first book is *Who Are the Hmong People?* This book teaches about the Hmong people, their history, and their culture and traditions. This excerpt from the book tells about the history of the Hmong people's journey to the United States and family traditions. I have also written a book that teaches the alphabet in Hmong. I'm going to make a library of Hmong books. I welcome anyone interested in helping to make this dream come true.

WHO ARE THE
HMONG PEOPLE?
FIRST EDITION

Dr. Kha Yang Xiong

©2019

To learn more about Dr. Xiong and her books, or to contact the author, go to: https://www.hmongchildrensbooks.com/.

Path to Citizenship

Were you born in the United States? If so, you are automatically a citizen of this country. But people born elsewhere can also obtain U.S. citizenship. The process is more complicated, but it can be done. Here's how.

It's Automatic

A child born outside the United States today is still considered a citizen if at the time of birth the parents are U.S. citizens and:

❏ Both parents are U.S. citizens and at least one parent lived in the United States or its territories before the child's birth. For example, Michael Smith is born in Argentina. Both of his parents are U.S. citizens when he is born, and his mother lived in the United States before his birth. So Michael is a U.S. citizen.

❏ Only one parent is a U.S. citizen, and that parent lived in the United States or its territories for at least five years before the child's birth, two of which were after age 14. For example, say that Michael's mother is an Argentine citizen and his father is a U.S. citizen. Michael is a U.S. citizen if, before his birth, his dad lived in the United States the required amount of time.

❏ One or both parents become naturalized U.S. citizens, and the child is automatically naturalized by "derivation," or by deriving their citizenship through their parent(s). The child has to be a lawful permanent resident with a green card and live in the U.S. legally and physically with the naturalized parent.

The Green Light

Someone born outside the United States (or a U.S. territory such as Guam or Puerto Rico) and whose parents are not U.S. citizens has a more involved route to citizenship. First, he or she must become a legal permanent resident of this country. This is often called having a "green card," officially known as a Permanent Resident Card. The most common ways to get legal permanent residency are:

❏ A close relative (parent, adult child, spouse, or sibling) who is a U.S. citizen or permanent resident applies for, or **sponsors**, the person.

❏ An American employer applies for the person because the immigrating person has the skills and education for a job that the employer wants to fill but for which the employer could not find any Americans to fill.

❏ The person invests $1 million in a new company in the United States and employs at least 10 full-time legal U.S. workers. Or they invest $500,000 in a new company that is creating jobs in an area where there is high unemployment.

❏ The person applies as a refugee or an asylee because the individual has a well-founded fear of persecution in his or her home country. Seeking **asylum** means someone is asking for political protection from another country because they cannot return to their own country. An asylum-seeker must prove they faced persecution in their home country due to race, religion, nationality, or political opinions. The request for refugee status must be made from outside the United States. Asylum requests are made once the person is in the United States. If approved, the U.S. government will provide protection and aid to those immigrants and their immediate family members.

❏ He or she wins the once-a-year immigration lottery. This lottery is open only to people from certain countries that don't have many legal permanent residents already in the United States. However, the future of the immigration lottery is uncertain, as the program may be discontinued after 2021.

All these situations require sending in many forms and filing fees to a U.S. Citizenship and Immigration Services (USCIS) office. A hopeful citizen-to-be must also submit official documents, including a birth certificate, fingerprints, and photographs. The person must undergo a medical examination and show that he or she will not become a financial burden to the U.S. government. It may take from 1 to 22 years to process a permanent residency case. The time varies depending on how the individual is applying (through family, through employment, as a refugee, etc.), what country they come from, and how many others have applied ahead of the person.

> **Sponsors** means to assume responsibility or vouch for a person.

©C. Sherburne/PhotoLink/Photodisc/Getty Images

> A U.S. passport confirms a person's citizenship and offers protection and aid while traveling abroad.

10 Steps to Naturalization

Understanding the Process of Becoming a U.S. Citizen

 U.S. Citizenship and Immigration Services   M-1051 (04/19)

U.S. Citizenship and Immigration Services offers printed pamphlets and online resources in many languages to help guide new immigrants.

If an application is approved and an interviewing officer decides that the candidate meets all the requirements, he or she will be issued a green card. This card allows the person to live permanently in the United States.

It's Perfectly Natural

After establishing legal permanent residency, a person may apply to become a U.S. citizen. This process is called naturalization. To become a naturalized citizen, a candidate must:

❏ Be at least 18 years old. If a child is younger than 18 but a parent becomes a naturalized citizen while the family is living in the United States as permanent residents, the child becomes a citizen automatically.

❏ Have lived in the United States as a permanent resident for five continuous years (or three years if married to someone who has been a U.S. citizen for at least three years).

❏ Have lived for at least three months in the state where they are applying.

❏ If a candidate is serving or has served in the U.S. military, they can apply for citizenship, even if they have been stationed or served in other countries. They must not have been dishonorably discharged from the military.

❏ Be a person of "good moral character" and behave in a legal and acceptable manner.

Byenvini Ozetazini
Yon gid pou nouvo imigran

May be reproduced for classroom use. *Toolkit Texts: Short Nonfiction for American History, Industrial Age and Immigration,* by Stephanie Harvey and Anne Goudvis, ©2021 (Portsmouth, NH: Heinemann).

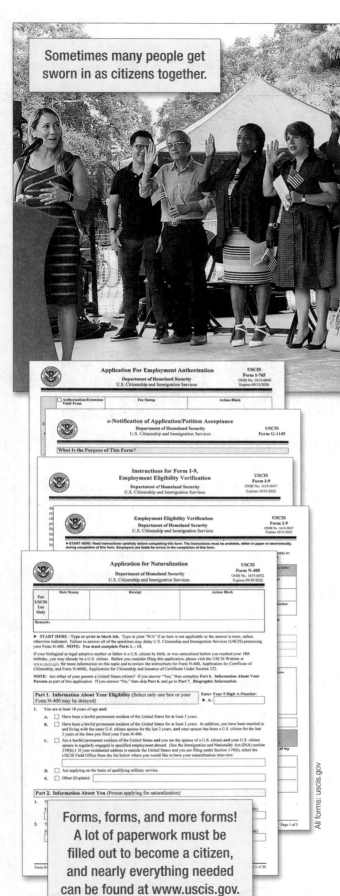

Sometimes many people get sworn in as citizens together.

©Paul Hennessy/Alamy Live News

All forms: uscis.gov

Forms, forms, and more forms! A lot of paperwork must be filled out to become a citizen, and nearly everything needed can be found at www.uscis.gov.

❑ Pass a test showing that they can read, write, and speak simple English and knows basic facts of U.S. history and government. Children and, in some cases, disabled or elderly people do not have to take this test.

❑ Promise to support and defend the United States and its Constitution.

In addition, the citizen-to-be must submit a naturalization application and a filing fee to a USCIS office. Criminal and national security background checks are completed to show that the person intends no harm to the country. Then, an immigration officer interviews the candidate. If the officer approves the case, the candidate will receive an appointment to a swearing-in ceremony. These events are often held in auditoriums, where thousands of people are sworn in as citizens. It is a time of celebration, with people waving American flags. At the end of the ceremony, the new citizens receive naturalization certificates and may apply for U.S. passports—the ultimate proof of U.S. citizenship. And, hopefully, they've planned a big party to kick off their new lives as U.S. citizens!

For many immigrants, the freedom to vote and have a voice is both a privilege and a responsibility.

May be reproduced for classroom use. *Toolkit Texts: Short Nonfiction for American History, Industrial Age and Immigration*, by Stephanie Harvey and Anne Goudvis, ©2021 (Portsmouth, NH: Heinemann).

Rights and Responsibilities

Citizens are official members of a nation.
No matter how someone becomes a citizen, all citizens are equal.
They enjoy special rights and have certain responsibilities, too.

Born with Rights

Jus soli, or right-of-birthplace citizenship, guarantees that all people born in the United States or in the U.S. territories are automatically citizens. *Jus sanguinis*, or right-of-blood citizenship, means that a person with at least one parent who is a U.S. citizen is automatically a citizen. The U.S. Constitution gives Americans basic rights. It allows freedom of speech and freedom of religion, and safeguards other rights, too.

Power to the People

Only citizens have certain rights. Citizens ages 18 and older can vote. Voting lets people decide who will run local, state, and national governments. In some states, citizens can vote to make or change laws, too. Only citizens can hold political office.

Adult citizens are asked to sit on juries. Juries decide issues of fact in court cases. Citizens also can get a U.S. passport. When traveling in other countries, a U.S. passport officially confirms a person's identity as a U.S. citizen and extends national protection while they are abroad.

Certain jobs go only to citizens. To be employed by the federal government, for example, one must be a U.S. citizen.

Duties of Citizenship

Along with rights, citizenship also has responsibilities. Citizens owe allegiance, or loyalty, to the United States. Citizens must support and defend the U.S. Constitution and obey laws. Like all citizens, they must pay taxes. They must respect other people's rights and opinions. Citizens must defend the United States, too. Sometimes that means that they must serve in the military.

From Refugee Camp to New Hampshire

Pramila Khatiwada immigrated to the United States from Bhutan with her family because they faced persecution. Like other Bhutanese citizens from the Lhotshampas ethnic group, they were not allowed to practice their cultural or religious traditions freely. Most Bhutanese refugees have been forced to leave Bhutan in the past 20 years. According to the United Nations, about 105,000 people have lived in refugee camps in Nepal since the early 1990s.

My name is Pramila Khatiwada. I live in Manchester, New Hampshire. My city is small and kind of beautiful. I live in a Nepali neighborhood where everyone is nice and friendly. I am 14 years old. I have one brother and one sister. They both are younger than me. My father has a job at the airport and my mother and grandmother study English. I go to Manchester West High School, which is near my home.

Today I am very happy to share my feelings about my time in a refugee camp and my life right now in United States. First, I will tell about my family. They are from Bhutan, a small landlocked country in South Asia. In Bhutan, it was hard to live and work all day and night for food and other things. There were no trucks or tractors and the land was very mountainous. My parents' families had their own houses and places to grow food and had enough money to buy new clothes and other things they needed. They were happy. Then the king said that if they didn't leave his country, he would kill them. The Bhutan government tortured our Bhutanese refugees. The Bhutanese king didn't like our parents' culture, dress, and religious customs. He said, "If you will follow my rules than you can stay in my country, if not, you have to go to Nepal."

My parents and their families decided to leave. Our parents thought that our culture was important so they went to Nepal. They didn't bring anything with them. They were forced to stay in refugee camps in Nepal, where they made small houses from bamboo and thatch. After four years, I was born in that small camp. My family was very happy because I was the first baby in our family.

They loved me and took care of me. I started to grow up day by day. When I was six years old, I got the opportunity to go to school in my camp. There was one school near my house made of bamboo and thatch.

The school had no electricity and we had to sit on the ground. The teachers moved from room to room, using books given to them by the United Nations. It was cold and wet and students cut large banana leaves to use as umbrellas when it was raining!

The camps were dangerous places because some people at night would come and kill people to steal gold earrings and other valuables. The houses were not strong and did not protect us from bad weather or bad people. Many people got sick because we cooked our food over an open fire and the people breathed in the smoke. People were often injured and there was no hospital or clinic.

Eventually we got the chance to leave the camp. My parents wanted to go America, so they started the third-country resettlement process. When the process was done, we got ready to come to America. When I heard that we were leaving this camp and going to another place to live forever, I felt very badly because I knew I would miss my friends, my cousins, and my neighborhood. But then I realized that going to America would make my future bright and better than in camp. I have never thought in my life that we would get this opportunity to live in America. We put our important papers, some clothes, and money in our bags. A lot of friends, neighbors, and cousins came to my house, and I was really sad because I didn't know if I would ever see them again. At last when we left camp, we said goodbye to everyone.

We flew to New York, and then on to our new home, Manchester. I felt happy and kind of sad. I have been in New Hampshire for one year and 10 months. I am learning a lot about America, and I like my new life in a new country. I now have a chance to go to a good school, and to learn another language. There are books, computers, and equipment that I didn't have in Nepal. We get our lunch at the school. My house is strong and I feel safe with my family. Here I can do things and go to my friends' houses, to the library, and to the park. My dreams may come true. I want to be a nurse and help other people. Someday I would like to visit Nepal again, but I want to live in the United States and become a good citizen.

By Pramila Khatiwada, *Faces*, ©2010 by Carus Publishing Company. Reproduced with permission.

100 Percent Colombian

Juan Sebastian Arevalo Cortes immigrated to the United States from Columbia with his family. Although Colombian immigrants are relative newcomers to the United States, the number of Columbian people coming to the United States began increasing greatly in the 1980s and 1990s. Political and economic problems in Columbia have motivated people to leave the country. By 2008, Colombians were the largest South American immigrant group in the United States, making up 30% of all South Americans in the United States.

My name is Juan Sebastian Arévalo Cortés. I live in an apartment in Cambridge, Massachusetts. Cambridge is like a baby who is sometimes quiet, but when you take away its bottle, it screams and cries and it makes your head explode.

The name of my school is Haggerty. I think Haggerty sounds like an elf name. But I like my school a lot because there are a lot of options for activities. There is no limit to what you can do. If you have a hidden talent, do not keep it to yourself. It is such a great feeling to be on the stage with the lights shining on you and to hear the applause; you feel like it is your first real moment of life.

The subjects that I take are math, science, social sciences, literature, English, music, art, and physical education, and I like all of the subjects because each one has its own fun touch. But if I really have to choose one, I would say art is my favorite because in art you have the right to express yourself freely. It is almost as if art was just a world of imagination where nothing and no one can bother you. Only you have the power to enter into your world of imagination; this is the reason I love art.

I am in sixth grade and there are three words that describe this grade: "hard, but fun."

In August, I turned 12, but I don't feel any different. At the beginning, I kept forgetting that I was 12 years old, but afterwards I adjusted to my change of age. I am looking forward to being 13, because I want to be a teenager.

I have a brother named Joshua Alejandro Arévalo Cortés, who is 16 years old. He is a good brother when he is not in a bad mood. We have a lot of things in common. For example, his friends tell me that I look a lot like him and we both like watching and drawing cartoons. We also have the same sense of humor.

My mother studies Spanish literature at the University of Massachusetts (UMass) and when she finishes she is going to study nursing. She is also a Spanish tutor at UMass and works part time at Shaw's grocery store. I inherited my artistic talent from my mom's side of the family. My father also studies at UMass, but he studies Women's Studies. I think he should study to become a chef because he cooks very well. I believe he is doing this because right now he is working as a waiter at an 'all you can eat' restaurant. From my dad I inherited an artist's eye, because both of us like Frida Kahlo, a Mexican artist.

My best friend is Oscar Medina Vargas. He is probably the most honest person on this planet, and he's also fun, courageous, friendly, and funny. Oscar is the definition of a true friend.

I make my own videos for fun, because there really isn't anything cooler than making videos that people like. Although my videos haven't been viewed much, I don't mind because at least there is one person who likes my videos. Her name is Shannon and I give her thanks for watching my videos. When I'm grown up I want to be an actor, a musician, and a video game designer. Yes, the dream may seem a little impossible, but I am a person who believes nothing is impossible. I am going to achieve this because I have faith that I can.

For vacations I go to Colombia. I went to Colombia about two weeks ago, and seeing my family was a spectacular experience. I hadn't visited in such a long time that when I saw them, my heart raced. The worst part was when I had to leave. I cried at the airport because I didn't want to leave. However, I realize that Colombia is in my heart, and that I am 100 percent Colombian.

The Colombian I admire the most is my great-grandfather because he was the type of person who, if you heard someone talking about him, they would say, "He was old, but he had a big heart." I want to be like my "teddy bear" grandfather. This is what I called my great-grandfather because he was loving and honest. Long live my "teddy bear" grandfather.

The best part about being an immigrant is that you can scream from the window saying, "I'm an immigrant and I am proud to be one." The worst part of being an immigrant is that when you tell someone you are an immigrant, they immediately think that you are here illegally, and this infuriates me.

The most notable differences between Colombia and the United States are the languages, education, cultures, food, family values, region, religions, people, landscapes, cities, towns, economies, and most importantly, the love.

I miss all the Colombian food, because nothing is the same when you prepare it here rather than in Colombia. This is because the Colombians put flavor in the food, but you need Colombia to complete the food that my parents make.

The children of Colombia value their country, family, and friends. We actually follow the rule that Americans talk about so much, "treat others the way you want to be treated." I'm not saying that all Colombian children are perfect or that all American children are mean. I just think that we are not just taught the value of respect, but we are also made to act on it.

It was my parents' decision to come to the United States. I only know that all of my father's family lives here, and I'm guessing that's why we came. I don't feel I belong here, and every time I visit my country I want to stay.

I don't remember the first time I came here because I was only two years old. The last time I went to Colombia was three weeks ago. When I came back I had many urges to cry because I didn't want to leave my grandparents and mostly my uncles.

I like Colombia better than America because I was born there, it's my heritage, and it's where the people I love are. But I have to accept that the United States offers me more career opportunities for the future. I am 100 percent Colombian and proud of it.

By Juan Sebastian Arévalo Cortés and Emily Bryer, *Faces*, ©2010 by Carus Publishing Company. Reproduced with permission.

The Dreamers Here to Stay?

DACA recipients and their supporters rally outside the U.S. Supreme Court on June 18, 2020.

By Marcia Amidon Lusted. May be reproduced for classroom use. *Toolkit Texts: Short Nonfiction for American History, Industrial Age and Immigration*, by Stephanie Harvey and Anne Goudvis, ©2021 (Portsmouth, NH: Heinemann).

It seemed like a huge relief for the thousands of undocumented children and teens. On June 15, 2012, President Barack Obama announced the creation of a program that was meant to protect minors who had come to the United States without authorization when they were young children. These children and their undocumented immigrant families were in constant danger of being deported if their illegal status was discovered. This meant that they could not get drivers licenses or a part-time job or apply for college financial aid. But they had lived almost all of their lives in the United States. They might have come from another country, but they thought of themselves as Americans and lived like other American young people.

Obama's program was known as Deferred Action for Childhood Arrivals, or DACA. DACA was created by the Obama Administration after it was unable to persuade Congress to pass the Development, Relief, and Education for Alien Minors (DREAM) Act, which was first introduced in 2001 but was never successfully voted into law. Because of this act, young undocumented immigrants were called

"Dreamers." When President Obama announced the DACA program, the more than 700,000 young Dreamers thought that they might finally be protected from deportation (sometimes called "removal"). They could finally live their lives like other young Americans, going to college and working and able to receive government benefits.

How did DACA help young immigrants?

It gave them temporary permission to live, work, and study in the United States, without the worry of suddenly being deported if they were discovered to have an undocumented status. For a teen or young adult who might have come to the United States as a very young child, it allowed them to apply for two-year, renewable periods of "deferred status," meaning they would not be considered undocumented during that time. But getting DACA status meant that they had to meet some conditions. When the program began in 2012, they had to be younger than 31 years old. They also had to prove that they had been living in the United States since June 15, 2007, and that they had arrived in the United States before the age of 16. They could not have a criminal record, and they had to be either enrolled in high school or college or be in the military. They could renew their DACA status every two years and remain in the United States as long as they kept meeting the requirements. However, DACA did not guarantee that they would be able to become U.S. citizens or even be given the right to live in the United States permanently by getting a Permanent Resident Card, also called a green card. Only Congress can provide a pathway for permanent resident status for Dreamers through federal legislation.

Who are the Dreamers?

Of the 700,000 Dreamers in the United States, most came from Mexico, El Salvador, Guatemala, and Honduras. There are also several thousand from Asia, mostly from South Korea and the Philippines. Dreamers now live in every state in the country, with the largest numbers in the states of California, Texas, New York, Illinois, and Florida.

However, DACA protections were in jeopardy after President Obama left office and President Donald Trump was elected. On September 5, 2017, the Trump administration announced that they wanted to end DACA. They said that it was unlawful because only Congress had the power to give undocumented immigrants the type of status that DACA offered, not the president. As a result, no new DACA applications were accepted, but after several court cases on behalf of people who already had DACA protection, the decision about deporting existing Dreamers was put on hold.

Immediately, people began protesting at the White House and the Justice Department, as well as in many U.S. cities, about the ending of the DACA program. Mark Zuckerberg, founder of Facebook, wrote, "It is particularly cruel to offer young people the American dream, encourage them to come out of the shadows and trust our government, and then punish them for it." President Obama wrote, "Whatever concerns or complaints Americans may have about immigration in general, we shouldn't threaten the future of this group of young people who are here through no fault of their own, who pose no threat, who are not taking away anything from the rest of us."

But in November 2019, the Trump Administration argued in front of the Supreme Court that the DACA program should end. Trump believed that the Department of Homeland Security, which is in charge of border security, has the right to terminate the program and that the courts do not have the right to challenge them. In June 2020, the court decided that the Trump Administration could not legally end DACA.

On January 20, 2021, in one of his first acts as president, President Joseph Biden issued an executive order that the Department of Homeland Security take all appropriate actions to "preserve and fortify" DACA. This allows DACA recipients, many of them students, to remain in the United States—living, working, serving in the military, and going to school. In addition, President Biden has urged Congress to pass legislation making Dreamers eligible to apply for permanent residence in the United States with a path to citizenship in five years, a message of hope for all Dreamers.

Walking the "Trail of Dreams"

In January 2010, four student activists left Miami, Florida, to walk to Washington, D.C., to protest in favor of a Dream Act. They called their march "The Trail of Dreams." Felipe Matos, Gaby Pacheco, Carlos Roa, and Juan Rodríguez, all college students from Miami, made the walk because they were discouraged by the lack of action taken to reform the immigration system. All four were excellent students, but because they were undocumented immigrants, they would become "ghosts" once they finished college because they did not have legal status, and they could not get jobs and build careers. They wanted to urge President Obama to take action.

The four students were joined by hundreds of others in Washington, some who were also undocumented immigrants and others who believed that they should have the right to stay. The undocumented protestors put themselves at risk, because they could have been discovered by U.S. immigration authorities and instantly deported. But Gaby Pacheco said that she marched 1,500 miles from Florida to Washington so she could say to President Obama, "We just want a chance." Two years later, she and her fellow immigrants received that chance when Obama announced the DACA program.

Four "Trail of Dreams" student activists, including Gaby Pacheco, left, and Felipe Matos, right, walked 1,500 miles from Florida to Washington, D.C., in 2010 to advocate for the Dream Act.

©Sarah L. Voisin/The Washington Post via Getty Images

By Marcia Amidon Lusted. May be reproduced for classroom use. *Toolkit Texts: Short Nonfiction for American History, Industrial Age and Immigration,* by Stephanie Harvey and Anne Goudvis, ©2021 (Portsmouth, NH: Heinemann).

Courtesy of Marissa Molina

Marissa Molina

First Dreamer to Sit on the Metropolitan State University Board of Trustees

Marissa Molina, center right in the back row (above), attended a rally outside of the U.S. Supreme Court with other Colorado DACA recipients in November 2019.

Marissa Molina came to Denver, Colorado from Mexico with her parents when she was nine years old. As is the case with many families immigrating to the United States, Marissa's parents came in search of a better life for their family, but they did not have legal documentation. Later, Marissa became eligible for the Deferred Action for Childhood Arrivals (DACA) program, which allows children who were not born in the United States to remain in the country legally, attend school, and get jobs. These people are referred to as Dreamers because they dream of living a productive life, making a contribution to their community, and becoming citizens of the United States.

When Marissa entered high school, she told her high school counselor that she did not have the proper papers needed to apply for college. Although he was not exactly sure how to help her, he told her that he would "walk with her on her journey" and she would "never be alone." His guidance gave Marissa the confidence to move forward.

With the support of her parents, her high school counselor, and others in her community, Marissa attended and graduated from college. After graduating, she went to work, and eventually became the Colorado

State Immigration Director for an organization that advocates for common-sense immigration reform and to increase access to opportunities for the immigrant community.

In 2019, Colorado Governor Jared Polis appointed Marissa to the Board of Trustees of Metropolitan State University (MSU) in Denver. Since 25% of the students at MSU are Latinx and many of those are Dreamers, Governor Polis chose Marissa because he wanted someone who was qualified for the position and also understood the Dreamer experience. She is now making history as the first Dreamer in Colorado to sit on a university board. Additionally, Marissa is the youngest board member to ever sit on the MSU board.

Marissa at her college graduation.

Marissa is grateful to her high school counselor for his encouragement to this very day. She is also thankful for the support of her college teachers. But she is most appreciative of her parents who have been there for her every step of the way. When she learned that she had been appointed to the university board, she called her mom and said, "This is for you, because you didn't give up on me and my dreams and you were willing to sacrifice to do whatever you could to get me here. And because you did that for me, I'm going to make sure that there are 10 and 20 and 30 kids behind me who have someone who is going to fight for them like you fought for me."

Marissa's goal now is to make sure that all students, including Dreamers and others, have the same opportunity that she had to go to college and have a successful career. Marissa Molina is a young woman who is making a difference.

The board of trustees is the governing body for a university. At Metropolitan State University, members of the board are appointed by the governor of the state. Members of the board work together to select the president of the university, decide on policies for the university, and provide guidance to help faculty and students.

For Kids, Crossing the U.S. Border Illegally Involves Fear and Hope

A girl living in Maryland shares her family's experience of coming to the United States.

By Luz Lazo
October 1, 2019

Evelyn Hockstein/For *The Washington Post*

Wendy plays at an apartment complex in Silver Spring, Maryland. She traveled from El Salvador with her sister and parents, who said they left their country because they feared gangs and didn't earn enough money to support the family.

Editor's note: This article was published in the Washington Post *in October 2019. At that time, families who were hoping to immigrate to the United States were being detained at the southern border and often separated from their loved ones.*

You might have seen the images of thousands of people detained at the United States' southern border in the past few months. Many of them are kids traveling from Central America alone or with family. They want to live in the United States but don't have permission to do so.

Because of a law, some of them have been released and allowed to live with family already in the United States while the government decides whether to let them stay or deport them (send them back home).

Americans disagree on how many immigrants, or people who come from other countries, should be allowed to come to the United States and stay. Immigration is a complicated issue. It's about numbers, but it's also about people.

Wendy, an 11-year-old, is one of those people. She came to the United States with her parents and an older sister in May. It took them one month to travel about 1,500 miles from their home in a small village in El Salvador to the U.S.–Mexican border. They traveled by foot, bus, and car, and crossed the Rio Grande—the river that divides Mexico and Texas—on a raft.

Seeking asylum means someone is asking for political protection from another country because they cannot return to their own country. An asylum-seeker must prove they faced persecution in their home country due to race, religion, nationality, or political opinions. In contrast, a refugee is someone who has been legally recognized under the 1951 Convention to be a refugee. People arriving at the U.S. border have the right to request asylum without being criminalized, turned back, or separated from their children.

"I was afraid I was going to drown," said Wendy, who now lives in Silver Spring, Maryland. The entire trip was long and scary, she said. Wendy and her family spoke with KidsPost on the condition that their last name not be used.

Along the journey, the family split up, and Wendy crossed the border with only her father. They surrendered to U.S. Border Patrol officers and were taken to an immigrant processing center in McAllen, Texas. There, Wendy was taken from her father and placed in a big, windowless room occupied by other immigrant girls and women.

Wendy says she stayed there four days. She had ham and cheese sandwiches and water for dinner. She wasn't able to shower, and one night the room was so crowded that there was no space to lie down to sleep. When she became cold at night, she said, she used aluminum foil as a blanket. During the day, she said, she mostly sat in silence and prayed quietly.

After the fourth day, she said, someone called her name and told her it was time to go.

"I was so happy," she said. "I wanted to see the sunlight."

Wendy was reunited with her father, and their relatives sent money for plane tickets to Washington, where their family would host them. Her mother and sister joined them in Maryland in early June, after a similar experience at the border. Wendy's family hopes to get a permit to stay in the country. They have to get an attorney and go before a judge. The process can take a long time. Because they are here illegally, they also could be deported.

Wendy's parents say they took the risk to come from so far away because they didn't earn enough money at home to support the family, and they were afraid of gangs that hurt people and steal their money.

Madeline Taylor Diaz, an attorney with Ayuda, an organization in the D.C. area that helps immigrants, says that people such as

May be reproduced for classroom use. *Toolkit Texts: Short Nonfiction for American History, Industrial Age and Immigration*, by Stephanie Harvey and Anne Goudvis, ©2021 (Portsmouth, NH: Heinemann).

Wendy and her parents come here for better jobs, education and freedom. And in recent years, many have come fleeing crime, violence, and persecution in their home countries.

"It is a crisis," said Taylor Diaz. "A lot of people are coming because they are truly afraid of staying back home."

Officials have been debating what should happen to these families.

President Trump and his supporters don't want undocumented immigrants to cross the border until they have the proper documents. They favor building a wall along the Mexican border to keep out undocumented people.

Trump's administration also announced in October 2019 a change for those who enter the country illegally. They would be sent back to their countries quickly or sent to Mexico while waiting for the U.S. government to consider their immigration requests. . . .

In the past 11 months, U.S. authorities arrested almost 1 million immigrants, nearly double the 2018 total, at the southwest border, which stretches almost 2,000 miles from southern California to the southern tip of Texas at the Gulf of Mexico. More than 70,000 were children traveling alone.

Taylor Diaz and others think that the United States should welcome immigrants.

"Helping immigrants is like helping our neighbors," Taylor Diaz said. "The kids are just like the kids you go to school with. Treating them fairly is part of the American tradition."

GLOSSARY • GLOSARIO

Border • frontera
Kids • niños
Family • familia
Immigrants • inmigrantes
Countries • países
Immigration • inmigración
River • río
Trip • viaje
Permit • permiso
Jobs • trabajos
Crisis • crisis
Undocumented • indocumentado

Wendy is adjusting to life in the United States. Her parents are trying to enroll her in school. She likes eating hamburgers and going to a park to swing as high as she can. She had never seen trees change colors in autumn before, and she can't wait to see snow. But she still misses her friends and grandparents.

"They also miss me," she said.

Throughout U.S. history, immigrants yearning for better lives settled in the nation

The United States is known as a nation of immigrants. It has had waves of migration since its founding.

In the mid-1800s, a large wave brought more than 14 million immigrants, mainly from Germany, Ireland, and other northern and western European nations, according to the Pew Research Center, an organization that studies U.S. immigration. By the turn of the 20th century, there was another wave of migration, this time involving people from Russia, Italy, and eastern and southern Europe. After 1965, most immigrants came from Asia and Latin America.

Many came to the United States for work or to reunite with family. Others were fleeing religious and political persecution and were in search of freedom. These immigrants are known as refugees, because they are seeking protection in the United States.

In the 1970s and 1980s, some Americans became more concerned about people entering the country through the U.S.–Mexican border without a permit.

Those concerns led to increased security along the southern border, and it drove some of the immigration policies that are in place today. Illegal immigration, mostly from Mexico and Central America, grew in the 1990s and early 2000s. Many of those migrants came to work at farms and in other low-paying jobs. Most left their children in their home countries.

The flow of undocumented immigrants slowed after 2007 for about a decade. A big surge happened this year, driven in part by the arrival of families, children traveling alone, and refugee seekers from Central America. This influx of migrants has ignited a crisis. Experts say people are coming because they can't find jobs in their countries, which are dealing with high levels of poverty and violence. The government has been debating how to control it.

The United States now has more immigrants than any other country. The majority of immigrants—35.2 million as of 2017—are in the country legally. About 10.5 million immigrants are undocumented.

Undocumented immigrants wait to be processed by the U.S. Border Patrol in McAllen, Texas, after they entered the United States in May. There has been a sharp increase in 2019 in the number of people entering the United States without documentation. Many have been families or children traveling alone from Central America.

Ricky Carioti/*The Washington Post*

May be reproduced for classroom use. *Toolkit Texts: Short Nonfiction for American History, Industrial Age and Immigration,* by Stephanie Harvey and Anne Goudvis, ©2021 (Portsmouth, NH: Heinemann).

Frankie Parrish/International Rescue Committee

Imagine being forced to flee your country to escape to safety.
If you were lucky, you had time to pack a few belongings.
If not, you left everything behind and ran.

Refugees: Who Is Helping?

Above: International Rescue Committee (IRC) workers help to reunite children with their families in Burundi.

Refugees are people who must leave their home country or region for their own safety or survival. No one chooses to be a refugee. War or natural disaster can strike anywhere in the world, forcing large numbers of people to seek help in refugee camps. People may also become refugees if they are persecuted or oppressed due to their race, religion, nationality, social activities, political views, or membership in a certain group.

Life in the camps is disorienting and difficult. Many organizations around the world have been established to help meet the basic needs for food, shelter, and medicine.

The United Nations (UN) is a group of countries that meet regularly to promote peace and cooperation between nations. In 1951, the group wrote a document describing the rights of refugees. At the time, many people had become refugees because of World War II. The UN established rules for helping these people settle in other countries.

UN Photo/Fred Noy (149573)

School girls attend classes in a school built by the United Nations High Commissioner for Refugees (UNHCR) in a refugee camp in Sudan. Schools teach girls in the morning and boys in the afternoon to provide education to the many refugee children in Sudan.

offering asylum. Refugee status is an official decision made by a country providing asylum. Many people who are seeking asylum have not yet been approved. Until they receive refugee status, they are known as asylum-seekers. After they are approved, they are welcomed into their host country. The host country is expected to provide them with civil rights and access to social services.

Another organization that helps refugees is the **International Rescue Committee** (IRC). The IRC responds to the world's worst **humanitarian crises** and helps people affected by conflict and disaster. In more than 40 countries and in 26 U.S. cities, the IRC provides clean water, shelter, health care, and education support to refugees.

Refugees Today

In 2017, the number of refugees rose to 25.4 million around the world, according to the UNHCR. Refugees from Afghanistan, South Sudan, and Syria account for the most refugees worldwide. Each of these regions has been devastated by war and oppression. Many people have been forced to flee their homes. About 5.4 million Palestinians are part of a longer-standing group of refugees. More than 8 out of 10 of the world's refugees are from poor countries. Over half of all refugees live in cities. They tend to settle in communities with people from their home countries.

The group originally limited its definition of refugees to include only those from Europe. In 1967, it expanded the definition to include refugees from any conflict or disaster.

Today, refugees can seek asylum in 147 different countries. Asylum is the protection from oppression or hardship offered by another country. The **United Nations High Commissioner for Refugees** (UNHCR) is part of the UN. It helps refugees and countries

A **humanitarian crisis** is an event that threatens the health, safety, or security of a community or other large group of people. This might be a natural disaster, such as an earthquake, flood, or drought, or a man-made crisis, such as a violent conflict or war.

UN Photo/UNHCR/R Chalasani (384472)

Kosovo children carry bread to their families in refugee camps in Albania.

Internally Displaced Persons

Not everyone who has to leave home ends up leaving their country. In some places, people are not safe in their homes because of natural disasters or war. Refugees who move within their country are called "internally displaced persons," or IDPs. Today, about 40 million people around the world are IDPs. For example, Sudan, a country in eastern Africa, has one of the largest IDP populations in the world. That is because for over 20 years, a war between north and south Sudan forced millions of people from their homes. By the end of 2017, around 4.4 million Sudanese people were IDPs. Other countries with large numbers of IDPs are Colombia, Iraq, Somalia, and Pakistan.

Environmental Refugees

Environmental refugees are people who must leave their homes because of environmental disruption. Natural disasters like earthquakes, hurricanes, and floods often force people to flee. Environmental disruption can also be man-made. In the 1990s, about 100 million people were forced to move because of dam building projects. Disruption usually happens when the water held behind the dam floods towns and villages.

In addition, climate change is causing people to seek refuge in other places. Human activity contributes to climate change.

Survivors of an earthquake in Pakistan stand outside of tents provided by the UN High Commission for Human Rights (UNHCR). Refugees often need help with basic needs, like clean water, shelter, and food, after natural disasters.

UN Photo/Mark Garten (108799)

In places where people depend on their animals for survival, helping refugees also means helping care for their animals.

Activities such as burning fossil fuels (like oil and gas) and cutting down forests add greenhouse gases to the atmosphere. This traps the sun's heat, making the Earth warmer. The rising temperature causes glaciers to melt, making sea levels rise. It also leads to droughts and floods. Environmental refugees affected by climate change are often called climate refugees.

The **International Red Cross** is a group that helps refugees. It estimates that there are more environmental refugees today than refugees from wars. The UN stated that 36 million people were forced to move because of natural disasters in 2009. About 20 million of those had to move because of climate change. Like IDPs, environmental refugees are not protected under international refugee laws. In fact, most of them are IDPs as well. They are not promised the same protection and assistance as other refugees. Many international groups see that environmental disruption is a growing problem. It may also increase the number of traditional refugees. The UN says climate change makes it harder for people to access food, water, and other resources they need to live.

Fast Facts

These nations have the most refugees, asylum-seekers, and internally displaced people in their borders (2017):

Colombia: 7,747,365
Syria: 7,033,119
Democratic Republic of the Congo: 5,144,932
Iraq: 4,501,786
Turkey: 3,789,320

Countries of origin of refugees, asylum-seekers, and internally displaced people (2017):

Syria: 13,288,372
Colombia: 7,901,909
Democratic Republic of the Congo: 5,374,765
Afghanistan: 5,336,582
Iraq: 4,809,858

Source: UNHCR, the UN Refugee Agency

The POWER of MUSIC

Liz Keller-Tripp

What is the power of music in times of crisis?

How can the arts help us find and hold onto our humanity?

Hadi Eldebek of the Silkroad Ensemble plays for students with two other musicians, Mike Block (cello) and Shane Shanahan (percussion).

The Silkroad Ensemble, a group of musicians who play many different instruments, believe in the power of music to connect with and support children in difficult circumstances. Since 2015, members of the Silkroad Ensemble have led arts and musical workshops for Syrian refugee children in Jordan and Lebanon. The children's families are part of the estimated 4.8 million people who have fled Syria since the current conflict started in 2011. Most of these refugees from war have settled in the neighboring countries of Jordan, Lebanon, and Turkey. Another 6.5 million Syrians are displaced within their own country living in refugee camps. Too often, people in these camps do not have access to adequate food, water, and other basic needs.

We sat down with Hadi Eldebek and Liz Keller-Tripp from Silkroad to talk about their experience working in refugee communities in Lebanon, and the power of music to heal and inspire children in times of crisis.

By Hadi Eldebek and Liz Keller-Tripp, *Dig*, ©2018 by Carus Publishing Company. Reproduced with permission.

What was the main goal in Lebanon?

Liz: This was an intimate and important opportunity for us to explore, as individuals and as an organization, how we can best use our roles as artists, storytellers, and fellow humans to support displaced populations. In addition to a goal of connecting and sharing with the students and teachers, our visit also involved research, and we were lucky to have such willing and wonderful research partners.

What was it like working with the students?

Hadi: The workshop took place in the classrooms of Shanay School, with students ages 6 to 10. Shane and I started by playing a piece of music, then asking the students what kind of moods, colors, and stories the music conveyed to them. After, we showed them our instruments and talked more seriously about the music we were playing, including the techniques we use and the rhythms. Shane even got them to clap along while we were playing. The students did not stop smiling. We couldn't have been happier.

Can you describe a highlight and a challenge from the week?

Hadi: Sometimes, the environment was a bit of a challenge for us. The rooms were pretty cold. There was an old gasoline heater in the middle of the room, but it didn't seem powerful enough to warm the whole area. However, the optimism of the children was THE highlight of the week. We are talking about kids who themselves or their parents have faced major difficulties caused by the war as well as the challenges related to living in the new place. So, to see the level of energy and enthusiasm that they had was hopeful and encouraging.

Liz Keller-Tripp

Lori Taylor

Silkroad musicians Mike Block and Hadi Eldebek play for students. Jusoor is a nonprofit organization based in the United States that supports Syria's development and helps Syrian youth realize their potential.

What feedback did you receive from students and teachers?

Liz: We were so honored by the smiles and greetings that met us as we entered and left the classrooms. We heard from our Jusoor partners that they still talk about our visit, which makes me both happy and determined to continue learning from and working with them.

What is the value of focusing on music in these workshops?

Hadi: The music in these workshops brought joy, education, and culture to all the participants—students, teachers, and staff. It was communal, especially when the principal and one of the teachers started to sing along and dance the traditional folk dance known as dabkeh. It gave hope and memorable moments of happiness as they learned about the musical traditions we presented.

How did your identity as someone visiting, or returning from, the United States shape your experience and the work?

Hadi: I lived my childhood in Lebanon before moving to the States for college. So, returning to Lebanon to give back to these kids was important for me. I am grateful for the work the Silkroad and Jusoor have done to make it happen.

Liz: [There was a special moment when] at the end of the visit, a group of about 15 young women from various classes, who had been quiet next to male classmates during our visits, enthusiastically approached me and a female colleague just wanting to say hi (all we could really say to each other) and to take pictures together. That moment meant 100 different things to me. As a very small step toward being able to connect more deeply, I am beginning Arabic language studies and will be based in Beirut for several weeks. It's not enough to say marhaba ["Hello!"] and shukran ["Thanks!"] and call that a meaningful interaction. I want to go back and talk to those girls more than I could this time, to get their stories and share their experiences.

In your opinion, what value do the arts have within education? What do you think the value is for Jusoor students?

Liz: What comes through so clearly during the class visits the Silkroad Ensemble has made is that teaching, learning, and understanding are enhanced and, in some cases, even made possible through the arts.

Liz Keller-Tripp, one of the authors of this article, stands in the middle, surrounded by students at the Shanay School.

Old Towns

Photo by A. Wodarek

New Life

In West Fargo, North Dakota, 5th graders take part in designing a natural playground for The Fargo Project World Garden Commons in 2016.

Today, the issues surrounding refugee resettlement—how many people to accept and from which parts of the world—are often debated. But many small towns and cities in the United States are discovering that refugees from other countries can bring new life to their communities.

Across the United States, especially in rural areas and the center of the country, many small towns are experiencing a population decline. Young people are leaving for better jobs in other places. The populations that remain are often older. Many employers cannot find enough workers to fill jobs. Many of these small towns are in trouble.

A Positive Impact

However, many towns like these are beginning to welcome refugees to their communities. Arrivals from other countries, such as Somalia, Syria, and Iraq, are often young people who are willing to fill vacant jobs. They settle in the community and start raising families, and

By Marcia Amidon Lusted. May be reproduced for classroom use. Toolkit Texts: Short Nonfiction for American History, Industrial Age and Immigration, by Stephanie Harvey and Anne Goudvis, ©2021 (Portsmouth, NH: Heinemann).

they rent apartments and shop for food and pay taxes. Their presence creates a healthier economy. As they become part of the community, these refugees also bring a new cultural perspective to places that have been populated mostly by older, white Americans. A multicultural community also attracts younger people and families from other parts of the United States and can persuade local young people to remain.

Welcome from Mayors

Several small town mayors signed a letter recently saying that they had accepted Syrian refugees and would take more. When some governors and members of Congress called for an end to the arrival of refugees from Syria, the mayors of several other small towns protested. They signed a letter that noted "the importance of continuing to welcome refugees to our country and to our cities." According to the mayor of Fargo, North Dakota, refugees from Somalia, Iraq, and Bhutan have contributed to strong population and economic growth.

Strong Protests from Some

Welcoming refugees to rural America isn't without controversy. Some residents worry that the newcomers will take over their community, or that there isn't enough room for them, even though many of these towns have empty apartments buildings and homes. They fear that refugees will take jobs away from local people or make the community more dangerous.

Yet this is untrue. Research shows the opposite: communities with refugees actually became safer. In addition, refugees contribute to the economy and impact society in meaningful and positive ways. Sadly, the number of refugees accepted into the United States has fallen to record lows. This decrease affects refugee families and also the towns and cities across the United States that have welcomed and been strengthened by refugees in recent years.

New Lives

Still, many American communities are enjoying a new energy, as younger people and families begin to populate their towns. New churches, stores, restaurants, and other services open in storefronts that used to be empty. Factories that were on the brink of closing due to a lack of workers are now operating at full capacity. Throughout the United States, refugees from all over the world are bringing old towns back to life.

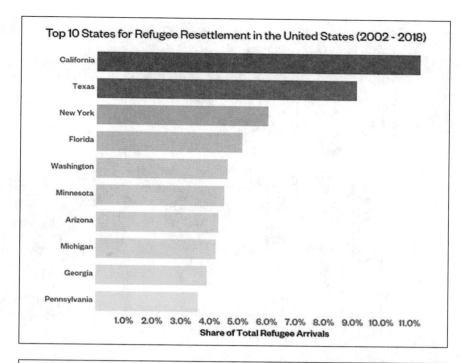

Top 10 States for Refugee Resettlement in the United States (2002 - 2018)

States listed top to bottom: California, Texas, New York, Florida, Washington, Minnesota, Arizona, Michigan, Georgia, Pennsylvania

Share of Total Refugee Arrivals (1.0% – 11.0%)

Top 20 Countries of Origin for Refugee Arrivals in the United States (2002-2018)

Country	Share of Total Refugee Arrivals
Myanmar	18.3%
Iraq	15.1%
Somalia	10.9%
Bhutan	10.1%
Dem. Rep. Congo	6.5%
Iran	5.1%
Cuba	4.9%
Ukraine	3.8%
Russia	2.3%
Sudan	2.3%
Liberia	2.2%
Syria	2.2%
Eritrea	2.1%
Vietnam	1.8%
Afghanistan	1.7%
Laos	1.7%
Ethiopia	1.6%
Burundi	1.3%
Moldova	1.0%
Sierra Leone	0.5%

Top and bottom: Originally published in Social Education 83, no. 6 (November–December 2019), the *Journal of National Council for the Social Studies*, www.socialstudies.org
New American Economy (2019, June 20). Refugee Resettlement in U.S. Cities. From https://data.newamericaneconomy.org/en/refugee-resettlement-us

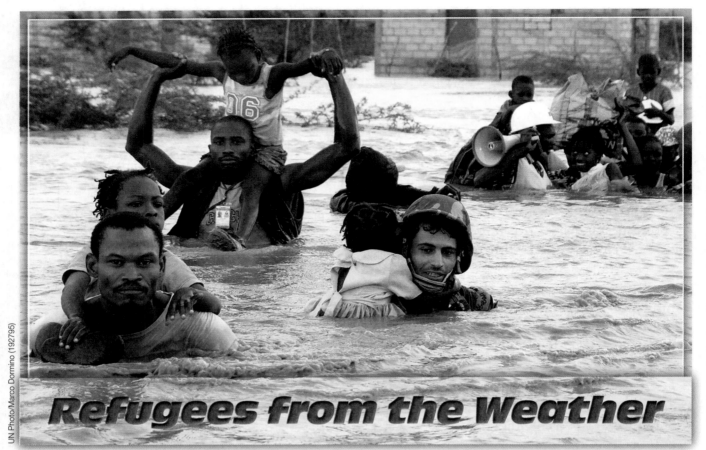

Refugees from the Weather

Editor's note: This article was updated in 2020 to reflect the current situations that environmental refugees face and the statistics on climate change and refugee populations around the world.

They've been called envirogees, environmental migrants, and climate refugees. These sound like fancy terms, but for the people they describe, it comes down to one thing: these people are forced to leave their homes and look for new ones, all because of changes in the global weather.

Refugee usually describes someone who is forced to leave their own country and seek safety somewhere else because of political issues, such as war or persecution. But a climate refugee is forced to leave home because of changes to their environment created by a warming climate and more unpredictable weather. These changes include **droughts**, flooding, rising sea levels, and changes in weather patterns, including more extreme hurricanes and other storms. These changes make it very difficult for families to farm and grow their food, get clean water, and make a living. These problems often force families to go to areas where they might have a better chance of survival.

Drought: A long period of very dry weather with little rainfall that leads to a shortage of water.

Warmer Temperatures

Many climate scientists are predicting that temperatures around the world will continue to go up. These warmer temperatures cause the sea levels to rise. According to a 2018 report by the UN Intergovernmental Panel on Climate Change

Rescuers (above) help the victims of Hurricane Ike, which struck Haiti in September 2008.

(IPCC), Earth's climate is now changing at a faster rate than scientists previously thought it would. With the climate changing so quickly, the problem of climate refugees will only become bigger. According to the International Red Cross and Red Crescent health organizations, more people are now forced to leave their homes because of environmental disasters than because of war. And more than half of the world's refugees could actually be classified as environmental refugees.

Leaving Home

Many places in the world have already seen changes that are forcing people to leave their countries and become refugees. On the island nation of Kiribati, in the Pacific Ocean, whole villages have disappeared because of rising sea levels. Saltwater has destroyed land and crops, contaminated fresh water, and flooded buildings and roads. In addition, people on Kiribati are no longer catching as many fish as they used to because rising ocean temperatures are ruining coral reefs and reducing the fish population. These problems have forced them to resettle in new places.

In the first six months of 2019, 49,000 people in Somalia were forced to leave their homes because not enough rain came during the rainy season, which caused extreme drought. This made it difficult to grow crops or care for livestock that people needed to survive. Many climate refugees are leaving their homes only to find themselves in crowded places that may not be able to handle the number of people that arrive there. For example, the refugee camps in the country of Kenya are overwhelmed and have little room left to help the many Somalis who come seeking refuge.

Not Enough Water

In other parts of the world there is not enough water to drink due to changing weather patterns. In 2019, the city of Chennai, India almost ran out of water for its 10 million people when the city's reservoirs nearly completely dried up. Many residents were forced to move out of the city. And Chennai is not alone. A government report predicts that 21 of India's major cities might soon run out of water.

In Pakistan, people await buckets of clean water to drink after flooding ruined their usual sources of this vital resource.

From the American Southwest to Somalia (above), droughts are devastating.

Rising Sea Levels and Raging Wildfires

Even in the United States, people are being forced to relocate because of climate change, becoming refugees within their own country. Residents of Isle De Jean Charles, a small town in Louisiana, live on a small piece of land connected to the mainland by a bridge. The town has been flooded by rising sea levels and saltwater and is slowly sinking. The government has given the residents a $48 million grant to relocate to the mainland. In Western states, an increasing number of severe wildfires, caused by a hotter and drier climate, are forcing residents to relocate after losing their homes. As of December 2020, nearly 10,000 wildfires burned across California, making 2020 the largest wildfire season in California's history.

Challenges and Solutions

As more and more parts of the world experience extreme environmental changes, people living in poorer countries will suffer more than people who live in wealthier countries. Climate refugees will still arrive in many countries as they try to find a place where they can get food and water, and realize a better life for their families.

What can we do about climate refugees? For those who have been forced to flee because of climate change, it might be impossible for them to ever go home. Scientists predict that the global temperatures will continue to rise and effects such as droughts will increase. Many big changes must be made soon in order to slow climate change. Scientists are working on methods that may allow crops to grow despite the changing environment. Countries that are less affected by climate and weather disasters could provide aid (both money and supplies) to countries where there are people suffering from environmental disasters. Both the countries where people are forced to flee, and the countries accepting these climate refugees, will have to develop plans for handling the movements and needs of many people. The time to begin planning for this worldwide crisis is here. Above all, now is the best time for people, including young people, to focus on the climate challenges facing our planet and to work together to solve these problems.

Climate protection activist Greta Thunberg speaks to participants of a climate demonstration in Italy in April 2019.

©Daniele Cossu/Alamy

Young Climate Activists

Climate change has become an increasingly dire issue for the world, and young climate **activists** have been playing a greater role in advocating for change. Their voices are being heard as they become more and more visible in the media. In 2018, a young girl from Sweden named Greta Thunberg sat outside the Swedish Parliament building every school day for three weeks. She was protesting the lack of action on climate change. Her school strike started a world-wide movement called Fridays for Future (FFF) and many students and adults began to protest outside of their parliaments and local city halls all over the world. More than 100,000 kids from all over the world have joined FFF. Greta traveled to the United States in September 2019, where she addressed the United Nations, saying, "My message is that we'll be watching you. This is all wrong. I shouldn't be up here. I should be back in school on the other side of the ocean. Yet you all come to us young people for hope. How dare you! You have stolen my dreams and my childhood with your empty words."

Another youth climate change group, Earth Guardians, began as a high school in Maui, Hawaii, in 1992. Students learned about environmental awareness and studied social movements. Since then, Earth Guardians has grown into an environmental organization based in Colorado, which trains young people to be effective leaders in the environmental, climate, and social justice movements around the world. Earth Guardians' Youth Director, Xiuhtezcatl Martinez (pronounced Shoe-Tez-Caht), comes from an Aztec heritage. At 19, he is a hip-hop music artist, writer, and climate activist. He has been speaking about environmental issues around the world since he was 6 years old, and was 1 of 22 young people who filed a lawsuit in 2015 against the federal government. The suit argued that the government was denying their constitutional right to life, liberty, and property by ignoring climate change. Martinez has said, "It's not about being an activist. It's about recognizing the power you have to make a difference. It's important to capture that spark and fire within young people, and I think our generation

An **activist** is a person who works for political or social change by using strong actions, like public protests, marches, or boycotts.

is very versatile. With our access to technology, we can communicate more easily than past generations, which gives us an opportunity to turn every issue into a public showing or celebration, like marches and protests. On the streets, as young people, we ask, what do we want to build? What do we want to leave behind?"

Young people of all ages are stepping up to protest and demand climate change action for the sake of their futures. Alisa Nesterenko, an 11-year-old who moved to the United States from Ukraine, attended the September 2019 Climate Strike in New York City. She wrote, "Us children are going to have to save the planet, so let's start today. Let's grow a plant. Even if it's just one or two, it will still help. Grow it like it was your own son or daughter, because our love and care for the planet is what will save us."

Earth Guardians' Youth Director, Xiuhtezcatl Martinez, leads a rally on the steps of the Colorado Capitol Building on February 20, 2017. Hundreds gathered and marched in support of a court hearing on fracking and climate change.

Students participate in the Global Climate Strike march on September 20, 2019, in New York City. Crowds of children skipped school to join a global strike against climate change, demanding adults act to stop environmental disaster.

Bibliography

Our passion for historic reading goes way beyond this book. Here is a list of terrific, engaging books and resources to keep history alive in your classroom.

INDUSTRIAL AGE, INVENTIONS, AND INNOVATION

The Boy Who Harnessed the Wind by William Kamkwamba and Bryan Mealer. Illustrated by Anna Hymas. Young Readers' Edition. New York: Puffin Books. 2016.

Electrical Wizard: How Nicola Tesla Lit Up the World by Elizabeth Rusch. Illustrated by Oliver Dominguez. Somerville, MA: Candlewick. 2013.

Girls Think of Everything: Stories of Ingenious Inventions of Women by Catherine Thimmesh. Illustrated by Melissa Sweet. New York: HMH Book for Young Readers. 2018.

Grace Hopper: Queen of Computer Code (Volume 1) by Laurie Wallmark. Illustrated by Katy Wu. New York: Sterling Children's Books. 2017.

Hidden Figures by Margot Lee Shetterly. Illustrated by Laura Freeman. Young Readers' Edition. New York: HarperCollins Publishers. 2018.

The Industrial Revolution for Kids: The People and Technology That Changed the World by Cheryl Mullenbach. Chicago, IL: Chicago Review Press. 2014.

Whoosh! Lonnie Johnson's Super-Soaking Stream of Invention by Chris Barton. Illustrated by Don Tate. Watertown, MA: Charlesbridge. 2016.

Library of Congress: Primary Source Sets: Industrial Revolution in the United States http://www.loc.gov/teachers/classroommaterials/primarysourcesets/industrial-revolution/pdf/teacher_guide.pdf

CHILD LABOR / LABOR

Brave Girl: Clara and the Shirtwaist Makers' Stroke of 1909 by Michelle Markel. Illustrated by Melissa Sweet. New York: Balzer + Bray. 2013.

Breaker Boys. How a Photograph Helped End Child Labor by Michael Burgan. North Mankato, MN: Compass Point Books. 2011.

Good Girl Work: Factories, Sweatshops and How Women Changed Their Role in the American Workforce by Catherine Gourley. Minneapolis, MN: Millbrook Press. 1999.

Kids at Work: Lewis Hine and the Crusade Against Child Labor by Russell Freedman. Illustrated by Lewis Hine. New York: Clarion Books. 1998.

On Our Way to Oyster Bay: Mother Jones and Her March for Children's Rights by Monica Kulling. Illustrated by Felicita Sala. Toronto, ON, Canada: Kids Can Press. 2016.

Strike! The Farm Workers' Fight for Their Rights by Larry Brimner. Honesdale, PA: Calkins Creek. 2014.

The Triangle Shirtwaist Factory Fire: The History and Legacy of New York City's Deadliest Industrial Disaster by Charles River Editors. Scotts Valley, CA: CreateSpace Independent Publishing Platform. 2014.

Library of Congress: National Child Labor Committee Collection https://www.loc.gov/collections/national-child-labor-committee/about-this-collection/

Library of Congress: Primary Source Sets: Children's Lives at the Turn of the Twentieth Century http://www.loc.gov/teachers/classroommaterials/primarysourcesets/childrens-lives/pdf/teacher_guide.pdf

URBAN LIFE AND THE GREAT MIGRATION

The Dream Keeper and Other Poems by Langston Hughes. New York: Knopf Books for Young Readers. 2011.

Duke Ellington: The Piano Prince and His Orchestra by Andrea Pinkney. Illustrated by Brian Pinkney. New York: Hyperion Books for Children. 2007.

The Great Migration: An American Story by Jacob Lawrence. New York: HarperCollins Publishers. 1995.

The Great Migration: Journey to the North by Eloise Greenfield. Illustrated by Jan Spivey Gilchrist. New York: HarperCollins Publishers. 2010.

Harlem Stomp! A Cultural History of the Harlem Renaissance by Laban Carrick Hill. New York: Little, Brown Books for Young Readers. 2009.

Jake Makes a World: Jacob Lawrence, a Young Artist in Harlem by Sharifa Rhodes-Pitts. New York: Museum of Modern Art. 2015.

Jazz Age Josephine: Dancer, Singer—Who's That, Who? Why, That's MISS Josephine Baker, to You! by Jonah Winter. Illustrated by Marjorie Priceman. New York: Atheneum Books for Young Readers. 2012.

Josephine: The Dazzling Life of Josephine Baker by Patricia Hruby Powell. Illustrated by Christian Robinson. San Francisco, CA: Chronicle Books. 2014.

Langston Hughes by Milton Meltzer. New York: Ty Crowell Co. 1968.

Muddy: The Story of Blues Legend Muddy Waters by Michael Mahin. Illustrated by Evan Turk. Atheneum Books for Young Readers. 2017.

Poetry for Young People: Langston Hughes by David Roessel. Illustrated by Benny Andrews. Sterling Children's Book. 2013.

Richard Wright and the Library Card by William Miller. Illustrated by R. Gregory Christie. Lee & Low Books. 1997.

A Splash of Red: The Life and Art of Horace Pippin by Jen Bryant and Melissa Sweet. New York: Knopf Books for Young Readers. 2013.

Story Painter: The Life of Jacob Lawrence by John Duggleby. San Francisco: Chronicle Books. 1998.

Visiting Langston by Willie Perdomo. Illustrated by Bryan Collier. New York: Square Fish. 2005.

When Marian Sang: The True Recital of Marian Anderson by Pam Munoz Ryan. Illustrated by Brian Selznick. Scholastic Press. 2002.

Zora! The Life of Zora Neale Hurston by Dennis Brindell Fradin. Illustrated by Judith Bloom Fradin. Clarion Books. 2019.

National Museum of African American History and Culture
https://nmaahc.si.edu/

Library of Congress: Primary Source Sets: Harlem Renaissance
https://www.loc.gov/classroom-materials/harlem-renaissance/

IMMIGRATION: HISTORICAL AND PRESENT DAY

Brothers by Yin. Illustrated by Chris Soentipiet. New York: Philomel Books. 2006.

Dear America: Notes of an Undocumented Citizen by Jose Antonio Vargas. Young People's Edition. New York: Dey Street Books. 2019.

Dreamers by Yuyi Morales. New York: Neal Porter Books. 2018.

The Day You Begin by Jacqueline Woodson. Illustrated by Rafael López. New York: Penguin Random House. 2018.

The Distance Between Us by Reyna Grande. Young Readers Edition. New York: Simon and Schuster. 2016.

Emma's Poem: The Voice of the Statue of Liberty by Linda Glazer. Illustrated by Claire A. Nivola. New York: HMH Books for Young Readers. 2013.

Enrique's Journey: The True Story of a Boy Determined to Reunite with His Mother by Sonia Nazario. Young People's Edition. New York: Delacorte Books for Young Readers. 2013.

Her Right Foot by Dave Eggers. San Francisco: Chronicle Books. 2017.

Home of the Brave: 15 Immigrants Who Shaped U.S. History by Brooke Khan. Emeryville, CA: Rockridge Press. 2019.

Immigrant Kids by Russell Freedman. New York: Puffin Books.1999.

In Search of Safety: Voices of Refugees by Susan Kuklin. Somerville, MA: Candlewick Press. 2020.

Ink Knows No Borders. Poems of the Immigrant and Refugee Experience by Patrice Vecchione and Alyssa Raymond. New York: Seven Stories Press. 2019.

Just Ask! Be Different, Be Brave, Be You by Sonia Sotomayor. Illustrated by Rafael López. New York: Philomel Books. 2019.

Let Me Tell You My Story: Refugee Stories of Hope, Courage and Humanity edited by Twila Bird. Sanger, CA: Familius. 2018.

Migrations: Open Hearts, Open Borders by various authors. Somerville, MA: Candlewick Studio. 2019.

One Green Apple by Eve Bunting. New York: Clarion Books. 2006.

Refugee by Alan Gratz. New York: Scholastic Press. 2017.

We Are Here to Stay: Voices of Undocumented Young Adults by Susan Kuklin. Somerville, MA: Candlewick. 2020.

We Are Displaced: My Journey and Stories from Refugee Girls Around the World by Malala Yousafzai. New York: Little, Brown and Company. 2019.

When Jessie Came Across the Sea by Amy Hest. Illustrated by P.J. Lynch. Somerville, MA: Candlewick. 2003.

Who Belongs Here? An American Story by Margy Burns Knight. Illustrated by Anne Sibley O'Brien. Thomaston, ME: Tilbury House Publishers. 2020.

Library of Congress: Primary Source Set: Immigration
http://www.loc.gov/teachers/classroommaterials/primarysourcesets/immigration/pdf/teacher_guide.pdf

Library of Congress: Primary Source Set: Mexican American Migrations and Community
http://www.loc.gov/teachers/classroommaterials/primarysourcesets/mexican-americans/pdf/teacher_guide.pdf

National American History Museum: Many Voices, One Nation exhibit
https://americanhistory.si.edu/exhibitions/many-voices-one-nation

The Danger of a Single Story. TED talk by Chimamanda Ngozi Adichie
https://www.ted.com/talks/chimamanda_ngozi_adichie_the_danger_of_a_single_story?language=en

"I Learn America: One High School, One School Year, Five New Americans." Video from New Day Films.
www.ilearnamerica.com; www.newday.com

"Waking Dream: Young, Undocumented, Future Unknown." Video from New Day Films.
http://inationmedia.com/waking-dream/

MAGAZINES

Cobblestone, an American history magazine for grades 5–9

Dig, an archaeology and history magazine for grades 5–9

Junior Scholastic, a current events and social studies magazine for grades 5–8

Kids Discover, a social studies and scientific magazine for grades 3–7

The New York Times Upfront, a current events and social studies magazine (both national and international news) for middle and high school students

Scholastic News, a curriculum-connected current events news weekly online for grades 1–6

US Studies Weekly, a U.S. history newspaper for students in grades K–9

WEBSITES

Kids Discover: www.kidsdiscover.com

Library of Congress: www.loc.gov

PBS: www.pbs.org

Smithsonian Museum: www.si.edu

Works Cited

Allington, Richard L., and Peter H. Johnston. 2002. *Reading to Learn: Lessons from Exemplary Fourth-Grade Classrooms*. New York: Guilford Press.

Anderson, Richard C., and P. David Pearson. 1984. "A Schema-Theoretic View of Basic Processes in Reading Comprehension." In *Handbook of Reading Research*, Vol. 1, edited by P. David Pearson, R. Barr, M.L. Kamil, and P. Mosethal, 255–91. White Plains, NY: Longman.

Cervetti, Gina N., Carolyn A. Jaynes, and Elfrieda H. Hiebert. 2009. "Increasing Opportunities to Acquire Knowledge Through Reading." In *Reading More, Reading Better*, edited by E. H. Hiebert. New York: Guilford Press.

Goudvis, Anne and Stephanie Harvey. 2012. "Teaching for Historical Literacy." *Educational Leadership* March 2012: 52–57.

Goudvis, Anne, Stephanie Harvey, Brad Buhrow, and Anne Upczak-Garcia. 2012. *Scaffolding the Comprehension Toolkit for English Language Learners*. Portsmouth, NH: Heinemann.

Graves, Donald H. 2003. *Writing: Teachers & Children at Work*, 20th Anniversary Edition. Portsmouth, NH: Heinemann.

Harvey, Stephanie, and Anne Goudvis. 2005. *The Comprehension Toolkit: Language and Lessons for Active Literacy*. Portsmouth, NH: Heinemann.

———. 2007. *Toolkit Texts: Short Nonfiction for Guided and Independent Practice* (Grades PreK–1, 2–3, 4–5, 6–7). Portsmouth, NH: Heinemann.

Keene, Ellin Oliver, Susan Zimmermann, Debbie Miller, Samantha Bennett, Leslie Blauman, Chryse Hutchins, Stephanie Harvey, et al. 2011. *Comprehension Going Forward: Where We Are and What's Next*. Portsmouth, NH: Heinemann.

Pearson, P. D., Elizabeth Moje, and Cynthia Greenleaf. 2010. "Literacy and Science, Each in the Service of the Other." *Science* April 23 (328): 459–63.

Romero, D. 2013. "The Power of Stories to Build Partnerships and Shape Change." *The Journal of Community Engagement and Scholarship (JCES)* 6(1): 11–18.